TARNISHED CITY

Vic James is a current affairs TV director who loves stories in all their forms. Her programmes for BBC1 have covered the first one hundred days of Trump's presidency, the 2016 US election and Brexit. She has also twice judged the *Guardian*'s Not the Booker Prize. *Gilded Cage* is her first novel, and an early draft won a major online award from Wattpad for most talked-about Fantasy. She has lived in Rome, Tokyo, and now London.

You can follow Vic on Twitter: @DrVictoriaJames
www.vicjames.co.uk

By Vic James

The Dark Gifts Trilogy

Gilded Cage
Tarnished City
Bright Ruin

VIC JAMES

TARNISHED CITY

The Dark Gifts Trilogy

Book Two

PAN BOOKS

First published 2017 by Pan Books
an imprint of Pan Macmillan
20 New Wharf Road, London N1 9RR
Associated companies throughout the world
www.panmacmillan.com

ISBN 978-1-5098-2149-5

A CIP catalogue record for this book is available from the British Library.

Typeset by Palimpsest Book Production Limited, Falkirk, Stirlingshire
Printed and bound by CPI Group (UK) Ltd, Croydon, CR0 4YY

Visit www.panmacmillan.com to read more about all our books
and to buy them. You will also find features, author interviews and
news of any author events, and you can sign up for e-newsletters
so that you're always first to hear about our new releases.

For my brother, Jonathan.
Thank you for doing the numbers-thing,
so I got to do the words-thing.

CONTENTS

Prologue

Jenner

Jenner reined his horse to a halt, and it stamped and snorted in the long blue-black shadow of the trees. He'd pushed the stallion hard.

He glanced over his shoulder, back towards the great house. Kyneston glittered in the darkness. He didn't think they'd seen him go. He didn't want any of his family to witness if he succeeded. Or failed.

This was Abi's last chance. He couldn't fail.

Despite Jenner's desperate appeal, Father had decreed that Abi and her parents must go to Millmoor, banished to the slavetown because of her brother's crime. The car would come tomorrow, so Jenner had to get her out tonight.

He stepped forward and placed his hand against the softly glowing Kyneston wall. The moss tickled his palm, but he pressed harder until he felt the brickwork beneath his fingers. And summoned by his touch, here it came – the flowing, leaping light. It was as if the mortar between the bricks had turned to liquid gold.

1

Now Silyen, as the family's gatekeeper, would know he was here. He didn't have long.

Jenner had first met Abi at this wall just seven months ago, when he and Silyen had brought the Hadleys into the estate. Tomorrow, Sil would cast them out again – unless Jenner could do something he had never managed before. As a Jardine, he could wake the gate. Being Skilless, he was unable to open it.

His heart was in his throat as the molten ironwork took shape. Skill-light flowed upward then unfurled into flowers and vines, fire-feathered birds, and writhing beasts. As a last incandescent loop burned around the family monogram, Jenner marvelled at its beauty. He hadn't allowed himself to wake the gate for nearly a decade, because it was almost worse than nothing, to be granted this one miracle and no more.

'I remember the year you turned thirteen,' said a voice right beside him. 'You hardly left the wall alone. And then you stopped. I always wondered: did Father beat you to keep you away, or did you simply give up?'

Jenner whipped around, outraged and disbelieving. How had Silyen got here so fast? And how had Jenner not heard him approach?

'Seeing if you'll fare any better than Leah and baby Libby?' Silyen asked, because he could always follow up one obnoxious observation with something even worse. 'It happened right about here, you know. All we need is

Gavar, and Abigail herself, and we could have a little re-enactment.'

Jenner lifted his hand off the wall. He flexed his fingers, which itched to slap his little brother. He wasn't rising to the bait.

Or was there an opportunity here? Sil was so capricious, you never knew when he might unexpectedly prove obliging.

'How about *you* open the gate? For Abigail.'

'And defy Father's wishes?'

'When have Father's wishes ever meant a damn to you? Or anybody's wishes, other than your own?'

'Well,' Sil said pleasantly, 'seeing as you put it like that . . .'

His brother dusted off his hands and turned back towards the treeline, where his black horse patiently cropped the grass. Silyen must have been in the woods.

'No, wait! I'm sorry.' Jenner grabbed Sil's arm. 'I'm just all wound up. Please. Abi could have been killed when the East Wing exploded. And now, what's happening with her brother – she'll be in shock. Millmoor is the last place she deserves to be.'

'In that case' – Silyen turned back – 'have a go at it yourself. It's what you came out here for, isn't it? To see if *wishing* might magically make it happen.'

His brother's voice was sing-song, taunting. And only the knowledge that Sil's Skillful reflexes would protect him stopped Jenner from lashing out.

'Do you work at being this hateful, Silyen, or does it come naturally?'

'There's only one person you hate, Jenner, and that's yourself. But don't let the fact that you have an audience deter you. I've watched you try and fail to use Skill your whole life.'

Jenner hadn't thought he could yearn to open the gate more then he already did, for Abi. But the furious desire to prove Silyen wrong blazed through him.

He gripped the wrought ironwork and pulled. As he did, he remembered how he had seen Leah desperately doing the same, all those months ago. He'd arrived just in time to watch Gavar raise his gun and shoot her – an act he'd found incomprehensible at the time, and still did not understand.

The gate favoured him no more than it had Leah and baby Libby. Despite its deceptive radiance, the ironwork was cool beneath his fingers.

And it didn't matter that he had known it would be so. Had known it would be useless. Rage and bitter disappointment welled inside him.

'Satisfied?' he yelled at Sil, humiliated by his own stupid hope.

Which was when he felt it trickling inside his wrists, inside his veins. It licked warm along his fingers, as if he held them over flames. It felt as much a part of him as his hot blood.

Skill.

Jenner's head snapped up to stare at his brother, and he saw in Silyen's dark eyes a tiny flicker of fire reflected from the gate. But his brother's face didn't reflect the hope that was surely radiating from Jenner's own. Sil was frowning.

Which was when Jenner realized that something was very wrong. The gate still wasn't opening. Skill might be flowing in his veins, but it was as if his wrists had been slashed and it was pumping straight back out again. Jenner uncurled his fingers to stare at them in disbelief, as if he might see the hot gold dripping from them uselessly.

He clamped one hand around his wrist, as if to staunch the flow. But he knew it would be futile. And then the warmth ebbed. The last sensation of Skill drained away.

Silyen was staring at him.

'I thought, maybe . . .' his brother said. Sil's tone held none of his earlier malice. It was almost uncertain. He shook his head, wild hair falling to cover his face. 'You'd better go break the bad news to Abigail and her family.'

'What did you do?' Jenner breathed. 'What *was* that?'

'An experiment.' Sil raised his chin defiantly. 'Sometimes experiments don't work.'

'How dare you?' Jenner cried. 'How dare you play with me like this? I'm not one of your experiments. I'm your brother – much though you and Gavar wish it otherwise.'

'I've never wished you weren't my brother,' Silyen said quietly. 'And I'm sorry.'

'Sorry enough to open the gate, so Abi can escape?'

The contrition left Sil's face so fast Jenner wondered if it had been there at all.

'Not that sorry, no. You should tell the Hadleys what Father intends. Leave it till the morning, though. I need to hand Luke over to Crovan tonight, and it'd be better if they don't know until it's done. They deserve a night's sleep – and I don't want them interfering.'

Sil whistled for his horse, which trotted over and stood placidly as he swung himself onto its back. His gaze lingered on the wall. Then Silyen twitched the reins in his hand, and was gone.

Jenner turned to look, too, in case by some final whim of his brother's the gate was swinging open.

It wasn't, of course. Brightness was leaching from it. Birds and beasts fading back into nonexistence. Vines and flowers shrivelling. The brilliance dimming.

Jenner examined his hands. He'd felt it there, for that fleeting minute. Skill inside him, as vital as blood or breath. How was it possible that he lived and walked and talked without it?

In that instant, he would have given anything to have it. Anything at all.

When he looked back up, the gate was gone.

1

Luke

They came for Luke that night.

At that morning's farce of a trial, Luke had been found guilty of a crime he couldn't remember but was certain he hadn't committed. Then Gavar Jardine had dragged him from Kyneston's East Wing. He'd slung him in here, a small chamber beneath the kitchens.

It was stone-walled, chilly and unlit. Groping around in the darkness had identified only a thick wooden counter and some empty barrels. The air had a musty sourness that seeped into your skin. Kyneston wasn't the sort of place to have dungeons, and besides, the Jardines didn't need to lock people up to restrain them. So this place must be a part of the wine cellars.

Which meant that close by, life was going on as normal. And Kyneston was still full of hundreds of Equals. So much had happened since the ball where Chancellor Zelston had died: the East Wing's annihilation and restoration, his own trial, Crovan's Skillful fight with Jackson and its catastrophic end. The Equals would doubtless linger at the Jardine estate to pick over it all. Slaves would be up and down to the kitchens and cellars regularly, too.

One of them would have keys for this room. Or could get word to Abi, who could surely find some.

So Luke had spent the next few hours banging on the door to attract attention. When his fists became sore, he kicked it instead – though he knew better than to imagine he might kick it down. He shouted until he was hoarse, then rested his voice and redoubled his pummelling, before shouting some more.

But not even this physical commotion was as exhausting as the confusion in his brain. In whatever direction Luke turned his thoughts, he ran into the same dead ends of incomprehension and ignorance.

Someone had killed Zelston, and it had to be Luke himself. But only the deed was his. Not the intention.

Doc Jackson had defended him. Yet Jackson was an aristocrat, an Equal, and so had also deceived and betrayed him. Luke's memories of the past twenty-four hours were a maze in which he wandered, utterly lost.

As the day wore on and no one came, Luke sagged against the door, drained. Eventually he must have fallen asleep slumped against it. When he woke, it was because the door had been opened from the outside, causing him to spill forward over the boots of someone on the threshold.

The person's identity was hard to make out, thanks to the dazzle of a star-bright light they cupped in one hand.

'I'm not the rescue party,' said Silyen Jardine. 'Sorry.'

Get up, some tiny voice in Luke's skull urged him. *Run*.

But he was shattered, and no part of him obeyed. Neither his leaden legs nor his bruised hands. Luke opened his mouth, but only a croak emerged. The Young Master screwed up his face and slid his feet out from under Luke's huddled body.

The Equal folded his fingers and extinguished the light. The next thing Luke knew, Silyen was crouched over him in the darkness, one hand curled in the collar of his now filthy white shirt, the other pressed against his temples. Luke shuddered at the touch. When the Equals were done hurting you on the outside, they could always hurt you some more on the inside.

But there wasn't any pain.

'I have questions,' Silyen whispered. 'And right now, you're the best chance I have of finding some answers.'

The Equal's cool fingers trailed down the side of Luke's face. When he gripped Luke's jaw, for a mad moment Luke thought the boy was going to bend down and kiss him. But it was more intimate and far worse than that. Something inside him writhed and leapt at the Equal's touch.

And Silyen must have felt it, too, because that creepily radiant smile lit his face as if he'd conjured back his Skilllight. His hand moved down to Luke's neck, and Luke's pulse throbbed beneath the pressure of Silyen's calloused fingers, as if it might burst and spray them both with bright, arterial blood.

An image came unbidden into his head of Jackson on all fours in front of the Parliament of Equals, pure light exploding from every pore as Crovan triumphed. Luke closed his eyes against the unbearable memory. But Silyen was so close that Luke couldn't avoid the feather-trace of his breath as he spoke.

'If you don't try to escape,' Silyen Jardine murmured, 'I won't let him break you. Not beyond repair.'

Then the hand disappeared and Luke heard himself groan with relief. He opened his eyes to see Silyen brushing the knees of his jeans as he stood up.

'He's fit for travel,' Silyen announced, with his usual brisk carelessness. He was addressing someone who waited further along the dim passageway. 'I'll undo Kyneston's binding at the gate so he's all yours. Come on, Luke. Don't keep your new master waiting.'

The boy offered a slender hand to Luke, who stared at it then turned away and grabbed the door frame for support. Luke wasn't entirely play-acting as he laboured to pull himself upright, but it gave him a few precious seconds to think.

New master.

He had just worked it out, when the person waiting at the end of the corridor lifted a Skill-light of his own and

confirmed the deduction. Lord Crovan stood there, looking just as he had when Luke had taken his bag in
Kyneston's Great Hall only a few nights earlier. His over-
coat was already buttoned. *Fit for travel.*

In just a night and a day, Luke had become a murderer, a
defendant, and now a prisoner. In the uproar after Jackson's
duel with this man in a bid to defend him, Luke had barely
heard Lord Jardine utter the word that sentenced him. But
he remembered it now: *Condemned.*

Condemned and passed into the custody of Lord Arailt
Crovan, for transportation to the man's estate of Eilean
Dòchais, in Scotland. No word spoken of any release. No
word of any review of that sentence. You could almost hear
the sound of a thrown-away key rattling down a deep well.

Luke couldn't allow Crovan to interrogate him. The
man's Skill would discover Luke's memories of the Club,
and put his Millmoor friends in danger.

Yet Luke needed to know what had really happened at
the ball, to clear his name. Not just for his own sake, but
for his family's, too.

'My sisters,' he said urgently, turning to Silyen. 'Are they
okay? My parents?'

'Going to Millmoor,' Silyen replied. 'Safest place for
them, in the circumstances.'

Luke felt winded all over again. Now that he knew what
the Equals were capable of, the thought of his family far
away from them was a relief. But he knew first-hand the

11

horrors of Millmoor: the risky work, the casual brutality and injustice, the way Daisy's education and perhaps even her growth would be stunted in that pitiless place.

'Oh,' Silyen added. 'The little one stays here. Gavar's special request.'

Daisy was staying at Kyneston?

But Luke was out of time for more questions. Crovan paced down the passageway and stopped in front of Luke, eyeing him with faint distaste.

'Why the delay? I wish to be gone before the rabble wakes to yet another day of gossip and gluttony. You're mine now, boy. Come with me.'

Luke bit his lip and followed the man as he led the way back through the dim corridors of the great house. It would be madness to try and run. Even if he escaped Crovan and Silyen – which was unlikely – there was no way past Kyneston's wall. He'd be reduced to hiding in the grounds. Perhaps hunting him down would provide the Equals with a day's sport. Kyneston's stables certainly held dogs and horses enough for that, and the Master of Hounds would doubtless enjoy it.

No, the time for escape would be while they were en route. The drive to Scotland would take all day. Surely there would be stops along the way. His brain unhelpfully supplied images of Crovan striding into a motorway service station calling imperiously for coffee. That would certainly cause a diversion.

Don't try to escape, Silyen had told him. Well, Luke didn't plan to start following life advice from Silyen Jardine any time soon.

The rest of what Silyen had said made little sense. The Young Master had questions – presumably to do with Crovan – whose answers Luke would somehow help him obtain? It was a shame he hadn't told Luke what the questions were, then.

They were at the kitchen door of the great house, now. The one used for deliveries, from which, just a few days earlier, Luke had imagined he might smuggle himself into a vehicle and escape back to his friends in Millmoor. Back to the Doc and Angel. The betrayal he'd felt at learning their true identities still gnawed at the core of him.

A slave opened the kitchen entrance at their approach, and a draught enveloped the three of them as they stepped out into the night. Luke shivered from more than merely the chill. At Crovan's castle, he might be in a cell. Always cold; always in darkness. There might be a time he looked back fondly on his night in Kyneston's cellar.

But no. If he thought like that, then he would be a prisoner in mind as well as body. Broken and afraid. He was going to get out of this. He had to.

Outside, another slave held open the door of a gleaming vehicle. Its engine was purring and Crovan was already getting in the other side. A third slave held the bridle of

Silyen's tall black horse, and the Young Master swung lightly up into the saddle as the beast pawed and snorted.

'Get in,' snapped Crovan's voice from the car's interior.

'Please tell my family I love them,' Luke blurted to the slave holding the door. 'Tell them I'm sorry and I'll see them again.'

The woman stared ahead impassively. If she'd heard him, she gave no sign. Luke's resentment flared, before he checked himself. It was fear of the Equals that cowed people like this. Jackson had taught him that.

Jackson. Who was himself an Equal.

Luke wasn't sure he'd ever be able to forgive him.

'Please,' Luke begged the woman one more time, before ducking his head and getting into the car.

The vehicle didn't use its headlights; instead Silyen rode in front, casting a gentle glow of Skill-light. Luke craned his head to look back at the great house. Even in near darkness, Kyneston was majestic. Light glowed along the parapet and silhouetted the bell in the bright cupola. A few windows were still illuminated.

But Luke's eyes were irresistibly drawn to the golden light that writhed and pulsed along the ironwork skeleton of the vast East Wing. Luke had stood in it as it exploded, then just twelve hours later he had stood in it again for his trial. That impossible restoration had been Silyen Jardine's handiwork.

And the Equal's words in the cellar came back to him.

The ones Luke had pushed away and tried not to think about. *I won't let him break you. Not beyond repair.* A promise, of sorts. But also a threat. Repair. But before it – breaking.

Luke stole a look at the man next to him. Crovan was staring out of the window, seemingly indifferent to either Luke's presence, or anything else.

Luke was so tired of this. Of being used by the Equals. Just a pawn for Jackson. A thing for Crovan to break and for Silyen to put back together, each for their own unfathomable purposes.

He would never be free – Britain would never be free – until there were no more Equals. Simply ending their rule wasn't enough, because with power like that, even if they suffered setbacks, they would eventually win again. And again. And again.

They'd never stop winning.

He leaned against the car door, flexing his fists pointlessly. Despair wouldn't help him now.

Just as the car pulled to a halt, a dazzling brilliance flared in front, making the chauffeur swear and the vehicle swerve. It was Kyneston's gate.

'Out,' said Crovan, swinging his legs out of the car door. He turned his head to look back at Luke. 'Here's where you become mine, boy.'

And he smiled. He honest to goodness smiled, and it was the most awful thing Luke had ever seen. Luke's legs barely obeyed him as he climbed out.

Silyen was waiting by the gate, which fizzed with Skill-light as though made of the sparklers that Mum used to buy on Bonfire Night. What was it, this power? Where did it come from? What did it really do?

'Time to say goodbye,' said Silyen, his pale face luridly lit by the molten brightness. 'For now. I'm breaking your binding to Kyneston. Try to resist the urge to punch me just because you can.'

Inside Luke, something snapped. He almost heard it crack. He remembered the padlock on Dog's cage in the kennels – how Silyen had simply plucked it off and let the shattered pieces fall to the floor.

'You feel it?' asked Silyen.

He was looking at Luke intently, and Luke remembered the first time he had met this boy, after the nightmarish journey from Millmoor in the back of the Security van, when he'd had no idea where he was going. He'd dreaded a Security facility or a lifer camp. Instead he'd been brought to Kyneston. He'd been relieved, at the time.

'You feel it?' Silyen repeated.

Then Luke felt it.

Whatever Silyen had broken inside him – the slave binding to Kyneston – was insignificant compared to what still bound them. And Luke remembered what had happened at that first meeting. How the Equal had seemed to take him apart, like Dad working on an engine, then put him back together again with an extra piece added. How he'd

16

felt his whole self trickling like soft sift through Silyen's fingers.

His gut heaved. What was this connection between them?

He looked up and his gaze met Silyen's. The Equal's eyes were as black as that first night. However, they didn't shine as they had then, with the brightness of stars, but with the reflected liquid gold of the gate. Would his great Skill burn him up from within, this boy? Would it burn Luke with him?

A hand on Luke's shoulder pulled him around.

'Done?' said Crovan, looking at Luke but speaking to Silyen. 'Good. Let's get going.'

Beyond the gate, something thumped the air. Luke felt the whump of the chopper blades as a helicopter descended just the other side of Kyneston's wall.

So it wouldn't be a car, then. And you couldn't escape a helicopter. Luke might be desperate, but he wasn't completely mad.

In the split second between the gate opening and reaching the helicopter door, maybe? His eyes strained to see through the fiery gate. His few weeks as a groundsman told him they'd taken a route from Kyneston that led away from the road. Silyen had summoned the gate where the estate adjoined more parkland – better suited for a helicopter's descent.

'Pay attention.'

17

The back of Crovan's hand lightly smacked Luke's cheek. It dropped lower, and the Equal traced a line across Luke's throat as if miming slitting it. It was a surprisingly crude threat.

But then Luke choked as something cinched there. His fingers came up, clawing, as it constricted his throat. But he could get no purchase. The thing was snug around his neck, and so flat and fine that it lay smooth against his skin.

It was a golden collar.

Luke's panicked eyes darted up and met Silyen's in mute appeal. But the Equal was smirking.

Kyneston's gate swung open.

Abi

Jenner had delivered the unbearable news that Luke was already gone. Then the barely less awful fact that the rest of her family was to be split up: Daisy remaining at Kyneston, Abi and her parents going to Millmoor.

What she needed to do had instantly become clear. Once the journey to Millmoor was underway, she had feigned travel sickness so the vehicle pulled over – and then she had run.

That had been nearly a week ago. Now, she stood on a beach, as light from bars and restaurants spilled in bright slicks across the heaving sea. Abi inhaled the salt-sharp air. She was so close. Somewhere in the night was her goal: the island castle of Highwithel.

It was the home of Heir Meilyr Tresco, the young Equal-turned-revolutionary who had betrayed her brother in an unspeakable way – hijacking his mind and body to kill Chancellor Zelston.

Or had someone else yet unknown done that, and was

Meilyr instead her brother's friend and defender? If so, he had paid the highest price of all – his Skill – in an attempt to save Luke from the horror of Condemnation.

Which was it? She was so close to finding out.

Abi splashed into the sea and gasped at the cold. Water rushed into her trainers and saturated her jeans, making every step leaden. Coarse sand and fine pebbles shifted underfoot.

She *had* to find out, because by coming here she had left behind everything that meant most to her in the world. Her little sister, at Kyneston, in the keeping of volatile Heir Gavar. Her parents, who by now would be in the Millmoor slavetown and distraught at being separated from all three of their children. The young man she might love, if she dared to – the Skilless second son of England's most powerful family, Jenner Jardine.

And though it seemed the smallest sacrifice in that awful tally, Abi had given up the future she'd always imagined. She was a fugitive from her slavedays. Outside the law. Whatever lay ahead for her now, it was unlikely to be the hospital job and neat terraced house filled with a husband and kids that she had once envisioned.

This world was crueller than she had ever imagined when she submitted her family's slavedays application to the Estates Office nearly a year ago. Discovering the truth of it had cost Abi, and those she loved, so much.

She hauled herself up into a small boat, her long legs ungainly and the vessel rocking beneath her.

Luke had to be rescued. And Abi would make Heir Meilyr of Highwithel help.

The motion of the shallow hull subsided. Her jeans were soaked to mid-thigh, but she wasn't worried about catching cold. She'd bought a snug sailing jacket, and besides, her body would be busy oxidizing amino acids into an adrenaline rush to send blood pumping round her body.

She remembered the pre-med textbook in which she'd learned that. Being a doctor would have been a rewarding way to help people.

But Luke had dreamed bigger.

He'd fought against the slavedays and the Equals. To think that Abi had worried about his safety during the disturbances in Millmoor, when he'd been one of those causing trouble. The next time she saw her little brother, he'd get a scolding.

Because she refused to accept that there might not be a next time.

Abi dug into her jeans for the key to the boat's engine and fumbled to fit it into the outboard motor. Growing up with a mechanic dad didn't help much with things like this. But her skill set was expanding by the minute. First theft and flight; now burglary. She had acquired the key only an hour earlier – by breaking into the seal-watching tours office, down on the jetty.

The engine choked into life. Abi set her hand to the tiller and turned it experimentally. Satisfied, she sighted the red and green lights marking the exit of Ennor's inner harbour and steered the craft towards them.

This was her second attempt to reach Highwithel, Britain's most remote Equal estate, nestled at the heart of the Scilly Islands off the southwest tip of England. It had been a long journey.

After fleeing the car taking her and her parents to Millmoor, Abi had hitched a ride along the A-road to Exeter. Then she'd travelled by train to Penzance and by ferry to Ennor, the largest of the islands. There, she'd drawn a blank.

Ennor was a popular tourist spot. As you couldn't travel abroad until you'd completed your slavedays, the warm, windswept Scillies were as distant and exotic a holiday destination as Britain offered.

So on her first day here, Abi had tried a clueless-tourist-who'd-love-to-see-the-castle routine. This had been politely rebuffed by the local water-taxis. Abi sensed that the islanders were fiercely loyal to their lords. The Tresco name was everywhere, painted along the sides of humble fishing boats, and on the swinging sign of a weather-beaten pub. The locals wouldn't be sharing the estate's secrets with outsiders.

It would be down to her resourcefulness. The Scillies were an archipelago of 146 isles, but only 145 were shown on the map she'd stolen from the drawer in Kyneston's Estate Office, and none of them was named Highwithel. She tracked down an aerial photograph in Ennor's library, and compared them. They matched. So either the image was doctored as well as the map, or Highwithel didn't show up on photographs.

She'd tried to think laterally. The Equals would need supplies: food, and all the little luxuries an aristocratic family would want.

Ennor was a cheerful place – would all of Britain be like this if the local lords were kind, and not cruel? And amid its bright shopfronts one stood out as especially smart. Abi slipped inside. It was a swanky grocery, and on its shelves were a few eye-wateringly expensive London brands that the Jardines used. The only commoners who could afford such items were those who had done their days early and gone on to prestigious careers. She'd bet the Trescos were supplied from here.

There was no sign of an order book – the shop's system was computerized. But slipping round the back Abi saw boxes being carried down to the harbour, for delivery by boat. Each carton was neatly marked with the customer's name and destination island. Abi was sure her instincts were correct, so it would be a matter of watching the deliveries.

She'd spent two days on a bench along the harbour slipway, her brain fruitlessly turning over other ideas as she waited. Should she simply write a letter? No. She needed to look Meilyr Tresco in the eye as she demanded answers about Luke. What about contacting Jenner? She bought an over-the-counter mobile phone with some of the money she'd swiped from Kyneston, and several times her fingers hovered over the numbers for its estate office. But Abi wasn't sure how Jenner could help, and didn't want to risk involving him.

Then on the third day a large load had come down to the jetty, each box discreetly lettered 'TRESCO/Highwithel'.

Abi had sprinted away from the harbour and up to the island's highest point, a chapel where fishermen's families had once anxiously awaited their safe return during storms. She straightened up, ignoring the stitch in her side, briefly terrified that she had lost sight of the boat already. But no – there it was, far out in Ennor's west channel.

By the time it disappeared around a distant islet, she had a clear sense of its direction. Her map showed that the route led to three areas of seemingly open sea that she had identified as possible locations for the hidden island.

Her first attempt, the previous night, had found nothing. So here she was again in a different 'borrowed' boat, heading for the second location.

Looking back, one hand firmly on the throbbing outboard engine, Abi could no longer see the red and green harbour lights. The wind picked up as she nosed the vessel westward, raising wavelets on the sea surface as the boat began a choppy bounce.

Would she capsize and drown? Or would this little craft smash onto rocks, breaking her with it? Perhaps a current would swing her out into the wide, wide ocean, where she would perish of exposure and thirst. Then she'd never rescue Luke. He might die in Crovan's keeping, and that would kill her parents with grief, too. And then Daisy would be all alone.

Stop it, she told herself, fiercely. *Stop thinking like that.*

Abi touched the lifejacket clipped round her neck. She felt the plastic tube of the emergency flare in her pocket, and patted the tide chart and diagram of currents tucked inside her jacket. She'd caught herself doing this sort of thing several times, in the week since she'd run – small rituals of calming and reassurance. Abi recognized it as a distress response to the trauma of what had happened at Kyneston. It wasn't healthy, she knew, but it was hard to stop – not least because it helped quiet the voices.

Voices that insisted this was *all her fault. She* had told Mum and Dad that Luke and Daisy would agree to do their days if they did them together. *She* had suggested applying to an estate. *She* had failed to get Luke out of Millmoor quickly enough, before he'd ever become mixed up with Meilyr Tresco and his deluded plots.

And yes, she knew these thoughts weren't entirely rational. But even so, fixing everything felt like *her* responsibility. And she'd do whatever it took. Including piloting a boat barely bigger than a bathtub through the night to an invisible castle.

She passed dozens of islands, their pale cliffs gleaming and rocky shores lost in the blackness beneath. The moon was waning and cloud trailed over its face. The light was thinner tonight than it had been yesterday. Tomorrow would be darker still.

Here was the last inhabited island in this map-grid of sea. The windows of its solitary farmhouse were yellow rectangles hanging in the night, like golden portals to some world of Skill. Abi had made it this far yesterday before continuing west. Tonight, she would turn north.

Her hand on the tiller was stiff with cold, but she pulled the engine round, spitting out strands of hair as the wind whipped her sandy plait into her face and eyes. She opened up the throttle and sent the boat forward as fast as she dared. It skipped like a stone across the surface of the sea. Luke had always been able to skip stones so well – eight or nine bounces.

I'll get you back, little bro, she promised him silently.

Sea spray lashed her face. That was all the salt stinging her eyes was. That was what she could taste, trickling down her face to her wind-cracked lips.

Then the wind stopped. The spray stopped.

The engine stopped.

The boat stopped.

Had she broken the motor by pushing it too fast? How could she have been so stupid?

Abi bent over the engine, turning the key ineffectually. She took it out and tried again. Nothing. The sea slopped queasily beneath the little tender's fragile hull.

Then she fell against the engine as the boat began to move. She lay there, hands gripping the sides, as she realized what this meant.

It was being drawn by Skill.

All around, both sea and sky were black. She looked behind. The lights from the farmhouse were gone. She looked up.

The moon was gone. The stars, gone. There was only a deep darkness . . .

And then, before terror could consume her entirely, there was an island. Abi's heart missed a beat. Missed two.

Highwithel loomed, as lofty as its name suggested. The moon was visible again, and beneath its insubstantial light the island shone bone-white, mottled with shadow. Its flanks shifted eerily, like the sides of a living thing. Abi's lurching heart slammed into frantic life as the cliffs shattered outward into a hundred fragments. Her memory reeled back to the horror of Kyneston's exploding ballroom – until she realized it was seabirds. A mass of them, rising, wheeling and screaming.

At the summit of the island was the castle. It rose seamlessly from the rock, one graceful pinnacle piled on another, buttressed by sturdy arches. There were no battlements, but turrets and towers rose along the walls – would they have been watchtowers once?

Her craft moved at a steady, even speed. Abi had nothing to fear from the sea now.

But what about the island? What sort of reception would broken Heir Meilyr give her?

The shore was getting closer. Abi knelt upright in the boat, shielding her eyes from two lights burning ahead. One was a glowing golden ball that could only be Skill-light. The other was a high-wattage torch beam, white and harsh.

She was looking at the end of a jetty. Three people stood there. One was a tall, slender woman; the Skill-light she cupped illuminated her white-blonde hair and elegant features. An Equal. Another, her face shadowed behind the dazzling torch, was a scrawny kid with wild corkscrew hair. Between them stood Heir Meilyr.

The woman must be Bodina Matravers, the sister of Heir Bouda. Abi remembered how she and Meilyr had walked into Kyneston's ballroom side by side, just as they stood now. And Abi had seen her again in the chaos afterwards, bent over a slave crushed by a girder, bright as an angel in her sequinned dress, and supernaturally strong. She had freed the man, then healed him.

Were the pair of them Luke's allies?

Or his betrayers?

The little boat glided towards the jetty. The kid set down the torch and crouched, throwing Abi a rope. Why didn't Heir Meilyr do it? Abi wondered. This was his island. Did he think it was beneath him? One more task to leave to a slave – just like killing a Chancellor?

Securing the boat, Abi glanced up for a ladder and found herself instead looking into the young Equal's face. Neither the warm Skill-light held by the woman beside him, nor his trim beard, concealed his ravaged features.

As part of her university prep, Abi had volunteered at the hospital where Mum worked. She'd seen faces like Heir Meilyr's on wards there. The sort of wards where people spoke in gentle voices, and where you sometimes heard muffled sobbing behind the curtains. He was leaning heavily on a cane.

'Abigail Hadley,' he said, his voice hoarse. 'I'm Meilyr Tresco. "Doc Jackson" is how your brother knew me. Welcome to Highwithel.'

Abi braced her feet against the bottom of the boat as she stood.

'This isn't a social call,' she said. 'I'm only here for one reason. I'm going to get my brother back.'

Tresco passed his cane to the slavegirl at his side, and with Bodina holding his arm to anchor him, he stiffly bent down and extended a hand.

'That makes two of us,' he said.

She didn't miss the spasm of pain that crossed Tresco's

29

face as he helped her over the top of the sea-slick ladder and onto the jetty. His duel with Crovan had wrecked more than just his Skill.

They led her along the causeway to treacherous stone steps cut into the cliff. And then came a surprise. The kid with the electric torch wasn't a slavegirl – or not anymore, it seemed. She introduced herself as Renie, a friend of Luke's from Millmoor.

'I'll take Abigail ahead,' Renie said to the Equals, without a trace of deference. 'Explain about us all.'

Bodina Matravers nodded, her hand still firm on Heir Meilyr's arm.

And as Renie and Abi started up the cliff stairs, the girl began her story. There had been a group of them, she said. The 'Millmoor Games and Social Club'. Bodina Matravers had broken them all out of the slavetown as soon as Luke was transferred to Crovan's custody.

'We didn't know she was an Equal,' Renie explained. 'Nor Jackson. I mean, Meilyr. That's taking a bit of gettin' used to.

'But Dina came and found us, one by one. Said Luke had been arrested and was being questioned by one of *them*, so the Club might be discovered even if he wasn't saying nothing. She rounded us up in a van, and the Security guards just looked the other way when she drove us outta Millmoor. That'd be the Skill,' the girl added reflectively. 'Always wondered how she did it. Figured it was just 'cause she was pretty.'

The kid gave a low cackle that sounded old beyond her years. Renie was a natural tale-teller, and Abi found herself fascinated as the girl explained how the Club had started out simply doing good in the grim slavetown. She felt a flush of pride when Renie narrated her first encounter with Luke.

'He rescued me from those nasty fellas, and I never did thank him properly for that. But I will. Don't you worry, we're all as set on getting him back as you are. The Doc – *Meilyr* – won't rest till it's done.'

After Heir Meilyr had learned of the doomed Proposal to abolish the slavedays, the Club's activities had escalated. They committed acts of sabotage against Millmoor's administration. And finally, there had been the January riot.

'Luke was part of all this?' Abi still couldn't quite believe it.

'Part of it? He came up with the best bit – he shut down the Machine Park. He's good, that boy. If a thing needs doing, he says so, and worries about the hows of it later.'

That sounded like Luke all right, Abi thought, scrabbling at the cliff face for purchase as her heel slipped. The seabirds circled and called distractingly overhead. She felt a pang at the thought of her brother's life in Millmoor, close to these people she'd never met.

If only she and Luke had talked more during their

weeks together at Kyneston. He'd kept all this bottled up. Was that because he'd known how much she'd disapprove? Or was it because the assassination of Chancellor Zelston had been planned even then, and Luke was willingly a part of it?

That was the third scenario in all of this. The one she hadn't wanted to think about. Luke could have been used by Meilyr Tresco. He could have been used by someone else entirely.

Or he could have volunteered to do it.

But no. Abi could imagine Luke getting into all sorts of scrapes – yes, even the lawbreaking that Renie had described. But to shoot a man in cold blood? A man who had done nothing wrong, other than be the figurehead of the Equal regime. Who had even proposed the abolition of the slavedays. Luke wouldn't have done that willingly, she was certain.

They were dizzyingly high now. Abi paused to catch her breath and looked down – not her best idea, as the yawning darkness made her head spin. The golden glow of Skill-light was far below. Heir Meilyr was having a hard time of it climbing the stairs.

'What's wrong with him?' Abi asked, watching the heir's painful progress. 'I mean, I know about his Skill. I was at Kyneston when it happened. But this is just walking up steps. You don't need Skill to do that.'

Renie's pinched little face screwed up. She really cared

about Meilyr, Abi realized. That spoke in the heir's favour – but Abi would still be making up her own mind.

'It's pain,' Renie said. 'Terrible pain that won't go away. That's what Dina says. She's tried using her Skill to help him, and so has all his family. Jackson – *Meilyr* – says he's like a leaky bucket. He can feel them pour Skill into him, but it just runs straight out.'

As they watched, Bodina's soft Skill-light began to move rapidly towards them. Leaping the steps faster than any normal person could have managed, the Equal girl was soon with them. She wasn't the slightest bit out of breath.

'Go on,' she told them. 'I'm going to have to carry him, and I'd rather he had some privacy.'

'Carry him?' said Abi disbelievingly. Then she remembered that girder. This slender girl could probably carry a baby elephant if she had to.

'He won't be able to talk to you any more tonight, either,' Dina said. 'He sends his apologies. There'll be a room for you near the others. Renie can show you one. You must be tired, too.'

Her last words were more instruction than question. The Equal girl then turned and ran lightly back down the steps.

Abi groaned. But it was true, she *was* exhausted. She'd barely slept this past week, between worrying about Luke, worrying about her parents, worrying about Daisy, and keeping half an ear out for the police. She'd expected them to barge into the small hotel in Ennor at any minute, where she'd checked in under a false name.

But she had made it here. For now, just for tonight, she could rest.

She let Renie lead her up the last few turns of the cliff stairs, and into the great, dark entry hall of the castle. Tiredness weighed on her with every step. The girl took Abi through a maze of narrow corridors, then finally pushed open a door. The torchlight fell onto a narrow bed made up with a thick woollen blanket.

'Why don'tcha take this one?' Renie announced. 'I'm just across the way.' The kid looked into Abi's eyes, her urchin face wiser than her years. 'Let yourself sleep. Don't feel guilty. You'll need to be strong for Luke.'

'Thank you,' Abi said, before stepping in and gratefully closing the door. She'd barely pulled off her clothes before her head hit the pillow and she was sleeping deeply for the first time in days.

When she woke, it was already light. She wasn't sure what had dragged her from unconsciousness. Some distant noise. Screaming seabirds, perhaps. Or waves crashing onto rocks far below.

Abi lay there, marshalling her thoughts. Today she would find out the truth of Zelston's killing. She'd discover if Meilyr Tresco would fight alongside her to rescue Luke. His words on the jetty last night had been promising.

For the first time in a week, Abi let herself feel a small ray of hope.

A knock at the door interrupted her ruminations and she quickly sat up, pulling at the blanket.

'Abi?'

She recognized that voice.

But that was impossible. He was at Kyneston. How would he know she was here? How could he get here?

'Abi, it's me. Can I come in?'

'Yes!' she yelped, jumping up and tugging at the bottom of her T-shirt.

Then Jenner was through the door and seized her in his arms. He picked her up and spun her around. Her head kept on spinning when he put her down, because he was kissing her as if he had believed he would never see her again.

And Abi kissed him back, because she had believed she would never see him again.

How could they say he had no Skill, this boy? Because his hands on her skin burned as if they were full of golden fire. His grasp on her hip was fierce enough to bruise.

Perhaps she hadn't lost everything. Not quite.

'How did you know?' she asked, when they drew apart for a moment to look at each other. 'That I was here? How did *you* get here?'

Jenner tipped his head to one side, and the sun through

the tower window caught those freckles and the Jardine bronze of his hair.

'The map,' he said, smiling. 'The minute I heard you'd escaped from the car, I remembered I'd seen you by the map drawer. When I checked, the one for the Scillies was missing. So I contacted Armeria Tresco, to alert her that you might turn up.

'There was lots to do at home, after what happened. But I left Kyneston as soon as I could so I'd be close by. My family thinks I'm on an estate-management tour of some of our properties. Dina called me late last night to say you were here, I made it to the coast and she came for me in the chopper this morning.'

The helicopter landing. That was what had woken her up.

'Ow!' Jenner rubbed his arm where Abi had smacked him. 'What's that for?'

'Because,' she scolded, after first administering an apologetic kiss, 'you could have given me a lift. Now give me a moment to get dressed. Then let's go find out how our hosts will help me rescue my brother.'

3

Luke

When Luke opened his eyes, it was into a world as bright as Skill – like a room on fire.

He came awake with a jolt.

The space around him wasn't just fiery. It was shaking. As his eyes adjusted he saw the interior of a helicopter, and it all came back: leaving Kyneston; the gate.

The collar.

His fingers went to his throat and found it. A flat band, flesh-warm and skin-tight.

Luke looked up. Opposite, Arailt Crovan was studying him. The man's eyes were hidden behind round-rimmed glasses, but the tilt of his head recalled a bird watching a worm.

The source of the golden light wasn't Crovan, but lay outside the helicopter's windows. With a wary glance over at the Equal, Luke strained against his seatbelt and looked.

It was a molten sunrise of such beauty that it took Luke's breath away.

During his childhood, his family had holidayed on the Yorkshire moors, or among the soft hills of the Peak District. No overseas travel, of course, because none of them had done their slavedays. But Luke had never minded. He loved racing Abi to the top of some windy summit, or helping Daisy count the rocks piled in wayfarers' cairns.

But what lay beyond the window was lovelier than anything he had ever seen. Far out was the sea. An island stretched lazily along the horizon, its ridged back basking in the dawn.

Inland pooled an immense spill of gold – a loch. The black shape jutting at the heart of it should have marred its glory, but instead lent it a dark magnificence.

The castle was taller than it was wide, and until halfway up there were no windows at all, only sheer walls of stone. Its upper parts were lacerated with arrow slits, their placement giving no clue to the layout of the space within. At the top was a vast casement, more lead than glass. Set at one corner was a turreted tower topped with battlements. The immense stronghold stood on an outcrop of rock at the centre of the loch. There was no bridge that Luke could see.

'Eilean Dòchais,' Crovan said, with evident satisfaction. 'The seat of my family for a thousand years. The name means "Hope Island", which Silyen finds vastly amusing. But I think it rather fitting. This is where society hopes that you Condemned will be contained, and where I hope to further my own researches, with the assistance of all of you.'

He turned from the scene outside to face Luke. The sunrise flared in the lenses of his spectacles, turning his eyes into discs of gold, resembling a death-offering to pay passage into the next world.

'It's where my guests hope that their punishment will end one day. Many of them hope it will end quickly.'

Crovan leaned back in his seat, his expression unreadable. Luke tried to ignore the fact that everything inside him had just melted into pure, liquid fear. He clenched his fists and curled his toes to remind himself of his own body. Of its strength, built up in Millmoor and by labouring on the Kyneston Estate. Of his determination, which he'd found in the slavetown, too. Of his family, and his friends, who were also in danger and might still need his help.

He wouldn't let this man break him. Wouldn't submit to the horrors of this deceptively beautiful place. Wouldn't think of Dog, who'd been a soldier and had murdered Equals, who Crovan had somehow reduced to a creature crawling on all fours on the end of an old woman's leash.

With a smooth movement, the helicopter dove towards the castle. It jerked as the pilot adjusted the controls – they were landing on the shore, not the island – then settled down the final few feet to the ground.

'Out,' said Crovan, and Luke complied.

His hand went to the band about his throat. Was that Skillful compulsion? Or just reflexive obedience?

The truth was, everyone in Britain wore a collar they couldn't see. Millions of people, unquestioningly obeying the Equals. Slaving for ten years in appalling conditions. Subject to rulers they couldn't choose or criticize. Confined to a country they couldn't leave until their days were done. And accepting it all as normal.

Better to wear a collar you could see. That way you never forgot.

The chopper lifted into the air. It hovered for a moment, the metal eye of a whirlwind that flattened the yellow heather and sedge, then spun and flew back the way it had come. They both watched it go, then Crovan turned his back on Luke and walked away towards the castle.

Now would be the moment to run. Despite Silyen Jardine's enigmatic warning against trying to escape, Luke didn't intend to be Crovan's guest for long. He bolted in the direction the helicopter had disappeared.

Running on the heather was almost impossible. The shrub bunched at ankle-height and while it appeared dense, each time Luke's feet came down they plunged through the bush and tangled in the twisty stalks beneath.

When he fell, he wasn't sure if it was Crovan's doing or just a misstep. Something snatched at his heel and he hurtled face first into the scratchy heather. He lay there for a moment, panting, trying to fight down his disappointment.

A shoe pressed into the small of his back, where his shirt – still the one spattered with gore from Chancellor Zelston's murder – had ridden up to expose skin.

'They all try,' said Crovan, as his heel dug into the base of Luke's spine. 'They all give up. You will, too. Now come.'

Luke promptly picked himself up, and this time as Crovan strode away towards the loch he trotted obediently behind. This new compliance was Skill, Luke was certain. But it didn't feel like he was being made to do anything. It was as if he wanted to. The sensation itched and crawled across his skin. Under it.

They walked across the moor, Equal and Condemned, until they reached the gravel shore of the loch. The water was shallow and glassy, magnifying the pebbles and grit of the beach. It was impossible to judge how deep it was further out, where it turned to glinting black.

Luke was no great swimmer, but the loch was land-locked so it wouldn't have tides or current. The distance from island to shore wasn't impossible. The water was sure to be cold, but the exertion would warm you up. There might be no alternative – looking up and down the beach, Luke still couldn't see a boat or bridge.

'You can't,' said Crovan, startling Luke from his thoughts. 'Swim, that is.'

'Why's that? Are you keeping the Loch Ness Monster in there or something?'

'Try if you wish. I wouldn't advise it.'

They liked this, Luke thought. All these Equals. Taunting you with their superior knowledge and their creepy power. It was pathetic. Bullies in the playground did the same, confident their victim's curiosity would get the better of him, even when he knew it was a trap.

Luke's curiosity got the better of him.

He needed that information. When he escaped, he'd have to get across the loch. If one option wasn't going to work, better to know that now.

He crouched and examined the water more closely. It looked entirely normal. The smell was almost intoxicatingly fresh, zinging with ozone.

Then he saw it. Tiny sparkles of gold which he had mistaken for refracted sunlight. They bobbed in the water like a trick of the eye. Luke remembered a geography lesson one afternoon, when their teacher had been sick and the supply had played them a film about oceans. One scene had showed a kayak slicing through a sea at night, leaving a rippling blue glow in its wake. Bioluminescence.

Luke looked at the shimmering water warily. He'd bet his entire, non-existent, worldly goods that this was no natural phenomenon. An unnatural one, maybe.

'I'm sure I remember Meilyr telling us all about your bravery,' Crovan observed.

Luke dug his fingers into the gritty beach, fighting down his anger. Crovan was toying with him.

But he did need to know.

Hesitant, he dabbled his fingers into the shallows.

And screamed as what had looked like water turned out to be acid. His whole body convulsed with the shock of it. He could feel his skin melting, his fingerbones corroding and washing away on the sparkling, shining wavelets. He fell backwards onto the beach, sobbing and cradling his ruined hand.

His eyes squeezed shut with the horror of it. He'd been so stupid. So unbelievably stupid, playing the hero and planning an escape, when he should have simply focused on surviving this place, this man.

'I forgot to mention its name,' Crovan said, from a world made distant by pain. 'Loch nan Deur, the Lake of Tears. My family, like the Jardines, guards its privacy.'

Luke forced open his eyes, and through the blur saw faint amusement on Crovan's face. Rage welled up inside him and he lunged. All he had to do was knock the man down in the shallows. If necessary, he'd wade in and hold him under, if it was the last thing he did.

Which was when two things happened. The compulsion exerted by the collar slammed him to the ground.

And as his arms came up to break his fall, Luke saw that his hand was not, after all, half gone.

Fingers. Skin. Everything still there. Intact.

In shock, Luke lay motionless, his cheek pressed against the coarse, gritty sand. His thoughts raced to make sense of everything. The lake wasn't acid. Those wicked glints of Skill had worked on . . . what? His body, to make him feel pain? Or his brain, to make him think it? It was like the bed of blood he'd hallucinated at Kyneston after hours of Crovan's interrogation. He could no longer trust the evidence of his own senses.

Wait, he admonished himself. Wait and learn. No more escapes, no more attacks, until it's all figured out.

'Watch,' said Crovan.

The Equal stepped backwards into the water.

Luke was prepared not to be impressed. It stood to reason that if it was Crovan's or his family's Skill that infused the loch, it wouldn't hurt him. But what happened next was astonishing enough that Luke was mesmerized.

Where Crovan moved, the water moved away from him. It flowed with a smooth, almost magnetic repulsion. For a space around the Equal, the loch bed was exposed.

'Come quickly and keep close,' said Crovan. 'If you don't stay on my heels, the water will claim you. I think you have an idea by now of how that would turn out.'

Luke didn't need telling twice, he scrambled to his feet and plunged after his new master.

It was cold within the loch, and as they moved further in, the water grew deeper. Reached head height. Continued to rise. Soon, the claustrophobia was intense. It would have been pitch black, were it not for the gentle glow of Skill all around them. It was like being at the bottom of a well. What did they call those deep pits in dungeons – oubliettes? Forgetting-places.

His family wouldn't forget him, Luke knew. At least his parents and Abi would be safe in Millmoor. Mum and Dad had useful professions that the Labour Bureau would recognize, while Abi's perfect grades had included Chinese, so Millmoor's Bank of China call centre would snap her up. She'd be bored out of her mind, but she'd be away from the deadly intrigues of the Equals.

He was worried sick thinking about his little sis at Kyneston, with the Jardine heir her only protection. Hopefully Gavar would grow tired of having Daisy around once Libby was old enough for school. Then she'd be sent to Millmoor to join the others.

If anything happened to him here, would they even be told?

Luke only just caught himself in time as Crovan stopped abruptly. Their passage was blocked by a wall of rock, into which was cut a series of glistening steps. They had reached the island.

As Luke followed Crovan up, careful not to lose his footing, a chill wrapped around him. His fate here was close.

They broke free of the water's edge. The castle rose above them, vaster than it had appeared from the shore. The walls were blank and massive, flaring slightly at the base. Not even a mouse would be able to climb them.

Set into the wall directly ahead, separate but side by side, were two doors. They stood twice Luke's height, made of weathered wood banded with iron. Two words arched across each, incised deep into the stone and picked out in gold. Neither door had a knocker, a keyhole, or any visible means of opening. Mounted above both was a large stone shield carved with the device of a lightning-struck boat.

'The Crovan arms and my ancestral motto,' said Luke's new master, indicating the words. '*Omnes vulnerant; ultima necat. All hours wound; the last one kills.*'

'Cheerful,' said Luke with a bravado he did not feel. 'Very welcoming.'

'Each door opens only one way,' Crovan continued. 'This opens from the outside, the other from the inside.'

At the Equal's touch, the left-hand door swung inward. Someone stood just over the threshold – a finely dressed man who looked to be in his late twenties. Was he Crovan's son and heir? But no, the Equal sat alone in parliament.

'Master,' said the waiting figure, a strained edge to his voice. 'Thank goodness you're back. You've been gone so long.'

As the man wrung his hands anxiously, Luke glimpsed, beneath the silk scarf knotted at his open collar, a golden band like his own. The man noticed Luke standing there, and his fawning expression hardened.

'You're not alone, Master?'

'Evidently not,' said Crovan tersely. Then he turned to

Luke and continued: 'This is the Door of Hours. You Condemned don't do days, you do hours. There are so many more of them.'

Crovan stepped over the threshold. Luke watched him, reluctant to follow. What awaited within these walls?

'The other door,' he said, stalling for time. 'Does that one have a name, too?'

'That is the Last Door.'

The speaker was a girl. She wove her way between the other two and came forward. Skinny and pale, she was no older than Luke himself. She wore a plain black dress, and her golden collar was bright against her thin neck. Her voice was clear, as were her cool grey eyes.

'Remember the motto: *ultima necat. The last one kills.* You don't want to walk through that door – not until the day you want it so much that nothing will stop you.'

Luke stared at her.

'It kills you? How?'

He conjured up images, none of them good. A guillotine, dropping from above. A poisoned door handle. Perhaps concealed blades that shot out from the walls and skewered you as you stepped over the threshold.

'The "how" is immaterial,' Crovan said. 'It takes your life, as all things that kill do. Luke, enter. Coira, this is Luke Hadley. Show him to a room and see that he is presentable, then bring him to breakfast.'

The irresistible compulsion of the band drew Luke over

the threshold. And as he felt his body comply with the will of his new master, Luke knew for certain that this was how it had happened – the murder of Zelston. Someone had used Skill to make his body do their bidding and kill the Chancellor. Then he had been made to forget his own part in it.

But who? Crovan himself? Lord Jardine? The Equal he had known as Doc Jackson?

Perhaps even Silyen Jardine?

The door slammed shut behind him. He glanced back, only to see something even more startling – the door was gone.

'You look like someone tried to kill you,' said the girl. Coira. She was studying his appearance sceptically. 'Or that you killed someone. Given that you're here, I'm guessing it's the latter.'

The blood that covered his shirt had long since dried and stiffened, and was slowly turning brown. He'd not been permitted to clean up before his trial – his appearance proclaimed his guilt without Lord Jardine having to say a word. He was also streaked with feculent muck from the Kyneston cellar.

'Luke has been Condemned for slaying Winterbourne Zelston,' Crovan clarified.

'The Chancellor?' said the man with the cravat.

'Yes, Devin.' Crovan spoke as if to a slow-witted child. 'Chancellor Zelston is dead. Britain is now once again governed by Whittam Jardine, as interim Chancellor in an emergency administration. My hunch is that the emergency will prove sufficiently dire to require him to stay on in that capacity for some time, if not indefinitely. Come, I'll tell you all the details.'

And Crovan led away the man – Devin – leaving Luke and the girl standing by themselves.

'I didn't do it,' Luke said immediately.

He had no idea who this girl was, or whether he'd ever see her again after this morning, if Crovan's next plans for him involved a cell or a kennel. But for just this brief moment he wanted someone to believe him. He'd not expected to find anyone of his own age here, let alone a girl.

But Crovan's words had turned her mood.

'That's what they all say,' she said. 'I hope for your sake that whatever you did to him was quick. Follow me.'

You're not here to make friends, Luke reminded himself, as Coira walked off. *You're here to survive – and escape. You're here to find out anything you can about the Equals, so you can use it against them.*

But maybe there *would* be allies here. The Condemned were those handed the very worst punishment by the Equals. Those not wrongly convicted, would have already committed some atrocity to land them in this place. They had reason to hate the aristocracy, and experience of acting on that hatred.

Luke remembered his Millmoor friends with a pang:
nervy Asif and the cheerful, improbable tech wizards that
were Hilda and Tilda. Violence had never been part of
their plan. But perhaps fighting the Equals justified using
every means available. Luke would keep an open mind
about his fellow prisoners at Eilean Dòchais – assuming he
wasn't being led to solitary confinement.

Where he was being led, he noted with some astonishment, was through rooms as luxurious as any at Kyneston
– albeit festooned with tartan and armour, and ornamented
with the occasional taxidermied animal head.

As he followed Coira through thickly carpeted corridors,
he kept waiting for the moment their path would turn
downward to dungeons below, or would pass through a
locked iron door to a corridor of cells. But no. The walls
were hung with sepia portrait photographs and garish oil
paintings, many depicting Eilean Dòchais itself, often amid
scenes of battle. In one, the castle's silhouette was lit up by
vivid swirls of what could be either the northern lights, or
scintillations of Skill.

There were even weapons hung on the walls – bayonets
and pikes, crossed swords and axes – though Luke doubted
he could simply creep down one night and grab one, hack
open the door and flee.

'Let's try this room,' said Coira, stopping outside a door.
'Blake is alongside, which is why nobody wants it, but it's
got a lovely view.'

She turned the handle and led Luke into what looked like a posh country hotel room. A large double bed was positioned facing a window that looked out across the loch. There was an over-stuffed armchair (more tartan) and a heavy, carved wardrobe. The air was slightly musty, but Coira unlatched the windowpane and a trickle of fresh air seeped in.

'It won't open any wider,' the girl said, fastening the latch. 'So don't go getting any ideas. I'll fetch you something to wear – you look about Julian's size. Bathroom's through there. I'll be waiting outside in ten minutes to take you down.'

Then she was gone before Luke could say anything.

This was all some elaborate joke. It had to be. Maybe you were given a few days of this, to make it ten times more painful when you were finally dragged to the dungeon in chains.

But right now, Luke didn't care. He threw off his filthy clothes and went into the bathroom. He could have stood under the shower for ages, letting it scald away everything his body had endured in the last forty-eight hours, but he remembered Coira's ten-minute warning and leapt out the second he was clean.

He laughed in disbelief at the clothes she had laid on the bed: a three-piece suit made of fine but slightly hairy fabric (was it tweed?), a crisp white shirt, and a tie. He had no idea what to do with the tie.

There was a knock on the door and Coira's head poked round. Her eyebrows went up at the sight of the limp tie-ends loose in his hands.

'Let me,' she said, knotting them briskly. 'Come on, you mustn't be late for breakfast.'

Then she was off again, and Luke was hurrying after in trousers that were an inch too short and boots that were a size too small, but at least weren't spattered with the mortal remains of Chancellor Zelston.

He should talk to her, this girl. Was she one of the Condemned, like himself? Or simply a house-slave, like those at Kyneston? It was impossible to tell from her dress, which was more formal than anything Luke had ever seen a girl wear, but also plain and well-worn.

'How long have you been here?' he asked, as he followed her through a gothicky-looking door inset with panes of coloured glass. 'Are you just doing your days, or, or . . .'

He trailed off as she turned on her heel. She looked furious. Luke could have put his head in his hands. Talking to girls was difficult enough under any circumstances, but surely he deserved to catch a break.

'We're all killers – or worse. Some of them will try and tell you otherwise, or claim they acted for a great passion or a grand ideal, but we all have blood on our hands.'

Luke didn't know what to say. Even on his past form, this was going disastrously.

'Ask, if you like,' she goaded him. 'I can see you want to.'

Fine. She could have it her way.

'All right: who did you kill?'

'I don't know.' Coira lifted her chin defiantly. 'He's taken that from me. He's taken it from some of the others, too, although most get to remember. But I was young when I did it, because I can't remember ever being any place other than this. So it must have been another child. An Equal one. Happy now?'

She met his eye challengingly. Luke couldn't bear to hold her gaze.

The pity of her situation overwhelmed him. And his heart fluttered as he realized how easily Coira's story could become Daisy's. Two children. An accident. It could only have been an accident. Yet for Coira to have been sent here – collared from childhood. It was inhumane.

But they weren't human, were they, the Equals?

'Here we go,' Coira announced, opening yet another door before Luke had a chance to compose himself. For a split second he was back in Millmoor, with Renie ushering him in front of the Club for the first time, all of them sitting around that knackered office table.

Then the spectacle of the room he'd just entered registered in his brain.

It was nothing he could ever have imagined.

4

Abi

'I'm sorry,' said Abi, feeling not sorry at all. 'Would you say that again? Because I thought I heard you say that rescuing my brother wasn't a priority right now.'

Highwithel's occupants were gathered in its great hall: Abi and Jenner, Meilyr and Dina, Renie and the Club, Lady Tresco and her two daughters. Everyone sat on benches along an imposing table made of sea-polished driftwood. All except Heir Meilyr, who had placed himself at the top. A small, malodorous dog was wandering around their feet, huffing loudly. Abi stared at its mistress, the woman who had just spoken – Bodina Matravers.

The hall windows were stained glass, depicting historical maritime scenes. The light streaming through them imparted a chilly blue lustre to the Equal's white-blonde hair. Did Bodina resemble her sister, icy Heir Bouda, more than Abi had realized?

'Luke isn't our *immediate* priority, no,' said Dina. 'We must get the measure of Whittam Jardine's new regime.

Which means, Jenner, that now you know Abigail is safe, you need to leave. You'll have to accept the Quiet about what you've seen and heard here. We can't risk you giving away anything, even accidentally.'

'No.'

The word was barely out of Abi's mouth before Jenner said equally vehemently, 'I'm not leaving.'

The others all looked at them. Abi focused on the Club members – she had barely mastered their names. The sisters: Hilda and Tilda. The pair she'd thought were Renie's parents, but weren't: Jessica and Oz. The young guy who jiggled all the time and struggled with eye contact: Asif.

And Renie. Beside her, the kid was bristling.

'The first thing you did was come for us,' Renie told Bodina. 'Because you thought this Crovan guy would search Luke's memories and see us all. You didn't hesitate. You came. We've gotta do the same for Luke.'

'Luke rescued me as much as you did, Doc,' said Oz, appealing to Meilyr. 'Went right into that prison in a fake uniform. And unlike you, he didn't secretly have Skill to save his neck if anything went wrong.'

'The situation with Luke is entirely different,' snapped Bodina. 'This isn't walking past half-witted guards. Arailt Crovan is one of the most powerfully Skilled individuals in Britain. Probably *the* most powerful, given that no one alive has ever damaged a person's Skill the way Crovan did Meilyr's.'

Abi's fury warred with her incomprehension. The Dina Matravers she had seen in the aftermath of the Kyneston explosion had been compassionate and powerful, not hesitating to heal a slave. She had rescued the Club members immediately, once they were put at risk by Luke's interrogation. Why was she not going after Luke now? It made no sense.

'I'm not Skillful enough to take on Crovan by myself,' the Equal continued. 'Meilyr can't help me yet – and obviously Jenner can't help at all. Plus, it's not just Crovan we'd have to worry about. That castle of his, Eilean Dòchais, is full of ancient and exceptionally nasty power. All sorts of legends surround it. Until Meilyr is recovered, there is no way we can risk a rescue for Luke.'

Abi was ready to snap, and she felt Jenner angrily push back the bench, ready to rise and remonstrate with Bodina. But someone else spoke before either of them.

'I won't recover. Look at me.'

Meilyr Tresco's voice was calm and clear. At the far end of the table, his youngest sister stifled a sob.

Highwithel's heir rested his cane against the arm of his seat and hauled himself upright. He reached out, his arms trembling with the effort, and his fingers twitched, palsied. Abi saw a vein throb at the side of his throat. How on earth had he made it down those steps last night? Why had he done that just to greet her? Abi's only claim on this man was that she was Luke's sister.

Maybe that was all the claim she needed. She looked at Meilyr. The others in the Club were plainly devoted to him. Abi had come here half convinced that she would be confronting a man who had exploited her brother's devotion and turned him into a walking weapon. She no longer believed that was true.

But if Meilyr hadn't done that, then who?

'Don't push yourself,' Dina told him. 'Last night was too much. You should be in bed.'

The heir gave a tight, mirthless laugh.

'I've been in bed half the day ever since I came here. Isn't that right, Mother?'

He looked down to the far end of the table to where his mother sat. Lady Armeria Tresco appeared to have aged a decade from when Abi had last seen her, at the Debate Ball. She nodded.

'You just need to rest,' insisted Dina.

'No, I don't. No amount of rest will fix my Skill. There's nothing left to fix.'

'Skill can't be destroyed. It's not possible.'

There was a panicky edge to Dina's voice now. Somewhere beneath the table her little dog, sensing her distress, started a thin, unhappy whine.

Meilyr reached out and took her hand, and Abi saw the shine of tears in Dina's eyes.

'Dina, it's not coming back.'

The Equal shook her head. She turned her hand in

Meilyr's grasp and her fingers tightened on his. He jerked back, but she held on, a frown creasing her forehead. Was she working Skill on him?

The members of the Club were watching them. Jessica pressed a hand to her mouth. Beside Abi, even Renie had stopped squirming.

'Please don't,' Meilyr said. 'DiDi, stop it.'

He snatched his hands back, wincing at the abrupt movement, and lowered himself carefully into his chair.

'Where does it go?' Dina pleaded. 'It's like I'm pouring it away into nothingness.'

'That's because there *is* nothing, not any more. It's like there's a hole inside me, and the wind will just blow through it forever.'

As Meilyr wiped sweat from his brow, Abi saw the tears overflow from Bodina's eyes and spill down the Equal's cheeks. And at last she understood.

The Equal girl's refusal to go after Luke this instant was partly because she believed Meilyr would recover, and she wanted him at her side for the rescue. And doubtless partly because she was terrified of confronting the person who'd done this to the man she loved. But mostly, Abi sensed, what had happened to Meilyr was so monumental, so devastating, that no one else's pain made an impression on Bodina Matravers right now. And despite what that meant for Luke, Abi couldn't find it within herself to hate the Equal for that.

A hush fell over the room – until Jenner broke it.

'Life goes on without Skill,' he said. Beneath the table, his warm fingers gripped Abi's knee reassuringly. 'I'd say I'm proof of that, and so are all your Millmoor friends here.'

'Meilyr's not like you,' said Dina fiercely. 'He's going to get better. You've never had Skill. You were born without it.'

'I'm not sure that's true.'

At the far end of the table, Lady Armeria Tresco rose from her place. Abi had heard her discussed disparagingly by Lord Jardine and Bouda Matravers at Kyneston. She was estranged from her husband, a minor noble who had taken her family's name on marriage – but who had not, in her judgement, lived up to it. But with her chin held high and intelligence in her keen blue eyes, she looked a woman you didn't underestimate.

'I remember one time at Kyneston, when you were small, Jenner. You know how Meilyr and your brother Gavar would sometimes play together, being the same age. This was just a few weeks before Silyen was born, and your mother was exhausted, so we were sitting in the sunshine talking and keeping half an eye on the three of you. Then a wail goes up from my boy.'

Lady Armeria stopped by her son and lowered a hand to the back of his chair.

'Gavar had taken something of his, a toy or a book, and had torn it or broken it. He was such a little brute. So

Meilyr was going puce and demanding justice, as we Trescos do.' She smiled fondly, and the tips of her fingers brushed her son's cheek. 'Then *you* leaned across, Jenner. You couldn't have been older than four. You picked this thing up and gave it back to Meilyr, and you said – I remember this clearly – "Better now."'

'And it was fixed?' Abi blurted, gripped by the story.

'It was fixed. I distinctly remember congratulating Thalia that she had a good-hearted boy who would grow up to use his Skill well.'

Everyone was quiet. Jenner had removed his hand from Abi's knee and was sitting very still. Abi chewed her thumbnail to stop herself saying anything more. She remembered Jenner telling her, that time in Kyneston's library, that Lady Thalia had tales of his infant Skill. He had dismissed them as a mother's wishful thinking. Surely he couldn't ignore this?

But his response wasn't what Abi was expecting.

'So what happened?' said Jenner calmly, lacing his hands together on the table. 'Did Crovan make a social call shortly after and rip out my Skill while no one was looking? I don't think so. Mother has stories like that too. The time the gardener brought her a bunch of rosebuds cut from the garden, and I made them all bloom. But of course rosebuds open when brought into a warm house. And that toy was never broken. It would simply have been children squabbling.'

'How can you say that?' Abi said. 'Why would she make it up? Or your mother? Don't you want to have been born with Skill?'

His vehemence was so sudden, so startling, that Abi never saw it coming.

'Want to?'

Jenner's hands slammed against the table as he shoved the bench back so hard the others wobbled. Beneath the freckles, his skin had gone the mottled pink Abi was used to seeing on his father and older brother. Never on Jenner, though.

He stormed away across the hall, this boy she thought she loved, then spun back to face them all accusingly.

'You don't get it, do you? Just like *she* doesn't get it.'

He pointed at Bodina. His voice was louder now. More like shouting. More like Gavar.

'It's *gone*. It went before I even knew what it was. And Meilyr's right, it isn't ever coming back. All I'm left with is a gaping hole where it used to be, and all I can do is pretend it never existed. Because if I have any hope, that means I'm looking into that hole, and the last thing its emptiness will swallow – is me.'

The only sound was the muffled sobbing of Dina Matravers. She'd picked up her dog and buried her face in its fur while her shoulders shook.

Abi was trembling, but not with fear. She could never be afraid of Jenner, even in the grip of this terrible passion.

Because she recognized it for what it was. A self-loathing buried so deep she had never suspected its existence.

She thought of the first day she'd met him, at Kyneston's gates. The easy, practised way he had alluded to, and dismissed, his lack of Skill. She remembered the library, where he had shown her the little portrait of Sosigenes Parva, the Skilless child erased from his family line. The bitterness in his voice as he'd pointed out the empty cage, the dead flower, the noteless music – everything that symbolized how his world looked, to those with Skill.

Now she knew the awful truth. The empty cage, the dead flower, the noteless music. That was how Jenner's world looked to Jenner himself.

'But you have filled that hole.'

It was Meilyr Tresco, taking a few painful steps across to where Jenner stood.

'You have filled it with kindness, and with integrity. Kyneston's slaves are well treated, under your supervision. You manage the Jardine land to benefit its tenants and workers, more than for your family's enrichment. You will be an example to me. Your family is the most powerful in the land, yet you are the best of them.'

Jenner looked at Meilyr, his chest rising and falling as he drew in breath that seemed to pain him.

'I *could* have been the best of them,' Jenner said, wiping a hand across his face. 'And even now there are nights when I lie awake thinking that I would gladly be the worst

– cruel like my father, callous like Silyen, reckless like Gavar, all rolled into one – if only I could have Skill.'

You don't mean that, Abi wanted to say.

But of course he meant it. It would have been more surprising if he didn't. His whole life had been lived in a society that told him he was worthless. Abi sprang to her feet.

'That's because we've got it wrong,' she cried. 'No world should prize the merely Skillful over the truly good.'

'It shouldn't,' said Jenner. 'But it *does*. Do you think you can change it, Abi? Do you, Meilyr? Or how about you, Dina? Because good luck with that.'

He fixed Abi with a last, terrible look, then strode out of the hall. Abi sat shell-shocked as the great doors of sea-wracked wood slammed behind him.

At a light touch on her shoulder, she turned.

'I'm sorry,' said Meilyr quietly. 'For allowing Jenner to feel that we all think being Skilless is a fate worse than death. He has lived with that every day of his life. I'll apologize to him.'

Abi watched the Highwithel heir for a moment.

'This world, that prizes the Skillful over the good,' she said, 'do you really think it can be changed? Does my brother think that, too? Will you tell me what happened to him?'

'Yes,' said Meilyr Tresco. His eyes were very clear, and

something about the way he spoke made Abi shiver. 'Come to me this afternoon and I will.'

As Meilyr led his mother and Dina from the hall, the Club members turned to Abi with a tumult of support. They wanted Luke back too, they assured her. Dina would come to her senses soon. Even if she didn't, the rest of them would do it without her.

Nobody said a word about Jenner's exit.

'We shut down Millmoor without Dina,' Renie said fiercely, and Abi could have hugged her.

But it would be madness to risk a rescue without at least one Skilled Equal. Dina Matravers had to come round. Because there was no one else.

Was there?

Abi needed space to think, so she went where she always thought best: a library. Highwithel's was magnificent. She curled up in a corner chair, hidden from view, with an age-spotted historical tome on the great estates that contained a chapter on Eilean Dòchais. From the old engraved plate illustrations, it looked every bit as beautiful as Highwithel.

There were two island estates in the whole of Britain, and she and Luke were at them. Abi wasn't superstitious, but it felt almost like a sign. They were on parallel journeys. Like her, Luke would have crossed water to a Skill-bound castle he could not easily leave. What had he found there? What was happening to her little brother in that awful place?

Those accusatory, insistent voices started up again, so when Meilyr's sister arrived to show Abi to the garden, the interruption was a relief.

The castle garden was a walled oasis of lush flowers and fruit trees, occupying one of Highwithel's highest court-yards. It was walled on three sides and open to the sea on the fourth, but rather than the gale Abi anticipated with such exposure, barely a breath of wind stirred the surround-ing greenery.

She went to examine the view, only for her legs to stop co-operating when she realized that what she had taken for a terrace was actually a platform, jutting out way too far and stomach-turningly high over nothing but the heaving sea below.

'You can't fall.'

Which was just as well, because the unexpected sound of Meilyr's voice made Abi start. She turned and saw him sat in a low canvas deckchair.

'It's called the "law ledge" and it's warded by Skill. My ancestors used to throw wrongdoers off there. Smugglers, slavers, crooked revenue men, pirates, the lot. You could say we Trescos have always had a robust approach to jus-tice.'

His words were light, but his expression grave. Abi

noticed the deep lines at the corner of his eyes. Once, this man had smiled often. But not any more.

'So you're willing to use any means necessary to dispose of the unjust? Like making a commoner boy kill a man whose politics you don't agree with?'

The heir's face clouded, and he forced himself to stand. Abi wished he wouldn't. The sight of him struggling made her heart well up with pity, and she needed to be tough.

'No,' he said. 'No, that's not my way. But, Abigail, I'm pretty sure I know what happened to your brother.'

Abi's legs went limp beneath her, as if Heir Meilyr had pushed her to the brink of the ledge and forced her to look down.

'Tell me.'

'There is a man, an Equal: Lord Rix. He shares my belief, and Dina's, that the slavedays are unjust. But he also nurses a deep hatred of Whittam Jardine. It goes back to their youth. Rix loved a commoner woman, but Whittam – to curry favour with Rix's father, an influential man – arranged for her to be packed off to a slavetown.

'Rix has been an ally to me and Dina. He works in his own way, on the parliamentary Justice Council, to protect commoner interests. Sometimes he tips us off about arrests, miscarriages of justice. He hides under a veil of contempt for the common folk. He tried to get Gavar Jardine's mission to Millmoor voted down as beneath an Equal's dignity, when in reality he was trying to protect Oz and everything we were working towards.'

Lord Rix. Abi turned the name over in her mind, trying to fit it to a face from the formal announcements at Kyneston's ball. Then an earlier memory swam up. A tall, thin man smoking a fragrant cigar. Stopping her in the corridor during the debate preparations.

'When we discovered that Luke had family at Kyneston,' Meilyr continued, 'Rix suggested we get him transferred so that he could assassinate Lord Whittam. The act would take out Jardine, and make Luke an icon for the unrest we hoped to spark in Millmoor and across the country. But I refused point blank. I wanted Luke to be reunited with you all at Kyneston. Not used like that. Never to pay that price.'

Horror twisted Abi's guts, because she had just remembered the conversation she'd had with Rix that day. He had enquired about her brother, the famous Millmoor escapee. He'd asked her to point him out.

And Abi had told him: a blond boy with an axe, working in the estate grounds.

Something roiled in her stomach. Guilt. Anger.

'So you think Rix tried to compel Luke to kill Lord Jardine. But something went wrong and the Chancellor was shot instead?'

'Yes. I don't know what. The gun must have misfired, or someone moved just as he pulled the trigger.'

And the missing piece in Meilyr's account clicked into place in Abi's brain.

'There's a slave binding at Kyneston. Silyen Jardine lays it on us all at the gate. Jenner told us about it – it means we can't hurt any of the family. There were four of them together that night: Lord Whittam, Lady Thalia, Euterpe Parva, and the Chancellor. Zelston was the only one who wasn't family, unprotected by the binding. Even if Rix intended for my brother to shoot Jardine, the only person Luke would have been *able* to harm was the Chancellor.'

That was how it had happened. It had to be. It was almost a relief to know. Abi looked at Meilyr Tresco. Surely her own face mirrored the awful, guilty understanding that dawned in his.

But Meilyr Tresco's guilt was a useless thing.

He had known that Lord Rix wanted to use Luke for murder. He should have reported Rix when the man first mentioned his plan. He should have found and warned Luke the minute he arrived at Kyneston to attend the debate. He should have turned Rix in at Luke's farce of a trial, never mind that he hadn't known about the binding, which made it all fit together.

One missed opportunity after another. What use was his regret now? None at all.

The anger that had been bubbling away inside Abi erupted.

'You let this happen,' she heard herself shout, as she

grabbed Meilyr's shoulders and shook him. 'You practically *made* it happen.'

Then something slammed into her and lifted her off her feet. Abi gasped as she was tossed through the air, just as she had once seen Bouda Matravers thrown by Gavar's Skill. She went down hard against the stone ledge, banging every bone and joint as she hit.

Shame and fury consumed her. It wasn't only Meilyr. Even if Rix was ultimately responsible, and Meilyr culpable, Abi had also let Luke down. They were both to blame for the nightmare that had engulfed her little brother.

And Meilyr was in chronic pain, yet still she had seized and shaken him.

Abi rolled onto her front to hide her face, hating herself.

But Meilyr had struck back. He had thrown her through the air. His Skill was returning. Abi sat up, breathing hard. Could this ugly fight have brought about something so wonderful?

Like a giant's hand, another surge of Skill shoved her to the brink of the ledge.

She screamed, but came to a halt just in time. Her head and shoulders were jutting out over the edge of the platform. Whatever Skillful wards Meilyr claimed made this place safe, they weren't there now. Abi stared numbly down. It was hundreds of feet to where the sea bit and slavered at the rocks below.

Was this how it would end, with Luke unrescued, her

parents unknowing, and her sister alone? With Jenner still wrathful and disappointed with her?

'How dare you? You know the state he's in.'

The voice was female and enraged. A hand pulled Abi's shoulder round and another slapped her so hard that dark spots wheeled before her eyes.

But Abi barely had a chance to see her assailant before the woman was yanked backwards, and in her place, looming over Abi, was a taller, broader figure, the late afternoon sun glinting bronze in his hair.

'Abi? Tell me you're okay.'

Jenner crouched down, turning his back on the drop, the raging sea, and pulled Abi against him. One hand smoothed back her hair from her face, checking for injury.

'I'm not letting you out of my sight,' he said. 'And I won't get angry like this morning ever again, I promise. I'm so sorry – will you forgive me?'

His brown eyes looked anxiously into hers. His kiss begged her forgiveness – and she gave it.

When Jenner half lifted her back onto her feet, Abi saw the other pair standing there: Meilyr Tresco and a flushed and trembling Bodina Matravers. What had just happened?

Then she understood, and her heart broke for Highwithel's heir all over again.

'That was her,' she said to Meilyr, 'not you. For a moment I thought your Skill . . . I'm so sorry.'

Meilyr was sombre.

'I reckon all four of us here have things to be sorry about,' he said. 'And me most of all. Dina came looking for me, and Jenner was with her, trying to find you. They didn't catch us at our finest moment.'

Abi shook her head.

'But they did. We worked out what happened the night Zelston died. Which means that Luke is innocent. Now we just need to prove it, and then they'll have to let him go.'

'Abigail Hadley,' said Meilyr Tresco, 'we shall and they will. And it begins now. Dina just told me that my mother and I have been summoned to Westminster – Lord Jardine has called his first parliament. We'll be gone in a few hours. Everyone I need to speak to will be there.'

'And if they won't listen,' Abi said, 'we'll figure out how to get into Crovan's castle ourselves.'

5

Gavar

Gavar had lost count of how many drinks he'd had in the parliamentary Members' Bar that night. He tossed the last of the Jura down his throat and signalled to the barman for more.

'Make it two,' said a voice beside him.

Had Gavar been less fuddled, the smell of the cigar smoke would have told him who stood there. As it was, he had to turn before he recognized the voice as belonging to Rix. The rest of the place had emptied out. Just how late was it?

'Mind if I join you?' said Rix, eyeing the empty glasses lined up on the counter. 'I'm steeling my nerves for tomorrow's big event.'

Gavar wasn't aware of any upcoming event. And Rix could have danced naked on a table for all Gavar cared. He grunted assent.

'Just give us the bottle,' Rix instructed the barman. 'Then

close up for the night. Everyone else overdid it on Lord Whittam's hospitality at Kyneston.'

'I don't want to hear that name,' Gavar slurred. 'No.'

His father. Always his father. The man was running the country again. And what was the first thing he planned to do? To humiliate his eldest son, of course. To take the only good thing in Gavar's life – his daughter – and proclaim to the nation that she was worthless. A baseborn nothing.

Rix indicated two high-backed armchairs by the fire. Gavar shrugged, but followed. Rix now had the bottle of malt, after all.

'Is this about the mooted Bill of Succession?' Rix asked, refilling Gavar's glass and pouring one for himself.

What did the man think? That Gavar drank like this every night for absolutely no reason?

Oh, wait.

'Your father won't rule Britain forever, you know. This is an interim administration. And the bill may not even pass.'

'It'll pass. I know what I've heard round the dinner table at Kyneston. Half of parliament has been moaning in private for years, wanting to go back to how things used to be. He's just giving them permission to say those things in public again. Denying baseborns the family name. Requiring them to do days. They'll be tying baseborn babies in sacks and throwing them in rivers next.'

Gavar leaned back in his chair, winded by his own

vehemence. Rix was eyeing him thoughtfully. Gavar was about to tell him where to get off when the man spoke.

'I had a child, too. Like yours. A boy. And for years, I never even knew – thanks to your father.'

Gavar blinked, and pulled himself upright.

'The mother?' he asked. 'She was—'

'A commoner, yes. This was more than a quarter of a century ago. I'd gone back to Oxford to give a talk, and afterwards at High Table she was seated next to me, this beautiful creature. Turned out she was brilliant as well – doing research comparing the legislative structures of countries ruled by our kind, with those governed by the unSkilled. We had a lively dinner discussion, and neither of us wanted the evening to end. So it didn't. It went on for months – the happiest of my life.'

'Then she got pregnant but never told you?'

'She got pregnant and did tell me. And I told my father. Announced that I wanted to marry her, and that the succession of Far Carr could skip me and go to my cousin instead.'

Gavar had never had that conversation with his father. He'd never had the courage. And if he was honest with himself, though he had loved Leah, he wouldn't have renounced Kyneston for her willingly. He had believed he could have both, and Bouda would just have to suck it up. Once, many a cottage on a great estate had housed a common-born family.

What if he'd had to choose, though?

A pointless thought. He drained his glass and poured another before speaking.

'Your father didn't take it well,' Gavar said.

It wasn't a question. The previous Lord Rix had been a noted statesman, rumoured to be the power behind the Chair of not one, but two Chancellors. He was also famously choleric; a man more admired than liked.

'He did not. We fought; he threatened to disinherit me. But that would have been freedom for me – of sorts. So I imagined I had the upper hand. Then she disappeared.'

'Disappeared?'

'She began her days. She wrote to me saying that she had chosen not to be an obstacle between me and my inheritance. I only found out later that it was all arranged by your father – and my father rewarded him handsomely for it, with a seat on the Justice Council.

'Whittam was cunning even then, you see. He sent someone to her with a large sum of money, pretending that I had sent him to pay her off and provide for an abortion. She refused, of course. So then came an appeal to her decency: that she begin her days, to save me from scandal. A place at Arden was promised – the model slavetown near Stratford-upon-Avon, the one that tourists see.

'But that was a lie, too. She was sent to Portisbury, Bristol's shadow. An awful place then, as now. It was a miracle she didn't lose the baby. But he was born there. Raised there.

And though she never spoke ill of me to him, he grew up believing that I had cast his mother off and wanted him terminated.'

The tale was so horrible that Gavar had forgotten to take even a sip of his whisky. He gulped it down now. Then his own story rose up and overwhelmed him.

'Leah ran away,' he heard himself say. 'I adored her, but we argued all the time. I wanted my father to recognize Libby, our daughter. She said a quiet life was safer for both of them. She was so strong, but she was afraid of my father. I think she was afraid of me, too, at the end, and that's why she ran, to escape both of us.'

Gavar hung his head. He'd never spoken of the shame he felt to anyone. He wasn't sure why he was telling Rix now, except that the guy had always been easy to talk to, and Gavar had been pierced by his admission about his lost child.

'And you killed her,' said Rix. 'Didn't you?'

'I . . . I . . .' Gavar hunched in his chair. *I didn't mean to*, would sound ridiculous. *I hardly knew I did it*, would be even more absurd.

Yes, when he'd learned that night that Leah had gone, he had raged. But he had leapt on his motorbike and given chase in order to keep her, not kill her.

It had happened at the gate. The blazing sight of it had set off something in Gavar's brain. After that, he'd hardly known what he was doing – until the moment he had stood over Leah, gun in hand, and heard their daughter howling.

No. He couldn't talk about this. And he certainly wasn't going to spit out a confession that could be used against him. His anger flared again. At Rix, for asking all these questions. At his brothers, for being there when it happened and not stopping him. At his father, for his contempt for the little girl who was Gavar's whole world. But mostly – always – at himself.

'I'm done for tonight.' He banged down his glass and rose unsteadily to his feet. 'I've had enough of your questions.'

'Wait.' Rix caught his arm as he pushed past the man's chair. 'You don't have to live in your father's shadow, Gavar. Doing your father's bidding. That man has destroyed your happiness, and mine, and now he wants to destroy your child's. He'll destroy our country, too.'

'Get off me.' Gavar shook off Rix's hand. He could hear his voice rising. 'I've nothing to say to you.'

And thank goodness he knew the route from the bar as well as any corridor at Kyneston, because his eyes were blurred with tears as he stumbled from the room.

He woke in the morning refreshed in body, if not in spirit, and cursed his efficient Equal metabolism. But when the pantry slave delivered his breakfast, he left the Bloody Mary he'd ordered untouched upon the tray. He wanted to be alert today, for the beginning of parliament and Father's new regime.

He took his place in the House of Light at the last possible moment. Leah had filled his thoughts all night, and he had no desire to speak with Bouda. Especially now that a new date had been fixed for their wedding. Nor did he wish to see if Meilyr Tresco had dragged himself back from Highwithel – or what state he was in if he had.

Barely a moment later, the trumpets sounded. Father might be only an interim Chancellor, but he was denying himself none of the trappings of office.

The session was beginning with that most ancient of ceremonies, the Investiture. The acclamation of debutant peers and heirs usually took place at the first session of each parliamentary year, in May. Father had brought it forward, cloaking his coup in the velvet and ermine of tradition.

Gavar averted his gaze as the first pair was announced: his eager night-time pupil, Heir Ravenna, and her father Lord Tremanton. They knelt to receive their ermine at Father's hands, before proceeding to their obscure estate seat.

The second pair, though, drew his unwilling attention – and that of everyone else in the House. A repulsive snort from directly behind told him that Bouda must have prodded her humongous father awake.

'Of Lindum, in Lincolnshire,' quavered Hengist, the

ancient Elder of the House. 'The Lady Zelston and Heir Midsummer.'

The late Chancellor's younger sister had outlived her entire family. She'd been a schoolgirl when her eldest brother and parents were killed instantly, when the light plane her father was piloting had crashed. And her middle brother, of course, was only a week dead – gunned down by the commoner boy that Gavar himself had fetched out of Millmoor.

There were those, Gavar knew, who might dream of a cataclysm overtaking their family, erasing the line of succession that stretched before them. But Lady Flora Zelston's black skin was dull with grief, and her haggard face showed that she was not one of them.

And then there was Heir Midsummer.

Lady Flora's eldest child was a postgraduate at university – in Brighton, rather than Oxford or Cambridge, which surely explained her ridiculous half-shaved hairstyle and the bar piercing her ear. Her chin was high and her expression defiant as she stared around the chamber. She did not look like the heir of a doomed line. She looked like trouble.

Neither she nor her mother had been present at the hasty trial of the Millmoor boy, now Condemned to Crovan's custody. What had they been told? Did they believe the official version of events: that he was some sort of lone-wolf terrorist, radicalized in the rioting slavetown and brought to Kyneston by unhappy chance?

As Midsummer and her mother knelt before the Chancellor's Chair, the girl turned to stare over her shoulder directly at Gavar. Her dark eyes burned with unmistakable hatred. Did she imagine that she knelt here between a father and a son who had connived at murder for the sake of power?

Gavar stared back, feeling an angry flush creep up his neck. Let her think what she would. The Zelstons were not among the great families. Her uncle had risen to the Chancellorship through his smarmy ways, and without him, they would return to being provincial nobodies.

Gratifyingly, Midsummer looked away first, having to bow her head to murmur the formula of fealty. He saw her shoulders shift uneasily as Father draped the ermine mantle around them.

Two more installations followed, and Gavar's thoughts had wandered, when the final pair of names pronounced by old Hengist jerked him upright.

Surely he'd misheard?

But if he had, then the four hundred Equals seated around him were mistaken, too. The surging noise in the chamber threatened to lift the vaulted roof right off. Striving against the din, Hengist repeated himself.

But words were superfluous as the great doors swung open and Gavar saw him standing there. He'd acquired a new jacket for the occasion, but his hair was uncombed as ever. From where Gavar sat, the customary mischief and malice shone in those familiar black eyes.

Father half rose from the Chancellor's Chair in disbelief as Hengist announced them a third time,

'Lord Rix of Far Carr, and Heir Presumptive Silyen.'

Heir presumptive. As Silyen was not a blood relation of Rix, an act of Skill would be required to confer inheritance.

What was Rix thinking? Gavar remembered his greeting from the previous night – *Just steeling my nerves for tomorrow*. No wonder.

As the pair walked forward to stand before the Chancellor's Chair, the uproar died away.

'Explain yourself,' said Father.

'The precedent is well established,' Rix replied. 'Your own ancestor Cadmus was adopted from the Parva line to become the Jardine heir.'

'Cadmus was first-degree blood kin, as all adoptions in living memory have been. But Silyen is no kin of yours.'

'Indeed. This is an adoption of merit.'

'Merit?'

Silyen, who had kept poker-faced up till now, permitted himself the hint of a smirk. Gavar wanted to smack it off his smug, sharp face.

'Surely, Lord Chancellor, your youngest son's recent feats demonstrate exceptional merit? The revival of Euterpe Parva, and the no less astonishing restoration of Kyneston.'

'Why adopt an heir?' Father asked. 'You can easily marry. Pass your estate into the keeping of those of your blood.'

'A fusty old bachelor like me?' Rix gestured to his immaculate self and drew laughter from a few parliamentarians. 'I think not.'

Behind him, Gavar heard the heel of one of Bouda's stilettos grind against the wooden floor. Rix was godfather to both Bouda and Bodina. Perhaps she had imagined that Far Carr would pass to them one day.

'I need only to ensure that my estate has a deserving inheritant,' Rix continued. 'Now that your son is past his eighteenth birthday, I can think of no finer candidate.'

Far Carr was a dreary place: a hundred mostly empty square kilometres of Suffolk – forest, reed beds, and a scrabbly stretch of coast. Far Hall was a tumbledown medieval pile from the time of the kings. Silyen would be welcome to it – if he could get it, because now Father had turned his attention to him.

'Is being a member of the Founding Family not enough, that you push yourself like a cuckoo into another's nest?'

Silyen glanced up at the golden shadows that flickered ceaselessly across the glass walls of the House of Light, then back down to their father.

'My lord, you know better than anyone that it's knowledge I crave, not status. How astonishing it will be for me to sit in this hallowed House. How could I refuse Lord Rix's generous offer?'

His expression was rapt, almost childlike, and for the briefest of moments Gavar was thrown back to a time when Silyen was a tangle-headed toddler stumbling around the garden, his Skill wreaking innocent havoc. As the eldest, Gavar had kept a watchful eye.

But these days there was nothing innocent about his little brother's talent for mayhem. Silyen had instigated Zelston's abolition Proposal. And look how that turned out: overwhelming defeat, Zelston dead, and Father back in the Chancellor's Chair.

Gavar froze where he sat.

If Father had anyone to thank for his recapture of the Chair, it was Silyen.

That had to be a coincidence.

Surely.

Of course it was. Father had been as surprised as Gavar when Silyen told them all those months ago how he'd manoeuvred Zelston into issuing the Proposal. Father was just as surprised now, by Sil's appearance as the heir presumptive of Far Carr.

Wasn't he?

Gavar narrowed his eyes. What if the scene now unfolding was merely the latest in an elaborate piece of playacting? Could Silyen and Father have been conspiring all this time to return Lord Jardine to power? Which would make this latest development Silyen's reward.

Or was there even more to it than that? Was this Lord

Jardine manoeuvring his brilliant youngest son into parliament? Positioning him for future preferment – even, perhaps, succession to the Chair?

So Gavar wasn't surprised when Father soon announced himself satisfied. The adoption would proceed.

As Father took up an officiant's position between Sil and Rix, Gavar snorted. Bouda had made him attend several wedding rehearsals, which was what this ceremony resembled. Until Silyen pulled out a knife.

Sil ran a finger along the edge of the blade. It gleamed gold beneath his touch and looked sharp enough to kill.

Gavar watched his little brother hold out his right hand, palm splayed. Placing the point of the knife at the tip of his thumb, Silyen jabbed it deep into the soft fingerpad.

'I will defend your wall.'

Slowly, he drew the blade along the length of his thumb and dragged it round the heel of his hand, stopping in the centre of his palm. Blood welled up. Gavar could smell it from where he sat.

'I will uphold your roof.'

Silyen moved the knife to the top of his index finger. Stab.

Down went the blade, unpeeling a red seam in its wake.

'Your land is my land.' Stab.

'Your line is my line.' Slice.

'Your honour is my honour.' Cut. 'I ask you to be my lord.'

Silyen cupped a five-petalled flower of blood.

Despite himself, Gavar was on the edge of his seat at the grisly spectacle. As his brother opened out his hand, the edges of the wounds gaped wide, and blood spattered audibly onto the floor.

His patrician features blanching, Lord Rix offered his own hand, placing it palm down on top of Silyen's. Their fingers locked in an oozing handshake. It was all pretty disgusting, but nothing for Rix to be looking so queasy about.

Then Silyen spun the knife in his hand and offered its hilt to Rix, and Gavar understood.

'I unbar my gate to you. I open my door to you,' Rix intoned, holding the knife just above their clasped hands. 'My land is your land. My line is your line. My honour is your honour. I take you as my heir.'

His hand trembled for an instant before the knife flashed down. Gavar heard Silyen's pained intake of breath. Rix gave an agonized groan and let go of the handle.

The blade skewered their conjoined palms like a hand kebab. Father was watching avidly. Maybe it was the blood that riveted him; maybe it was simply the pain. The man was one sick puppy.

Lord Jardine rested his fingers atop the knife hilt.

'Blood has mixed with blood,' he declared. 'A kin bond has been sealed.'

Father pulled the blade. It came out clean.

Rix looked uncertainly at his hand as it began to heal. Silyen didn't spare his injury a glance. He wore a vague, faraway smile, as if high on Skill.

The light in the chamber was shifting oddly.

The House of Light was lit solely by the radiance from the world beyond – that creepy, shining realm that Gavar and most of the peers tried not to think about. Not thinking about it was usually easy. But not at this moment. Up above, something was happening on the other side of those glass walls.

Gavar wasn't the only one to have noticed. Around him, Equals stirred in their seats. Murmurs ran through the chamber and a sense of growing unease was palpable.

Was it getting darker? Or brighter? How could it be impossible to tell which?

Nobody knew what the shapes were that moved in the world beyond. They passed like clouds on a sunny day or the shadows of wind-tossed trees. But you only had to watch for a little while (Gavar tried never to watch) to understand that the movement was purposeful.

Right now, that movement was towards the walls of the chamber. Distant forms became larger and brighter, gathering there.

Then someone – several people – screamed as a gout of gold flared impossibly through the glass walls towards the trio on the Chancellor's dais. Rix cried out and recoiled. Father lifted an arm to cover his face.

And Silyen?

Sil was staring upwards, his arms wide, open-mouthed and breathing raggedly. Something about the sight of him made Gavar feel sick with apprehension. He wished his baby brother had never graduated from toddling round the garden turning blackbirds orange and making the housekeeper's cat bark.

What had Rix and Father done?

The light died almost as quickly as it had flared. The structure of the House appeared intact. Parliamentarians were looking around with relief, and conversation began to rise.

Father strode forward and made a hushing motion, and the assembled Equals quieted.

'Well,' he said, loud enough to be heard by those in the uppermost tier. 'Now you see why most of us prefer to get our heirs the way nature intended.'

Gavar heard Lord Lytchett snuffle with amusement behind him. Scattered laughter broke the tension in the chamber, and Father gestured for Rix and his new heir to kneel for their investiture.

The estate seat of Far Carr was in the fourth tier back, gratifyingly mid-rank. But as Rix staggered towards it, Silyen remained where he was. What now?

'As my son turned eighteen only two weeks ago,' Lord Jardine said, 'that makes him the new Child of the House.

Heir Brogan, you may return to your seat. Please pass the Chancellor's mantle to Heir Silyen.'

The dismissed Child moved faster than Gavar had ever seen anyone move in the House of Light. He left his spot at the side of the wooden throne, thrust the bundle of velvet into Sil's arms, and hurried to the estate seat where his mother waited.

Father settled into the Chair. He sat straight-backed, fingers gripping the armrests with an air of casual command. Silyen stood very close by.

Marvellous. Now Gavar had both of them to look at.

'Last week, you elected me Chancellor to deal with an emergency,' Father said, his leonine head turning to gaze sternly around the chamber.

'The events of the past months and weeks have revealed a shocking conspiracy among the common people of Great Britain. A conspiracy so extensive that it duped one of our own number with tragic consequences. He's here today and we are glad to see Heir Meilyr among us once more, after his regretfully necessary chastisement.

'But there have been no consequences yet for the prime instigators: the seditionists and rabble-rousers among the common people. In the coming weeks, I will introduce a preliminary raft of laws to regulate the proper status of the commoners, including baseborns. But my first duty as Chancellor is to protect our peace. So I take two initial steps, effective immediately.

'The first is the suspension of the parliamentary observers. Until cleared of any disloyalty, the commoners have forfeited their right to representation among us. The second is an even weightier task. I entrust it to two young parliamentarians of proven ability, both members of the Justice Council.'

Gavar sat transfixed by his father's stare. There was no escaping the direction Lord Whittam was looking – right at Gavar, and at the girl sat behind him.

'We must purge the slavetowns. With justice. But where necessary, without pity. To spearhead this I appoint Heir Bouda of Appledurham and – as proof of how seriously I take this threat – my own son and heir, Gavar.'

Because just when Gavar thought things couldn't get any worse, of course they always, *always* could.

6

Silyen

The Chancellor's Chair was a riddle disguised as a piece of furniture. Once, it had been the throne of kings. But not of the fabled Wonder King himself – only the low kings who came after. The Skilless.

How had that happened, Silyen wondered? How had power passed from those with Skill, to those without – before Lycus Parva's overthrow of Charles the First and Last had wrested it back again a thousand years later?

If you could understand that, you could understand how it might happen again.

Or how it could be prevented.

The day's session that had begun with his own investiture was over, and Silyen was alone in the deserted House of Light. He crouched down by the side of the throne and traced the worn carvings with his fingertips. As heir of Far Carr, he could now walk in and out of this chamber as he pleased. As Child of the House, his place was next to this Chair. It was perfect.

Rix hadn't wanted to adopt him. But he couldn't argue with what Silyen knew – that it was Rix's Skill that had Silenced Luke Hadley after the little mishap in the ballroom. That as good as pinned the crime on the man. So Rix had bought Silyen's discretion with an inheritance.

Now the deed was done, the lord of Far Carr couldn't take it back. Indeed, if anything were to happen to Rix, then the estate would pass entirely to its new heir.

Rix really hadn't thought it through.

Silyen stroked the bowed seat of the Chair. This was an entertaining game to play. He could see how it might obsess men like Father, and women like Bouda Matravers, to the point that they believed this was all that mattered: mastery of your peers, mastery of the country. But none of it mattered without mastery of yourself.

What would it take to make the Equals realize what they were truly capable of? More than the need to suppress a riot in Millmoor, that was certain.

'Hello? Silyen?'

Sil straightened up. Who was seeking him out here? The tapping of a cane on the marble floor provided the answer. Silyen watched as Meilyr Tresco limped across the chamber.

'It's been a few centuries since any of my ancestors sat in that,' said Meilyr, coming to a halt and raising his stick to point at the battered throne.

'Jory Tresco,' said Silyen, smiling. 'One of the best we ever had.'

When Napoleon had conquered the unSkilled countries of Europe and turned his covetous eye on Great Britain, Chancellor Jory Tresco had been waiting.

He had gathered together the Equals most Skilled in elemental manipulation. Being a true Tresco radical, he took pains to seek out talented women who he believed had an affinity for such work. Risking scandal, he took a group of them to Highwithel – for which one of Silyen's ancestors had attempted to impeach him. There, they worked in seclusion for more than a year. And when Britain's bold Admiral Nelson, acting as bait, had finally lured Napoleon's fleet up the coast of Spain and France towards Britain, the noblewomen had simply rolled up the sea behind him.

'It's memorialized in the windows of our hall at Highwithel,' said Meilyr. 'All the French ships falling off a cliff of water and smashing on the bed of the English Channel. Did it really happen, do you think?'

Silyen rolled his eyes. Meilyr's own ancestor had made it happen. The corridors of Westminster and half the great houses of Britain were hung with paintings of *The Grounding at Gorregan*. Barely two centuries had passed since that day, and already its events were regarded as half legend. Just as the deeds of the Wonder King had been consigned to folklore, judged too fantastical to be true. Silyen begged to differ. But that was a conversation for another day.

'I doubt you sought me out to talk about history,' he said. 'But I'm glad you've come by. I wasn't there to see what Crovan did to you, but from the descriptions I've heard, it must have been spectacular.'

A hurt, haunted look crossed Meilyr's face.

'Do you mind me asking,' Silyen continued – a phrase you only ever said when you knew perfectly well that your interlocutor would mind, and greatly – 'what it felt like? And how you feel now?'

'Actually,' said Meilyr, pushing himself erect on his cane, 'I have some questions for you. Perhaps we could trade answers?'

Which was intriguing. Silyen nodded and lowered himself onto the rim of the Chancellor's dais, swinging his legs over the edge.

'You first,' he offered.

'Would the binding that you place on all slaves at the Kyneston gate prevent someone who had been bound from, say, shooting one of the Jardines.'

'It would.' Silyen wondered who Meilyr's source was. Two possibilities presented themselves: Abigail Hadley, or the Dog. 'My turn: is your Skill merely damaged, or gone?'

'Gone,' said Meilyr. 'As far as I can tell. Dina hopes it'll come back soon. My mother hopes it'll come back eventually. But I don't think it's ever coming back. My next question: when you examined Luke Hadley after the shooting of Chancellor Zelston, did you find any evidence that

93

he had been Skillfully interfered with in any way? Compelled, Silenced? That sort of thing.'

'I did,' said Silyen.

It had to be Abigail who'd worked it out. She was smart enough, and had been missing ever since running from the Labour Bureau car. She must have fled to Highwithel. Which would also explain – Silyen couldn't believe he hadn't connected it before, though to be fair, Jenner's activities were usually of minimal interest – why his middle brother had gone to 'inspect the family properties' in Devon and Cornwall.

'And?' Meilyr demanded. 'Who?'

'If I told you, what would you do with that information?'

'I would make sure that an innocent boy is freed from Crovan's clutches, and that the person truly responsible answered for their crimes.'

'And how would you do that?'

'I'm sorry?'

'How would you *make sure that an innocent boy*, et cetera, et cetera?' Silyen waved a hand airily. 'Because I thought you tried that already, and it didn't go brilliantly for either of you.'

Meilyr Tresco stared. His fingers were white around the head of his walking stick; his breathing was harsh and appeared painful. Crovan had really done a number on him.

'I would confront . . . the person in question. And

whether he confessed or not, I would take what I know, and your evidence, to the proper authorities.'

'Meilyr, there are no proper authorities. There hardly ever were, but now there's just my father.'

'Surely your father would want to know if someone had made an attempt on his life? An attempt that only failed by accident. I doubt he'd be pleased to hear that one of his sons knew who the perpetrator was and hadn't told him. Particularly if the son had used that information to advantage himself.'

Meilyr pointedly lifted his gaze from Silyen, to the estate seat of Far Carr.

Sil smiled.

'Oh, I don't know. My father would probably give me a medal for cunning or something. But think for a minute, Meilyr. You want Luke Hadley out of Crovan's custody. Turning in an Equal you suspect of using him isn't going to achieve that. Guilt isn't an either/or thing in these sorts of circumstances. It spreads to everyone it touches.

'That Equal would be punished, most likely just as you were. My father gets to make another show of strength that will even further cow his already few opponents. Luke will stay right where he is, as a deterrent to the common folk. Is that really what you want? The person you're talking about was your ally once. He can still be useful to you, just as he has been useful to me.'

Meilyr hadn't taken his eyes from Silyen's face. The

man's internal struggles were plain to see. Poor, principled Meilyr. So worried about justice that he couldn't see logic.

'I can't let Luke suffer,' Meilyr said. 'Not when I'm to blame.'

'Well, technically,' said Silyen, 'I'm to blame, seeing as I'm the one that had Zelston introduce the abolition Proposal that started this whole thing off. But I'm not losing sleep over it.'

Meilyr's hands slumped at his side, the head of his cane banging his hip.

'The rumours said it was you. But I never understood why you'd do that. You're no abolitionist – not that I know of. What are you, Silyen Jardine?'

Which was a good question. Silyen thought about it.

'Curious.'

Meilyr half laughed, seemingly despite himself.

'You can say that again.'

Silyen smiled. 'You owe me a second answer, Meilyr. So here's my second question: When you realized what Crovan had done to you, did you want to die?'

The knuckles went white around the cane handle again. Meilyr Tresco actually lifted it, as if his hand itched to smash it across Silyen's face. There was something magnificent in the spectacle of Highwithel's heir warring with his own honourable nature.

When the cane struck the marble floor hollowly as

96

Meilyr let it drop back down again, Silyen was almost disappointed.

'Yes,' he said. 'Yes, I did.'

'I think,' Silyen said, jumping down from the dais and landing lightly on his toes, 'that we've covered everything. Now, if you'll excuse me, I need to go. I have an estate to restore – my Aunt Euterpe is returning to Orpen Mote, and she needs my assistance.'

Silyen sensed Meilyr watching as he left.

What would Highwithel's heir do? Silyen couldn't predict. Tresco was plainly desperate to get Luke away from Eilean Dòchais. Would he try and turn Rix in? He surely knew that wouldn't work.

Would he attempt to rescue Luke the old-fashioned way? That would be something to see. The wards on the ancient Scottish castle were fascinating. Silyen had taken an interest in them, and specifically Crovan's collaring, when crafting the act of binding for Kyneston's slaves. But though Meilyr was brave, bravery alone wouldn't get you into – or out of – Eilean Dòchais. Particularly when you no longer had Skill.

All the while they had talked, Silyen had been probing where Meilyr's Skill should have been. He'd encountered nothing. A void. Tresco didn't think his Skill was ever coming back. Silyen didn't think it was either. Meilyr was now Skilless, like Jenner.

Deep in thought, Silyen ran his fingers along the corridor

tapestries as he left the great chamber. Aunt Euterpe had scolded him for doing that at Orpen when he was a child and she still lay comatose at Kyneston, and they had walked together through the lost house of her memories.

What he had found at Orpen, in the journals of Cadmus Parva-Jardine, had raised questions about his brother's lack of Skill that Silyen longed to investigate.

Cadmus's fabled ability had gone unremarked in his youth. It was only in adulthood – after his first wife's death and the birth of his supposedly Skilless son – that word of his great Skill had spread. The reason for that was abundantly clear to Silyen: Cadmus had possessed no exceptional power, until his child was born. And that power had come from taking his son's Skill.

It was something never acknowledged in Cadmus's journals. So it had plainly happened accidentally. Involuntarily.

And Silyen would bet his newly minted title that something similar had happened between him and Jenner in their earliest childhood. The coincidence of his brother's lack of power and his own Skillful strength was too great.

So could Skill ever be restored? Or if Skill originated not in individual human bodies, but somewhere external – what they all called the World of Light – could it be drawn upon, and replenished?

Silyen had been spurred to re-examine these questions after what Crovan had done to Meilyr. Hence his confrontation with Jenner at the gate. Sil had wondered if Jenner's desperation to free Abi Hadley might spark some residual power. He had stirred up his brother with provoking words. And he had attempted a small transfusion of Skill, to see if his brother's body would respond to it and remember forgotten abilities.

But in the event, Jenner had proved unable either to retain transfused Skill, or generate more of his own. The resulting anger and raw hurt of his usually calm and affable brother had shocked even Silyen.

That encounter with Jenner proving fruitless, no light had been cast on what had happened to Meilyr Tresco. Had Crovan taken Meilyr's power, as Silyen believed he himself had taken Jenner's? Had Meilyr's Skill been destroyed? Or was there a third possibility? From the descriptions Silyen had gathered of the spray of gold that burst from Meilyr, of its rising and disappearance, had his ripped-out power somehow been flung back into the World of Light?

And what of the flare of brightness that had shot through the House of Light's shimmering ceiling after Silyen's adoption ritual? The two events pointed to one conclusion: that the barrier between this world and the World of Light was permeable. Penetrable.

Could Skill be drained out of this world – or pulled into it?

As he passed through Westminster's corridors, Silyen let his awareness unfurl and eddy around him, sensing the movement of the Skilled. There was Bouda Matravers, hurrying into a quadrangle on the left, a vitality both intense and controlled. No sign of Gavar near her, of course.

His perception spiralled upward and outward, until it encompassed the entire Westminster complex. He felt different, more connected, now that he was an heir – an acknowledged part of this place. Silyen paused in the corridor and closed his eyes. When he opened them, he gasped.

He was seeing a world composed of only bright and dark. Of Skill, and its absence. Behind him throbbed a power so blazing he dared not turn – the House of Light. All around were the glowing traces of hundreds of Equals: parliamentarians, their guests and family members, the second- and third-borns who would never hold office, but who worked here. Each individual was a Skillful radiance that flickered and flared. He tipped his head. Up high in the Chancellor's Tower moved an intense golden pulse: Father, prowling.

Dazed, Silyen leaned against the wall. A tangle of brilliance bore down on him, which he only belatedly realized was a person walking along the corridor. It stopped right alongside, and its proximity was hardly bearable.

'Are you all right?' a voice asked.

Silyen had no idea who it belonged to. Was incapable of responding.

'Whatever,' the voice said sniffily. 'Weirdo.'

The brightness moved on.

Silyen tried to focus. It wasn't just the dazzling hotspots of Skilled individuals that he could see. Around him, the walls of Westminster were faintly limned in light. He must be seeing the traces of Skill worked on the building through its history, he realized.

The lambent outline was sufficient to navigate through, and Silyen made his way to the low River Door that led from Westminster down to the Thames. It wasn't one favoured by parliamentarians. He pushed it open into a gust of wind and noise: the stop-start of clogged traffic, car horns quarrelling with pedestrians, tour bus guides describing the glories of the House of Light in more languages than even Silyen recognized. Britain's inhabitants might be unable to leave the country until the completion of their slavedays, but visitors flocked here from every corner of the globe.

Westminster Bridge was surely heaving with people, as usual. But in Silyen's Skillful sight, it was nothing but emptiness and darkness.

How much more beautiful it would be, golden and glowing. Filled with Skill.

A crawling pinprick of brightness distracted him – an Equal in a taxi, coming over the bridge – which was why he sensed nothing until the blade was at his throat, too late for his Skillful reflexes to kick in.

'That's you – dead,' a voice rasped in his ear.

Then it laughed, a repulsive sound.

Silyen closed his eyes and concentrated, momentarily

terrified that his normal sight had been burned away by his bright vision. But when he opened them again, the every-day world swam back into view.

And what a view. Dog stood in front of him, blade upraised to Silyen's neck and looking not a whit saner than when he had last seen the man – when he'd summoned the gate at Kyneston and released him in the aftermath of the East Wing's destruction.

Dog's strangulation of Great-Aunt Hypatia had gone undetected amid the general chaos. Her body, already purpling and puffy, hadn't been found until the next morning. The faint contusions around her neck were deemed an injury from the explosion; her death was attributed to a heart attack from shock. Only Silyen – and Abi Hadley – had seen Dog moving purposefully towards Hypatia, the leash wrapped around his hand.

Silyen sighed. 'I would say I've missed you,' he said, raising a hand and lightly pushing the blade away from his neck. 'But Mother instilled in me that a gentleman never lies.'

'You're no gentleman,' Dog rasped.

'I'm an heir, now, so mind your manners. No more knives at throats, please.' He glanced down. Dog appeared to have more than one knife. He had a whole bunch of them, held oddly in his hand. 'I presume this isn't a social call, to congratulate me on my elevation?'

'Need your help,' growled Dog. 'Been – busy. Need a

place – to lie low. I owe you – three debts, so – came to you.'

'I hate to break it to you, but that's not how debts work. The idea is that you help me.'

Silyen inspected Dog. He was still wearing the clothes in which he'd run from Kyneston, coveralls swiped off a peg in the kennels. They were thickly grimed, and coated with a dried substance that was mud, blood, or worse.

'I can't take you to our house on the Embankment – though I think Father plans on trading up from there soon. But I keep a little place for myself in Marylebone. Let's walk; I'll make sure we're not noticed. And put those knives away. What exactly have you "been busy" doing – burgling cutlery drawers?'

'Beautiful, isn't it?'

Dog opened his fingers and Silyen saw that he wasn't holding knives after all. Where his right hand had been was a replacement made of metal. Razor-sharp metal. Then he looked more closely and saw the leather webbing across the man's palm, the laces that criss-crossed up the back and knotted tight at the wrist. It was part glove, part instrument of torture. And that was when he realized what he was looking at.

'Black Billy's handiwork. I never knew you shared my appreciation of historical artefacts. You must have paid a visit to my relatives at Ide.'

'Nice,' said Dog, 'to see the old place – again.'

He bared his teeth in a grin, and dug his monstrous hand into the coverall's voluminous front pocket to conceal it. Side by side, they turned away from the river towards St James's Park, skirted Green Park, and kept going.

At Silyen's bolt-hole – a limewashed mews house in a quiet courtyard – he coaxed Dog into taking off the glove so he could examine it while the coffee brewed. It was heavy, made of mottled, folded and refolded crucible steel. Each finger was jointed. And each one was subtly different, varying in the length and width of its blade.

Every schoolchild in Britain knew the story of this glove: the final work of a blacksmith who, a century and a half ago, had led a revolt against his harsh masters. Black Billy had incited his fellow villagers to rise up against the Vernays of Ide – a branch of the Jardine family. But the peasants never stood a chance. While his closest confederates were summarily executed, Billy was tortured to death using the ingenious instruments he had first been Skillfully compelled to forge. Implements that had remained at Ide in the custody of the Vernays ever since.

Until now.

'For slicing,' said Dog, watching him sort through the various blades. 'For peeling. For segmenting. And there are – others, too. Not knives.'

He opened a flat leather pouch that hung from his belt and withdrew more implements.

'For ears,' Dog announced, holding up a delicate length

of metal. It curved in sinuous loops, with minuscule barbs along its length.

He picked out another. 'For eyes.' That one was more like an ice cream scoop for someone with a tiny appetite. Silyen grimaced. He hated ice cream.

'Souvenirs?' he asked. 'Or have you more practical plans?'

'A workman likes – good tools,' the man rasped. 'Getting them – was easy. The family was – away. Someone who knew me – let me in.'

'After what you did?'

'My leash – round his throat – may have persuaded him.'

Dog's abrading laugh again.

'This one,' Dog said, leaning in to touch the largest blade on the glove, heavy and serrated, 'will take off the head – of your cousin Ragnarr.'

Silyen poured himself a thin, hot stream of coffee and let that sink in. He sat back in his chair and raised the cup to his lips.

'Revenge is a beautiful thing,' he said. 'And I appreciate what you're doing to reduce my Christmas card list, but will I have any relatives left by the time you're done? What Ivarr did to your wife and unborn baby was unspeakable, but you killed him, his wife, and their children. My great-aunt made you her dog, and you've paid her back in kind – using the leash was a nice touch. But are you going after Ragnarr because of his older brother's deeds?

Because if that's how it works, I should have women Gavar has wronged knocking on my door morning, noon and night.'

'They did – everything together.'

Including, presumably, raping Dog's wife. Silyen took another sip of scalding coffee and let it warm him. Fine. Cousin Ragnarr wasn't someone Silyen would shed any tears over.

In fact, another killing of an Equal so soon after the assassination of Zelston would electrify the nation. Father would crack down harshly. That would oppress the common people further, while reminding them that Equals were vulnerable. Which would stir things up nicely.

And for the victim to be yet another of the Vernays of Ide, whose crushing of Black Billy's Revolt had made them a byword for Equal oppression of the commoners, and who had been the victims of the worst commoner slaying of Equals in living memory when Dog took out Heir Ivarr and his family five years ago?

Well, that was almost perfect.

'It seems to me,' he told Dog, 'that you'll be in need of somewhere more long-term to hide out. Luckily, I know just the spot. My aunt is expecting me at the ruins of Orpen Mote – we're going to rebuild it. No one goes near the place.' He proffered the steaming silver pot and a small cup. 'And it's only fifty miles from Ide. Coffee?'

Dog took the cup, and bared his teeth in what was once a grin but was now simply a horror.

They travelled out the next morning, the car driven not by one of the family chauffeurs but by a discreet fellow of Silyen's acquaintance. He dropped them at the perimeter of the woods that encircled the once-great estate, and they went forward on foot through the trees, then across fields where waist-high cow parsley, vernal grass and feathery vetch whipped at them as they walked.

Orpen had no gate worth the name, simply a plain iron four-bar set into a low stone wall. The boundary was marked instead by an immense ha-ha – a ditch to prevent animals crossing. And not only animals. Sil felt the tingle of Skill as he crossed the ditch's small bridge, its cattle grid rusted with long disuse. Dog shuddered as he stood on the grid. The touch of Skill meant nothing good to him.

'You don't have to come over,' Silyen said. 'The woods here have plenty of game. You could hunt. Practise. I'll find you at the end of the day.'

Dog patted the pocket of the overalls, and the blades within clashed dully. He nodded, turned his back, and loped off towards the treeline. The man would kill every Equal in Britain if he could, Silyen thought, watching him go. He touched his throat and remembered the scrape of steel there.

Aunt Euterpe was sitting in the garden just as she had

the first time he'd met her, when he walked into her mind as she lay slumbering at Kyneston.

But this was no fresh-faced twenty-four-year-old, sunning herself in a deckchair.

Aunt Euterpe's youthful beauty had been scraped away by the painstaking knife of sorrow, sculpting her delicate features into something austere. She resembled a funerary statue, set upon a crumbling line of masonry that might once have been an ornamental wall. Her dress was plain and black. And as he bent to kiss her cold cheeks he saw, pinned near her throat, an ivory badge bearing the Roman banner and standard of the Zelston coat of arms. Mourning attire.

Taking her hands, Silyen gently pulled her upright. Euterpe leaned against him, her head just reaching his shoulder, as together they stared at the charred remains of lost Orpen. She was his mother's sister, but sometimes, recalling the days of his childhood and adolescence they had spent together in this place, Silyen felt she was more like his.

It took a moment for him to realize she was crying. Reflexively, he put his arms around her and folded her against his chest.

'I wish you'd never woken me,' she said, muffled into his riding jacket. 'I wish I could have slept and dreamed forever. In our garden, Winterbourne was still alive. But here . . .'

'Here, *you* are alive,' he said. 'And you will be happy again. Look.'

He took his aunt's hand. Felt the Skill that throbbed there, almost like a second pulse. The strength of this woman.

He let Skill flow out of him. Felt it drip through his fingers like blood and drop into the soil. He'd become better, so much better at this, since the day the Hadley girls had caught him in the woods experimenting with the cherry tree.

What had lain dormant in the earth responded.

Clods of soil writhed. The first green shoot pushed up out of the ground. Then another. A third. A whole row of them. They grew, bushed and bloomed. At his side, Euterpe Parva watched as flower after flower unfolded, each a blood-red bowl of petals.

In the garden of Orpen Mote, the air was heavy with the scent of roses.

7

Luke

Luke had imagined various scenarios awaiting within the walls of Eilean Dòchais. A leash and obedience classes, perhaps. Maybe a dungeon. Certainly a cell. But never this.

He checked in the mirror as he knotted the black tie. The grandfather clock in the hallway had already chimed quarter past, so he toed on his polished dress shoes and hurried downstairs. In the castle's high central atrium, draped on all sides with antique flags and heraldic banners, Devin was waiting anxiously, just as he had hovered on the threshold when Luke first arrived.

A silver fob watch was in his hand. Devin waited for his master every night, and liked to ensure that the castle's other occupants were seated before Crovan took his place at the table.

As Luke pushed open the glass-paned doors to the dining room, he was greeted with a scene remarkably like the one at breakfast that first morning, when Coira had dressed him in Julian's clothes and brought him down. He'd thought, at the time, that he was hallucinating.

Two chandeliers glittered at each end of the windowless room. Along one wall hung a tattered battle standard emblazoned with the now-familiar motto: *Omnes vulnerant; ultima necat – All hours wound; the last one kills.* Against the opposite wall stood an immense glass case housing a tableau of stuffed game animals – pheasants, deer, pine martens, all grimacing at the indignity of their afterlife.

But the most striking thing about the room was the people gathered in it. A dozen were already present. Their full number would be twenty one: mostly men in immaculate black tie, though there were three women in bright evening dress. Servants circulated with glasses of champagne. It was how Luke had always imagined the Equals lived, behind the walls of their great estates: luxurious and carefree.

Except everyone here was Condemned. These were no party guests, but prisoners of the state, sentenced to Crovan's keeping at Eilean Dòchais.

Luke hunted for his place card around the table, and found it almost directly opposite where Crovan sat. To his right would be Julian. He didn't need to read the namecard to his left, as the seat was already occupied.

'Hello, Luke,' said Lavinia, tipping up her face. 'Don't

you look handsome tonight? Are you going to give a lady a proper greeting?'

Luke had learned Lavinia's name easily, given how few women were here. She was bird-tiny and at least a decade older than his Mum.

He had no idea what constituted a 'proper greeting', until she presented her rouged cheek. It would be just like kissing your grandma, Luke told himself, as he bent over her – except at the last minute, Lavinia turned her head and met him full on the mouth. Luke felt her lips part expectantly and recoiled, gagging. He wiped her scarlet lipstick from his mouth and coughed to cover the gesture, but any hope of discretion was dashed when Lavinia shrieked loud enough for the entire room to hear.

'No lip-kissing, you naughty boy. I know I'm irresistible, but my mouth is only for darling Braby.'

Luke burned with mortification, and matters weren't helped when the first pair of eyes he met across the table were Coira's, filled with scorn.

Then Coira was gone, carrying a great silver platter through to the kitchen. She wasn't one of the 'guests' – as those who gathered every morning and evening around this table styled themselves – but a servant. Although apparently she possessed some authority over the others.

'Hands off the ladies, Luke,' came a voice from over Luke's shoulder. 'Evening, Lavinia, you gorgeous fossil.'

Lavinia simpered as Julian pulled out his chair and sat down.

'Got you, did she?' Jules muttered quietly, pushing his floppy hair out of his eyes. 'Sorry I didn't warn you. Quicker than a striking snake, that one.'

'Thanks for nothing.' Luke stole a look at Lavinia, who had picked up a silver salt cellar and was admiring her reflection in it. 'Who on earth is *darling Braby*?'

'*Darling Braby* is the reason she's here. Our lovely Lavinia is doing her days on Lord Brayburn's estate, when they start up a little fling. He toys with her, gets bored of her, drops her.

'Now, you or I might respond by feeling sad, maybe a touch used. Lavinia slashes the brakes on his wife's car, which crashes doing eighty on the motorway, killing both Lady Brayburn and Braby's dowager mother. She also beats his five corgis to death with a poker. Apparently it was the corgis that made him push for Condemnation, rather than just slavelife. Ah, a refill.'

The attendant circulating with a bottle of champagne flinched as Jules wrapped his fingers around her arm. Luke saw that beneath her grey tunic, her hand and wrist were horribly bruised and covered with burns and contusions, some of which looked fresh.

What had happened to her? Was it a kitchen accident? Luke might have thought so, were it not that he'd noticed some of the other attendants also bore visible injuries. One man limped, another was missing a couple of fingers, a third wore an eyepatch. Others were more freshly marked, with cuts and bruises. Was this where the horror happened – below stairs, where the servants lived? Did Crovan torture them down there?

But why only them, when the other half of the Condemned lived upstairs, as extravagantly as any lord or lady?

'Such a relief the seating's rotated,' Julian was saying. 'I've been next to Blake for the past week. Not only is he an unspeakable pervert, he has absolutely no conversation.'

Jules had conversation. Plenty of it. It turned out he wasn't only closest to Luke in height and build – which was why Coira had swiped some of his clothes for Luke that first day – he was also close in age. He'd been an undergraduate when he was Condemned – at the behest of a powerful Equal lord who had wanted to put an end to Julian's relationship with his daughter, a fellow student.

In the outside world, Luke and Julian would have nothing in common. But here at Eilean Dòchais, Luke couldn't believe his luck at having a fellow inmate who was not only young, but also – like Luke himself – the victim of Equal injustice.

Coira slipped back into the room, picked up the small brass bell that sat by the hearth, and rang it. Luke watched the quick, quiet way she moved. Jules was obviously watching, too, because he leaned over and whispered in Luke's ear.

'She'd be cute, if only she'd stop scowling.'

Luke thought the scowling kind of suited her. But when she saw the pair of them, heads together and looking her way, the scowl deepened into something close to anger.

Fine. She probably hated him for having a place at the dinner table while she was scurrying back and forth with plates and dishes. All the below-stairs residents of the castle probably hated Crovan's 'guests'. But Luke hadn't chosen where he'd been put or how he was being treated. And he certainly wasn't going to ask to be sent below just so Coira would stop giving him the side-eye.

The bell had heralded Crovan's entrance, and the guests all rose to their feet as he issued a clipped 'good evening' and seated himself in a chair pulled out by Devin. A procession of grey-clad attendants bearing steaming silver tureens entered through the service doors.

'Cock-a-leekie,' Julian said approvingly, picking up his spoon. On Luke's left, Lavinia was content to inhale the steam.

The rattle of metal against china drew Luke's attention to the other side of the table. The server approaching Blake was having difficulty holding the dish properly. As she set it in front of him, broth slopped across his jacket and he snarled, twisting to deliver a vicious backhanded blow that sent the woman to the floor.

Luke couldn't believe it. He stood so fast he almost upended his own bowl. Only the width of the massive mahogany table prevented him from reaching over and hauling Blake up by the lapels.

'What are you doing?' he shouted. 'You can't just hit her.'

Blake looked up, blinking his watery, almost lashless, eyes.

'That's where you're wrong, new boy.'

Then Coira was there, helping the woman up. She led her from the room, then returned and bent over Blake's jacket with a cloth, wiping the satin lapel.

'You'll clean that properly later, bitch,' the man snapped. 'And if that happens again, you'll feel it too. They're your responsibility.'

'Master.' Luke couldn't believe he was actually saying that word, but calling out Blake was worth swallowing a little pride for. 'You can't let him behave like this.'

Crovan looked up. Dabbed his moustache with his napkin. His eyes were remote behind the lenses of his glasses, like specimens beneath a microscope slide.

'Sit down, Hadley. We're eating.'

Blake shot Luke a look of gloating triumph. In disbelief, Luke looked up and down the table at his fellow 'guests'. Mostly, their gazes were fixed on their plates. The few that were watching were doing so with a detached curiosity. Luke shook his head.

'Is no one . . . ?'

Nope, no one else appeared to be outraged – or even

greatly surprised – by what Blake had done. Julian's hand tugged at Luke's jacket. The meaning was plain. *Sit down.*

It made no sense. Okay, so the slap was a small abuse compared to what Luke had expected to witness in this place. But the opulent surroundings, the formalwear, the pretence that this was the world's longest house party, only served to heighten the awfulness of Blake's behaviour.

Luke shook his head, and sat.

One course followed another – venison casserole, then a dessert of baked cream with raspberries – but Luke found the feast difficult to choke down. What was he not under-standing about this place? He was no nearer an answer when a chime rang out: Devin, tapping a wine glass with his butter knife to attract attention.

'Please follow our master. One of our number has decided to leave us tonight.'

A murmuring arose around the table. Luke was non-plussed. *Decided* to leave?

'What does he mean?' he asked Julian.

'You'll see. You're lucky – it doesn't happen often. I've been here three years, and this is only the third time. Come on, you'll want a good view.'

Julian hustled him along to the entrance hall, into which Luke had stepped on his first day. Candles were lit in the wall sconces. In the wall in front there was only one doorway, not two. Only one lintel, inscribed with two words: *Ultima necat.*

'Where's the other door?' Luke whispered. 'I saw it disappear when I came in.'

'We can't open it from inside,' said Julian, taking a deep swig from the glass he'd brought with him, then gesturing at the blank wall, 'so we don't need it. That's the only door any of us can open.'

The guests formed a semicircle. Behind them, the servants, clad in their plain grey tunics, were filling the remaining space. It was the first time Luke had seen them all together, and their numbers were evenly matched with the guests.

A hush fell as Crovan arrived, people moving back to let him through. The lord of Eilean Dòchais came to a halt in the centre of the space – and as Luke watched, two people entered, hand in hand.

His breath caught when he saw that one of them was Coira. The other was the woman Blake had hit at supper. She looked tired, and the fresh bruise blooming on her cheek was not the only visible injury. Coira squeezed the woman's hand, and something eased a little in Luke's chest as she stepped back, leaving the other standing alone in front of their master.

'What was your crime?' he intoned.

The woman replied in a voice that was hoarse, like the scraping of a rarely opened door.

'Eleven years ago I sabotaged the BB plant in Portisbury slavetown, before an official visit from Lord Lytchett and

Lady Angelica Matravers. My plan was successful and Lady Angelica was killed.'

Another act of protest in a slavetown, Luke thought, his heart jolting. So it wasn't just Jackson and the Club in Millmoor that wanted to fight.

But this woman had wanted to kill. The Club had never done that.

Was that what it would take to make a difference? Was that the direction the struggle against the Equals had to take? He remembered his own fury with Crovan on the shore of the loch, the feeling that he could have knocked the man down and held him under. Would he have done it? Then Luke realized the identity of the woman's victim, and it staggered him. Lady Angelica Matravers. Wife of Lord Lytchett – and, therefore, the mother of Bodina, who Luke had known in Millmooor as 'Angel'. Despite her mother's murder, Angel championed justice for commoners. It hardly seemed possible. When right and wrong were so tangled up, how could you ever pull them apart?

Crovan looked at the serving woman. The candlelight danced in the lenses of his glasses.

'Why did you do it?'

'My son had died from ill treatment in Portisbury. Because of that, I hated the Equals.'

'And now?'

'Now I understand that you are our better selves. Now, I love the Equals.'

She knelt on the ground, reached for Crovan's hand, and kissed it.

And the Equal did something more nauseating than anything Luke had imagined happening in this place – he touched his fingers gently to the woman's forehead, like a blessing.

'Your crime is gone. Your hours are done.'

Luke felt sick. Who was this monster, to offer absolution to a woman he had abused?

'Your hours are done,' the assembled onlookers echoed.

Crovan traced the bruise on the woman's face, and beneath his fingers it faded away. He took her hands in his, unexpectedly gentle, and raised her to her feet. Luke saw her flex her fingers freely once he let them go. His touch passed lightly over her: shoulders, sternum, hips. Her exhaustion sloughed off, skin and eyes seeming to glow in the candlelight. She'd not been a beautiful woman, but Luke could see the beautiful things she'd been: strong and fierce and unafraid.

'All hours wound,' said Crovan, lifting his hand away. '*Omnes vulnerant.*'

'*Ultima necat,*' the woman said. 'The last one kills.'

She looked past Crovan, at the door. As she went to it, Luke couldn't tear his eyes away. The latch lifted cleanly, and with a single pull, she swung the door wide.

It was raining outside: a rare March shower. The night sky over the loch was purple-dark, and the air rushed in, cool and clean. Luke luxuriated in the freshness of it. He'd not set foot outside since arriving at the castle. How tempting it was, how easy it would be, to walk through that door right now.

But though he couldn't quite understand *how*, he was pretty sure he knew *what* lay on the other side of the Last Door. And it was nowhere you came back from.

The woman glanced back over her shoulder – then stepped through unhesitating, her face upraised to the rain. Her life left her like a sigh, and she crumpled on the other side of the threshold.

Luke could barely believe it. Where a split second ago there had been a woman, living and breathing, there was now just a huddled body. He stared at her, lying there.

'I know, I know.' Beside him, Julian sounded almost apologetic. 'It's pretty underwhelming, right? I keep on hoping for something . . . more, but they're all like that. Still, we got our refill.'

The young man tipped his head back and drained his glass.

'To the eerily departed,' Jules said, and hiccupped.

How were they going to move the body? What happened if you put your hand through the Last Door? Unbidden, a memory came to him of the searing waters of Loch nan Deur.

His first question was answered when Coira came and put her shoulder to the door to push it shut.

121

'You're just going to leave her there?' Luke demanded.

'Yes,' she replied. 'Or would you like to go out and bury her?'

She gestured at the doorway. Luke's skin prickled.

'No,' he said quickly. 'No. But it doesn't seem right.'

What about this place did? Nothing at all.

'Don't worry,' Coira said, closing the door. Luke heard the latch drop. 'The eagles come.'

Eagles. Luke shook his head in disbelief.

'This departure gives me the opportunity to make an adjustment to our household,' said Crovan, drawing all attention to him.

'With Luke Hadley's arrival, the dining table has become a little crowded. And now that we are one down below stairs, it seems the ideal moment.'

Luke froze. Did that mean what it sounded like it meant? At his side, he sensed Julian taking a step back, moving imperceptibly behind him.

Crovan looked slowly round at his 'guests'. The tension in the room fizzed like Skill.

This was it. This was where the week-long illusion that Condemnation meant dressing up and playing at being an Equal came crashing down. Luke would be going down-stairs – and he'd be finding out exactly how the servants came by their injuries. Perhaps he'd even find others down there, men like Dog, caged and chained.

Perhaps he'd join them.

'Lavinia,' Crovan said, and Luke nearly toppled forward as Julian's fist thumped him between the shoulder blades. 'I'm afraid our time together up here has come to an end. There's nothing more I can do with you. I'm sure you'll adjust to your move below. And if not, as you've just seen, there is an alternative.'

The incomprehension on the older woman's face was awful to see. Hands pushed her roughly from behind – one of the other guests – and she was thrust, stumbling, into the centre of the circle of onlookers.

She realized what was happening then.

'No!' she screeched. 'No, you can't! Braby is coming for me soon.'

Coira stepped forward and took Lavinia by the hand, shaking it gently to bring her to her senses.

'No!' It was a birdlike squawk. 'Don't touch me! Only Braby touches me.'

'Not any more,' said a voice from among the guests.

Who had spoken? Was it Blake, with his loose mouth and watering eyes? Lavinia's eyes darted around, terrified.

'Stop it.' Luke stepped forward, his legs and mouth somehow acting entirely without permission. 'She's frightened. She doesn't have the strength to work hard. I'll go.'

Crovan turned, the reflection in his spectacles sliding from candle-bright to stone-blank.

'Oh no,' he said. 'That won't do. You and I are barely getting started, Luke Hadley.'

And as Lavinia began to sob, Luke felt cold all over, as if somewhere behind him the Last Door had just swung open.

'Please,' Coira said to Crovan, her arm around Lavinia's shaking shoulders. 'Can we lock the kitchen door tonight? It's her first night. Give her a chance to get used to it.'

'She knows all about it,' said Blake. 'She's watched – she's even taken part. Now it's her turn.'

'Nobody asked you,' Coira said, whipping round, fury in her eyes.

But Crovan was already shaking his head.

'No exceptions,' he said. 'I'm amazed you keep asking. The door stays unlocked. Hadley, it's time you and I talked. Meet me in the library in ten minutes.'

'What?'

But Crovan was already striding away.

Coira was in Blake's face, her finger jabbing.

'If you go near her, I'll kill you.'

'Yes,' drawled Julian, from Luke's side. 'Bit old for you, isn't she? How old were Lady Towton's daughters when you started giving them "extra tuition" on the side? Seven and nine, wasn't it? Still, given the limited supply in here, I suppose you can't afford to be picky.'

'You can't talk,' snarled Blake, before stalking off.

Julian sighed theatrically.

'What on earth was that about?' Luke said, looking from Julian to Coira and back again.

'Let's just say Blake wasn't Condemned for murder,' said Jules. 'The murder of innocence, maybe. But look, Lord Arailt will explain everything. Why this place is . . . the way it is. What's expected of those of us who live upstairs.'

'Nothing's *expected*,' said Coira, her voice swollen with disgust. 'Blake and the rest of you choose to do it.'

She turned her back on the pair of them and led a trembling Lavinia away.

'What does she mean?' Luke asked Jules. 'What are we expected to do?'

Julian shifted uneasily. 'That's for Crovan to tell you.'

Which sounded ominous. Luke doubted it meant a bathroom-cleaning and bin-emptying rota.

The library appeared deserted when Luke went in. It was almost pitch dark. Only a faint glow from around one jutting bookcase told him that Crovan was already there. He followed the glow of the Skill-light, and found Crovan in an armchair, a book open in his lap. The man took his time finishing a page before looking up.

'Have a seat, Hadley.'

Luke did. Was that the collar? He had almost – and the thought turned his stomach like a dodgy kebab – forgotten it was there.

'Let me ask you a question,' Crovan said. 'Do you consider yourself to be a better person than us Equals? Do we seem unkind? Cruel?'

'Of course. What you did to Dog. What Gavar Jardine

125

did to the mother of his child. The way you treat the servants here – I've seen their injuries. And the slavetowns – they're horrendous, even though they don't have to be. People would probably work harder in better conditions, so it's not just cruel, it's stupid.'

'Hmm.' Crovan made a noncommittal noise. Luke rubbed his palms down his trousers. They were sweaty and prickled with fear. He could have just lied, but what was the point? Equals could probably sense things like that, and it wasn't as though Crovan would have believed a denial.

'And you think you commoners are, therefore, morally superior to the Equals?'

This question was less straightforward, but: 'Yes, I would say so. Normal people aren't perfect. We do terrible things. But you Equals don't even seem to realize how monstrous the things you do are.'

This conversation was awful. Every word out of his mouth felt like one step closer to a trap he would surely fall into. Crovan was studying him closely.

'Morality is nothing to do with it, Hadley. This is a common error I see among many of the Condemned sent to me here. Those whose crimes arise from their idealism. Like the woman who left us this evening. Or like you.

'You imagine that you are better than us. You are not. Only weaker. A world in which your kind ruled would not be improved. It would be merely diminished. And that is one of the lessons my household is designed to instil. Come with me.'

Crovan rose, and led the way from the library. Luke's eyes roamed frantically for something, anything, that he might hit this man with. Knock him unconscious. Escape. But no, the collar would prevent it. They descended the stairs, and Luke found himself unexpectedly back in the dining room.

Crovan paused, his hand on the door to the kitchen.

'Those who are sent to me, I divide in two. Half live as Equals do. The other half remain in servitude. To those who are my guests, I give power over those who serve. The collars prevent servants harming or physically restraining guests, just as they prevent all of you from harming me. But guests may harm servants with impunity.

'Many guests enjoy frequent visits below stairs to do exactly that. Some hold out, just as you will. But out of boredom, out of frustration, they all give in eventually – just as you will.'

Luke's head spun. What was Crovan saying?

'Harming? Why on earth would those of us up here want to hurt any of the others?'

'Because,' said Crovan, 'that is human nature.'

He pushed open the door and the sound, magnified by a deep stone corridor, clawed at Luke's ears.

Somewhere down below, a woman was screaming.

127

8

Luke

'The strong dominate the weak,' Crovan continued. 'Men over women. British over inferior races. Equal over commoner. It is the natural way of things. As you saw this evening, I require those who would leave me to understand and acknowledge that, before I can grant them the mercy of the door.'

Luke could barely think, with the hideous sound of that thin, high wail echoing up the passageway. But you didn't need to think to know that what Crovan was spouting was the vilest stuff imaginable.

These people. Their power. The good they could do with it, and the evil they chose instead.

Another shriek. Luke pushed past his master. Who cared what Crovan would do to him? Whatever was happening down there had to be stopped.

'It's what you truly are, Luke,' Crovan called after him, as he sprinted down the corridor. 'All of you.'

Luke pulled up in the doorway of a huge kitchen. He

took in the bare impression: stone walls, an immense fireplace and wooden tables. It looked centuries old, maybe dating from the time of the kings.

His eyes went immediately to a group of people gathered at one end of the room. There was a trio of men in black-tie evening dress – Luke's fellow guests. One of them held a struggling fourth man, clad in a servant's grey tunic, in an armlock. Two women stood backed against the table. One, her evening gown half ripped from her bony shoulder, was Lavinia. In front of her, arms outstretched, stood Coira, spitting her words into the face of the nearest man.

'Don't touch her again, Blake, or you'll be sorry.'

'You never learn, do you?' Blake said. He was smoking a thin cigarette, and Luke noticed with horror what looked like livid burn spots on Lavinia's exposed shoulder. 'You can't be in two places at once. I think my friend here has some unfinished business with Josie downstairs.'

Blake thumbed over his shoulder to the third man, who gave a slow, lazy grin.

'So . . . Josie? Or Lavinia? You may be our master's pet, and untouchable, but you can only protect one of them.'

Luke realized what Coira was going to try at the same time as she moved. Grabbing Lavinia's arm, Coira spun the older woman round and pushed her towards an open door on the far side of the room. But the man behind Blake was equally fast – and bigger. He snatched at Lavinia with one hand and at Coira with the other. He somehow missed, or

129

failed to keep hold of Coira, and she slipped between his fingers. The girl cursed, a ragged, furious sound, and ran to the door.

'Josie,' she called down, with a yell that sounded too big for her skinny chest. 'Hide!'

Then she turned to the man holding Lavinia.

'Let her go.'

She launched herself at him, fingers clawing for his face, and he roared. Which was when Luke snatched up a fire iron from the massive open hearth and raised his voice.

'You heard her. Let Lavinia go.'

The room went quiet.

'New boy.' Blake's voice was curdled with scorn. 'I really wouldn't interfere.'

'I'm not interfering,' said Luke, lifting the fire iron. 'I'm stopping this right now.'

'You think?' said Blake. But a note of uncertainty had come into his voice. He took a small step back towards his more powerfully built accomplice, who was struggling to hold Lavinia with one hand while fending off Coira's raking fingernails. Was he seeking his goon's protection?

No.

Whip-fast, Blake grabbed Lavinia by her long wispy hair and forced her head down. Plucking the cigarette from his wet mouth he pressed it against Lavinia's scrawny neck. The woman shrieked again and the sound turned Luke's stomach.

'Every step you take,' said Blake, 'I'll burn Lavinia another beauty spot. And she's so ugly' – he twisted his hand in the woman's long hair and forced her tear-and-snot-streaked face towards Luke; her eyes rolled wildly with terror – 'I reckon it'll take quite a few to make her beautiful.'

'You do that,' said Luke, hefting the iron bar in what he desperately hoped was an intimidating fashion, 'and while your hands are full, I'll bash your brains out. Your friends are both busy, so it'll be just you and me. I'm half your age and worked in Millmoor's Machine Park, which I reckon makes me twice as fit. So how about it?'

Blake snarled as Luke sprang. The man pushed Lavinia to one side, and darted around the table, keeping it between him and Luke.

'Lavinia, get downstairs,' yelled Coira. 'Go!'

Luke had no opportunity to see if the older woman made her escape, because Blake was reaching beneath the table. Reaching, not fumbling. He knew what was down there.

One hand whipped up to throw a heavy, flat blade fast in Luke's direction. A meat cleaver. Luke swerved and swore. He rested a hand on the pitted tabletop to steady himself – which was when Blake stabbed it with a carving fork.

Luke howled with pain, but even as he did so, something else urged him on – the knowledge that, if Crovan's description of how the collars worked was true, Blake wasn't used to people able to fight back.

He jumped up onto the table and lashed out. He was wobbly, poorly positioned, but just close enough to clip Blake's skull, sending the man reeling.

'Luke!'

Luke turned towards Coira's warning cry just in time to see an iron skillet descend towards his head. The third guest had released the struggling serving man and come to Blake's aid.

Luke raised a desperate hand, but it was too late.

The pan connected with the side of his head and he went down into hot, black darkness.

The touch of something scalding brought him back up again.

'Ahh!' He shrank away.

'It's only a cup of tea,' Coira said, folding his fingers around it. 'I don't believe tea cures everything, but it's a good place to start.'

Luke blinked. He was sat on a bench in the kitchen, his back propped against the table. He doubted Coira would be giving him tea if Blake was still tormenting Lavinia somewhere nearby, but he looked around to check anyway. They were alone.

What else had happened? He remembered the skillet descending, and reached up his other hand to feel around his skull. The hand hurt – it was bandaged – but not his head.

'How?' he croaked, taking a grateful sip of the tea.

'Crovan,' she said. 'And are you really okay? Because he said you would be, but he's a sadist, so that could mean anything from "still hurting" to "in absolute agony".'

'My hand hurts, but my head's fine. Which is weird. And where's Lavinia? That bastard Blake.'

Luke clenched his fist angrily, then yelped at his injury once again.

'Crovan appeared as soon as you went down.' Coira settled herself on the bench beside him, and Luke found her presence as warming as the tea. 'He was angry. Sent Blake and the others back upstairs immediately. Rhys – the guy with me – went to check on Lavinia. So I was the only one here when Crovan healed you. But just your head, so it's not about sparing you pain. He must have been worried about concussion or brain injury. I've never seen him do that before. Why do you matter, Luke Hadley?'

Startled, Luke looked up. He mattered?

I won't let him break you. That had been Silyen Jardine's promise at Kyneston's gate. *Not beyond repair.*

'I have no idea,' he told her truthfully.

'Thank you for trying,' Coira said. 'That was brave.'

'Not bravery; just reflex. And it feels like all I do is *try*. I want to change things for the better, but only seem to screw up even worse.'

'Well, if killing Chancellor Zelston was your idea of changing things for the better, then maybe you're right.'

'I didn't,' said Luke, stung by Coira's words. He shifted upright from where he'd let himself slump against her. 'Yes, I held the gun, but I have no recollection of doing it. One of them must have used me.'

Coira looked at him. Her assessing gaze reminded him of someone, though he couldn't place who.

'I didn't,' Luke insisted. 'And I'm not staying here. Nor can you. What just happened, that's happened before, hasn't it? Have they . . .' And the idea that stabbed into Luke's brain was more excruciating than any carving fork. 'Have they ever done anything like that to you?'

If she said 'yes', he'd find that iron bar again and go kick Blake's door in right now.

She didn't say 'yes'. But her answer was unexpected.

'They can't,' she said. 'They can't harm me, in the same way that none of the servants can harm the guests. They've tried, but you saw how it is. They can't even keep hold of me. Blows don't land. The collar prevents it somehow. It's how I knew I could get involved, without the risk that Blake would start using me as a human ashtray too. So you see, I'm not all that brave, either.'

'That wasn't what I saw earlier,' Luke said, then flushed pink all the way up to his ears because he was so rubbish at this saying-nice-stuff-to-girls thing, and he hadn't meant it like that anyway. 'But I don't understand. Crovan explained the set-up of this place, and it seemed pretty simple: we guests can hurt you servants, and clearly we can hurt each other. But you can't harm us.'

'No one can hurt me,' said Coira. 'I think it's because I was a child when I came here, and even Crovan isn't that evil.'

Luke said nothing. He wasn't convinced that there were any limits to Crovan's depravity.

'How old were you?' he said finally.

'I came below stairs when I turned thirteen, I think. Birthdays are a bit hazy, but it was four years ago. Before then, I was upstairs. This place is all I can remember. I've no recollections of the time before, or of my parents.'

Which was the worst thing Luke had heard yet. To take away memories of your family. Your past. Of who you truly were. It was like Dog, who didn't even know his own name, only that he had once had a wife whom he loved, who had been abused and had killed herself. *I only remember what he let me keep*, Luke heard the voice rasp in the darkness of Kyneston's kennels. *And that's just the bad things*.

Would Crovan do that to Luke, too? Would he end up not caring about escaping, because he had lost any memory of who and what he would be escaping to?

'There has to be a way out of here,' he said. 'You and me, Julian, we're so young. We can't spend our lives like this.'

'Julian's not who you think he is. I saw you talking at

dinner earlier, when you were both looking at me. I see him looking at me a lot.'

'Well, who wouldn't?' said Luke, then immediately wanted to bury his face in his hands. Okay, Millmoor hadn't been a good place to sharpen his social skills, but honestly.

But Coira appeared amused, a little, for when he looked up she was smiling.

'I don't know,' she said. 'Maybe I'm wrong. He's never laid a finger on me. It's just I sometimes get the feeling he'd like to. As for getting out, well, Rhys and I have explored everything we can think of. The boat. Any way the collars might let us incapacitate Crovan, even though we can't actually harm him.'

'There's a boat?'

'Don't get excited. It's moored on the far shore of the loch, so you probably wouldn't have seen it from the helicopter. It brings over our supplies once a week. There's a watergate down below, with double doors kept locked so we're never in the dock at the same time they are. And yes, yes.' Coira held up her hand because Luke had been going to interrupt. 'There is a way around that. We managed it about a year ago; Rhys stowed away. But the boat never made it to the other side.'

'It sunk?'

'No, it just . . . couldn't get there. It stopped. The engine was running; there was no wind; it could go left or right, but not forward. There must be some Skillful boundary that none of us Condemned can cross.'

Luke put down his mug in disbelief. He'd known this wasn't going to be simple. Escaping a deadly castle surrounded by a loch full of pain, while wearing a magical collar that let your Skillful jailer jerk you around like a puppet, was always going to be a tall order. But he'd never doubted it could be done.

But this? Even if you overcame all of those things, for there then to be some boundary that you couldn't cross? It must be like Kyneston's wall, he supposed, responsive only to the Equal family.

'So, what?' he said to Coira eventually. 'You're saying we should just give up? Accept our lot, until the day we finally crack and walk out of a door that kills us? Because I'm not doing that. I've got a family that needs to know I'm all right. I've got people to fight for.'

'Oh, no,' said Coira, standing and pulling Luke to his feet, careful of his bandaged hand. 'The only thing more impossible than getting out of here is accepting that you'll never get out of here. But you're going to need your strength, which means you need sleep. So no more questions, for now.'

Coira led him through the maze of the castle's corridors. Through the dining room, the high atrium where the heads of stag and elk hung next to the guns that shot them, and up the stairs.

'I know the way,' Luke protested. 'You should go back. Lavinia will need you more than I do.'

'Don't be so sure of that,' Coira countered, with a meaningful nod at the door next to Luke's as they turned onto his landing. Blake's room. 'Lock your door tonight. And maybe tomorrow, you'll find a leak in the ceiling and will need to move.'

Luke grinned. She was smart this girl. Smart like Abi. And brave like Angel.

Except Angel wasn't who Luke had thought she was. She had been daring, but it had all been done with the knowledge that her Skill would protect her. His infatuation with the beautiful blonde woman felt like a lifetime ago. He darted a glance at Coira. Making the same mistake with someone in here would be a bad idea. A very bad idea.

But hey, it was fine to have an ally in your escape plans, wasn't it?

'Are you all right?' said Coira, looking at him curiously. 'Or are you having some kind of delayed head injury thing? Because you look a bit—'

'No,' Luke said hastily, mortified. 'No, I'm fine.'

As he closed the door, he thought he heard a faint snort of laughter.

But if he went to sleep buoyed by the discovery that he wasn't the only one in here desperate to get out, he woke in an altogether more sombre mood.

This place was horrific. People were encouraged to prey

on each other, simply to justify Crovan's dehumanizing ideas about Equal superiority. And if what Coira had said was correct, Luke was trapped here by his collar. He didn't just have to find a way out of the castle; after that, lay some kind of boundary that functioned like the Kyneston wall. And despite his experiences with Silyen Jardine, he didn't know nearly enough about how such a thing might work.

He didn't know anything about it at all.

So: a perimeter, and a collar. His hands went to his throat. It was more like a ribbon than a collar: soft and supple. So close to the skin that you couldn't get your fingers under it. So smooth, in fact, that when Luke stroked his fingers down his throat, he could hardly tell when he reached the band.

Almost as if it had become part of his skin.

His stomach lurched as he scrabbled with his fingernails at the edge of the collar, but could get no purchase. The band was indistinguishable from his flesh.

He ran to the small sink in the corner of his room and retched.

When he had finished, and had washed and wiped his face, he could hear Blake moving around next door. The man and his cronies would surely have it in for Luke after last night's misadventure. So remembering Coira's suggestion, Luke sploshed some water on the floor and went down early before breakfast to ask Devin for a change of room.

'Oh,' said Devin, after acquiescing fussily. 'Our master will see you again this morning. He's asked me to bring you up at eleven o'clock, so meet me here five minutes before. Don't be late.'

That didn't sound great. Was Luke in trouble for intervening last night? Well, no one had told him he couldn't. And maybe Luke would have a few questions for Crovan.

Blake appeared as he was relocating his few things – you could hardly call them possessions – to the new room. Luke tensed for a spat. The man was sporting a tight, puffy black eye from where Luke had clipped him last night. Its pink rims streamed as he peered balefully at Luke.

'So he did fix you. That's like giving water to a starving man – it just prolongs the agony. I'll enjoy watching your mind being broken apart, Luke Hadley.'

'I won't start with your mind, if you try anything again like you did last night,' Luke said, attempting to sound as tough as he could while holding a pile of folded shirts and underpants. 'You and your friends need to stay away from downstairs.'

'Or else?' Blake lisped.

Luke didn't dignify that with a response. Call the encounter a draw – though it didn't seem that Blake would be getting his goons to beat Luke to a pulp anytime soon. It sounded more like he was relying on Crovan to wreck Luke for him. Which wasn't reassuring.

'I have a question,' Luke said loudly, as Devin ushered

him into Crovan's presence a short while later. Devin tutted audibly at his audacity as he withdrew.

'Hmm?' Crovan was looking out of the window of the high, wide room, his hands clasped behind his back.

'Those below are punished. They're terrorized, and they live like servants, doing all the work. While those of us above live like house guests at Kyneston – we dress for dinner and drink champagne. But we're all here because we've been Condemned. So why don't you punish us too?'

Crovan turned. 'You think I don't?'

'Not that I've noticed.'

'Not that you've noticed. Indeed. Which means that either my guests go unpunished – or I mete out their pain privately, away from prying eyes. So, welcome to my *private* apartments, Luke.'

Crovan permitted himself a smile. A thin one, as if sketched lightly by a portraitist uncertain whether the expression belonged on that face. His words sent a chill through Luke.

He looked around, but there was nothing out of the ordinary here. An intricately stuccoed ceiling. An immense leaded window overlooking the loch. Old and expensive-looking furniture. The door Luke had come in, and then another on the far side.

'You know that I believe in a natural order, Luke. Well, I also believe in a natural justice. To my guests, I give back their crime in kind.'

'What does that even mean?'

'Allow me to show you.'

And before Luke could say that no, he'd do perfectly well without being shown, thank you, Crovan pulled a rope pinned to the wall. Out in the corridor, a bell rang. And moments later, Devin stepped back into the room.

'No,' Luke said, apprehension rising. 'No, Devin, you're not needed.'

'Master?' Devin looked between them, confused.

Crovan circled the man. He stopped behind him and put a hand on his shoulder, like a proud headmaster presenting his top pupil.

'Let me tell you Devin's story. Devin needs to be needed. He was the indispensable assistant to an elderly lord. Catered to the fellow's every whim: bathed him, dressed him. Was like a son to him. But as this old gentleman approached the end of his life, he had one last, all-consuming wish: to see again his two children, from whom he'd been estranged for many years. So Devin promised to find them.'

'My lord?' Devin was looking uneasy.

'After a few months of searching, Devin reported that he'd located them. But they were wary, he said. Doubtful of their father's love. Perhaps if he could prove it to them in some way. A gift, maybe?

'The gift Devin suggested was an expensive one. But no matter. The love of a child is priceless. Over the months that followed, there were more gifts. Letters. Promises of visits. The old lord was anxious, because he knew his health was failing. But he had every confidence in Devin, his surrogate son.'

Crovan patted Devin's shoulder. Let his hand rest there. Gripped powerfully with a suddenness that made the man cry out in surprise.

'You've made your point,' Luke said. 'You can stop now. I can imagine how this ends.'

'It ends like this,' said Crovan.

Devin's scream tore at Luke's ears.

He couldn't see what had happened, at first. But then Devin's hands came round to clutch the front of his black dinner jacket and the blood became visible, running freely over them.

Another scream. Against Devin's white dress shirt, blood welled from a deep wound that had appeared from nowhere in the middle of his chest. The man howled.

'Master,' he begged. 'What? Please stop.'

'You see Devin was jealous. And Devin was greedy. He'd not done a thing to locate his lord's children, and he'd spent all the money. Frittered it away on gambling and cocaine. The occasional rent boy. His master was bound to find out eventually. And when he did, Devin turned on him. Most of us Equals could have withstood such an assault – our Skill would throw off any assailant. But this poor fellow was so old. So ill and weak. It still took Devin twenty-three stabs of the knife to finish him off.'

Devin screeched. Another wound sheared along his collarbone, gushing crimson.

'Now he imagines that he is my most trusted servant. My right-hand man. He opens doors for me, pulls out my seat when I sit for supper and when I rise. Every time I do this he cannot believe it.'

Crovan lifted Devin's chin and made the whimpering, sobbing man look him in the eye.

'I only keep you near me to make this so much sweeter. And then . . .'

Crovan turned to Luke with the air of a conjurer presenting his final, most spectacular trick.

'All gone.'

Devin groaned and collapsed to the floor. He wobbled, unsteady, on his knees. Hands fluttered to touch himself all over.

The lord of Eilean Dòchais knelt down beside his servant, all solicitude.

'How are you, Devin? Have a seat. You broke a glass and managed to cut yourself quite badly – just look at the mess you're in. But I've fixed you now.'

Shaking, Devin allowed himself to be helped to an armchair. He looked down at his bloodstained shirt, face pale with shock. He stammered out copious thanks to Crovan, and his hand trembled as he drank down a shot of whisky the Equal passed to him.

Luke was pretty sure he was trembling himself. He'd not seen anything more horrifying in his entire life.

'You do that – to all of us?'

Was this to be his fate? A brutal cycle of infliction and forgetting. Luke remembered the mess that had been Zelston, spattered across the ballroom floor. The tide of blood. Horrifying – but quick.

For Luke, Crovan would wound, but not kill.

It would not be quick.

'Well, in your case,' Crovan said, his eyes unreadable as ever behind his gleaming spectacles, 'I will be making an exception. You see, for you, I have special instructions.'

9

Bouda

At this rate, the only opportunity Bouda would have to speak to Gavar about the slavetown purge would be on their honeymoon. Perhaps she could make creative use of some silk scarves, then when he wasn't in a position to escape, get out her ministerial dispatch box and take him through the paperwork.

For now, she was well served in her advisers. One was Bouda's own appointment: the former Millmoor Overseer. She had been the first to suggest using special measures on the prisoner Walcott and hadn't shrunk from giving the order to fire during the slavetown's riot. The other was the Security man Kessler, whose recruitment had been Gavar's sole contribution to the task his father had given them.

She'd initially thought Kessler a mindless brute. But quickly discovered he was that most useful of creatures: a mindful brute. He'd asked if he needed to relinquish his baton and stun gun now that he was no longer serving

Security. Bouda had told him that on the contrary, his new position might merit an expansion of his arsenal.

Kessler had grinned at that. He might be Gavar's recruit, but Bouda had a feeling that he'd scented where true authority lay.

'I was aware of this underground railroad between Millmoor and Riverhead,' the Overseer was saying, her finger drawing a line between the two slavetowns on the wall-mounted map of Great Britain. 'It smuggles technology and information and facilitates the illicit movement of people. But it was never clear from which of the two places it was being masterminded.

'After the revelation about the Tresco heir's activities in Millmoor, it was tempting to lay this at his door too. But I now have reason to believe that the railroad operates from Riverhead. And here's a surprise – the ringleader may be a woman.'

Bouda wasn't surprised. She knew all too well how easily women were overlooked and assumed to be of less consequence. Yet women were capable of feats of Skill as powerful as any man. Anyone who doubted that – and there were many, still – need only look at what Euterpe Parva had done at the Debate Ball.

So why not a woman leading the sedition in Riverhead? Bouda could almost picture her: older, with authority. Lean and hardbitten by life, but charismatic. Able to stir up the law-abiding slaves with rabble-rousing talk. Revelling in her secret network. Imagining she was playing the Equals at their own game.

Not for much longer.

There was a rap on the door behind them. Her secretary put his head round it and had barely got out the word 'Speaker' before the door banged open. Speaker Dawson, the woman who led the commoner Observers of Parliament, barged past him into Bouda's office.

Correction: who *had* led the OPs, before Lord Jardine had suspended them. Four hundred years of history, established by Cadmus Parva-Jardine himself, swept away in a single emergency decree.

A second figure slipped in after Dawson. The Speaker's son, Jon Faiers.

Bouda still remembered the audacious way he had spoken to her after the Second Debate, that windswept night on the cliffs at Grendelsham. How he'd professed to admire the Equals and their rule. Bouda had at first thought it a simple – and grossly inappropriate – come-on. Had she not been shaken by her encounter with Lord Jardine, she would have dismissed him instantly.

She should dismiss him now. If his mother had no right to be in here, he had even less.

Faiers caught her looking. Bouda frowned and turned her attention to his mother.

'. . . been nearly two weeks,' Dawson was saying. 'Lord Jardine was explicit. "Until cleared of disloyalty," he said.

Well, we are ready and waiting to be examined – and cleared. There's no disloyalty among the OPs.'

'We'll be the judges of that,' Bouda said. 'And if what you say is true, then there's hardly any urgency to investigate, is there? As you can see, we have before us a more immediate task. Rooting out those whose disloyalty is blatant. Twenty slavetowns. Twenty investigations.'

'We could assist with that,' Dawson said. 'Your enquiries will progress more easily with our co-operation.'

'Are you suggesting that we need your help?' Bouda asked, narrowing her eyes. 'That sounds as though you are questioning our competence. Which sounds an awful lot like disloyalty.'

At Bouda's side, the Overseer scoffed. Dawson screwed up her face as she tried to think of a response that wouldn't dig her deeper.

'Leave us, Speaker Dawson,' Bouda said, exasperated by the woman's presence. 'Or should that simply be "Dawson", as you have forfeited your right to speak for anyone at all. Don't bother us again unless you have something concrete to offer. Names. Information. And given your current status as a person under suspicion, it's best you don't come yourself. Send someone else. Him, maybe.'

Bouda indicated Faiers then immediately turned back to the map. She'd intended it to be a gesture of dismissal, but had felt herself flush as the words left her mouth. What had possessed her to say such a thing?

Behind her, she heard a low 'Goodbye, Heir Bouda' that could only have come from the commoner. His mother was out of the door with no words at all.

Bouda set her shoulders back. The woman was an irritation and her son was an irrelevance. That was all there was to it.

She sleeked her ponytail around her neck and studied the map.

'There are two other sources besides the line my team is pursuing,' the Overseer continued, as if the interruption had never happened. 'The Highwithel heir must have known this woman. And there's the boy that killed the Chancellor. The one in Lord Crovan's custody. Given that the railroad ran between Riverhead and Millmoor, he may have met her.'

The Highwithel heir.

Meilyr had been at the opening of parliament. His attendance had shocked Bouda to the core. The effrontery of it, of course. But also the look of the man. With his gaunt face and walking cane, Meilyr was a shadow of the carefree boy who just a couple of years ago had been a welcome visitor at the Matravers estate.

The change in Meilyr had begun when his mother had brought him on to the Justice Council. The Trescos were commoner sympathizers from time immemorial, of course. But as the council debated labour and living conditions, and tackled unrest, Meilyr's criticisms had become sharper, his arguments more strident.

Then he had disappeared.

Should Bouda have guessed that he had somehow become mixed up with commoners? Could she have done more to protect her little sister from the inevitable heartbreak?

And what of Meilyr's absurd attempt to speak up for the boy who had shot Zelston? He had as good as claimed responsibility for the act himself. What had been done to him was horrifying – Bouda remembered the golden mist, and Meilyr's anguished howl – but his own actions had made it necessary.

Well, Crovan's interrogations of the commoner boy might confirm if Meilyr had indeed been involved – not just in the Millmoor debacle, but in Zelston's death too. They could also clarify Whittam's belief that he had been the intended target.

And now there was a further question for Crovan to probe: whether the Condemned boy knew the identity of this Riverhead leader. Bouda dictated a memo to Eilean Dòchais to that effect, then dismissed her aides. She needed a few minutes to herself to think.

DiDi had gone with Meilyr and his mother, when they fled from Kyneston back to Highwithel. Bouda hadn't heard from or seen her sister since.

Perhaps DiDi was angry with her for being so closely

allied to Whittam Jardine, who had authorized Meilyr's terrible punishment.

Bouda pushed down the hurt she felt at that idea. DiDi would see, eventually. Everyone would.

Whittam wanted only to make their country strong again. To maintain Britain's influence in a world whose axis of power was balanced precariously between the Skilled and unSkilled nations. Between the Skilless Triad of France, Russia and the Union States, and the Skilled Three of Japan, Britain and the Confederacy.

Bouda thought it absurd that there was even a semblance of balance. In any conflict, the unSkilled nations would surely be unable to resist the Skilled, despite their powerful military forces. But international disputes these days were settled in the boardroom, not on the battlefield. And there, the unskilled Triad constantly sought to undermine Skilled power. They invoked so-called 'human rights' – such as moaning about the slavedays – in an attempt to constrain the way the Three could use Skill in governance and the economy.

The Triad wouldn't get the upper hand. Not when the allegiance of China was unknown. That vast country still boasted Skill, but its practitioners had withdrawn from everyday life, living monastically on the high Himalayan plateau. In day-to-day affairs, China conducted itself as if Skilless. And so both blocs sought to bind the powerful nation to a closer alliance.

In these uncertain times, Britain needed Lord Jardine, and should be thankful to have him.

She would update Whittam on her progress, she decided, setting off to pay her soon-to-be father-in-law a visit. They needed to discuss some other irritants, as well, such as whether Zelston's seat on the Justice Council would pass to Lady Flora and Heir Midsummer. Bouda sincerely hoped not. Midsummer was unbearable: as zealous as the Trescos, and crassly entangled with a commoner woman to boot. Her mother had been the third in line. Neither of them had been meant to get anywhere near the House of Light. As was obvious by how grossly unsuited they were.

Bouda's route took her through tapestry-hung corridors to an immense winding staircase. Lord Jardine had taken over the Chancellor's suite at the top of New Westminster Tower. Its principal chamber was oak-panelled on three sides; the other side was entirely glass with views over the House of Light.

During Zelston's incumbency, Bouda had visited it only for the annual Chancellor's drinks party. In between working the room with small talk, she had studied the portraits that lined the walls: the likeness of every man (they were all men) who had ever held that great office of state, from Cadmus onward.

Every fourth portrait, or thereabouts, was of a Jardine. Bouda knew all the names, and the family stories and scandals that explained a gap. And now that Whittam was

Chancellor once more, the suite was again a locus of Jardine power. The rooms were practically an annexe of Kyneston. You felt as if you might open one more door and find Lady Thalia sewing in the Great Solar, or Silyen up to no good in the library.

Except these days, you might find Silyen right here in Westminster, Bouda mused, as she stepped into the brass cage lift to the top of the tower, Skill-crafted to admit only Equals.

She still couldn't understand why her godfather Lord Rix had installed Silyen as his heir.

She would have quizzed Rixy about it, but that would be in poor taste, given the gossip circulating about her and Dina's expectations of Far Carr. DiDi wasn't the sort of stuff an heir was made of, but Bouda had expected to inherit and eventually pass the estate to one of her children. The eldest would have Kyneston, the second would take Appledurham, and a third child at Far Carr would have created a dynasty to last generations.

Added to the loss of Far Carr was the sheer exasperation of having Silyen in parliament. Bouda liked to deal with known quantities. For years now she had observed people's alliances and weaknesses, desires and vulnerabilities, filing them away in her head for the day they would become useful. The day she took aim at the Chancellorship.

She didn't have a clue what was going on in Silyen's head.

And neither did his father, she thought, as the lift chimed for its destination. It was a novel and unwelcome experience for both of them.

Bouda rapped on the door to the suite and felt Skill tingle across her skin like fingertips. The door opened just wide enough for her father-in-law's head to appear in the gap.

'Bouda,' he said, raking back that silvering tawny hair and smiling his lion's smile. 'Do come in. Imogen was just leaving.'

The woman on the sofa as Bouda stepped inside did not look like she was just leaving. She wasn't wearing enough clothes, for a start.

This wasn't the first time Bouda had walked in on such a scene. She suspected Whittam did it deliberately. He could easily have fabricated a pretext to keep her waiting outside while the woman dressed. This was Whittam testing her limits, to see if she complained or criticized. Bouda pressed her lips together and said nothing.

'Family business,' Lord Jardine told the woman, snatching something brightly coloured and flimsy off the floor and tossing it in her direction. She stood, shaking out the blouse and slipping it on.

'Always so busy, Whittam,' she said, in a little-girl voice. (And how was that supposed to be seductive? Bouda thought, revolted.) 'Don't work too hard.'

'Goodbye, Imogen,' he said, holding the door open. 'Until next time.'

The woman paused to blow him a kiss on the threshold before the door was shut firmly in her face. Bouda had placed her. She was the third wife of an elderly Midlands lord – one of the minority who had not backed Lord Jardine's coup.

'Revenge?' she said. 'Or recruitment?'

Her future father-in-law unstoppered the decanter that stood on a side table.

'Both.' He poured a generous measure. 'The best revenge on an enemy is to make him want to be your friend. And the best sight in the world is the expression on his face when you plant a knife in his back anyway.'

He passed the whisky to Bouda and poured another for himself. They touched glasses and smiled.

'What brought you here, dear daughter? Not long now till I can call you that. My son doesn't know how lucky he is, winning a prize like you.'

Whittam reached for Bouda's jaw and cheek, turning her this way and that like a jeweller looking for a flaw in a diamond. He wouldn't find one.

Her father-in-law's fingers were warm and strong. Bouda wondered where his hands had been, just minutes earlier.

'Of course,' Lord Whittam continued, 'Gavar didn't win you. I did.'

His fingers squeezed once – Bouda could imagine the red marks they'd leave on her skin – and released.

'I've come about the Millmoor boy,' she said. 'To ask if Crovan has secured any information of use to our investigations into the slavetowns.'

Whittam's mood changed in an instant. He banged down the now-empty glass and went to his desk.

'Nothing substantial,' he said, sifting the papers and snatching one up. 'He's only carried out one interrogation so far because, as I found in the Middle East, the process takes a toll on the subjects. Loss of mental faculties, and so on. I can't have the prisoner's mind turned to mush before Crovan has discovered what's needful.

'So the boy will be examined weekly, which should give us at least a couple of months before he's a drooling idiot, and Arailt is confident he'll have answers within that time.'

'Perhaps . . .' Bouda hardly dared say it. Lord Whittam's moods, like his heir's, were unpredictable at best. 'Perhaps it is all as it seems: a boy, radicalized, and sent to kill a Chancellor. No larger conspiracy, no Equal involvement beyond what Meilyr has already confessed.'

'No. The one thing Crovan has found is evidence of Skillful tampering with the boy's mind. Masking his memories with the Silence, perhaps, or an initial act of compulsion. Maybe both. But it proves that one of our kind was behind this. And when that gun came up, it was pointing at me.'

Could he be right? Of course, if Whittam was the true target, then the motive could be anything at all. Bouda thought of the woman on the sofa. Any number of cuckolded husbands might want to take a pop at Lord Jardine. Gavar would have been top of her list of suspects, except all the Jardines knew family members could not be harmed by one of their own slaves.

'I had Silyen make an attempt on the boy's mind, in the hours before the trial. But he found nothing. Perhaps I should have given him longer. But Silyen himself insisted I send the boy to Crovan for further searching, and we all know it isn't like my youngest son to make a modest assessment of his abilities.'

More new information. Bouda turned it over, unsure what it meant.

'Perhaps he didn't want to lose face by failing, so soon after his triumphs in reviving his Aunt Euterpe and rebuilding the East Wing?'

'Perhaps.'

Whittam did not sound convinced. Bouda wasn't either. But neither did she have another explanation – yet.

'I have not seen Silyen since his adoption,' Lord Jardine said, refilling his glass. Bouda frowned. It wasn't even midday. 'Which is not in itself problematic, although his mother misses him. He has gone to Orpen Mote.'

'Orpen? But that's a ruin.'

'Not any more. Silyen and his aunt Euterpe are restoring

it, apparently. First Kyneston, now Orpen. I thought I was raising a Skillful prodigy. And when he came to Westminster I imagined it might be the beginning of a political career. But it seems my youngest's true vocation is as a jobbing repairman. What a frustration, the pack of them.'

Lord Jardine banged down his glass. Refilled it yet again.

'But not you, eh? My diligent, dutiful daughter.'

Lord Whittam eyed her. Around his blue-green pupils, the whites of his eyes were pink and bloodshot.

'Tell me, Bouda, what do you think of my children. Are they not all defectives? Gavar a wastrel, Silyen without a shred of responsibility, and Jenner of no use to anyone.'

It was no more than Bouda thought privately. But she doubted that Lord Jardine would wish to hear her true assessment of his family. Where was this leading? Was her future father-in-law finally about to admit what she had waited all these years to hear – that his son's wife, and not his son, would make the best head of the family's next generation?

'It seems unlikely, does it not,' Whittam continued, gesturing to the portraits that surrounded them, 'that a family like mine would throw up such specimens. Even Silyen, so powerful, is flawed in so many ways. The boy is ungovernable and unnatural. And yet what a line they come from.'

Lord Whittam took Bouda by the elbow and steered her towards the portrait-lined walls. The first they passed over without comment. Cadmus Parva-Jardine needed no elaboration.

'Ptolemy Jardine,' Lord Whittam said, pointing to Cadmus's heir and successor. 'He entrenched his father and grandfather's revolution, and ensured that our rule would last forever. His son, Aristide Jardine – Harrower of Princes. He executed not one, but three imposters who claimed to be inheritors of the extinguished throne.'

Bouda looked at Aristide. His was one of the most handsome faces in an already handsome line. He was almost beautiful. His destruction of the Pretender Princes was similarly flawless.

Rather than punish those commoners who had backed the first imposter, Aristide had granted a three-day holiday for the working folk of London. The city became one immense fairground. Stalls distributed free pies and beer, sweetmeats and wine. Hawkers gave away ribbons and trinkets; jugglers and fire-breathers performed in the streets, and dogs fought bears in the public byways. At its culmination, drunk on liberty, licence and liquor, the revellers surged into a square where the terrified pretender was tethered naked to a post. The Londoners had torn him apart with their bare hands.

Seven years and another two pretenders later, when Great Britain had unsurprisingly run out of royal claimants, Aristide instituted the Blood Fair as an annual holiday. The worst offenders against the Equal regime were publicly dispatched during a day of revelry. The grisly tradition had continued until two centuries ago. Bouda had always admired Aristide as the pinnacle of Skillful statecraft.

They walked past more portraits. More Jardines.

'Jerrold Jardine,' Whittam said, pausing in front of one showing a smiling young man whose long copper hair was tied back with a knot of sea-green ribbon. 'Jerrold the Just. Known to you, no doubt, from his friendship with your ancestor Harding Matravers, who first lifted your line from obscurity. A playboy in his youth, Jerrold found greatness in the Chancellorship. There was a time when I imagined Gavar might do likewise. Now I'm not so sure.'

'Why are you telling me all this?' Bouda asked. She knew these paintings, these faces and histories, as well as those of her own ancestors that hung at Appledurham.

Then she gasped as her father-in-law's hand closed tightly around her arm and thrust her back against the canvas. She turned her head away as Lord Whittam put his face close to hers, and found her eyes meeting the knowing, painted gaze of Jerrold.

'I tell you because there is taint in this line,' Whittam rasped. The alcohol fumes on his breath tingled across Bouda's skin. 'Taint that must have come from my wife's family. My wife is only weakly Skilled. And you know her sister's degeneracy. Euterpe's desire to crossbreed her ancient line by marriage to Zelston, her inability to control her emotions, and the violence of her Skill that almost destroyed Kyneston itself.'

What Euterpe Parva had done the night Chancellor

Zelston was killed was something Bouda would never forget. It was grief made into pure power.

In the moment before the ballroom exploded, Bouda had felt as though everything inside her was being crushed down impossibly small. And the terrifying thing wasn't that unimaginable pressure; it was the apprehension of what might come next, when that force released its grip. Bouda had felt for a moment as though she might fly apart into a million tiny pieces. And then Kyneston's East Wing had shattered instead.

'Taint from my wife's line is in my sons,' Whittam continued, his other hand coming up to take Bouda's chin and force her face back towards him. 'In Gavar, your affianced husband.'

His words froze Bouda where she stood. She was not married yet. Not mistress of Kyneston. Not yet the mother of heirs. All could still be lost – and with it, Bouda's hopes of the Chancellor's Chair.

'What are you saying?' she asked, hoping it didn't sound like a plea. 'Do you no longer wish Gavar to marry me? My line may not be exalted, but it is strong. We are wealthier even than you. I am Skillful; my children will be both beautiful and clever. If what you believe about your line, in this generation, is true, who better than someone like me to breed out that taint?'

'Oh, I'm not talking about you breeding it out,' said Whittam. He stepped closer, and she felt him against the length of her body. The hand that had been around her arm let go, and began to move lower.

'Gavar is my image,' said the lord of Kyneston, his mouth against Bouda's ear. Was it only the alcohol on his breath that made his words sting and scorch? 'No one will ever know. Let's make sure that taint is never bred *into* you.'

His mouth attacked hers. His knee pushed forward between her legs.

Bouda felt her Skill coil inside her – the protective reflex held on a trigger, her body uncertain whether or not this assault was a threat.

Was it?

She didn't want Lord Jardine. But then she didn't want his son, either. She wanted the Chancellorship.

Whatever it took.

Like bringing a savage animal to heel, Bouda quelled her body's Skillful instincts. She let her arms fall to her side. She parted her lips beneath her father-in-law's hungry mouth.

All around them, the painted likenesses of dozens of Jardines watched. Proud. Intelligent. Powerful.

Hers would join them, Bouda thought, as she tipped her head back.

Even this was worth it.

10

Abi

Meilyr had come back from Westminster without a pardon for Luke, and though Abi had told herself not to get her hopes up, it was hard to contain her dismay.

He had confronted Rix, who had denied any involvement. And he had spoken to Silyen Jardine.

'Silyen more or less confirmed that Rix worked Skill upon Luke,' Meilyr said, holding himself carefully in one of the library armchairs as Abi and the Club members huddled around to listen.

'More or less?' Renie scoffed. 'What good is that?'

'He has to tell someone,' Abi insisted. 'The Equals need to know who's responsible – and his father wouldn't be happy to learn that Silyen was withholding something like that.'

'You lived alongside him,' said Meilyr wearily. 'Do you think Silyen Jardine has ever been made to do anything in his life? And he'd probably withhold information purposely to make his father unhappy. He sparked all this, you know.

He did a deal with Zelston to raise the abolition Proposal, in exchange for waking Euterpe Parva.'

Abi sat back, astonished.

Silyen? He would have been . . . well, maybe not the last – his father and Bouda Matravers took that title – but one of the last people she could imagine advocating abolition. Everything about him reeked of belief in his kind's superiority.

But that was a mystery for another day.

'Well,' she said, forcing down her disappointment that there hadn't been an easier way to do this, one that was reasonable and fair. But if there was one thing she'd learned, it was that the Equals didn't do *fair*. 'It's just as well we've been busy with an alternative while you've been away. I'm not saying we give up on Rix. You've said he won't confess willingly, so we should consider pressure, or passing on an anonymous tip-off. But here's what the rest of us have been doing while you've been in London.'

'An escape plan?'

Something kindled in Meilyr Tresco's tired eyes, and next to Abi, Renie bounced in her seat to see it. Abi nodded.

'Bodina did the field work, with Oz, Jess and Renie. Asif, Hilda and Tilda and I did the desk research.'

Which played to everyone's strengths, but had also saved Abi from working with the woman who had nearly shoved her off a cliff. Jenner had refused, at first, to depart

Highwithel and leave the two of them together. But she had made him go back to Kyneston, at least for a little while, so as not to arouse suspicion. She also wanted him to keep an eye on Daisy while Gavar was in London. It had broken her heart to make him swear not to tell Daisy that he knew of her big sister's whereabouts.

Bodina pulled out a phone, laid it on the library table, then dialled a pay-as-you-go number. When it crackled into life, she hit the speakerphone, and the voice was unmistakable despite patchy reception.

'Bit gusty,' bellowed Oz, once a coded greeting had been exchanged. Dina asked whether he was in a suitable place to talk. 'You bet,' came the answer, warped by wind shear. 'I'm looking at it right now. It's one beautiful place. Tall and dark, in this loch that kinda glitters.'

There was some indistinct muttering, then Oz boomed out again. 'Jess says to tell you it matches those photos you sent, Tilda. The satellite ones. Every detail's the same. He hasn't had a nice new bridge put in, sadly. But there's a boat tied up on the far shore, and something like a gate or little dock on the island itself. We've not seen anyone use it, though. We've not seen anyone outside at all – on the island, or those jutty bits at the top of the castle.' Another muffled exchange; Oz's laughter. 'The battlements.'

When the call wrapped up, Abi and Dina unfolded their plan to Meilyr, with Renie chiming in excitably, too.

'So Abi's told you what we've discovered about the

castle,' said Dina, when Abi had finished explaining what she'd found in Highwithel's library. During her sleepless nights, she'd kept the terrors at bay by trawling antiquarian history books for information about the castle layout. 'But Crovan is the key. He's the only one at that place with Skill, and we know he has no scruples about using it.'

'So we've gotta get Crovan out of there,' Renie breathed, leaning towards Meilyr. 'And you'll never guess who came up with how. Asif.'

They all turned to where Asif sat, sunk deep into a chair with his knees drawn up. He cringed and waved his hands.

'Don't all go looking at me. Poorly socialized introvert over here. And it's a pretty simple plan.'

'Those are the best,' said Meilyr, smiling.

It was good. Abi knew. She'd gone over it again and again herself.

'My sister is secretary of the Justice Council,' Dina said. 'So it makes sense that she would notify its members if they had an emergency meeting, yes? Tell me if I'm wrong.'

'You're not wrong.'

As Meilyr listened, he reached out for Dina's hand, and Abi saw some of the tight unhappiness that had gripped the Equal girl for the past days ease a little. She admired them, this pair, even if she found Dina hard to like. They didn't have to be doing this – any of it. They had put aside their privilege to combat the abuses perpetrated by their kind.

And yet, something inside Abi insisted. How did that

sentence end? *And yet they have less to lose?* That wasn't right, because Meilyr had already suffered a loss no commoner could ever understand.

And yet it isn't their fight? Maybe that was it.

No matter. They were all in this together now – and Abi needed them, both of them, if they were to rescue Luke.

'I'll send him a memo from my sister requiring his presence; I know her handwriting. And I'll telephone, too. It's easy to make my voice sound the same. Then while Crovan is travelling to London – we can't wait till he gets there, because that's when he'll discover there is no meeting – I'll go to the castle,' Dina was saying. 'I'll pose as Bouda. Say that the prisoner Hadley is needed for examination by the full council. That's plausible, because his people will know Crovan has gone to London for a Justice Council session.'

'We know the boat's there, to get us over to the castle,' Renie chimed in. 'And Tilda's photos show a helicopter pad – the one Crovan uses. 'Cause we're posing as legit, we can just fly in and out with the Highwithel 'copter. And that's it.'

The kid looked at Meilyr triumphantly. You could see him thinking over what they'd suggested, examining it for flaws.

'I warned you it was simple,' said Asif, jiggling one leg, while they all awaited the heir's verdict. 'It's not going to work, is it? I knew it wasn't going to work.'

'No,' Meilyr said, slowly shaking his head. 'No, I think

it's going to work just fine. I'm coming too, of course. I'm still a member of the Justice Council. My presence will corroborate the story for whoever is in the castle, while reassuring Luke.'

Dina looked like she wanted to protest, but Renie was nodding enthusiastically.

'It's like when you and Luke got Oz out of the security lock-up,' the kid said. 'The pair of you walked in like you had a right to be there and they believed you.'

Abi suspected that the earlier break-out hadn't been quite that simple, and that Skill had been involved. But this scheme was essentially the same. It rested upon one thing: Crovan believing the summons.

Had Luke felt as nervous before Oz's rescue as she felt now? He couldn't have done. He was merely rescuing a friend. She was going in for her little brother.

Renie was elbowing her in the ribs. The kid nodded at Meilyr, who had apparently asked her a question.

'I said, I know you've been working from some strange old sources, but is there anything you can tell us about the castle? Why the prisoners don't all escape every time Crovan leaves? Maybe he locks them all into their cells, but I'm sure I've heard legends about Skillful safeguards.'

'The books aren't clear. There's one old folk tale I found . . .' She ferreted through the volumes stacked within arm's reach, pulling out one stamped with Celtic patterns. 'It's called *The Necklace of Eile An Dòchais* and it's a comedy, if you'd believe that. It says – and other sources confirm this – that the castle has two doors. One, you can only go in. The other, you can only go out. Here's the twist: the one that leads out is deadly. It kills you, unless it's opened by a Crovan. Which would be quite a deterrent to escape, if it were literally true.

'There are references here and here' – she plonked two heavy history books down in front of Meilyr – 'that throw some light on it. The Crovans are one of the ancient baronial families, the *mormaers*. In the Middle Ages, Scotland was embroiled in one power struggle after another: assassinations, usurpations, you name it. The *mormaer* Crovan built the doors to protect his family. But it seems that because of that deadly door, entering the castle became proof of good faith. So the Crovans became known as peace-brokers and deal-makers, and Eilean Dòchais was used to exchange hostages during the endless *mormaer* disputes.

'Then there's the lake. The loch is infused with Skill and apparently causes excruciating pain to any who come into contact with it. So the prisoners can't swim across – and the boat is kept on the far side of the lake. Given the sort of crimes the Condemned have committed, I daresay Crovan doesn't worry too much about the local people developing sympathies and rowing over to get them.'

'Could they build a boat?' Renie wondered out loud. 'I dunno, turn a table upside down and paddle across?'

'That might be possible,' Abi admitted. 'Which all suggests he has other safeguards. Someone left in charge when he's away. Or, like Meilyr said, he simply locks them all in cells.'

Or ties them up with collars and leashes.

'One last thing,' she said. 'I have to come as well. Luke will probably recognize you, Dina. Especially if Meilyr's there. Hopefully he'll understand that it's a rescue. But it's possible Luke believes *you* used him to murder Zelston. He might even think you're abducting him to kill him, to prevent Crovan seeing you as the Angel of the North in his memories. Who knows what state his mind will be in by now?

'So I'll come, too. The real Bouda would travel with an aide or assistant. That will be me. I'll wait in the boat – but if anything goes wrong and Luke starts resisting, I'll be there to reassure him straight away.'

'And I'll wait with the chopper,' Renie announced. 'Be a lookout. We'll have Tilda's headsets so we can be in touch.'

And that was it. Their plan. It was chancy, but they'd tested it from all angles and it could – should – work. *Please let Meilyr agree*, Abi thought. Every day knowing Luke was captive in that place was unbearable.

Meilyr pulled the two history books towards him; his fingers stroked the gilded edges of the pages contemplatively.

'Let me think on it tonight,' he said. 'And talk to my

mother. But I think you're right – this feels like the best chance we've got. Renie, would you be brilliant and carry these books to my room for me?'

Nobody saw Meilyr the next morning, and Abi thought the suspense was going to finish her off. She couldn't eat a mouthful of breakfast, her stomach was so knotted. She was sitting in the Great Hall staring with equal desperation at her lunch when the tap of a cane told her that Highwithel's heir had arrived. His mother was on one side of him, Dina on the other.

'It's done,' he said to Abi and the Club members present. 'A message has been dispatched summoning Crovan to an emergency session of the Justice Council in two days' time. Dina will call tomorrow morning to confirm that he has received it and is preparing to travel to London. When we know he's leaving, we leave too. We'll follow the same route Dina did when she took Oz and Jess to scope out the castle – up to Mallaig, then on to Eilean Dòchais tomorrow evening.'

Abi's mouth went dry. In thirty-six hours, she'd have Luke back. She pushed her plate away. She wouldn't be able to eat another thing all day.

What would they do once reunited, both of them fugitives? Assuming they both made it out of this. There would be no pardons from Lord Jardine's regime. Bouda Matravers would discover that her identity had been used as part of the imposture to free Luke, and would waste no time hunting them both down. Where could they go? They could hardly live here at Highwithel. Only one option seemed possible: to flee the country.

The Skilless nations of the Triad – Russia, France and the Union States of America – granted automatic asylum to those fleeing abusive Skilled regimes. Would one of them admit Luke and Abi? And their parents and Daisy would be free to travel abroad, even emigrate, once their days were done. Was this how it would end, with the Hadleys reunited and settled somewhere in small-town America, with new lives?

A life that wouldn't have Jenner in it, because as one of Britain's elite – despite having no Skill – he wouldn't be permitted across US borders. But that was a sorrow for another day.

In the morning, Bodina confirmed that her call had been successful. A brief conversation with Crovan had revealed that he planned to depart after four o'clock. So Luke's rescue was on for that evening, and Highwithel spun into action.

The Club's data people were staying behind.

'I guess we've gotta sit this one out, Doc,' Hilda said.

'But you keep those comms open in case there's anything you need,' Tilda added.

Asif and Meilyr exchanged a goodbye awkward even by the standard of man-hugs. Thanks to Meilyr's pain and Asif's jitters, there must have been a clear foot of air between them.

'You tell your brother we can't wait to see him,' Tilda

173

said. 'And that the food here's a whole lot better than back in Millmoor. That'll get him hurrying.'

They chuckled, but Abi knew the sisters, too, would each be a bag of nerves until they were all safely back – and Luke with them.

And to finish it off, as the helicopter rose swiftly and smoothly away from the island with Dina at the controls, Abi discovered that she got airsick. Even the moment when Highwithel simply disappeared, as they reached its Skillful concealing boundary, was little distraction. Abi closed her eyes and concentrated on breathing exercises for the remainder of the flight, not wanting her stress to trigger a panic attack or flashback to the horrifying explosion at Kyneston. Sometimes it did. Occasionally, she opened her eyes to see Renie watching her. Once, the kid reached over and squeezed her hand sympathetically.

She'd recovered sufficiently by the time Dina's voice crackled over the headset announcing that they had crossed into Scotland, and Abi found she could look down. They had mostly flown north over the Irish Sea, but off to the right she could see the curve of the Scottish coast. How absurdly beautiful it was from the air. She could trace the course of rivers, the contours of hills. The colours were bright and fresh and clean.

And then, far off, something that wasn't. A writhing ball of smoke, steam and fire. Carlisle's shadow: Rockdale slave-town. It soiled the landscape around it.

Abi wanted to look away, but didn't permit herself. Luke had been in a place like that for months. Somewhere worse than that. It was no wonder he had been spurred to protest. Abi vowed never to judge him for it again. In fact, as toxic gusts billowed up from Rockdale, for the first time she felt proud of her little brother's choices.

They landed at Mallaig, refuelled and rested, and waited. Dina had already assumed the persona of her sister, wearing a formal dress and austere nude lipstick, her hair sleeked back in a ponytail. The transformation was almost flawless, even to Abi, who had seen the Matravers heir on numerous occasions at Kyneston.

She remembered coming round in the Great Solar at Kyneston, in the company of Jenner and his mother, an excruciating pain in her head. And Silyen in the library weeks later, explaining that she had witnessed a row between Bouda and Gavar, and Bouda had Silenced her for it. For such a small thing, to cut a swathe through Abi's memory. Bouda Matravers embodied all that was worst about the Equals. Their unquestioning superiority and utter indifference to any who were not their own kind. Abi should judge Dina more gently. The Matravers sisters had grown up in the same environment, with the same opportunities, and yet how different Dina's choices had been.

Jessica arrived, and briefed the four of them.

'We never saw a helicopter take off,' Jess said anxiously.

'He should have gone by now. That's why Oz stayed there, to watch.'

That didn't sound good. Was their plan derailed before it had barely begun?

'You wouldn't see it,' said Meilyr. 'Remember when you came to Highwithel – and when you left. How the island just disappears from the air? There are ways of Skillfully hiding comings and goings.'

And the alarm that had bubbled up inside Abi died back down again.

'The boat is on the opposite side of the loch from where you'll land,' Jess said.

'Not a problem.' Dina batted away the information with a flick of her hand. Her mannerisms, voice, were all changing. It was disconcerting – but also reassuring. Luke's freedom depended on the conviction of this performance.

'Why's it kept there?' Renie asked. The kid always had 101 questions. 'A bit inconvenient for Crovan, isn't it?'

'It's for food supplies,' Jess said. 'So it's on the side closest to the nearest village. Goes back and forth a couple of times a week, just like Highwithel – which was how Abi found us, remember? You're more like your brother than you think, Abi.'

The woman squeezed her shoulder reassuringly. And wasn't that a novel experience – being compared to her brother, with the comparison intended to flatter. Pride warmed Abi from the inside out.

They had set their departure time for 6 p.m., just as the light would be fading, which gave them another half hour. Meilyr and Dina had stepped away, perhaps to discuss a few last things, while the other three chatted. Abi slipped into the corridor of the little airfield's departure lounge to find the loo for the second time (because really, if anything justified needing an anxiety wee, this whole situation did) and saw them standing there, silhouetted against the glass.

Dina was leaning into Meilyr's chest, her head was tucked under his chin, and one of his arms was around her.

'Thank you for doing this,' Abi heard Meilyr say softly. 'You mean the world to me. Always have.'

'Nothing's changed,' Dina replied, with a fierceness that was all her own. 'First we get Luke back. Then we fix you.'

The Equal girl went up on tiptoe and wound both arms around his neck and kissed him. As Meilyr's palm cupped her face, the kiss went on.

Abi looked away and retreated, letting the door close soundlessly. She'd try again in five minutes, opening it really noisily this time.

That was the problem with Equals. They were cruel autocrats filled with unimaginable power.

But they were also just human.

By the time they got back in the helicopter, Abi was about ready to puke with nerves. Was this how Luke had felt, when he had played those 'games' for the Club that Renie talked about? She used to think 'courage' was a reckless, slightly stupid thing. She understood it a little better now. It was doing what was right, even when every shred of self-preservation screamed against it.

Would Luke recognize the rescue for what it was, and be able to play along with it? Abi desperately hoped her brother's mind wasn't already broken, so he'd be able to understand what was happening. But she remembered the state of Dog and had to concede that it might be too late for that.

She looked down at the small coil of cable in her lap. An earpiece, to connect her to Renie back on shore if there was any alert. Meilyr was also mic'd up. Abi and Renie would be able to hear every word.

Then as Dina banked the helicopter, there it was: Eilean Dòchais. She'd seen many images of it in the course of her research: from foxed watercolour plates, to line engravings, to the high-res satellite photographs that Tilda had turned up on some restricted database.

But she had never imagined it would be this stunning. Evening's approach had stretched the sun's rays, and the loch glittered and sparkled. The arrow slit windows were like golden wounds in the black hide of the castle, dripping fiery blood. How could so beautiful a place hide such evil?

The chopper settled on its runners and they were out, ducking under the blades that whirred to a halt. Renie gave a small salute as the three of them set off. Dina grumbled about the impossibility of walking on heather in Bouda-style power heels, and Meilyr laughed at her.

She had no more luck on the loch shore, her shoes sinking into the fine gravel. But by this time, she was more Bouda Matravers than Bodina, and said nothing as she closed her eyes – and reached out – and –

The boat rounded the far side of the island, gliding towards them. It nudged the shore. After the stories she'd read about the waters of Loch nan Deur, Abi was glad to see sturdy handrails on the boat's side. The thwarted med student in her was curious about the water's pain-imparting properties, but now really wasn't the time to investigate.

Meilyr clambered on board with great difficulty. It was plain that the journey had taken a terrible toll. The helicopter's vibrations must have exacerbated his pain. His cane clattered against the railings as he used both hands to haul himself up. Abi looked away as Dina reached down to help him.

Then the boat moved off and Abi stared up at the castle. She didn't expect to see Luke's face at a window looking down at her, of course. And there hardly were any windows. But just knowing her little brother was in there somewhere, so close, made her heart sing.

Steps rose from the waterline near the front of the castle, and Abi looked up at the two doors that greeted them. Both were closed. The inscription above was hard to read without her glasses, but the books had told her what it said. *Omnes vulnerant, ultima necat.*

All hours wound, the last one kills.

Abi shuddered, and set about securing the boat. She was pretty inept, but from here on in, Dina was Bouda, and there was no way Bouda Matravers would risk breaking a nail by performing servants' work.

'Don't forget,' Abi whispered, as the pair disembarked. 'Stay outside. Don't go in. We don't know the truth about those doors, and it's not worth taking chances.'

Then the two of them were off up the steps. Abi positioned herself near a rocky outcropping, where she was mostly concealed, but had a good view of the left-hand door. She touched a finger to her earpiece, and heard Renie whisper 'Good luck', and some faint heavy breathing that could only have been Tilda or Hilda listening in from Highwithel.

The great door had no visible handle or other means of opening it. Dina rapped on it once. Twice. The she stepped back and straightened her shoulders, sleeking her ponytail as Abi had seen Bouda do.

Abi's heart stopped in her chest when the door creaked inwards. She could just about see what was going on, but the sounds of it were horribly magnified through her receiver.

'May I help you?' said a man at the door, politely. From

what Abi could see, he was young-ish and clad in a smart suit. Some kind of butler?

'I am Heir Bouda of Appledurham, Secretary of the Justice Council. This is Heir Meilyr of Highwithel, another council member. I know that your master left a few hours ago. It is frustrating that we were unable to reach him – our departures must have almost coincided. It would have saved me a journey.'

Abi could almost imagine Bouda's disdainful expression as Dina spoke. She was good at this. Meilyr extended his hand so that the man could inspect the Tresco signet ring he wore, confirming his identity.

'We are here for the Condemned prisoner, Luke Hadley. Chancellor Whittam wishes Lord Arailt to examine him in full council, so that we can see what progress has been made in the investigation.'

'I . . . see.' The man sounded uncertain, hesitant. Abi exulted. This was exactly how they'd imagined it. Perhaps Dina was even exerting a little Skillful persuasion on him, if she didn't consider that a violation of her principles. 'Let me just go check. I need to consult. Wait here a moment, please.'

He turned away from the door, and in Abi's ear Renie let out a low exhalation and a 'Niiiiice.'

Excruciating moments passed, then Abi saw two new figures arrive. They stood back in the entryway and were almost entirely in darkness, but was one of them about Luke's size?

'Heir Bouda.' The voice was male, crisp and clipped. Scottish. Perhaps a Crovan relative? Abi's heart lurched again. Maybe it wouldn't be so simple after all.

'Such a pleasure,' the man was saying. 'You look quite refreshed from when I saw you last. One might almost say you look two years younger. The resemblance to your lovely sister is uncanny. And Heir Meilyr. Happier circumstance than when we met last. How are you bearing up?'

In her ear came a low, appalled 'No' from Renie. But Abi had worked it out, too.

'Lord Arailt,' said Dina, her chin high, still persisting with their pretence. 'I was under the impression from our conversation this morning that you would be travelling to London.'

'I lied,' said Crovan – because that was who this was, Abi grasped, as every organ turned to concrete inside her. 'Just as you are lying now, Bodina. But I applaud your brazenness. There's just one thing that puzzles me.'

Abi saw Crovan's head swing between the pair of them.

'I never attend meetings of the Justice Council – not even emergency sessions. Your sister knows this. Every member knows this, Meilyr included.

'So I've really only one question: Meilyr, what on earth were you thinking?'

11

Luke

'Champagne o'clock,' Jules called it. The hour before dinner at seven.

The guests were gathered in the billiard room, and from where he sat at a table in the library next door, Luke could hear the clink of glasses and bubbling laughter. His friend was telling a convoluted anecdote about a romantic punting trip with his Equal girlfriend, Athalie, during which Jules had discovered that he had no knack at all for steering the flat-bottomed boat. He had chivalrously persisted in attempting to navigate Oxford's rivers, and mishap after disaster had ensued, from all of which Athalie had used her Skill to extricate him.

Luke wished he could be in there with them. It sounded almost as funny as last week's yarn about how they had kidnapped a stuffed dodo from the University Museum and driven it in Athalie's sports car to parties around the colleges.

But no, here he was, in the library. Doing an Abi. Who would have thought it?

From his conversation with Coira, it was plain there was one major obstacle to escape: it wasn't getting out of the castle or leaving the island, it was the loch boundary.

Sitting down with Silyen Jardine for a nice cup of tea and a chat about how such a thing might work wasn't a possibility, so Luke was trying the only way he could think of to find out more – his sister's preferred option of simply hitting the books.

He'd also started keeping a journal – something else Abi had done, and for which he had once teased her, imagining her egghead tribulations recorded in obsessive detail. (Looking back, Luke wished he'd been a less annoying little brother.) He'd swiped a book from a dusty cabinet, some old one on heraldry that had lots of blank pages on the reverse of the coloured illustrated plates, and scribbled a few notes in it daily. Luke wasn't sure what was wrong with him, but he was getting a lot of headaches these days, and sometimes his thinking felt muddled. Writing things down really helped.

He was jotting down a final thought, ready to join the others, when he heard it – a distant juddering sound. There was a stir from the billiard room next door. His fellow guests were crowding at the window. Luke closed his journal, stashed it in the usual place behind a low shelf of obscure books, and went to see what was causing the fuss.

It was a helicopter.

'Other than Crovan's, I've not seen one of those in the

three years I've been here,' Julian said next to him. 'No one ever visits. That's our gossip for the next few weeks taken care of.'

Luke pressed his face to the glass as the chopper set down. So helicopters never came to Eilean Dòchais, but now, just weeks after his own arrival, here one was. Was it because of him? A pardon, secured by a confession from whomever had used him to murder Zelston at the ball?

He didn't dare let himself hope.

The chopper's passengers disembarked. There were three of them. Discerning more than that was impossible, because the glass in the billiard room window was centuries old, in thick, small panes. Wordlessly, they all watched the visitors' progress across the heath and down to the lake shore.

'Two women and a man,' someone called as the trio neared. 'He's got a stick.'

'How are they going to get across?' someone wondered. The answer came a minute or two later, when the boat sailed into view.

'That'll be Skill,' Julian said. 'They're Equals. Come on.'

Jules shouldered his way through, and led the twittering group of guests into the stair-lined central atrium. Glasses of champagne still in hand, they hung over the banisters, gawping. When two heavy raps came on the Door of Hours, a hush descended. Devin passed below, hurrying through to the entrance hall.

Luke's hearing was pretty sharp, but he couldn't make out

the conversation, only that it was a woman speaking. After a brief exchange, Devin returned. Seeing the assembled guests bannister-hanging, he gestured impatiently. Then his eyes caught Luke's and lingered, before he passed into the deeper part of the castle. A prickle went up Luke's spine. This was about him. He knew it.

Devin returned with Crovan.

'Hadley,' their master said, halting and looking up. 'Your presence is requested. Come.'

All eyes swivelled to him. Luke's legs wobbled, but the compulsion of his master's instruction was irresistible. The huddled guests parted to let him through, and he descended the staircase.

In the entrance hall, Crovan went to the Door of Hours – which had magically materialized and stood ajar – while Devin laid a hand on Luke's wrist, keeping him back.

'Heir Bouda,' Crovan said. 'Such a pleasure. You look quite refreshed from when I saw you last. One might almost say you look two years younger. The resemblance to your lovely sister is uncanny. And Heir Meilyr. Happier circumstance than when we met last. How are you bearing up?'

Meilyr. Luke started to shake. He'd known this man by a different name: Doc Jackson.

So who was the woman? The blood rushing in his ears drowned out her response. Luke craned for a glimpse, but could only make out a gleam of white-blonde hair.

Angel. They'd come for him. Just as he and Jackson had rescued Oz.

'I lied,' Crovan told Angel. 'Just as you are lying now, Bodina. But I applaud your brazenness. There's just one thing that puzzles me.'

He turned to look between them and Luke shifted again for a clear view. There they were, side by side, just as they had been in Kyneston's ballroom the night his world had fallen apart. Immaculate and impressive, Equal authority personified, although – Luke felt a churn of horror and pity – Jackson looked a shadow of himself. His face was hollow and grey.

'I never attend meetings of the Justice Council – not even emergency sessions. Your sister knows this. Every member knows this, Meilyr included. So I've really only one question: Meilyr, what on earth were you thinking?'

'Luke, is that you?' Jackson said urgently.

The voice of this man – the one who had taught Luke that he could dream bigger and do more, but who had broken Luke's trust by concealing his true identity – drew him forward. Devin didn't try and stop him.

'It's me,' he said, standing beside Crovan within the doorway.

What would happen if he bolted for it right now? Why had the pair of them simply come to the front door like this, like they were his mum and dad picking him up after school?

And what lies had they told, that Crovan had apparently seen through?

'Meilyr?' Angel turned to the Doc. 'What is he saying? You knew he wouldn't go to London?'

'I knew there was a chance, yes. Among parliamentarians, Lord Arailt is somewhat infamous for attending only once a year. Most of his peers like it that way.'

Incredibly, Jackson – Meilyr – smiled at Crovan like they'd shared a joke. Crovan gave a small huff of amusement. What was this?

'I don't understand,' Angel insisted. 'Why take that risk?'

'There's no risk.' Meilyr squeezed her hand, which was when Luke noticed that he now held a cane. Was the sick look just an act, and any minute now he would whack Crovan round the head with it so they could all escape? 'We're just standing here having a conversation.'

'Long way to come for a conversation,' Crovan said. 'And I'm afraid I've no room for two more for dinner. So you've had a wasted journey.'

The door began to swing shut, when Meilyr thrust the cane inside.

'You know he's innocent.' Meilyr pushed the door back wide, so Luke could see them both plainly. Three people had come over in the boat. Where was the third person? Was it another Equal? Maybe even Silyen Jardine?

'If you haven't seen it in his memories already, you will. He was used, then Silenced – we believe by Lord Rix. Luke is innocent. Let him go. We'll take him back to London and keep him under house arrest while investigations continue – at a Matravers property, so Dina's sister and Jardine are satisfied he's secure. But he doesn't belong among the sort of people you have here.'

'I'm afraid that's not my decision to make, Meilyr.'

'Since when were you a stickler for the rules, Arailt?' Angel said. 'People die here in your custody and you notify no one for months. The man you twisted into a dog for Hypatia Vernay, the one who murdered Heir Ivarr and his family, you didn't do a good job there. After her death at Kyneston, he escaped.'

That cut through even the panic Luke was feeling now, as his future was debated on Crovan's doorstep. So Silyen had kept his word and freed Dog.

Would Silyen keep his word to Luke? A promise that was conditional on Luke not trying to escape.

But this wasn't escape, was it? This would be a perfectly legitimate release.

'The answer is still no,' said Crovan, maintaining the weirdly polite tone of this conversation, as if the three of them were friends debating where to go for dinner. Even when the Equals hated each other, they had more in common than they did with those not of their class. 'Now please leave.'

Jackson and Angel – Meilyr and Dina – didn't move. Luke held his breath.

'Let's try this another way,' said Meilyr.

And he stepped over the threshold into the castle.

At Luke's side, Devin stirred and disappeared back inside. Was he going to get backup to restrain Meilyr? Then a voice called from outside the castle, and Luke's blood ran cold.

'No, don't go in!'

He would have recognized it anywhere, but he needed to see her to believe it. Over Meilyr's shoulder, Abi had darted into view.

The third person on the boat.

Luke had no idea how his sister had got here, and with this pair. Silyen had said she was going to Millmoor with their parents, so plainly he did lie after all. Abi shouldn't be within miles of this place. What were Jackson and Angel thinking of, bringing her here?

'Oh, Luke.'

His sister saw him, and came to a stop, as if the mere sight of him winded her.

'Abi.'

'You're . . .' her words trailed off as she checked him over, just as she'd been doing her whole life, after playground scraps, or when he'd fallen off his skateboard. *In one piece*, he wanted to say. *Surprisingly untortured*. But also, *scared witless*.

Thank you for coming for me, he wanted to say. And, *Mum and Dad are going to kill you*.

He didn't say any of it, but Abi nodded, and turned to Meilyr. 'You shouldn't have gone in. We don't know enough about how these doors work.'

'We're out of options, Abigail. We hoped he'd be gone; he isn't. We hoped he'd see reason; he hasn't. But there's one more thing to try. You got the gist of it in those books you read, the *mormaer* histories. I discussed it with my mother, and she confirmed it. As law lords of the sea, the Trescoes did something similar.'

He braced his cane against the floor and lifted his chin. At Luke's back, there was movement, but he was transfixed by the scene unfolding as the Doc spoke.

'I claim the right of honourable exchange. I offer myself as hostage in Luke's place. May my life be forfeit as bond of my good faith.'

'Meilyr, what?' Dina's voice was panicky.

'It's how this castle was used for centuries,' Meilyr said, without taking his eyes off Crovan. 'Your ancestors built these doors for their own security, but they became a test of honest intent. Truces were forged here, because someone who entered could only leave with the say-so of the lord or heir. The Crovans are hostage-keepers. So I'll stay. Luke goes. Take him to your sister, Dina, and tell her everything. Luke must be examined – she can do it herself, if that's what it takes to satisfy her. Then when he's proclaimed innocent, I will be free to go.'

Silence fell. Luke looked at Jackson, his friend and

mentor, and their eyes met. The Doc smiled, eyes crinkling, and his face was full of its familiar determination.

How could Luke have ever doubted him? Doc Jackson left no man behind.

So it took a moment to register the sound he was hearing as laughter. Crovan's laughter. It began as a snicker, but grew into a full-throated guffaw. Luke stared in astonishment. They all did. Meilyr was visibly incensed, and his fingers curled tight around the head of his cane.

Crovan wiped the corner of each eye theatrically.

'Oh, Meilyr. What happens here isn't diplomacy; it's punishment. And even if it wasn't, we live in the twenty-first century, not the twelfth.'

'The laws still apply.' Meilyr stepped forward, furious now. 'You have to—'

He reached out to – what? Strike Crovan? Shake him?

They never discovered, because Meilyr's skull blew apart.

12

Luke

Someone screamed, and Luke wasn't sure if it was himself, or Angel. For a mad moment he thought it was Meilyr, until he saw the gore spattered over the walls. Saw the slumped body, half the skull missing, slopping blood and brain onto the cold granite floor.

He turned. They all did. Devin lowered the gun in his hand. It was a long-bored hunting rifle, doubtless a Crovan family heirloom.

'Nobody threatens my master,' he said.

Something inside Luke broke at that. He leapt at Devin, fists flailing, hardly hearing his sister scream his name.

But his blows never landed. Instead, he was thrown sideways against the wall, striking the stone hard and sliding to the floor. A loud sound made him look up. The gun in Devin's hands had broken in two. Crovan's Skill at work. The man was snapping a reprimand at his servant, but one more exasperated than angry, as if murder was no worse than a broken dish or spilled soup.

Luke was dazed with the horror of it. Meilyr – Doc Jackson – dead. And in such a way. No heroics. No chance. Luke howled as if his heart was breaking.

His heart *was* breaking.

Look at the world, Jackson had told him once, in Millmoor. *Not at the ground.*

But Luke looked at the ground now. Jackson's blood was pooling there, the dark puddle of it widening across the flagstones. Crovan had stepped back fastidiously to avoid it. In the doorway, Angel was crouched on the threshold, as close as she could get without crossing over. Abi stood alongside, one hand on the Equal's shoulder, comforting or restraining her. Perhaps both.

It felt to Luke that nothing would ever happen. They would all be trapped in that instant forever, unmoving, save for the expanding pool of blood. It would creep outward, and outward, and eventually swallow them all up, just as he had imagined himself drowning in a bed of blood at Kyneston, after Jardine and Crovan had interrogated him.

That had been a delusion, though. This was all too real.

Then movement broke the spell. Coira.

She came forward and knelt by Jackson's body. From the belt at her waist she pulled the white cloth she always carried, and gently wiped the ruin of Jackson's face. The cloth crimsoned immediately, so she turned it and found another clean corner, and another.

She folded the towel and tucked it back in her belt, then reached for Meilyr's hands, laying them across his breast.

'Take your last look,' she said softly, to anyone that needed to hear.

Luke didn't want to. He wanted to hide his face and never look again at the ruined thing that had been Jackson. But he did.

Beneath the devastation of his skull, the Doc's beard and serene expression looked like nothing so much as the statues you saw on the cracked and neglected tombs of the kings from centuries ago: those Henrys and Richards and Edwards from a time before the Equal Revolution. This fierce, flawed, honourable man. Luke let himself weep.

'Help me,' Coira said.

She motioned for him to take Meilyr's arms, under the shoulders, and stood waiting by the feet. Luke picked himself up, staggering against the wall, and obeyed. Moving was better than thinking.

The Doc was surprisingly heavy.

'What are you doing with him?' Angel choked out between great gulping sobs. 'Give him to me.'

'There's only one door anyone can leave by,' Coira said. 'Equals and Condemned alike.'

And she led Luke away from the open Door of Hours, where Angel and Abi were silhouetted against the glowing sunset, towards the closed Last Door. She set down Jackson's feet and put her hand to the latch.

Luke cried out when she pulled it open. The sun was a ball of fire so bright he had to shield his eyes.

'Luke?' Abi's voice was panicked. 'Luke, are you okay?'

His sister hurried to the other side of the Last Door, Angel with her, and the two of them stood side by side, watching them.

The shock of seeing Abi here was incredible. Luke had a million questions for her. How had she found Doc and Angel? Had they rescued her? Where were the rest of the family? Were they safe?

He started towards them, but Coira laid a warning hand on his arm.

'You know you can't go through,' she said.

'Enough of this.' Crovan's voice was cold. 'Sling the body out and be done with it.'

Luke could barely see the outline of the Last Door through his tears. He and Coira shifted Jackson's body till his boot heels rested against the lintel. Coira came to kneel next to him, setting both her hands to one of the Doc's shoulders. Luke followed her example, trying not to look at the ragged bone and pulpy mass above Jackson's eyebrows where his skull had been.

On her count of three, they pushed. Jackson's legs were across.

Angel had crouched, her face in her hands, unable to watch. Which left Abi to lift the Doc's feet as Luke gripped his hands. Luke looked at his sister as they lifted the body of his friend. It was impossible that the space between them was death itself.

Abi was checking him over frantically.

'Are you okay?' she whispered.

'Yes,' Luke said. 'This place is . . . But, yes. Daisy?'

'At Kyneston with Gavar,' Abi said. She paused. 'Safe.' It didn't sound like she thought so. 'And Mum and Dad are at Millmoor. They're fine.'

There was no way she could know that, Luke thought unhappily.

'Luke – no!'

A hand grabbed the back of his shirt so suddenly Luke almost dropped Jackson.

'You can't go through,' Coira said fiercely. '*Look.*'

Luke's hands were close – so close – to the threshold. He trembled.

'It's true – the doorway actually kills?' said Abi, shocked, pale beneath her freckles.

Luke nodded. 'I've seen it. I'll put down his shoulders and you'll have to pull the rest of him to your side.'

'I'll take him,' Angel said, straightening. And as Luke and Abi laid Jackson down, the blonde Equal pulled him to her and gathered the body gently into her arms. She did it with surprising ease. That would be the Equal's unnatural strength. Angel could have broken Devin's neck with a single blow. Grief made his thoughts ugly, and he wished she had.

'We will speak of this to no one.' Crovan had come to the doorway to address the two outside. 'Meilyr's death was unfortunate, but he brought it on himself. You are trespassers here. Furthermore, Miss Hadley is a fugitive while you, Bodina, are believed by everyone to be a spendthrift good-time girl. I presume that no one else is privy to your involvement in Meilyr's unfortunate politics, and that you would like it to stay that way.

'So you will leave as you came. Invent a story. I'm sure everyone will be saddened but not greatly surprised to hear that Meilyr Tresco took his own life. I don't think he ever recovered from the loss of his Skill, do you? And of course, no Skill means no self-protective reflex. Meilyr will be the first Equal in history to have committed suicide. What a distinction.'

'How dare you,' Angel blazed. She stood, cradling the Doc's body. Luke felt the crackle of static that he now knew presaged Skill. 'I'll kill you for what's happened here.'

'I highly doubt it, Bodina. But do feel free to keep trying.'

Crovan slammed the door in both their faces, too quickly for Luke to take a final look at his sister.

'She will kill you,' Luke said. 'And I'll help her.'

Crovan assumed an air of long sufferance.

'Clearly the good manners practised in my home haven't rubbed off on you yet, Hadley. Don't make promises you can't keep. Now get cleaned up before dinner. I won't have you at table looking like that. Devin, come with me.'

Then Crovan was gone, as if he'd just answered the door to nothing more consequential than a parcel delivery.

Luke swayed where he stood. His mind churned. Abi. Jackson. Angel.

When Coira came and wrapped her arms around him, laying her head against his chest, he said nothing. But neither did he push her away. After a few moments, she gave his ribs a squeeze before stepping back.

'You heard what he said. Go get clean. I'll have this place mopped.'

The crowd of guests along the staircase had broken up. Devin must have chased them off.

Devin. As he trudged to his room and there stripped off his gore-grimed clothes, Luke tried to focus. For Devin to kill to defend Crovan, given what his master did to him, was unimaginable.

But Devin didn't know what Crovan did to him, of course. Their master made him forget each time. He'd left Luke with that memory, though. As he stood under the shower, Luke recalled the entire encounter, including Crovan's last words: 'For you, I have special instructions.'

If Crovan could take Devin's memory of the awful assault he had perpetrated on him, then what had he torn from Luke?

And would he steal the memory of what had just happened?

Luke leapt out from beneath the steaming spray. The

water swirling down the drain had been pinked with Jackson's blood, but now ran clean. He towelled himself dry and dressed quickly. Checked his watch. Still twenty minutes until dinnertime. Everything that had just unfolded had taken barely quarter of an hour.

He hurried down to the library, retrieved the battered heraldry book that he had concealed, and ran with it back to his room. He didn't have long enough to record everything that had just happened, but scribbled down the most important things.

Jackson and Angel came to rescue me. Abi with them. (How?) I said Lord 'Rix'(?) made me kill Zelston. Devin shot the Doc – defending Crovan. Coira & I put Doc through Last Door. Crovan told A+A to say it was suicide.

He thought a moment, then tore out a page.

WRITE IN THIS EVERY DAY, he wrote in block capitals. *THIS IS ALL REAL. TRUST WHAT'S IN HERE, NOT WHAT YOU REMEMBER.*

He folded the sheet in half, and tucked it over the top of the cover so it would be the first thing he saw. Then he slid the book under his pillow, where he couldn't miss it.

He ran down the stairs to dinner. Devin was waiting, fob watch in hand. He frowned as Luke approached.

'Cutting it fine, Hadley.'

The man tutted. Luke stared at him. Barely half an hour earlier he had blown out the brains of the man Luke had admired most in the world, and now he was reproving his timekeeping as if nothing had happened.

As if he couldn't remember something had happened.

Crovan had got to him already.

Luke thought of the book now safe beneath his pillow, and shivered.

13

Gavar

Families, Gavar thought with some exasperation, were more trouble than they were worth. If his wife-to-be's sister's ex had to jump off the cliffs of Highwithel, he could at least have waited till after the wedding.

As it was, no one had heard from or seen Dina since the news of Meilyr Tresco's death had broken a few days earlier. Bouda was half hysterical that her sister was going to skip the wedding altogether, while Father was grouchy that people might attempt to pin the death on him. Meilyr had been popular, despite his wacky politics, and the note from Armeria Tresco – she had sent a copy to each member of the Justice Council – was explicit that her son had been suffering a deep depression since the loss of his Skill.

Mother, of course, was carrying on as if nothing had happened.

'You look lovely,' she said, pinning the pink rose button-hole to Gavar's lapel. 'My handsome boy, my first born, all grown up and getting married.'

While he was indisputably handsome, Gavar highly doubted he looked lovely. He probably resembled a man going to his own execution – which in a way, he was.

The wedding of the century was finally happening, and half of Equal society was there to celebrate it. The other half was either too *arriviste* (Mother's exclusion criterion) or of the wrong political persuasion (Father's criterion) to be invited.

Mother kissed him on each cheek, dry little kisses that entailed contact between the minimum number of skin cells to constitute an actual expression of affection. Then she gathered her skirts and hurried from the room intent on some further nuptial errand. Checking place cards, perhaps. Or that the correctly shaped wine glasses were matched to each vintage served at the reception.

Kyneston had filled up again: guests, cars, slaves. There'd been a time when Gavar had relished these occasions. He'd strut around at the Debate Ball every year as if he already owned the place. Kyneston's Heir and, through his teenage years, the Chancellor's eldest son, his portrait destined one day to join that of his father on the walls at Westminster.

Here he was, the Chancellor's son once again. But these days, Gavar could take it or leave it. Even the fringe benefits were no longer as appealing as they had been. A high point had been his nineteenth year, when his conquests had gone into double figures over the course of the Third Debate weekend. Dozens of well-bred women who had tried and failed to get their hooks into him would be sitting there witnessing his union with Bouda.

Some spectres would mercifully be absent from the feast. Crovan had sent a polite note of regret – he didn't do social events. Which worked for Father, who was doing some adroit back-pedalling. Yes, he had sanctioned Meilyr's punishment, ran Lord Whittam's line. But Crovan had carried it out. The creepy Scottish lord, never top of anyone's guest list, was for the time being firmly *persona non grata*. And Father, like the cunning old fox he was, had managed to distance himself – but not so much that people would forget he was allied to a man with the terrible power to strip Skill.

It was all frankly depressing. Gavar pulled out a packet of Sobranies and lit up. Bouda didn't approve of his occasional ciggie habit. Hopefully she'd smell the smoke on him when she joined him at the altar.

Would Dina show up? She was supposed to be her sister's bridesmaid, but Gavar hadn't spotted her yet and there were now just a couple of hours until the ceremony. Gavar hadn't been permitted to see Bouda all morning – which was fine by him – and he could only imagine she was having paroxysms at the thought that her sister might miss her big day. She'd been noticeably less distressed at the death of the man her sister had loved.

As for Gavar's siblings, well, Jenner was predictably doing his bit: issuing directions to everyone from caterers to florists. He'd even given the wedding photographer a tour of the grounds, to pick out the most scenic spots in which the happy couple could pose. (Bouda had specified that Kyneston was to be visible in the background of all the formal portraits.) Jenner was trying to be helpful, but plainly didn't realize that all the menial activity only made him seem more like the commoner he practically was.

Silyen's name had a question mark next to it on Bouda's reply sheet. Mother had received a short note last week, penned in Sil's borderline illegible hand, stating that he was with Aunt Euterpe at Orpen.

And Aunty Terpy herself? Who knew whether the Woman in Black would show?

'I know she's your aunt,' Bouda had said, frowning down at her seating plan, 'but she's a bit of a conversation killer, isn't she, and I can't think who I'd put next to her.'

Gavar gazed out the window of his childhood bedroom, across the wide vista of Kyneston's front lawns. It was now dominated by a gargantuan open-sided marquee made from cloth of gold. At each end of the parterre were linen-draped tables, ready to serve up the finest that Kyneston's wine cellars had to offer. Someone had even festooned the statues with swags of gold silk and chaplets of roses.

Sometimes Gavar wondered if his future wife was not a cold marble statue herself, somehow animated by Skill.

She and Father got along well enough, though. Bouda was an eager acolyte, ready to force through any of Father's legislation with the backing of her cronies. More than once Gavar had run into her on the staircase leading to the Chancellor's Tower suite in New Westminster. She was probably measuring up the place for curtains and picking out a colour scheme for when she took office herself.

Her appetite for power was unassuageable. When not plotting with Father, she was shut in what she'd laughably termed the War Room – the hub of the so-called slavetown purge with which they'd been tasked.

Gavar had precisely zero interest in purging slavetowns. His two trips to Millmoor had been quite sufficient. Millmoor was a ghastly place – needlessly so. Of course slavery wouldn't be much fun. But why make it quite so degrading? Surely the way to pacify the occupants of these hellholes was simply to make the places that bit more liveable. Then there'd be less dissatisfaction. Then there'd be fewer riots and unrest.

There you go: Gavar Jardine's prescription for peace in Britain.

Except it'd never happen. People like Father and Bouda, and many more besides, regarded the slavetowns as almost punitive. Punishing people for what? The crime of being born unSkilled? UnEqual?

'Daddy!'

Gavar hastily stubbed his cigarette out on the windowsill and flicked it towards the terrace beyond, before turning to scoop up his daughter.

Libby was toddling confidently now. And at some speed.

'Dada!' she squealed, as he lifted her high into the air. 'Kiss! Tickle!'

He gladly obliged, only a fraction later remembering to check that the door was closed so his daughter's happy shrieks couldn't be heard in the corridor. He needn't have worried. Daisy had it shut tight and stood there like a diminutive sentry.

'There's no way Libby wasn't seeing her daddy on his wedding day,' the girl said doughtily.

As at the fateful Third Debate, Father had ordered that Libby be neither seen nor heard during the festivities. Gavar had put up a fight, only for Bouda to grow strident and Mother to insist that he 'heed his bride's feelings'. It was news to Gavar that Bouda had any feelings, besides ambition and a patronizing affection for her father and sister, but cornered and outnumbered, he had backed down.

'Pretty,' Libby said, fumbling the flower from his button-hole.

'Just like you,' said Gavar, kissing his daughter's nose. 'Daddy's beautiful, clever little girl.'

Libby smiled at him, and though her colouring – the copper curls, the blue-green eyes – was all Gavar, details were emerging in her small features that reminded him painfully of Leah.

He put down his daughter, suddenly afraid he might

well up, and turned back to the window to compose himself. Guests were arriving for an aperitif before the ceremony. Gavar spotted his soon-to-be father-in-law, Lord Lytchett Matravers, readily locatable by the distinctive flow pattern of people squeezing around his gargantuan bulk. By his side was Bouda's godfather, Rix.

He remembered that conversation with Rix in the Members' bar at Westminster, the night before the man's shocking adoption of Silyen. How Rix had confessed that he, too, had a baseborn child – a boy he had not seen, or even known about for years. That son would be about Gavar's age. How did he feel about his father now?

Gavar looked down at his daughter. The very idea of being without her made his Skill tingle at his fingertips. Father had made no further mention of the proposed Bill of Succession that would degrade baseborn children. Gavar wondered if he was keeping it in reserve, a threat to hold over him, to ensure Gavar's compliance.

Well, Gavar had done everything expected of him, hadn't he? Including agreeing to walk down the aisle with that harpy Bouda.

Had Leah still been alive, would he be getting married today?

In all probability, yes. He was Kyneston's heir and duty came first, always. That had been instilled in him from when he was the age his daughter was now. Presumably even earlier. Father had presented his newborn heir with a stuffed toy salamander as big as the child himself. It had lain in Gavar's cot. He remembered its blank, black eyes.

This was where it led. A loveless marriage. And in time – if he could bring himself to do what was required – another heir.

He lifted his eyes from Libby, who was absorbed in the flower, to Daisy, to find the girl watching him.

'She'd understand,' Daisy said. 'Leah, I mean. I'm sorry, I don't know if that's who you were thinking of, but you seemed sad, and—'

'Thank you.' Gavar choked the words out, cutting her off. 'And for bringing Libby. I think the two of you had better go now.'

'Of course.'

Daisy took Libby's hand and led the little girl to the door. She went without protest. It was curious, Gavar thought, how the commoner girl – whose appointment as Libby's childminder had been intended as a discrete but deliberate slight to his child – had been the best thing to happen to his daughter in her short life.

'Say goodbye to Daddy,' Daisy instructed her small charge. Libby flapped her hand and lisped the words. 'Don't worry about us. I've got a place in the corner of the kitchens all sorted and Libby will be getting as big a piece of Daddy's cake as she can manage.'

'Cake,' Libby agreed, tugging Daisy out of the door,

drawn by the magnetism that sugary foods exert on small children.

'I'll press the flower, too,' Daisy added, as she disappeared, 'so she'll have it when she's older and will know that she was here, even though the photographs won't show it.'

Then they were gone. The only two people in the world who had the power to make Gavar feel at ease with himself: his bastard and a commoner kid who was still a child herself.

Being heir of Kyneston really wasn't all it was cracked up to be.

Father caught up with him as Gavar plunged into the throng on the terrace. He was in an uncharacteristically good mood – which was to say, sozzled already.

'Your big day, son. The day you become a man.'

Personally, Gavar would have set that day some ten years earlier, when on his fifteenth birthday he had convinced a particularly attractive parlourmaid that Heir Gavar deserved one extra-special present.

'Tonight, you show that wife of yours what us Jardines are made of, you hear me? Remember: family honour in all things.'

Faintly disgusted, Gavar turned his face away – seeing, as he did, something unexpected. Dina Matravers, talking to Jenner. As he watched, the blonde girl held something out to him. Jenner's face lit up. Strange.

'Bodina's here,' he said to Father. 'Do excuse me. I must make sure she knows where to go – she won't have much time to get ready.'

It was a convenient pretext. Dina Matravers was so beautiful it wasn't like she'd need much in the way of hair styling and make-up. Except as Gavar made his way through the throng, brushing aside greetings and well-wishes, he realized that no make-up on earth would conceal the transformation grief had worked on Bodina.

'Dina,' he said, touching her elbow. 'You made it.'

She turned from his brother, surprised. Jenner unsubtly tucked the thing in his hand – had it been a letter? – inside his waistcoat, and made his exit.

Gavar was shocked by the girl's appearance. She was as lovely as ever. But something had changed in her that had nothing to do with looks. The brightness had gone from her eyes. Even the pug in her arms was subdued.

Her sorrow touched something in him he'd not known was there.

'I'm sorry for your loss,' he said. 'So sorry.'

Was it empathy? Understanding, at least. Poor Gavar Jardine, heir of Kyneston, envied by all but understood by none. Well, now he and Dina had this in common: they had both lost the only person they had ever truly loved. He had shot his beloved, and hers had jumped off a cliff, not even her love enough to keep him in a world without Skill.

'Yes,' said Dina, looking him in the eye. 'Yes, I really think you are.'

Then she laid her face against his chest and sobbed her heart out.

They drew a few curious stares. Gavar wrapped his arms round her to shield her from prying eyes and shot his most quelling glare at the spectators.

At last she stilled. He heard a bubbling inhalation of snot as Dina looked up, tears sheening her cheeks.

'Well, that was unexpected. Thank you.'

'Not at all.'

Pug under one arm, she rummaged awkwardly in her handbag for a tissue.

'I didn't realize you were friendly with Jenner,' he said.

'Oh, you know.' When Dina finished wiping her face it was her familiar self looking back at Gavar. Bright-eyed. Smiling. 'Mutual acquaintances. I'd better get to my sis. Don't want to spoil your big day. She's taken over the Small Solar, right?'

Gavar nodded, and Dina was off, slipping easily through the press of people, sympathetic murmurs following in her wake.

Two hours and numerous glasses of champagne later, Gavar Jardine was a married man.

It took a lot of alcohol to have much effect on an Equal. Gavar knew where that threshold was and had ensured he'd surpassed it by the time he met his blushing bride at the altar. (And the only thing on earth capable of making Bouda Matravers blush, he thought, was a pot of pink pigment, generously applied.)

Bouda was clad in white, drawing a train of lace and feathers behind her like some albino peacock. With her ice-blonde hair, the effect was striking, and Gavar was drunk enough to think he might be capable of fulfilling his marital duties after all. But as he leaned in for the obligatory kiss, he saw the look in his bride's eye. The predatory gleam. The hunter's triumph. Bouda was more hawk than peacock.

With the exchange of vows came the moment Gavar had been steeling himself for, as their Skill touched and flared. He sensed Bouda at the very core of him, as if she had speared a manicured nail deep into the meat of his heart. Then it was over. He was grateful when she turned her back on him for the mantling.

Across her shoulders was a blue velvet cape, with the Matravers arms couched in silverwork. The device had been revised by her ancestor Harding the Voyager, and depicted a ship under sail. *Iter pervenimus* was embroidered beneath it. *I voyage to arrive.*

His wife had certainly arrived now, Gavar thought, as he removed the cape and replaced it with one of gold, bearing the Jardine salamander in scarlet. When they turned together for the applause of their Equals, her expression was nothing short of exultant.

The banquet that followed was every bit as excruciating as Gavar had imagined. The glass vastness of the East Wing reeked of a nauseating blend of flowers and cooked meat. It was filled from end to end with circular tables for their hundreds of guests, with the newly-weds in the centre of an elevated top table. His father sat on his wife's other side. In lieu of his wife's mother – killed years ago now in an industrial accident at a BB plant that could have been sabotage – Bodina was seated next to Gavar.

The girl was almost defiantly chirpy. To anyone who'd not felt the way grief had convulsed her body earlier, she might seem little altered from her normal self. A touch subdued, as was to be expected. But essentially the same, sparkly DiDi Matravers.

Stinker the pug had acquired a white bow tie, and Dina was holding it up to pose for photographs. Gavar recalled the memorable occasion the dog had somehow got shut in with him and Father in the Matravers' Mayfair drawing room, and devoutly hoped that Dina was watching what it was eating.

Her bridesmaid's speech was something of a surprise.

'We're here to celebrate love,' Dina began, rising to her feet in shoes so high-heeled the mere act of standing defied physics.

Before he could stop himself, Gavar rolled his eyes. The weddings guests, now equally intoxicated, laughed good-naturedly. They'd all enjoyed seeing Gavar the playboy finally being made an honest man.

'Love comes in many forms,' Dina continued, after the laughter had died down. 'That between partners, between siblings, between parents and children. All these are expected. Chosen. Sanctioned.'

A few people stirred at that. 'Sanctioned' wasn't the sort of word you'd expect to hear from DiDi.

'As you'll all know, earlier this week I lost the man I love, Meilyr Tresco. I'll never be sitting at a table like this with him beside me, as my sister and Gavar are here.'

More restlessness from the guests. It was in extremely poor taste to be talking about Meilyr's suicide on such an occasion. On Gavar's other side, his bride's body stiffened as Bouda sat upright and turned to watch her sister.

'Meilyr held views that weren't widely appreciated. Certainly not with my sister's new family. But all he really believed in was love.

'Not just love for those we know and have chosen, but for those we've never met and haven't chosen. The unSkilled. Commoners.

'As we sit in this beautiful place, enjoying the privileges of our position, we shouldn't forget to have love in our hearts also for the less fortunate. In fact, we forget at our peril our shared humanity.

'My sister and her husband embark upon a great enterprise. The creation of a new family. The next generation of this dynasty that first brought our kind to power. But that's not the only task ahead of them.

'They've been asked to purge the slavetowns. The goal is to keep the common people in line. To uphold our way of life. The belief is that this will require force. Repression. But to you, Bouda, and to you, Gavar, I say one thing: this, also, can be done with love.'

Bodina Matravers lifted her glass in salute towards bride and groom, then tipped her head back and drank. On the table in front of her, Stinker cavorted.

The wedding reception sat in excruciating silence.

It was broken by a loud and heavy handclap. Joined reluctantly by a few more. Then a smattering more besides.

Bodina Matravers sat down. Gavar became aware of his wife's hand curled around his wrist. Her manicured nails dug into the thin skin where the veins ran near the surface.

'Stop that,' she commanded.

Gavar looked down.

The noisiest applause had been his.

He'd never grasped why it took months of planning for a single day's event. But as one petal-and-confetti strewn stunt after another unfolded, Gavar began to comprehend.

To cover the awkwardness of Dina's speech, Mother had cued up the string quartet early, and over coffee and *petits fours* something like a normal mood had resumed. Next, he and Bouda toured the reception, stopping at every table to exchange platitudes and receive congratulations.

'Nice of your brother and aunt to make the effort,' said Bouda, as they neared the most obscurely positioned tables and saw the two empty seats that had been allocated to Silyen and Aunty Terpy.

'Best wedding gift they could give us,' Gavar murmured. 'Or would you have preferred a finale like the one they laid on the last time we should have been getting married?'

Bouda pressed her lips together and said nothing.

Everywhere they went, photographs were taken. Outside on the parterre, Gavar stood to one side as the photographer fussed to ensure she captured the moment when Bouda's bouquet went airborne above a pack of giggling women. He saw Dina also off to one side, watching.

He had no idea where the speech she'd delivered earlier had come from. He would almost suspect Meilyr of having written it. Except Meilyr was dead.

A sudden, intense sadness gripped him. Life wasn't meant to be like this, for any of them.

Maybe that was why he went to the kitchens to fetch Libby. There was one thing in his life that was perfect and that he wasn't ashamed of, and when he was lord of Kyneston no one would shut her away, so why shouldn't they see her now?

He hoisted his daughter onto his shoulders and bore her outside like a battle standard. Beneath the golden marquee, as twilight drew in, the Equals of Great Britain were dancing. On the lawns, children of sufficiently exalted lineage to have been invited were running and laughing, playing tag or croquet, or wrestling on the grass.

Heads began to turn as Gavar set his daughter down in the middle of them.

Libby toddled into the croquet, squatting to try and pick up a ball that was too large and too heavy for her tiny hands. A smiling boy bent down and offered it to her.

There was a commotion in the marquee. A woman pushed her way out and grasped the boy by the hand, hauling him up.

'Bedtime, Aubrey. Now.'

Libby wailed as her companion was dragged away, protesting.

For a brief moment, Gavar was tempted to go after the woman, to grab her by the hair and force her to her knees for an apology. He could feel his Skill smouldering and clenched his fists. He turned to the onlookers, daring another parent to walk past him to remove their child.

Then his wife was there in his face.

'Are you trying to shame me? First my sister, now you. Am I not allowed one day? Take her back to the kitchen.'

'No,' said Gavar. 'Why should I? She is mine, and Kyneston will be mine, and by the vows we took today you are now also mine and will obey me.'

'And you still obey the law of this land. And that will soon clear up any confusion about half-breeds like that child and where they truly belong.'

218

There was a roaring in Gavar's ears. He shook his head to clear it. It didn't diminish.

'Don't try that one. The Bill of Succession is just an empty threat of Father's, to keep me in line.'

'On the contrary.' Bouda's smile was so cold you could almost see her lips icing over. 'Your father and I have just completed the draft. It tidies up any ambiguity about the status of mixed offspring. They're to be removed from parental custody and sent to the UMUS homes in the slavetowns. We can't have anyone thinking they're something special, when actually they're an abomination that shouldn't exist.'

Gavar's anger detonated. For a moment, his vision flared so red he was unable to see. The roaring grew louder. His face scorched.

His vision cleared.

The cloth-of-gold marquee had gone up like a fireball.

14

Abi

'Gavar sent the marquee up in flames,' Dina said. 'Pandemonium everywhere. So I doubt my poor sister had the wedding night she wanted.'

The Club members were huddled around the vast hearth in Highwithel's hall. Although it was now late May, the fire was crackling. They all needed its cheeriness – for comfort, more than warmth.

'And it's got me thinking,' Dina said. 'We need to change. Isolated protests won't achieve a thing. The people now in charge of the country – including my sister – won't listen. And as we saw in Millmoor, forceful action inside the slavetowns is easily contained and quashed.'

Abi saw Renie nod her head and hug her knees a little tighter to her chest. She'd seen things no child should ever witness, Abi was sure of it.

'What are you saying, Bodina?' Hilda asked, when the Equal girl didn't elaborate.

'Well, she's not saying banners and marching in the

streets, is she?' said Jessica tartly. The woman looked at Dina. The toll of what had happened in the past week was evident in both their faces, sleeplessness and grief etching lines and smudging shadows. 'You're talking terrorism.'

Dina hesitated, and for a moment Abi thought she was going to pull back from a word like that. But she didn't.

'If you want to use that word, yes, I am.'

Abi sat back in her seat, her thoughts turbulent. Alongside Jess, Oz let out a sound neither of agreement nor dissent – more a sigh than anything. Were they ready for this, any of them? Was Dina in any fit state to be making decisions of this scale?

'Is that what you want?' Abi asked Lady Armeria, who was sat with them. 'Is that what you want your son's legacy to be?'

'Meilyr always favoured peaceful protest,' the Equal said, looking between Abi and Dina. 'However, my son is now dead.'

They had followed Crovan's directive on representing Meilyr's death to the outside world as suicide. If the true story of events at Eilean Dòchais came out, the depth of Dina's sympathies would be revealed, and her chance of ever gleaning anything useful from her sister would be lost. But they had told Meilyr's mother the truth.

'And that's exactly why no one should be making any decisions right now,' Abi protested. 'We're in shock, especially you, Bodina. You won't honour Meilyr's death by going against what he stood for.'

'How dare you.' Bodina leapt from her seat. In the hearth the flames soared, and kindling popped like a gun going off. Abi winced to hear it. 'You never even knew him. Your brother is the reason Meilyr is dead.'

'You and Meilyr are the reason Luke is in that monstrous place at all.'

'Actually,' said a new voice behind them, 'Whittam Jardine and the centuries of Equal privilege he stands for are the reason for all of it. But yeah, don't mind me, carry on fighting.'

The newcomer came closer. Abi stared in astonishment. She recognized this woman from the television coverage of Zelston's state funeral. She was athletically built, her hair half shaved. Piercings through ear, nose and brow gleamed against her dark skin.

The late Chancellor's niece. Heir Midsummer Zelston.

'You look terrible,' she said to Dina. 'But I guess you've got a reason. Come here.'

Midsummer opened her arms, and Dina went over and collapsed into them. Midsummer enfolded her, and held Dina as she cried and cried. Abi felt her anger leaching away as she watched. It was a miracle any of them were functioning, given the recent succession of events: the ballroom explosion, Luke's trial and Meilyr's punishment, and then the disaster at Eilean Dòchais. Abi knew the indicators of post-traumatic stress disorder. She could identify most of them in herself, and felt sure it would be the same for the others.

'I'm sorry I couldn't see you earlier,' Midsummer said, stroking Dina's blonde hair as she quieted. 'Funnily enough, me and my girl weren't on the guest list for your sister's wedding. But I got your message, and here I am. So what can I do, besides being a human-size handkerchief for you to wipe your snotty, pretty little nose on?'

Even Dina sputtered at that. Wiping her nose with the back of her hand instead, she took her friend by the elbow and turned her towards the circle of expectant faces around the hearth.

'Everyone, this is Heir Midsummer Zelston, a friend of mine and Meilyr's. I've asked her to join us because she's been part of this in her own way, up in Lincolnshire.'

Lincolnshire. Abi knew that the Zelston seat was Lindum – one of Britain's more extraordinary great houses. It was a sprawling oddity, built around various Roman remains. The vaulting red-brick structure that formed Lindum's hall had been an immense bathhouse, and mosaics still covered its floor.

The Zelstons traced descent from a consul posted to Britain by Rome's African emperor, Septimius. The lineage gave them the oldest pedigree of any family in Britain, though Abi had more than once heard Lord Whittam pouring scorn on it. His objections evidently stemmed from

personal animosity to Zelston. And also blatant racial preju-
dice – given a vile comment Abi once heard him utter
about the Chancellor's doomed love affair with Euterpe
Parva.

Dina had almost finished naming each of the Club
members for Midsummer, and as her turn approached,
Abi froze. There was only one connection she and Midsummer had in common: her brother had killed the
Equal's uncle.

'And this is Abigail Hadley,' Dina said. 'The sister of
Luke Hadley. The Millmoor boy.'

Should Abi apologize? Would that appear to concede
Luke's guilt? But to ignore it would be worse, surely?

Unexpectedly, Midsummer laughed, a frank, throaty
sound.

'You're tying yourself in knots there, Abigail. There's no
need. I know what your brother was Condemned for. I
know the price Meilyr paid for insisting that he didn't do it.
And I know that Meilyr had a theory that my uncle wasn't
even the target in the first place. What a mess, eh?'

Abi could have fallen over with relief.

'I don't believe my brother was in any way responsible,'
she said. 'But I know I need to prove that. I want to prove
it to everyone, but to you especially. I'm sorry for your loss.'

Midsummer's gaze was disconcertingly direct. Abi sorted
through what she knew about this woman, not much older
than herself. You never saw Midsummer Zelston in the

glossy magazines that papped Dina and her sister. She was a graduate student, Abi thought – and not at one of the Oxford or Cambridge colleges attended by almost all Equals. In Brighton, wasn't it? And she had a commoner girlfriend.

Yes, Midsummer Zelston wasn't your typical Equal.

But, Abi thought – and it was a thought that had been bothering her for some time now – *still an Equal*.

'You haven't got anything to prove,' Midsummer said. 'Not to me.'

'The Zelston seat is Lindum,' Dina said, pulling up a chair for Midsummer to join them by the fire. 'And you all know what's up there.'

'The Bore,' said Renie promptly.

Abi wasn't the only one to look surprised. The kid had street smarts, but she'd never struck Abi as much of a geographer. Renie shrugged, unperturbed, and pulled up her sleeve, pointing out a row of horizontal scars on the inside of her left arm. In the firelight, they shone silver-pink against her light brown skin.

Abi had noticed them once before, and had wondered if they were the result of some machine-inflicted accident in Millmoor, or – more likely, given her childhood – self-harm. It turned out they were neither.

'These ones are my littlest big brother Mickey and Uncle Wesley, my ma's brother,' Renie said, pointing to two of the scars. 'Sent to the Bore. Me mam: Edgemarsh. Da: Felfield

Secure Unit. My biggest brother Patrick: Dungeness Power Plant. And Declan, in the middle: Portisbury.

'I was only eight when we all got split up, and I was worried I was gonna forget them, so I made sure I didn't. But I didn't know where they'd all been sent till last year, after the Doc found me. I was doin' a game with Asif, keeping an eye out while he got into one of the Labour Bureau local servers. Him being brilliant, he got it done real quick, so we pulled my file to take a look. There they were, all my folks.'

There was an appalled silence.

'So yeah,' said Renie, looking at Midsummer Zelston and grinning that gappy smile. 'I know where the Bore is.'

'For any of you less clued up than our friend Renie, here,' Midsummer told the rest of them, 'The Bore is Britain's breadbasket: a massive agricultural area that's a Special Designated Slavezone – the largest in Britain. It takes people doing their days from all the big cities of the Midlands: Nottingham, Sheffield, Doncaster and Lincoln, the city nearest to my family's estate. It's mostly men, working the fields. A few women in processing and packing, but the women of the region are usually sent to Edgemarsh, which means couples get split up – just one more totally unnecessary hardship.

'There are lifers at the Bore, too. The place gets its name from the tidal bore river that runs in and out of the North Sea, so the direction it flows changes with the tide. There's a whole network of irrigation channels, with new ones needed all the time. Constructing them is the job of lifer gangs, guys supposedly guilty of the worst non-political offences – the political offenders are Condemned and go to Crovan. But in reality, even men with low-grade convictions get put in the lifer gangs.'

'Uncle Wes,' said Renie firmly. 'All he ever did was nick stuff. Quite a lotta stuff, mind you, but still.'

'Exactly. Now, my mother and I have spent years listening to grievances about conditions within the Bore. When my uncle was Chancellor, we were hopeful that change might happen. But no prizes for guessing who just killed reform of the Bore stone dead in his new regime, without even convening the Justice Council? Whittam and his cronies. So when word of that gets back to the lads I've been liaising with, things are really gonna kick off.'

'So here's what I'm thinking,' said Dina, leaning in. 'Millmoor by itself wasn't enough. And we didn't know how the authorities were going to respond. Now we know how they respond: with force. So we can still stir things up in a slavetown, but it should be peaceful – and big. My contacts in Riverhead want to co-ordinate a shutdown – something like your brother achieved, Abi, only across the whole city.

'But we should try something fiercer, too. Something destructive that will hit the system where it hurts, but where reprisals are harder. Not in streets, where people can be rounded up and shot. Nowhere with a single wall around it, so you can pen people in. The Bore is perfect.'

The Club had been listening attentively.

'It's a scale thing, right?' Hilda asked. 'Riverhead and the Bore together will get people's attention. Give them ideas. Then it'll spread.'

'Exactly.'

'I've got an idea,' said Asif, from where he was perched in the corner of the inglenook. 'It's a terrible one, mind you, but . . .'

'Out with it,' the Club members all but chorused.

'We're trying to change opinion. To empower people to stand up and speak out. Now, though most of us don't really know what Skill can do, we do know that it's what gives Equals their authority. So I was wondering . . .'

He trailed off, fidgeting even more than usual.

'Spit it out,' said Oz, thumping him on the shoulder. 'No idea can be that bad.'

But it was. Only it was also, Abi thought, brilliant.

'I was thinking we should tell people – the common people, I mean, 'cause only the Equals know about it so far' – Asif gulped, the Adam's apple bobbing in his skinny throat – 'that Meilyr had his Skill destroyed. If people know that can be done, then they know that Equals aren't . . . untouchable. Yes, it was another Equal that did it, but it seems symbolic.'

His suggestion was greeted with utter silence.

'I knew it was a terrible idea,' he groaned, hiding his face in his hands. 'I'm a horrible person. Ignore me.'

'No.'

That was Lady Armeria. Abi tensed for her response. Was this the moment she decided things had gone far enough, and threw the Club out of Highwithel to give her space to grieve in private?

'No, it's an excellent idea. Meilyr may be gone, but the things he believed will live on in your deeds. As his mother, I give you my blessing.'

And with that, the Club had a new mission. Oz and Jessica would go with Dina to Riverhead. Renie attached herself like glue to Heir Midsummer – and not merely, Abi suspected, because she hoped to find two of her lost family in the Bore. Asif, Hilda and Tilda would remain at Highwithel, where they'd push word about Meilyr out through anonymous channels. They'd also aim to crack the upper layers of the Riverhead Administration systems.

And Abi? What would she do? She had been accepted and trusted by this group, on Luke's account. But she'd never really been part of it. She and Meilyr had eventually seen eye to eye, but he was gone now. And while she knew that Bodina didn't blame her for what had happened at Eilean Dòchais, Abi had been the only witness to those tragic events. Abi suspected that would always divide rather than unite them.

And then.

And then there was the fact that Dina – like Meilyr – like Armeria – like Midsummer – was an Equal.

Abi wasn't sure why that mattered so much, but it did. As long as commoners kept looking to Equals to change things for them, then nothing was really, *truly* going to alter, was it?

And was she even signed up for this bigger political crusade of Dina's? That had never been her plan. She had come to Highwithel for one thing only: to try and get Luke back. So far, in that, she'd failed.

'Does Speaker Dawson know about any of this?' Abi heard herself say. 'She's the person who's supposed to represent commoner interests, and a commoner herself.'

The conversation turned towards her. It was Armeria Tresco who answered.

'That's an interesting question. The Observers of Parliament have little influence and even less power. Now, of course, they have none at all, since Whittam Jardine suspended them.'

'My uncle Winter wanted to bring the Speaker onto the Justice Council,' added Midsummer. 'He hoped it would be one of his last acts, before his term ended in two years' time, and he was attempting to build support for it. But it wasn't a popular idea. If Jardine hadn't just pulled off a coup that made murder superfluous, I would have assumed that my uncle truly was the intended target that night, and that the motive was to prevent his reforms.

'So I don't know about Dawson, but I'll tell you who is interesting – her son, Jon Faiers.'

'Her son?'

This was the first Abi had heard of Dawson's son, and she couldn't see why he'd be relevant.

'He works as her aide. Does a lot of the grassroots stuff – listening to people's grievances, trying to intervene with slavetown authorities, calling out the Labour Allocation Bureau, that sort of thing. I've met with him a few times about conditions in the Bore.'

Abi could have kicked herself for her stupidity. So there was someone she could have taken Luke's case to straight away, when he was first separated from them all and hauled to Millmoor. If only she'd known. Luke could have been retrieved before he ever met Meilyr Tresco. Every disaster that had stemmed from that could have been averted.

A deep and overwhelming sadness welled up in her. She clasped her hands in her lap to stop them trembling.

Most likely Faiers wouldn't have been able to do a thing. But still.

The truth was that Abi was fast running out of options. Their rescue attempt had ended disastrously. Speaker Dawson was frozen out of whatever influence she'd ever had. And Silyen Jardine had given Meilyr nothing but evasion. The Club wanted to rescue Luke, she knew. However, Dina was doing a good job of persuading them that overthrowing Whittam Jardine would be the best way to make that happen. Abi wouldn't be holding her breath.

Could Faiers help at all? Probably not.

But he was a commoner, like her, and one who knew the Equal world even better than she did.

Luke had trusted one Equal, Meilyr, who had lied about his identity; and had been used by another Equal, Rix, for his own ends. Well, Abi would see what help she might get from her own kind, while also assisting Dina's greater cause.

'I'll go and see him,' she announced. 'Faiers. If you think it's a good idea. I'll find out if we should bring him in on this, and maybe he'll have some contacts for us in the city. Things can kick off all over the country, but if we don't light a spark in London, then we've no hope of succeeding.'

'You'll get picked up by Security straight away,' Jessica pointed out.

'There are ways around that,' said Midsummer. 'Certain Skillful suggestions. I used them all the time at the God-awful boarding school I attended, so I could sneak out and see a girl in the village.'

'We can teach you how to hold yourself and what to wear to make things harder for CCTV,' Tilda said. 'And Asif here will be able to distort the eigenvectors on the photo the central Security database holds of you. We can't delete or replace it, because that would trigger alerts, but a little bit

of tampering should throw off their facial recognition software.'

'And I,' Renie announced, 'will give you a haircut after
which yer own ma wouldn't recognize you.'

Which settled the matter.

Just over twenty-four hours later, Abi was sporting a haircut that could only generously be described as an
'asymmetric bob', now several shades darker than her sandy
blonde. She and Renie were warily following Midsummer
Zelston through the streets of Hackney.

It was a rough neighbourhood. Walls and the sides of
houses were tagged with graffiti. The common people lived
here, in East London. Abi had never seen this side of the
capital before.

The city's magnificent heart – the House of Light, Gorregan Square and Hyde Park – was what visitors saw. It was
also where the Equals lived. Among them resided the international rich from other Skilled states. (And not only the
Skilled states. There were occasional scandals when a
Union American or French businessman was caught by
their country's government doing illegal business in Britain.)
West London was home to Britain's affluent professionals.
Mostly, such people had done their days early then pursued
lucrative careers. But a few, Abi presumed, hadn't yet put
their lives on hold for the decade of slavedays.

The system was designed to discourage people from
doing this. The state wanted the labour of the young and

healthy, not the ageing. Which was why children inherited the slavedebt of any parent who died before beginning their days. Most parents wanted to minimize the risk of passing on such a terrible burden, and did their days promptly once their children had left home.

Not all of them, though. Some people blithely ignored their obligation, until the deadline of their fifty-fifth birthday. The way they jeopardized their children for the sake of their own freedom was one more reason why these 'last-ditchers' were treated with scorn inside the slavetowns, and given harsh assignments. Abi still thought them selfish, but now she saw how well the system worked. Disapproval of parents who delayed their days was deserved – but the state was the ultimate beneficiary of the pressure to do one's days young.

Abi's thoughts were interrupted when Midsummer stopped outside a nondescript terraced house, the blinds pulled partway down. It didn't look much like a politician's office, but perhaps that was the idea. The Equal rapped on the door. No response. She pulled out her phone – a sleek, Union-made model, forbidden to commoners, capable of calling internationally and with unrestricted access to the internet – and dialled a number.

'Jon,' she barked. 'Got someone to see you.' Then she hung up and turned to Abi and Renie. 'He's a good 'un. A bit too pretty for my liking, but there you go.'

The door opened partway, and a man's head appeared in

the gap. Midsummer hadn't lied. Jon Faiers was exceptionally good-looking. Cropped brown hair and bright blue
eyes – eyes that were turned on Abi enquiringly.

'I've seen you before,' he said.

Shock rippled through Abi. Had he? And how did he
recognize her, despite all their precautions? Midsummer
seemed to think she had nothing to fear from Jon; that he
was an ally. But Abi felt her legs trembling all the same. So
to calm herself, she looked right back. If he had seen her,
then she had seen him. The only reason she could have for
not noticing a man as handsome as Jon would be that she
was with Jenner. And that helped her place him.

'You were at the Third Debate,' Abi said. 'You arrived
with the Speaker.'

'You were some kind of assistant,' he said, in the same
instant. 'At Kyneston, the night it all happened.'

They grinned at the shared moment of recognition.

'This isn't really a chatting-on-the-doorstep sort of
locale,' Faiers said, opening the door wider. 'Why don't you
come in?'

He put the kettle on, and rustled up a packet of biscuits.

'Custard Creams,' he said dolefully. 'I'm afraid I've eaten
all the Bourbons.'

Renie would have eaten them whatever they were, and
proceeded to crunch down half the pack while Abi told Jon
about Luke's plight. When she was done, he rocked back
in his squeaky desk chair and narrowed his eyes.

'So if your brother didn't do it, if it was an Equal who compelled him, then who?'

Abi hesitated. They had discussed turning Rix in once before, but Meilyr and Dina had pressed ahead with the rescue plan instead. Meilyr had once regarded Rix as an ally, while Dina was his goddaughter. Was that why the pair of them had argued against pursuing him?

Well, Meilyr was dead, and Abi owed Dina nothing. If the Equal wouldn't betray her godfather for Luke's sake, Abi had no compunction about doing so.

'Lord Rix.'

Her disclosure took Faiers by surprise. 'If he sympathizes with our cause, he does a good job of hiding it. Yes, I suppose I've heard about the occasional unexpected opinion. He's got a reputation for voting against rigorous detention and interrogation methods, for example. I think everyone just assumed the man was squeamish. Did Heir Meilyr ever say why Rix might want Jardine dead?'

What had Meilyr told her, all those weeks ago, in the high garden at Highwithel? That Rix had once loved a commoner woman, and that Jardine had packed her off to a slavetown. How strange that a simple, single act of deceit a quarter of a century ago should set up a lifetime of enmity that was causing such havoc now.

'He loved a commoner woman?' Faiers scoffed. 'Do any of them? You know what these people are like, Abigail. Could one of them love one of us?'

'Hey!' Midsummer spoke up from the corner of the ratty sofa, where she was slouched as easily as any Hackney local, and not looking at all like the heir to Britain's oldest estate and its longest line. 'You know that's not how it works, right? People can fall in love, Equal or commoner, male or female. The problem's not love. It's power. A girl doing her days might think she loves her master, but while she serves, she's not truly free to give her heart.'

'Jenner's not my master,' said Abi, stung.

'I was talking generally,' said Midsummer. 'But seeing as you've made it personal, here it is: Jenner might be the best of that bunch, but he's still a Jardine. If they had their way, we'd all be doing days to them, Equal and commoner alike.'

Abi bristled. Jenner was different. He was Skilless – it wasn't as though he could compel her to do anything.

And yet what Midsummer was saying was true. Abi cringed at those fevered novels she'd enjoyed only a year ago, in which hot Equal guys compelled and commoner girls submitted. She knew, now, about Dog's wife and little Libby Jardine's mother. She'd seen what Skill could do, and it wasn't sexy – it was terrifying and cruel. The way the slavedays warped human relationships was one more reason to hate them.

'What this info about Rix needs,' said Faiers, diplomatically moving the conversation on, 'is the right ear to drop it into. I've been watching Heir Bouda for some time. She's a woman going places – and in a hurry to get there. She sees Jardine as her ally, for now, and information like this could be valuable to her. I know Rix is her godfather too, but she's not a person to be bound by loyalties when her advancement is at stake.

'If Bouda confronts Rix and denounces him, then we could bring him down and it would help embed me deeper into her good graces. And while it might not secure your brother's release immediately, it could incline her to consider a pardon and release when, say, Chancellor Whittam rewards Bouda with the Chair of the Justice Council. So what do you think, Abi Hadley. Shall I tell her?'

Abi was stunned. Of course, Jon was painting a picture of the best possible outcome. But he wasn't making false promises about Luke's immediate release. He had answered with integrity.

She met Midsummer's gaze, looking for the Equal's approval. The heir gave a noncommittal shrug, but grinned.

And really, she had already given Faiers the information about Rix. Theoretically, it was out of her hands now.

'I think that sounds like a plan,' she said.

A loud crackling sound came from the other end of the sofa. It was Renie, tossing down an empty plastic wrapper.

'You know,' the kid said. 'The thing about plans is, they require more biscuits.'

15

Silyen

Was this real, or unreal? Silyen wondered, walking through Orpen's hallway, his fingers trailing across the dark wood panelling.

To be more accurate, was he touching the bricks-and-mortar Orpen Mote that he and Aunty Terpy had Skillfully rebuilt over these past weeks – a task much more intricate than the restoration of Kyneston's exploded East Wing? Or was he walking through memory-Orpen, where the pair of them had met during all those years his aunt had lain unconscious in her bed?

He ought to know the difference. More to the point, he ought to be disturbed that he *didn't* know the difference.

But he wasn't. The two Orpens overlaid each other almost seamlessly and Silyen walked easily in them both.

It was usually the furniture that gave it away. Restored-Orpen was still only half furnished; Mama and Jenner were locating suitable pieces from other family properties and sending them over. Memory-Orpen was crammed with objects and ornaments. It held everything that had filled the house during Aunty Terpy's youth, from tapestries and suits of armour, to the books in the library – including the cedarwood chest containing the lost journals of Cadmus Parva-Jardine.

Yes, objectively, Silyen knew that only one of the two was 'real', in the sense of physically existing in the present moment. But the memory-Orpen he'd visited in childhood, and occasionally slipped into now, felt no less real. In certain corridors and passageways, it was still possible to mistake the two versions of this place.

But there was no mistaking the third Orpen. The one made of Skill.

It wasn't constructed from wood and stone, nor from memories, but from power. It existed in the same bright-and-dark world he had perceived that day at Parliament. A reality composed entirely of Skill, and its absence. Everything in it was either void, or limned in light, like a sheet of black paper sketched on in gold.

This was the world he needed to see today.

Silyen was more practised than he had been at Westminster. On that day (the day of his adoption, and the conversation with Meilyr Tresco), he had glimpsed the bright world by chance. Now, he could look at it at will.

Silyen closed his eyes and opened them onto a shining outline of Orpen. Just as at Westminster, objects and spaces could only be discerned if they contained traces of Skill.

So this Orpen was no blank space, as the Skill-devoid streets of London had been. Because the entire structure had been magically rebuilt by Silyen and his aunt, the house appeared almost as solid as it did in the real world, albeit made entirely of dully shimmering gold.

Which was understandable. Quite apart from the latest rebuilding, Orpen had been riddled with magic for centuries. He looked to his left. There was a shining fissure in the soft glow of a windowpane, perhaps secretly repaired by a Parva child after a ball game mishap. High up, vivid bands of gold coiled around a chimney stack, the crumbling mortar Skillfully reinforced by some prudent lord or lady.

There was hardly a corner of this old moated manor that had not at some time been Skill-touched by its residents. Looking down, Silyen could even see glints scintillating through the moat drains far beneath his feet, the work of a practically minded Parva, keeping the channels clear.

Once, Skill had saturated even the most mundane aspects of an Equal's life – an art as lawful as eating.

With the advent of the slavedays, that had been set aside. Tasks once performed by Skill became the preserve of slave labour. That freed the Equals from having to think of such things – unSkilled housekeepers could instruct unSkilled slaves.

But what had been lost was incalculable: intimacy with one's Skill and a true understanding of all it could do.

Silyen made his way through the light-limned corridor

and up the staircase. In both restored-Orpen and memory-Orpen, this staircase was plain and dark, with smooth bannisters and thick, foot-hollowed treads. Walking in Skill, the stairs were likewise dim. Having never needed intervention beyond Silyen's own rebuilding, they bore only a faint Skillful trace.

But at the top of the stairs blazed a radiance to rival that of the House of Light.

In a cupboard.

It was a large walk-in linen cupboard, presently disused. It had been the same large linen cupboard in memory-Orpen, when it saw daily use. Silyen opened its door and ran his hands across the interior, feeling both the smooth wood of today's bare shelves, and the stiff, cool sheets stored here in the Orpen of Euterpe's youth.

But in the third, Skill-haunted Orpen, this space had served a different purpose entirely. Silyen wondered how he knew, and shivered.

He held reality up for the Skill-light to shine through and, beneath the present and the near past, discerned many more layers beneath. Orpen was a palimpsest of power. And *there* was the cause of the brilliance in this place, sunk centuries-deep. Silyen plunged down towards it, and surfaced in the exact same spot he had left.

Lustrous Skill engulfed the small cupboard. The light here was as absolute as the dark would be in a cave. Dazzled,

Silyen's eyes could discern nothing of his surroundings. He had to trust his other senses to know that he was not alone.

In the unseeing brightness, life began and ended. A woman screamed. A baby cried. A man wept.

The hairs prickled up Silyen's neck. He could feel the pulse of his Skill in every part of his body: throbbing in his earlobes, beating beneath his fingernails.

This large closet had been panelled off from the bedroom of which it was originally part. But once, it had all been one room. Silyen turned in a circle where he stood. Some inner sense told him that *there* was the bed on which, four centuries ago, Cadmus's first wife had struggled in labour. *There* was where their child Sosigenes had been born, the umbilical cord cut by a servant before the baby was handed to his father.

And *here* was where Cadmus had stripped his son's Skill. The violence of that act burned bright enough to sear through the centuries.

Why had he done it? And *how*?

Silyen walked forward. (Some small and irrelevant part of his brain told him that wasn't possible, because in restored-Orpen the panelled back wall of the cupboard blocked his way. But either the wall wasn't quite real or he wasn't quite real, because he was definitely walking forward.)

And he saw them: three bright flames.

Look closer.

Not flame. Each presence was not a single radiance, but a thousand threads of fire, all tangled together.

Two pulsed brightly, but one was unravelling into nothingness, like a fuse fizzing towards its own explosive annihilation. And it wasn't the latterly Skilless infant Sosigenes. His newborn form shone. No, the unspooling brilliance was his mother, in her fatal childbed.

This is how we die.

Loss of Skill didn't mean death – as both Meilyr Tresco and Jenner had obligingly demonstrated. But evidently, with death came this dissolution of Skill.

Mesmerized, Silyen watched what Cadmus did next.

Cadmus hadn't understood exactly what he was doing. The journals Silyen had read over and over in memory-Orpen's library made that clear. In them, his ancestor had connected the terrible night of his wife's death with his son's Skillessness, but he had never realized – or never acknowledged – that *he* was the cause.

Whatever Cadmus had done, it had been intuitive, unconscious. But the fabric of Orpen itself remembered.

And as Silyen watched, he finally understood.

He saw how Cadmus fastened one end of his child's Skill to its mother's golden thread. And how he joined the other end to his own. The Skill of all three were now tied together to make one tangled golden cord. Cadmus was attempting to anchor his wife in life. To be the strong rock to which her spirit was tethered.

The knotted cord held strong. But still his wife's Skill burned out like a bright fuse as her life ebbed.

And then his wife's thread was all burned away, and it was Sosigenes' Skill that was fizzing into the darkness. Cadmus recoiled and the conjoined thread broke. A tiny golden wisp floated after the rest into the dim. The remainder writhed and snapped back to its anchor – Cadmus.

Where there had been three bright flames in the room, now there was only one.

And though he could neither hear nor see it, Silyen felt Cadmus utter a raw howl that shivered right through him. He closed his eyes and trembled.

It was only the clashing of knives that brought Silyen round. They were so close he could feel them cut the air.

He took a deep breath. Tried to steady himself. Pushed away sensations that threatened to overwhelm him, to a distance from where they could be safely examined later.

'You're getting good,' he said, turning and opening his eyes back onto the real world. 'Although not good enough yet that I'd let you shave me.'

Dog grinned, and scraped the blades of Black Billy's glove against each other. They were thick with clotted blood.

'It's not a shave – I'll be giving – your cousin Ragnarr.'

Silyen looked at what Dog held in his other hand and rolled his eyes. Not again.

'Couldn't you go and kill a nice prime steak?' he said.

'Picking bones out of my dinner every night is becoming a little tedious.'

Dog hoisted the two brace of rabbits he held and emitted his barking laughter.

'Just be grateful – I didn't bring – the badger.'

Silyen grimaced.

'Anything interesting – in the cupboard?'

'You wouldn't believe,' said Silyen. He wiped his sweaty palms down his jeans. 'Things I need to think about. Come on, I'll put the kettle on while you get your furry victims ready for the pot.'

In the kitchen, Silyen filled the coffee pot while he watched Dog deftly use the array of Black Billy's implements to skin, gut and joint his kill. The man's proficiency had improved amazingly. He'd dispatch Ragnarr in a trice.

'You're not so – chatty today.'

'I think I just saw what I did to my brother. To both of them, in a way.'

Dog paused to rip the sheath of skin and fur expertly off a second rabbit, revealing the purple-pink meat beneath, swathed in gleaming membrane. He deployed the fine blade of the glove's little finger to nick it away. Job done, he grunted, so Silyen continued.

'I took Jenner's Skill when we were little. It's the only explanation for how he is, and how I am. I've no recollection of it at all. I must have been a baby.'

'So you were – born bad.' Dog wheezed in amusement.

'You wound me. No, it has to be that, because my ability and his lack of Skill would be a pretty massive coincidence, otherwise. But I never understood *how* it could have happened. I mean, there's precocious, and then there's performing dastardly deeds before you're even out of nappies.

'When I read Cadmus's journals, it was clear that he'd done the same, but didn't know it. So I realized it could be done accidentally. Unconsciously. The logical next step was to find out if it could also be done consciously, which inspired me to carry out a little experiment with Gavar and his baby.'

It hadn't been his finest hour. Silyen paused and poured himself more coffee. He'd finished the pot all by himself, but with Black Billy's glove on it wasn't like Dog would be able to pick up a cup without slicing his nose off.

Dog was watching, intrigued. And even though Silyen knew the man couldn't hurt him, that gaze was disturbing. Dog owed him three debts: a name, an escape and a life. Whose life would it be?

He put a hand to his throat. What would it be like to feel Dog's steel there, and your warm blood spilling?

He shrugged off his disquiet and continued.

'I was trying out ideas, wondering if Skill flowed between a parent and child. I wanted to discover if I could pull any of Gavar's Skill into his baseborn daughter. But I was doing it blind. It's only in the past year that I've been able to "see"

Skill, and only in these last few weeks that I've seen it with sufficient acuity to grasp how you might manipulate it.

'So I daresay I was doing it badly. That's what experiments are, doing things badly, until you do them better. I knew it was affecting Gavar. He would get headaches. He's always been moody, but his temper became even worse, if that's possible. And you know how it ended: that night at the gate. I wanted to see if little Libby could open it. I may have been overeager, and Gavar snapped. It was all most unfortunate.'

It was more than unfortunate. It was, if he was being honest, unforgivable. His Skillful meddling had tightened the bonds between father and child. But he hadn't foreseen how that would influence Gavar's reaction, when confronted with Leah trying to steal away with their daughter.

Silyen remembered Leah, fatally wounded and lying on the cold ground. He recalled Gavar's icy fury – *No one steals what's mine* – when the emotion he truly felt for the girl was a hot passion. And Jenner, bent over her as she died. What a mess. All Silyen had been able to do was walk away.

Can't you do anything? Jenner had called after him.

No, there had been nothing he could do. *No one can bring back the dead*, he'd told his brother. *Not even me.*

Not Silyen at Kyneston gate. Not Cadmus Parva at his dying wife's side.

Some things not even Skill could do.

'Enough of that,' he announced, hopping down from the countertop to peer over Dog's shoulder. 'If I may make a suggestion, add a little more black pepper. Last night's was woefully under-seasoned.'

'You can do it yourself – tomorrow,' growled Dog. 'I leave at dawn. Got a job to do. Your cousin won't know – what bit him.'

The man clashed his steel fingers, before picking up another rabbit and expertly slashing its fur from jaw to tail in one practised motion.

Which was when the roof of Orpen Mote blew off.

16

Silyen

Dog actually snarled, and if Crovan had progressed to giving the man hackles, they would have risen.

All around them, bricks shrivelled and crumbled, turning back into the ash they had been until Silyen and his aunt had begun their restoration. Silyen glanced up. Where the roof had been was now night sky. As he watched, the stars warped. Pots and pans were falling from the walls, clattering to the floor, their shapes blurring, melting.

'Out, quickly,' Silyen gasped.

Dog needed no telling. As they ran from the kitchen, the walls collapsed in a final puff of gritty dust. The floorboards scorched and withered beneath their feet as they ran. From behind came an almighty crash – the great iron chandelier in Orpen's hall smashing onto the stone-flagged floor.

Silyen set both hands to the front door and rammed through it. Where was his aunt?

This wasn't the first time.

Occasionally, over these past weeks, small portions of

Orpen had reverted to ruin. Silyen would turn a corner and find a room gone; a wall half missing; a passageway newly open to the sky. It was Aunty Terpy's grief, her potent, destructive Skill lashing out and undoing all their work. Silyen would simply pause, restore, and move on.

Not this time. This looked bad enough to devastate the house all over again, unless she was stopped.

'There,' Dog barked, pointing at the rose garden set on a terrace above the house.

In the thin moonlight Silyen saw Aunt Euterpe on her knees, clawing at the dirt. She looked just as she had that day a quarter of a century ago, when her grief over her parents' deaths and Orpen's destruction unleashed catastrophe. When Winterbourne Zelston had commanded her to be still, and she had been – through all the years that followed, until Silyen had found her in this same garden.

Silyen ran to his aunt, grabbed her shaking shoulders, and heaved her upright.

'Stop it,' he shouted. 'Stop. It'll all fall again.'

Euterpe's eyes were wide in her thin, pale face. The layers of Orpen flickered and superimposed. And she looked once more like the invalid girl he had met in the rose garden, and swapped stories with as they walked around the moat.

His friend. His sort of sister.

'I miss him,' Euterpe cried, tears streaking her soil-smudged face. 'I miss him more than I can bear. You

251

should have left me here, Silyen. Left me to dream of my Winter coming back.'

Silyen shook her fiercely. It was building again, that awful pressure they had all felt in Kyneston's ballroom before it exploded. Pressure as if your brain was inflating inside your skull, with violence the only release.

'Your Skill,' he hissed. 'Control it.'

Dog lurched over. He swung his head as if to dislodge the swelling pain. Blood trickled from his nose. With the hand that wasn't gloved in death, he slapped her.

'You'll kill us all,' he growled.

'I wish *I* was dead,' Euterpe shrieked. 'I wish I didn't have this Skill that protects me from myself. I wish I could be with him.'

Silyen froze. He released his aunt, who slumped to her knees. He closed his eyes, and opened them in Skill.

Aunt Euterpe was so dazzling he raised a hand to shield his vision. The raw power of this woman was astonishing. She pulsed brighter than any Equal he had seen, a writhing ball of energy.

What had he seen Cadmus do? Could he pluck and pull this coiling power and unravel her? Did he dare?

But he had to do something.

And she had said she wished to be free of Skill.

And Silyen was so *very* curious.

He bent over his aunt and gently tipped up her face. Somewhere beside him, in the inky darkness of the absence of Skill, Dog was raving. But Silyen spoke quietly and knew she would hear.

'I can take it – if you want.'

His aunt's reply was soft but unmistakable.

'I want you to take it. Please, I want you to.'

So in a world that was not quite *this* world – the world in which he had walked through cupboard walls that were no longer exactly *there* – Silyen thrust his hand into the heart of her. It was all he could do not to scream with the shock of it.

Look closer.

He looked. The threads of Euterpe's Skill whipped and sparked as Orpen's bright obliteration roared on.

This was hopeless. The intensity of the threads was too fast for his eye to see or his hand to catch.

Don't look, he told himself. *Feel. Reach.*

There.

A point of movement, whip-quick. Silyen seized it. The end of a golden thread burned in his hand.

'Please,' his aunt moaned. 'Take it.'

But how? He had no memory at all of what he had done to Jenner, while Cadmus's efforts had proved a disaster.

Sparks danced between Silyen's curled fingers. He hesitated. Then opened his mouth wide and crammed the brightness in.

And swallowed.

Was this what his father sought in alcohol? This giddying rush? Was it the palest shadow of this that Gavar and his Oxford friends were chasing, when eleven-year-old Silyen had caught them hunched over one of Mama's antique mirrors with a bag of white powder? Did Jenner feel even a fraction of this when Abi Hadley kissed him?

Silyen wouldn't believe it. Nothing could compare with this. Not the touch of tool-calloused hands on your skin and a muscled body straining against yours. Not sitting in the Chancellor's Chair, receiving the acclamation of one's Equals.

Nothing at all.

He wasn't drawing breath any more. He was inhaling pure Skill. Could feel it flowing from Aunty Terpy to him. He groaned and sank to his knees opposite his aunt. He wasn't sure which of them reached out first, but they embraced each other to keep themselves upright.

She was dimming, fading before his eyes. The pulse of her Skill thrummed through him. It was like receiving a heart transplant while your own still beat.

His head spun. A galaxy revolved inside it.

He tipped back his head and opened his mouth wide as the Skill poured in. He could feel it pushing at his fingertips, his toes, his ears, his eyes, as if it wanted to overflow and leak out of him. But he contained it.

'Thank you,' he heard his aunt whisper.

Her light guttered – and went out.

Silyen howled. Convulsed. Collapsed back onto the

cold, grey ground. He licked his lips and tasted blood – he must have bitten them. Raising his hand into his line of sight, he saw it was as bright as the sun.

He blacked out.

The glass of water in his face brought him round.

'Wouldn't want you,' Dog said, 'to sleep – through dinner. Know how you love – rabbit pie.'

Dog laughed and Silyen rubbed his face, disoriented. He was lying on a chaise longue in the antechamber of Orpen's hall. Everything appeared to be in place. There were walls all around, none of them letting in the night. He looked up. The roof was in place. A ripe meaty smell wafted from the direction of the kitchen, turning his stomach.

What had happened?

He must have asked that out loud, because Dog supplied an answer.

'I carried her – inside. Took her to – her room. She's sleeping. Went back – for you. You'd come round. Fixed it all – already. All this.' The man waved a hand to indicate the manor house around them. 'Nice work. Then you – collapsed again. Anyway. Dinner time now. Your favourite.'

Dog turned and disappeared back towards the kitchen.

Silyen wiped a hand down his face and through his dripping hair, then swung his legs over the side of the chaise longue. When his feet touched the floor his knees almost buckled with his own weight. It came back to him, then, how he had felt outside in the garden, after he had swallowed Aunt Euterpe's Skill. All fire and air.

Just existing in this body felt like an imprisonment worse than anything the Condemned endured.

He thought, briefly, of Luke Hadley.

But Luke could wait for another day.

With leaden steps, he crossed to the table. By the time he sat down, his appetite had returned. As he watched Dog carry in a large china platter on which stood a deep dish of rabbit pie, Silyen's thoughts turned to his aunt.

How would Euterpe be feeling? Exhausted? Liberated? Desolate? He had no idea. It had been plain, through the years, that her Skill disgusted her. What she had done when her parents died, and again in Kyneston's ballroom after losing Zelston, had terrified her. And out there, in the garden, she had begged him to take her Skill.

But would she regret this last, irrevocable decision? Because Silyen was pretty sure he couldn't give it back.

On the other side of the table, Dog had stopped in his tracks and was staring. Silyen twisted to look over his shoulder.

Aunt Euterpe was dressed all in white. It was a modest outfit, long and high-necked and unmistakably bridal. It must be the dress she had chosen for her doomed wedding more than a quarter of a century ago. On her head was pinned a small spray of antique lace and pearls. The tips of the shoes peeking from beneath her hem were also white.

'Here,' she said. 'Allow me.'

She walked to her customary seat at the head of the table and remained standing, gesturing for Dog to put the platter down in front of her.

'Thank you both for keeping me company these past few weeks,' she said. 'And you, Silyen, for all that you've done here. No aunt could ask for a better nephew – even if it took me a while to realize who you were when we first met.'

Her laughter was touchingly youthful. She looked right at him – those dark eyes, just like his, under curling dark hair, just like his. They were both Parva children. Were both of this line and belonged to this place.

'Thank you for today, especially,' she said.

Silyen didn't need Skill for something to tingle through him.

'Rabbit pie was a family favourite,' she told Dog approvingly. 'We had it often when we were little. His mother' – she nodded at Silyen – 'never cared for it much, but I always thought it delicious. It was Winterbourne's favourite. He asked for it every time he visited. Thalia used to tease me that I would serve it on our wedding day. And you know what? I intended to.'

She smiled at them both, her expression serene. That

smile was also Silyen's. And now her Skill was Silyen's, too. He didn't think she regretted it.

He held a plate towards her as she picked up the knife from the side of the platter to serve the pie.

'So much love,' Aunt Euterpe murmured. 'And so much to be grateful for. So very much.'

She lifted the knife too fast and too high and slashed her throat from ear to ear – no Skill left, now, to stop her.

17

Bouda

Bouda could not believe what Faiers, the Speaker's son, was telling her. That her godfather Rix was behind the Kyneston assassination, and that Lord Whittam – as he had always maintained – had been the intended target.

'A grudge twenty-five years old,' Faiers said, as he stood in her inner office having first asked for privacy. 'Coupled with a hatred for the new Chancellor's politics. Rix is a commoner sympathizer and always has been. He just masked it well.'

'Tell me how you came by this information,' Bouda insisted. 'Show me.'

'Please don't,' Faiers protested, as she readied herself to force the knowledge from his mind. 'The person this came from could be of much greater use to us in the future, if we let things unfold. Please let me protect their identity.

'If you doubt me, you could ask your brother-in-law, Silyen Jardine. He knows. He blackmailed Rix to secure his adoption as heir of Far Carr. Or ask Rix himself, though I doubt he'll sing all his secrets without encouragement.'

Bouda considered for a moment. She had never been adept at using her Skill for mindwork. She might not even be able to do it, which would be humiliating. And if she was successful, she might injure Faiers, and she felt oddly reluctant to do that – the man was useful, after all.

What he said made sense. Let him protect his source, for now.

But – her own godfather? It hardly seemed possible. Bouda prided herself on knowing what people thought and what they wanted. She relished digging up information, then squirrelling it away until its time came. Had she really missed something as huge as this?

And what should she do next? She could speak to her godfather privately. Surely she owed him that? The man was her father's best friend, a constant presence in the lives of the whole family. She remembered her parents, before her mother died, sitting on the great terrace of Appledurham roaring with laughter at some story Rixy had told.

But if what Faiers said was true, Rix might flee, if forewarned.

Bouda remembered the treacherous adoption of Silyen Jardine to Far Carr, which should have passed to her or DiDi. That betrayal was both the evidence and the justification she needed to take this straight to Whittam.

She turned to dismiss Faiers, only to find him watching her.

'Heir Bouda, if I may,' he murmured. 'When you find that my information is correct, I have two requests, if you would consider them.'

Faiers' impertinence had made an impression on her at Grendelsham, that night he had approached her on the clifftop. This was more obsequiously phrased, but impertinence nonetheless.

'Your kind do not make requests of my kind, Faiers.'

'Indeed, indeed.' He bowed his head, though not before Bouda saw his mouth twitch with amusement. 'But nonetheless, I would ask that you remember my loyalty in bringing this to you, and consider me for a place on your permanent staff.'

'You seem to mistake loyalty for duty, Faiers. You've done nothing more than is required.'

'Of course. But, a second request: once you have established Rix's guilt, I would appreciate a moment with him before his punishment.'

'What?'

'In your presence, naturally,' Faiers added smoothly. 'But, please.' He lifted his head to look at her then, and the humour was gone. Something like anger flashed in those sky-blue eyes.

'Why would you ask such an extraordinary thing?'

261

'I have my reasons. Should you grant my request, you will discover them.'

And then Faiers was gone, and Bouda could not remember if she had dismissed him or if he had simply left.

Well. Faiers was a piece of work. He had departed her presence equally abruptly that night at Grendelsham, just his cigarette smoke trailing on the wind. His words came back to her. *Your allies aren't always who you think they are – and neither are your enemies.*

Was Faiers her ally and Rix her enemy?

No. Equals had no need of commoners as allies, or as anything other than servants. Obedient ones. Although there could be a strategic benefit to bringing Faiers on side. As Speaker Dawson's son, his presence in some token role might allay commoner dissatisfaction at the suspension of their parliamentary observers.

She filed the idea away for consideration. But first: determining Rix's guilt, or innocence. She hurried to find Whittam.

'Bouda, always a pleasure.'

Her father-in-law took her by the wrist and pulled her inside the Chancellor's suite. He lifted her wrist to his mouth and kissed it, and it was all Bouda could do not to cringe away. Yes, she submitted to Whittam's pawings – and worse. But it was never without a reminder to herself of the prize that lay within her grasp with this man's backing.

After all, Whittam was only interim Chancellor. He would at some point have to step down and call an election for a new incumbent. Bouda knew there were a few parliamentarians who fancied their chances, but none, surely, who could resist the combined alliance of Whittam's backers and Bouda's own supporters – the same who had ousted Zelston.

No, the man now slobbering his way up the side of Bouda's neck would handpick his successor. Which meant Bouda had only one real rival: her husband, Gavar. Bouda had been furious with him ever since the debacle at their wedding. Although in hindsight his demented incineration of the marquee was potentially useful – a public demonstration of his uncouthness and instability.

And now this – the information Faiers had handed her. Surely this would cement her position as the worthiest candidate?

She pushed Whittam away as playfully as she could (and her Skill crackled at the end of her fingertips with the repressed urge to throw him across the room), and refastened the top two buttons on her shirt. Her father-in-law's spittle was tacky between her breasts.

'Irresistible as you are,' she said, pouting, 'I'm here for business, not pleasure. I've been passed some rather extraordinary information.'

And she unfolded everything that Faiers had told her.

'This supposed grudge,' she asked Whittam, who had

been brought sharply to his senses by her news. 'Is it true? What was it?'

'I can barely remember. He'd impregnated some commoner and his father wanted her packed off. So I sent some goon to her. The usual routine: first offer money, then offer promises. It would have ended with offering threats, but she gave in on the promises. It's always like that with these trollops. I had to do the same with Gavar's little slut – that was why she ran away that night – but then my son took matters into his own hands.'

Whittam laughed, and reached for the decanter that was never far from his grasp.

'So after all that time imagining I had some foe worth the name – an agent of our political enemies in the Triad states, or even this troublesome commoner woman in Riverhead – it was tragic old Rixy? No wonder he botched it and ended up killing Zelston instead. I'm almost insulted.

'And Silyen worked it out and fleeced him for an inheritance. I always knew that boy was brilliant.'

That stopped Bouda in her tracks. She had expected Whittam to rage at his son for withholding the name of his father's would-be killer.

'Brilliant? He knew of a threat to your life and didn't tell you.'

'Oh.' Whittam waved his glass, sloshing whisky on the floor. He appeared not to notice. 'Rix is hardly a threat – as events showed. And what price did Silyen exact for his knowledge? A seat in parliament. I always believed my youngest's great flaw was his lack of interest in politics. I supposed that as a third-born, he felt it was beyond his reach.

'But no. What did he do with his hold over Rix? Levered himself into the House of Light. With Gavar proving such a disappointment, it couldn't be better timed.'

Fear and fury wrapped around Bouda, tight and constricting. What was Whittam saying? That he could see a place for Silyen as his parliamentary protégé?

No. No, that could never be allowed to happen. Not Silyen, who she was quite certain spent his life laughing up his sleeve at his entire family. Who already had Skillful power enough to spare, and didn't need any more, of the political kind.

'After all,' Whittam was saying, oblivious to her turmoil, 'it could hardly be Jenner – though I can't deny it'll be satisfying to have all three of them in parliament now.'

'Jenner?' Bouda croaked. This day could hardly get more shocking.

'My wife's sister has passed away at Orpen. Seems she overtaxed herself with the rebuilding, or an accident of some sort. So the Parva title goes to Thalia, and as our only non-ennobled child, Jenner will become heir.'

'You would allow an unSkilled to sit in parliament?'

Which hadn't been the best way to phrase it, because Whittam's bloodshot gaze fixed on Bouda.

'I will welcome the second-born of the Founding Family to his rightful place – and so will you. Now bring in that godfather of yours, and let's put an end to this sorry business. To think that your family has harboured him under your roof all these years, and you never suspected a thing. But then women do have a weak grasp of such matters.'

Bouda stood there a moment, astonished that she had neither spontaneously combusted, nor that her Skill had blasted Whittam out of the immense window and sent him freefalling into the quadrangles below. It took everything she had to simply pivot on her heel, imagining Whittam's face beneath it, and walk calmly out. Behind her, she heard the clink of the stopper being lifted from the decanter yet again.

Bouda telephoned her godfather and invited him to dinner that evening. He readily agreed, with one of his usual roguish jokes, and Bouda hung up wondering if her father would ever forgive her.

Poor darling Papa – to have lost his wife to commoner terrorists, and now to learn that his best friend had been a sympathizer for years. Perhaps when she told Daddy what her godfather had done, she would tell him only the part about Rix's decades-old personal grudge, and not his deviant politics. Other than economic affairs, Papa had almost as little political interest as DiDi. He didn't need to know.

Then Bouda contacted Astrid Halfdan. Astrid was Skilled at compulsion and perception, which was why

Bouda had asked her to lead the interrogations for the slavetown purges. The woman had burned with a fierce hatred of the unSkilled ever since her little sister's abduction and abuse at the hands of a commoner maniac, a few years ago. She'd be glad to see a sympathizer brought to justice.

Kessler was ordered to be ready and waiting in the office that night, with two Security colleagues, all armed with tasers.

Bouda's hand hesitated before dialling the final number. She was astonished that she even had it, but there it was in the Westminster directory, logged under 'Speaker's aide'.

'Be at my office tonight at 9 p.m.,' she told Faiers, on hearing him answer. Then she hung up.

She reserved her godfather's favourite corner booth in the Members' dining room. She thought of inviting Papa, so they could have a final meal together. But no, it would prove too difficult to disentangle the pair of them afterwards.

She felt a twinge of something that couldn't possibly have been pity and certainly wasn't guilt as she poured her godfather another glass of champagne. And she listened to his droll descriptions of Far Carr's slaves' reactions, when told the estate had a new heir.

But then Rix turned the conversation, and Bouda's mood turned with it. He started asking light, mocking questions about the progress of the slavetown purges. But beneath the banter, he was probing. What had she discovered? Where were raids or further enquiries planned?

The champagne soured in Bouda's stomach. Faiers had been correct.

She checked her watch. A quarter past nine. Time to finish this.

'Come by my office,' she said. 'I can show you a map of the investigation's progress. Only if you're interested. You're so sweet to let me natter on at you.'

Bouda phoned ahead to Kessler, on the pretext of having coffee prepared, and the minute Rix walked through the office door all three tasers took him down. The surprise prevented his Skillful reflexes kicking in, and the combined force of it – enough to kill a commoner several times over – incapacitated him.

Rix writhed on the carpet, barely conscious, foam flecking the corner of his mouth.

'Bouda?' he moaned. 'What . . . ?'

'You know what,' she said. It was all she could do not to kick him as he lay there, this man who was practically family, who had betrayed her trust for so long. 'Astrid, do what you have to do.'

But before Astrid could begin her examination, Faiers stepped forward. Bouda had almost forgotten he would be there.

He delivered the kick that Bouda had only considered. More of a stamp, actually. Hard, to Rix's solar plexus. The man yelled out, curling up protectively. Faiers bent over the Equal and pulled back his dapper white hair, forcing Rix's head up.

'You imagine yourself a champion of the people, yet you discarded in a slavetown the common-born woman who loved you and was carrying your child?' Faiers said, his face very close to Rix's. His lip curled with contempt. 'You let that child grow up in misery, knowing he'd have to spend another decade there as an adult, because the clock doesn't start on your days till you're ten?

'And then you wooed her again, years later. You may have fooled my mother that you still cared for her, after everything. You may have fooled yourself that your half-hearted efforts on behalf of the common people made up for what you did. You may even think that your attempt on Jardine's life was right and just, because what happened was his fault, not yours. But you've never fooled me.'

Faiers stamped on him a second time. Rix groaned.

'Jonathan.' Rix spat froth from his mouth and tried again. 'Jonathan, it was Jardine. Your mother knows this. I was led to believe that she had turned against me, had abandoned me. It's why I never married. I still love her. I would love you, if only you'd let me.'

'I'd be ashamed to call you "Father". You deserve everything you get.'

Faiers stepped away from the prone man, cracking his

neck from side to side as if he'd finally set down a heavy load he had carried for a long time.

'Heir Bouda,' he said politely. 'Thank you.'

Rix's head fell back onto the carpet. The fight had gone out of him. Astrid crouched down.

'You understand what you're here for?' she asked. 'You're accused of causing the death of Chancellor Zelston when attempting to kill Lord Jardine, using a commoner boy as your instrument. We will be asking you questions to establish the truth of this allegation.'

'No questions,' Rix gasped. Plainly word had spread of Astrid's techniques. 'I admit it. I'm only sorry I never succeeded.'

'I'm afraid you don't get to avoid the questions.'

Astrid took a syringe and small vial from her pocket. Bouda bent down to watch as she picked up Rix's wrist and drove the needle in.

'Incapacitates even an Equal,' Astrid said. 'It's what the commoner scum who raped my sister used on her, for each of those nineteen days he had her.'

'Bouda.' Her godfather's hand clawed at her wrist and it was all Bouda could do not to shriek. 'Jardine is a monster. Take care.'

Then his grip loosened and his hand fell away, as Lord Rix's nattily dressed body went into violent convulsions.

'What's going on?' Bouda stepped back from the thrashing body. 'Astrid?'

Astrid inspected the vial. 'Correct dose. This shouldn't be happening.'

She knelt over Rix and pressed her fingertips to his chest.

'His heart. Perhaps the drug so soon after using the stun guns . . . But I don't think I can fix it. I'm not much good at healing.'

The woman looked up, but all Bouda could do was shake her head. She wasn't apt with healing, either. DiDi was better. Meilyr Tresco had been the best.

A final catastrophic tremor racked Rix's body, then he lay still on the carpet, beyond the help of anyone's Skill at all.

Bouda calmed herself. Let her breathing even out. Smoothed her skirt and sleeked her ponytail. Then she stood up straight.

'This is only how it would have ended anyway. You all heard the confession?'

Everyone present nodded.

'Very well. Deaths in detention do happen, especially when subjects resist questioning. No one was to blame. And crucially, we established the detainee's guilt prior to his decease. Astrid, please draw up an incident report, and we will all witness it.'

When Kessler's radio crackled into life, it was the last thing Bouda needed.

'Answer it,' she snapped.

Through the buzz of static, Bouda recognized the voice

of her other aide, the former Millmoor Overseer. What could the woman want at this time of night?

'There's a been a major incident,' Kessler said, twisting off the device. 'The Overseer's on her way. You two' – he snapped his fingers at his two Security companions – 'give Heir Astrid every assistance in removing the late Lord Rix to an appropriate facility. Heir Bouda, we need to get to a helicopter immediately.'

'I'll arrange that,' said Faiers. And when Kessler raised an eyebrow, 'I'm staff now, just like you.'

'What's happened?' Bouda asked, trying and failing to imagine what could be even more urgent than dealing with Rix's demise.

'Large-scale sabotage,' said Kessler grimly. 'In the Bore.'

Two hours later, their chopper was circling above Sector C of the Northern Bore.

The vast hay barns were burning.

It was the fourth attack of the night. Each target – another barn, an equipment depot, and a fertilizer store that had caused a vast explosion – had been hit on the half hour, miles from the previous location. These outrages were wide-ranging and co-ordinated.

Bouda watched through the windscreen. It was as if the sky itself was on fire, as incandescent strands of hay somehow became lighter than air and eddied upwards on thermals of their own making.

The doors to the largest barn fell away, revealing giant

stacked blocks of hay, blackened and glowing from within. Insubstantial flames shimmered across the mounds.

All around, headlights lanced into the darkness. A cordon of Security jeeps fanned outward through the dark fields, bouncing along rough tracks meant for trucks that brought the workers out and back each day, and for massive harvesting machinery. From the back of each jeep, figures leapt at intervals. Lamps fastened to their helmets sliced the night as they turned this way and that. Hunting.

Without a capture, there would be little usable evidence from this conflagration. Perhaps a distinctive form of accelerant that could be traced to a certain sector, or a specific workforce. Bouda doubted it would be enough.

The flames roared greedily. The barns were miles from any irrigation canal that might douse them. Bouda thought of her ancestor, Harding the Voyager – Harding the weatherworker, who had quelled storms and raised winds. He could have summoned a raincloud to extinguish this.

Something prickled uneasily within her at the thought. Her Skill was strong, she knew. But all she ever used it for was bickering with her husband, or subtly reinforcing suggestions to her clique of parliamentary followers. Yet what was the point of being Equal, if not to do things that the commoners could not?

If only she could call the wind and rain. Her fingers spasmed, as if to mock her.

'Back,' she barked into the headset. 'Let's go.'

But as they circled back to the massive administration hub at the centre of the Bore, it seemed her Equal senses were good for something, after all.

In the darkness: a man, running.

'There. You see him? Five hundred metres at two o'clock. Kessler, get in a shot that won't kill.'

None of the commoners had sighted the man at first, but the pilot dutifully angled the chopper and soon after came cries of recognition.

Air roared around Bouda's neck as Kessler slammed open the vehicle door. His gun cracked once and the man went down.

Not an entirely wasted night.

Back at the administration detention centre, the man was brought before Bouda and her team, while the Bore's own Security looked on.

'Locations are not good enough,' Bouda snapped. 'I need names.'

'I don't know any names,' he said.

Her hand flashed out. His hands were cuffed behind his back and he couldn't avoid the blow.

'Well, guess some,' she hissed. 'Who is popular? Who is dissatisfied? Who talks back?'

'Please, there are twenty thousand men doing days in the Bore. How could I know?'

At a nod from Bouda, Kessler drove the butt of his rifle

into the man's gut. The prisoner screamed and doubled over.

'What you did,' she said, 'was part of something bigger. So who told you to do it? And then I'll find out who told them. And then who told that person. Whoever is behind all this, whatever they intend, I will unpick it one stitch at a time until it all unravels. And then I will cut off the thread. So let's try again: I need names.'

She worked through the small hours and into the following day. By the time Bouda took a break for a few hours' sleep, she had unpicked seven stitches and had a location for what was planned that night.

The barley of Sector J, Eastern Bore, was the autumn planting: near ripe, with stalks that stood almost shoulder-height. Its harvest this year would be fire and choking smoke.

In the darkness, the flaming crops cast their own lurid light. From above, Bouda saw the fire advancing, a wavering but purposeful line. Behind it was a band of glowing embers. Further back, only the dead black of scorched earth.

The fire was spreading faster than anyone had anticipated. The destruction would be immense. The Bore's irrigation channels were also its firebreaks. This conflagration would destroy everything between those boundaries, and they'd have to hope that no sparks leapt the water to consume a new area of the fields.

To permit such devastation would be a victory for these agitators – even though a calculated decision had been made to let the fires take, in the hope of catching the men setting them.

Well, Security would take care of the perpetrators, but perhaps Bouda could be useful with the fire.

She was an Equal, after all. She had been reluctant to use Skillful mindwork on Faiers. She had been unable to heal Rix. But surely there was something she could do here?

Her mother-in-law, Thalia Jardine, liked to tell tales of her sister freezing Orpen's moat. And what of Gorregan, when the Equal women of Great Britain rolled up the sea and wrecked Napoleon's fleet? A large oil painting of the Grounding hung in the salon at Appledurham, and Bouda remembered the windows in Highwithel's hall that depicted the same scene.

Her fingers twitched again, just as they had last night. Then, she had thought it weakness. Tonight, she wasn't so sure. A sense of anticipation was building inside her.

'Get us as close as you can,' Bouda barked over the headset. 'Hover at ten metres.'

The chopper shied like a horse as it approached the flames. It was an easy drop for an Equal. Bouda swung both feet out onto the skid and jumped.

Coughing against the streaming black smoke, she ran along the smouldering stubble to the irrigation channel she'd sighted from above. Fell to her knees. Stretched down over the edge towards the water.

She'd thought she'd have to reach for her Skill, but it was already there, tingling in her fingertips. Bouda closed her eyes. She could sense every cell in her fingers, feel the Skill that pulsed there, and the swirling water, cool and quivering.

She felt the moment when, as if by osmosis, her Skill passed *into* the water and she knew it was at her command. It was dizzying. She reached out further. Felt the irrigation channel branch, and sensed beyond it the great inert mass of the canal.

Inert, but expectant.

Was this what Skill could do? Was this what she was capable of? It was almost unimaginable.

She called the river – and it came. This was turbulent water, alternately pulled downstream from its source and pushed back by the tidal bore from the coast. Bouda's Skill strove against the tide – then flowed out to the sea. She gasped, feeling the pull to dissolution by a power much vaster than her own. And called her Skill back again, drawing the water with it.

It built, gushing, spilling over the wide channel banks, mounting up into a great onrushing wave. Bouda's hands worked in the air, as if shaping the monstrous tide, and as it reached the flaming fields where she stood, she held it taut and dammed by nothing more than her own will.

Then with a downward smash of her hands, she sent the great wave rushing past her, surging onto the land, flooding the fields and extinguishing the flames. Bouda heard the hiss and the sizzle and felt the rising steam.

She was sopping wet and her hands shook, but something inside her roared and sang. She was very sure her heart was beating at twice its normal rate.

What had she just done?

What more could she do?

How had she lived without this?

18

Luke

'Hadley, I have news for you. See me at ten o'clock.'

Crovan rose from the breakfast table, so the rest of them rose to their feet too, remaining standing until their master had left the room.

'What's that about, eh?' Julian murmured once he was gone.

'No idea,' said Luke. 'It's "news", remember.'

What news might it be? A pardon for killing Zelston? A new investigation into that night's events? He highly doubted it.

'Well, you've got ages,' said Jules. 'Round of cards? Poker?'

Julian produced a deck from his pocket. He carried them with him at all times, ready to while away a quiet moment. And there were so many quiet moments – whole days of them, stitched together and laid smothering over Luke's life.

Maybe something would happen today.

'Luke, I need you for a moment.'

Coira had materialized beside them, and she took Luke gently but firmly by the elbow. He cast an apologetic glance back at Julian as she steered him towards the kitchen.

The castle's servants, others of the Condemned, bustled around clearing up. Someone at one of the sinks dropped a large pan and Luke flinched. An image flashed through his brain: a man in black tie stubbing out a cigarette on a woman's bare neck. A carving fork skewered through Luke's hand. Coira shouting.

What did it mean? He looked down at his hand. It was uninjured, unscarred. Had that been a memory? A night-mare given to him by Crovan? How could he not know which?

Coira led him into a small pantry. She tucked up her skirts and crouched down, straining to reach around a sack of potatoes. She tugged out a book and handed it to him.

'You didn't ask for it yesterday, so it must have become a black spot again.'

'What is it?' The spine proclaimed the book a history of heraldry. The edges of the pages were discoloured with age.

'It's your diary, sort of.'

A diary? How could he keep one of those and not know about it?

As if sensing his scepticism, Coira opened the cover and

Luke was astonished to see the title page covered in his own abysmal handwriting.

He makes you forget, it read. *This is how you remember. This is what you need to know about how this place works and what he does.*

'Why do you have it?' he asked, confused.

'You kept it beneath your pillow, but then you worried that Crovan would take it from you, or that Blake or Devin might destroy it. And' – she permitted herself a wry smile – 'you said that sleeping on it gave you neck ache.'

Luke turned the book over. A sheet of paper was folded around the back cover. He'd scribbled in emphatic capitals, as if anticipating his future scepticism: *WRITE IN THIS EVERY DAY. THIS IS ALL REAL. TRUST WHAT'S IN HERE, NOT WHAT YOU REMEMBER.*

'What he does to you,' Coira said, 'it affects your memory. You lose a bit – sometimes a lot – from day to day. Sometimes the memories come back. Sometimes they don't. So this book is your backup – except occasionally you forget about it, too. Have a read. I've got to get everything finished out there, but I'll come back when I'm done.'

Luke squatted against the shelves, and read.

Jackson and Angel came to rescue me. Abi with them . . . Devin shot the Doc – defending Crovan. Coira & I put Doc through Last Door.

There was more. Pages of it. The jottings, all dated, had

been made by him over the past month. Some were detailed – a long passage of rumination about the collars they wore, which Luke glossed over. *Skip: no point*, he had printed above what looked like pages about a boat that brought food supplies to and from the island. There was a summary of what he was accused of – the murder of Chancellor Zelston – and what had happened at his trial and Condemnation. One page bore the header *Devin*, and he'd scrawled a sentence over the top and underlined it: *Short version: not a nice man*. A section titled *Blake* had been even more succinctly summarized: *Monster*.

'I can't hope that this is an elaborate joke?' he asked Coira, when she came back some indefinable length of time later. His brain ached trying to take it all in. His heart ached trying to forget some of it all over again. 'I reckon Jules could forge my handwriting well enough. Or is there a section on him in here, too, that I've missed?'

'Nothing on Julian,' Coira said. 'Crovan knows he's your friend, so I reckon he's saving up the big reveal there so it really hurts.'

'There's something to reveal?'

'We've already had this conversation. I honestly don't know.'

'But you don't need to do anything like this?' Luke fanned through the book. 'Crovan doesn't take your recollection away from you like he does from me?'

'Not day to day, no. He took the main thing – the reason

why I'm here at all. But now, he never talks to me, or asks to see me. He looks right through me. The only reason I'm in charge of things below stairs is because I've been here so long.'

'But there's something else different about you. Everyone in this castle is either predator or prey – that's what it says in here.' Luke touched the book. 'The collars prevent the "servants" hurting the "guests", but not the other way around.'

The thought of what he'd read made his gut churn. Crovan's guests were punished by Crovan, but they could take out their sadistic urges on any of those living below stairs. All except Coira.

'You're not one of the guests upstairs. But you can't be hurt, like the other servants below stairs. You're special. Why?'

'I have no idea.' She hesitated. 'You know that I came here young, but I don't remember exactly when. I have no memories of any life before. But as a child, I would have been defenceless. So I think he did that to protect me.'

Luke's mind recoiled. To have known only this castle, this treasure chest crammed full of horrors, for your entire life? It was unimaginable. He thought of his old house in Manchester, where Daisy had run riot in the back garden and Dad had tinkered with cars on the driveway, and how unappreciative he'd been of his life back then, and the sheer stupefying normalcy of it. Where was Coira's family?

283

Then it hit him – a reason why Coira might have no memories of a place before Eilean Dòchais.

'What if you were born here? If your mother was the prisoner, not you?'

'Luke, I told you when you first arrived that I'm a criminal like everyone else here. I'm not making that up – Crovan said so. He's never told me what I did, only that it was awful. "The worst thing of all", was what he said. And what's that, if not killing another child?'

'Haven't you asked the others, if any of them remember when you came, how old you were, what was said about you?'

Coira turned her face away. A strand of brown hair fell down from where she pinned it back. He wanted to reach out and tuck it behind her ear, and fiddled with the book to stop himself doing anything so stupid. When she looked back, her agitation made him wish he'd never mentioned it.

'There's no one to ask. Those who were here through my childhood are dead or gone through the door, or don't know themselves any more. Lavinia was one of the first here, and she doesn't remember a thing apart from what *darling Braby* liked for breakfast and between the sheets.'

This girl had no roots, no anchor. No parents to share embarrassing childhood stories, or siblings to sass her, tease her, or just occasionally make her heart melt. Abi had always coached Luke through his exams. Daisy had been the one to get him out of Millmoor. He missed his family so much.

Luke wanted to promise Coira that one day, when they were far away from here, he would tell her stories of their time at Eilean Dòchais. She would finally have someone with whom she shared a history. But he was afraid it would come out all creepy and wrong, and besides, it wasn't as though their life here with Crovan was the stuff fond reminiscences were made of.

Crovan. They must have had the same thought at the same time, because Coira glanced up at the clock.

'Five minutes. You need to go and hear your news. I guess whoever's just arrived is something to do with it.'

'Someone's arrived?'

'A helicopter came in a quarter of an hour ago,' she said, taking the book and tucking it under her arm. 'And as you know, we never get visitors. It'd be too much of a coincidence.'

A kind of panic gripped Luke. Not Angel again, surely? And please not Abi with her. He never wanted to see his sister within a hundred miles of this place.

He hurried out of the kitchen, and up the square staircase to Crovan's apartments at the top of the castle, taking the treads two at a time. Devin was waiting outside the door to the upper floors, fob watch in hand.

'Cutting it fine.'

Not a nice man, Luke reminded himself.

Luke was ushered into Crovan's apartment. The lord of Eilean Dòchais was sitting at his desk by the window, sifting some documents.

'Thank you, Devin,' Crovan said. 'Send the girl up with a pot of coffee for my guest, please. Make sure it's hot.'

Devin bowed obsequiously, and withdrew.

'So, Hadley,' Crovan said, eying Luke through lenses that were a disconcerting cloudy white, reflecting the overcast day outside. 'Intriguing news. It appears that while in detention Lord Rix admitted responsibility for the slaying of Chancellor Zelston and the attempted murder of Lord Jardine.'

Luke couldn't believe it. A confession from an Equal? Hope blossomed inside him. He had purposely kept it dark and unwatered all these weeks, because to allow yourself to hope in a place where there was no mercy and no escape was the quickest way imaginable to drive yourself insane.

But then of course – of course – with his next words Crovan ripped that hope up by the roots and tossed it on the bonfire. Because that was what evil magical sadists did.

'Sadly, Rix then expired while in custody, so your precise involvement in the matter remains opaque. Given your prior history of violent sedition at Millmoor, Heir Bouda writes that your sentence of Condemnation stands, and the case is now closed. And of course, Heir Meilyr is no longer with us to plead for mitigation. You seem to be a dangerous young man, Luke Hadley: not one, but two of your Equal associates turning up dead.'

Luke's heart was heavy with the memory of Jackson, and his mind churned with this latest news, but his mouth was still doing its own thing.

'I'm happy to make it three, if you like.'

Crovan uttered a well-bred guffaw. From an armchair placed with its back to where Luke stood, a second laugh echoed it.

'Such wit. Oh – did you hear that splash?' Crovan turned back to the window, his expression quizzical. Luke had heard nothing, but then the Equals did have superfine senses. 'Ach, that'll be the key to your freedom, sinking all the way down to the bottom of my beautiful Loch nan Deur.

'No defender. No witness. You're all mine now, Hadley. Or should I say, "ours". I'm sure you remember my guest.'

'Hello, Luke.'

And as the curly dark head appeared round the side of the armchair, Luke realized he should have known it would be him.

'Silyen.'

The Equal swung both legs over the side of the chair and jumped to his feet.

'Have you missed me, Luke? And it's "Lord Silyen" now.'

Ennoblement had done nothing for Silyen's appearance. He was as dishevelled as ever, and there were dark lines beneath those dark eyes. How on earth had he come by his title?

'I'm presuming you didn't murder your father and brothers?'

'Luke.' The Equal's tone was reproving. 'We're no paragons of familial devotion, like you Hadleys, but even I have my limits. No, Lord Rix generously adopted me as his heir after the events at Kyneston. And then a few days ago he even more considerately passed away while in the custody of my sister-in-law. I'm sure she would have been more careful if she'd thought that through, but there you go.

'So I stand before you as the new lord of Far Carr. The investiture's in a few days, but I thought I'd come up here rather than go straight to London. Father's planning some ghastly parade to celebrate having the full set of us in the House of Light. You see, Mummy and Jenner are getting Orpen Mote now that my Aunt Euterpe is also no longer with us.'

Was Luke imagining it, or was that a glimmer of actual emotion on Silyen's sharp face?

Of course he was imagining it.

There was a knock on the door. That would be the coffee. And Luke knew who 'the girl' was that had been ordered to bring it up. He didn't want Coira in here with this pair. He didn't want Silyen so much as laying eyes on her. Nothing good ever came of catching Silyen Jardine's attention.

But a warning from Crovan stopped him in his tracks when he moved towards the door, so he could only watch as Coira stepped in, bearing a steaming coffee pot.

'Where shall I put it, my lord?' she asked Crovan, keeping her eyes down.

'Why don't you bring it to me?' Silyen said.

So she went over, gaze still firmly fixed on the rich Turkish carpet. She'd have a good view of the lord of Far Carr's dirty boots. Silyen reached out and plucked the cup from the tray.

He held it out expectantly. And Luke knew what he was going to do, dammit. He could see it from the smug way Silyen's mouth twitched up.

As Coira lifted the pot, Silyen lifted the cup. A little higher, and then a little higher again. Eventually she had to look up in order to see where to pour.

Luke's fingers itched to slap Silyen for his jerkish manners, but then he saw where the Equal's gaze was directed and it wasn't – as his eldest brother's would have been – lasciviously on Coira's face. Silyen was studying the golden band at her throat. Unlike the men at Eilean Dòchais, whose shirts and ties mostly hid their collars, Coira's plain black dress left her neck fully exposed.

When Silyen reached out and touched Coira's collar, she gasped and flinched. Luke had to fight to keep himself still. Crovan actually sprang up from his seat at his desk.

'Don't touch her,' he snapped at his guest.

'Oh, I'm sorry,' said Silyen, in his usual not-sorry-at-all way. 'I was just curious. Its effects are confined to this place, aren't they? I remember the Dog didn't have one when he went to Hypatia. You heard he slipped his leash after the business in our ballroom? He's such a bad dog.

'So how did you do it? Was it based on the principles of Gruach's necklace? I used something similar at Kyneston, but without the collar, obviously.' Silyen's eyes drifted back to Luke and lingered. 'Maybe I missed a trick.'

'Coira, leave us,' Crovan ordered.

'Thank you for the excellent coffee,' Silyen said, draining the steaming contents of the cup and placing it back on her tray. 'Just what I needed after that awful helicopter flight. How on earth can people bear to travel like that? So unnatural.'

He gave Coira his most brilliant smile, but she had already ducked her head. As she hurried past, Luke reached out and brushed her arm in a way that he hoped was reassuring.

'Enough. To business.' Crovan's brisk tone might as well have been accompanied by a rolling-up of sleeves. 'This decision by Bouda removes any concerns about one day having to present him in a fit state for re-examination. And the fact that we now know that it was Rix who Silenced him may assist us. Hadley, come and sit down. I don't want to be hauling you off the floor if you collapse.'

Crovan pointed to the armchair that Silyen had vacated. Luke didn't exactly sprint to it.

'What are you doing?'

'Looking for some answers,' said Silyen, shoving his hair carelessly off his face.

A memory stirred, deep in Luke's silted-up brain, and clawed its way to the surface.

The grey dawn before Luke's trial. Silyen curled in an armchair, and his whispered words: *You'll be useful to me, where you're going.*

And another memory. The Equal's breath coiling into Luke's ear in Kyneston's wine cellar: *I have questions. And right now, you're the best chance I've got of finding some answers.*

'Answers to what?' Luke said, trying to keep his voice under control. 'You just said that someone confessed to what happened at Kyneston, some lord who wanted to kill Zelston – or your father. What other answers do you need?'

'Oh, that's just facts, Luke. No one cares about facts. No, Arailt and I are interested in whether the Silence that Rix laid on you at Kyneston can be lifted or broken. The Silence is something of a specialism of my learned friend here. I'm sure you've noticed his fondness for it.' Silyen indicated Crovan, who gave a wolfish smile, before continuing.

'Everything we know tells us that the Silence and the

Quiet can only be lifted by the person who laid them. Half our world is built on secrets concealed by Skill. Just imagine what we'd discover if we could break them open.

'In your case, we now know who did it, and what he was trying to conceal, so we know the parameters we're dealing with. It's perfect test conditions.'

'You don't need me for that,' Luke protested, even as Crovan pushed, hard, in the middle of his chest and sent him down into the chair. 'This castle is full of people its lord has Silenced that you can practise on. Or if you need to know what about, then why not Silence someone's memory of what they had for breakfast, then do your research?'

'And I thought you were a revolutionary concerned about your fellow man, Hadley,' said Crovan. The only thing reflected in his spectacles now was Luke's own panicked face, horribly magnified. 'But here you are, trying to save yourself by offering up someone else. It's just as I said when you first arrived: you and your kind turn on each other without provocation. It's a mark of your inferiority.'

'What do you mean? Why is that me turning on someone else?'

'Because this sort of work breaks brains,' said Silyen Jardine, crouching down to Luke's level. And if Crovan's blank spectacles were disconcerting, Silyen's gaze was even worse. In its dark depths, something flickered like golden fire. 'Now hush – and remember what I promised.'

Silyen laid a finger to his lips, before retreating to an armchair directly opposite. He rested his chin in his hand to watch.

What did he think he'd be seeing?

Luke received his answer when his spine arched against the chair and his head snapped back with the ferocity of Crovan's incursion into his mind. If his thoughts were a tangle of confusion, Crovan's Skill was taking a machete to them, slashing a way through.

Luke whimpered. Crovan had hacked great holes in his memory already. There'd be nothing left of him but tatters by the time this was done. Each downward slice of the man's Skill hurt like a hot knife in Luke's head. But then, Crovan enjoyed pain. He inflicted bodily torture on people for amusement. Why should this be any different?

But it was different. It was worse.

He felt agony in every part of his body, as if all his blood had been drained out and replaced with the acid waters of Loch nan Deur. His fingers jerked uselessly, and in his neck the carotid artery pulsed like a jackhammer. He arched back against the armchair again, racked by spasms, and on his face the trickle of his own tears – sweat? snot? – scalded as it ran down his face.

He hated them. With his last, conscious, coherent thought, he hated them.

You have to – hate them. To beat them, Dog had said.

He'd dismissed Dog as a maniac.

Now he knew the man was right. Half right – because there'd be no beating the Equals.

Luke blacked out.

When he opened his eyes, he couldn't see properly. Momentarily, he was back in the van carrying him away from Millmoor, coming around in the darkness, not knowing where he was. He'd been afraid then, but certain that whatever faced him, he would bear up under it. He couldn't bear up under this, though.

Which was when he realized that the pain wasn't there any more.

Or that it didn't hurt any more – if you could have pain that didn't hurt, which Luke didn't think you could.

He blinked to clear his vision. It sharpened, but all the colour had gone. He was seeing in monochrome. But not black and white – rather, dark and bright.

He was standing in a field of rippling grass that stretched as far as he could see. Beyond, where he couldn't see, he somehow knew there were mountains. Behind, if he looked, would be trees.

He turned – and blinked against what he saw. Two flares of brilliance, almost too bright to bear. One was writhing, lashing like lightning strikes against a high dark wall. The other was a sun, blazing. Luke put his hand up to shield his eyes, which was when he saw that a thread of fire trailed from it, to him.

Astonished, he reached out towards the thread –

tentatively, afraid it might break. He didn't want it to break. It lifted and swayed beneath his touch, fine but strong, like golden spider silk.

When he turned back, someone was standing there: a young man with wild hair. The man's hand rested on the neck of a massive stag, its antlers branching and sharp. Above him, in the sky, an eagle screamed.

Luke shivered. Who was this? He squinted, as if that might make any difference. Was it some dream-version of Silyen – because, ugh, surely he was *not* dreaming about Silyen Jardine?

But no. What Luke had mistaken for messy hair was a nest of twigs and flowers, woven around the man's head like a child's pretend crown. His fingers were dug deep into the scruff of thick fur at the stag's throat, and with his other hand he petted the animal's nose. He was older than Luke had at first thought, and yet it was impossible to put an age on him.

His eyes were golden, like an owl's.

A thrill of terror and joy went through Luke. He wanted to run from this man. He wanted to kneel and pledge his life to him. He wanted to grip him by the shoulder like a comrade, and look him in the eyes.

'Am I dead?' Luke blurted at last. 'Or have I gone mad, and I'm imagining all this?'

'Neither.'

'Where are we?'

'Right here.' The voice was lightly accented and gently amused.

The man released his grip on his beast, and the stag huffed and snorted and trotted a few steps away. Luke saw, behind the pair of them, in the middle of the field, the faintest glowing outline of a door – like when you were little and your parents left the light on outside your bedroom at night.

The man reached towards the door and pulled it open. Luke gasped.

He saw himself, in an armchair, slumped and pale. Sweat plastered his hair to his forehead. Standing to one side of the chair, silhouetted against the window, was Crovan. At Luke's side, the tips of his fingers pressed to Luke's jaw, crouched Silyen Jardine.

'You see,' said the man, nodding towards the door. 'How close we are.'

An eagle dived low and mewed. The man – the king, Luke realized, though he wasn't sure how he knew – held out his wrist and, with a backdraft of wings, the bird came to him.

'Go now,' the king said. And though in that moment it was the last thing he wanted to do, Luke obeyed, and stepped through the door.

He blinked, opened his eyes, and saw Silyen's looking triumphantly back at him. Recoiling, Luke curled into the chair. His head ached and the beat of his own pulse was deafening.

Crovan picked up a piece of paper from the desk and crumpled it angrily, tossing it to one side. 'Unproductive,' he growled.

'Oh,' said Silyen, his face lighting up with one of those too-bright smiles. 'I wouldn't say that.'

19

Abi

Faiers had been as good as his word – yet it still hadn't been enough.

And now Rix was dead and it was all Abi's fault.

Yes, the man had ruined her brother's life and killed Zelston – a Chancellor who, in his own circuitous way, was trying to improve things for the common people.

But it was Abi who had revealed Rix's identity to Jon Faiers. Faiers had taken the information to Bouda Matravers. Bouda had detained and interrogated Rix – and somehow he had ended up dead. Whatever had happened to Rix at the end, that chain of events had begun with Abi. It was a heavy weight to bear.

At least the Equal had confessed before he died, so Abi hadn't traduced an innocent man. But she hadn't exonerated Luke either.

She sat up in the camp bed that Faiers had found for her, and looked around the dingy upper room of the Hackney house. It was full of filing cabinets stuffed with his casework.

The Speaker's son had shown her how the names were redacted, and cross-referenced to records elsewhere, so that no one would be compromised if the files were ever seized. He had taken Abi's phone and jailbroken it. The ease with which he and people like Asif, and Hilda and Tilda, talked about circumventing Security and surveillance made Abi realize how very much she had to learn.

Faiers had been gone for several days now. He had called Abi hastily to explain what had happened with Rix, and she had put him on speakerphone so Midsummer and Renie could hear too. Renie had wrapped Abi in a bearhug, as they heard Rix's confession had not been enough to free Luke.

'But one thing we hoped for has happened,' he continued. 'Heir Bouda was impressed that I brought that information to her. She's taken me on to her staff. Just think how that positions us – right inside the slavetown purge. And I'll be at her side when Jardine appoints her to chair the Justice Council, so we can press on Luke's behalf then too.'

'You really think he'll appoint a woman?' Midsummer had asked. 'And that he won't want to do it himself?'

'From what I've seen, that level of detail bores him. It's the sensation of power he loves, rather than its exercise. And Bouda has quite the fan base. All those slack-jawed provincial lords.'

Faiers called again, a day later, with the news that unrest was kicking off in the Bore.

'Get up there quickly, Midsummer,' he told the Equal. 'There have been arrests. Seven men so far – probably others to come. They'll be brought to London. Abi, there will be people Midsummer needs to get out of the Bore, ones the sweep didn't scoop up. You can help me with this – we'll need to get them to safe houses.'

'Not abroad?' Renie asked. 'Like the Doc did with Oz.'

'And what did Oz do?' Faiers said down the echoey line. 'He came straight back, because there's work to do here. What happened tonight was large-scale, the destruction of crops and infrastructure. Heir Bouda will want to publicize it widely, both the lawlessness and her success in catching perpetrators. She and Chancellor Jardine will use it to justify harsher measures.

'But this could be it. We could be building to something big. If Bodina Matravers succeeds in stirring up Riverhead, and the Bore rises, it could catalyze London. No change will happen without the city.'

Midsummer and Renie had prepared to leave straight away. Abi heard the young Equal on the phone to her mother, confirming what Faiers had just told them. In the kitchen, Renie butted herself against Abi's side.

'This isn't forgetting Luke, you know. 'Cause none of us will. Maybe Jon's right, and he'll be able to persuade Bouda Matravers to pardon Luke. Or maybe we'll have to fight their rotten government all the way to get things changed. But we'll do it. Luke's tough, he'll hold out. And the Doc didn't die for nothin'.'

Abi was too choked to speak as she wrapped her arms around Renie. She was so proud of her brother for inspiring friendship like this. But she wouldn't let any more of Luke's friends endanger themselves for him. Especially not this plucky little kid.

Then the pair of them had left, and Abi was alone in the Hackney house. Could she risk going outside? She wasn't sure, but she wouldn't change anything by hiding in here behind shabby net curtains.

So she followed what Hilda and Tilda had drilled into her, to help fool CCTV cameras: hair, make-up, glasses, hat and scarf, how to hold herself, how to angle her face so she could still look around, but without exposing herself to any facial-recognition algorithm. She hoped that Asif had well and truly distorted her eigenvectors, or whatever, on Security's database.

Then she had walked the streets of London all day long and well into the night. She didn't want to be picked up by Security – her heart was in her throat at every step. But if it turned out that she was an easy arrest, then far better that she be caught alone and out in the streets, so she didn't compromise anyone else.

She had stopped and bought coffee from a little cart, and picked up a copy of the free evening newspaper. 'BORE

BURNS', ran the headline, over a picture of a field of fire. She read the article avidly, but what she saw when she flipped over to page two was even more startling. They'd used a photograph of Jenner to illustrate it. She read the piece twice, then tore out the page and tucked it in her pocket.

At midnight, she had turned back towards Hackney. East London after dark was a place where you needed to be alert. But no one turned eighteen in Manchester without knowing the difference between the sort of streets it was okay to walk down, and those best avoided. She made it back to Faiers' base, and fell into the camp bed, exhausted. She'd even managed a night of unbroken sleep, not disturbed by nightmares of Kyneston or Eilean Dòchais.

And now here she was.

Abi made herself toast and reviewed her options. When Faiers returned, there would be work for her. She ached to be useful. When she was useful, she didn't have time to feel anxious or afraid – or to worry incessantly not only about Luke, but also about Daisy and their parents.

She didn't have time to miss Jenner.

But Faiers wasn't back yet. Which meant there was a different plan for today. She smoothed out the folded sheet of newspaper. At two o'clock, a public memorial for Euterpe Parva was to be held at the former Queen's Chapel. There would be two speakers: the deceased woman's sister and her nephew. These were the new lady and heir of Orpen Mote: Thalia Jardine, and Jenner.

The thought of Jenner's unexpected inheritance made Abi's heart clench painfully. He would be an heir – and one day, a lord. The gulf between them, already unbridgeable in any meaningful way, now gaped impossibly wide. As a Skilless second son, pitied and disregarded by his Equals, Jenner had been halfway to Abi's world.

Not any more. Equal girls who would never have looked twice at him might swallow the shame of an unSkilled husband, and weigh the possibility of unSkilled children, by fixing their eyes on his inheritance. Or perhaps one who loved Jenner simply for who he was might now find prejudiced parents easier to persuade.

Abi hadn't seen Jenner since their parting at Highwithel weeks earlier. She'd always understood their little romance was impossible, even when it was no more than a daydream at Kyneston. When she'd first realized he might feel the same, she had still felt it was hopeless.

And yet she was clinging tight to something equally impossible: justice and freedom for her brother, who had killed a Chancellor. So why not this?

No. She wasn't giving up on Luke. She wasn't giving up on Jenner either.

And she wasn't giving up on a changed and better Britain, in which neither of those two hopes had to feel like a dream.

Besides, joining the crowd of spectators would be useful. The place was sure to be crawling with Security, so it would be one more test of how visible she was.

Yesterday, Abi had roamed London on foot. Today, she tried public transport. Not the Tube – she knew how heavily surveilled the Underground system was – but the city's red buses. They were full of tourists, so her over-the-top scarf and sunglasses didn't stand out.

The holidaymakers were taking photo after photo on their phones as the bus rounded Gorregan Square. Here, the statue of Admiral Nelson stood on a tall column, ringed by great bronze lions. The monument loomed over a group sculpture of the Equal women whose Skill had brought his victory. Then a tourist spotted something, way down Whitehall, and with excited chatter in Chinese the group flocked to the opposite side of the bus. They proceeded to snap away at the coruscating magnificence of the House of Light.

Abi consulted a map and hopped off before the bus was diverted up Haymarket. Ahead, Pall Mall had been closed to traffic but was open to pedestrians. As she walked, Abi studied the classical facades of the gentlemen's clubs that lined it. They were rumoured to be especially popular with debauched younger sons who, with no burden of inheritance or expectation of a political career, need not mind their reputation. The street oozed Equal privilege.

The chapel was at the far end, on a curved carriage

drive. Abi knew its long and varied history, though she had never laid eyes on it before. It had been built for the French wife of the Last King. After the revolution, when the Equals disestablished the Church, it passed into the ownership of parliament. Aristide Jardine had held show trials there, to select victims for the Blood Fairs. When the fairs were eventually abolished, the infamous building instead became a venue for concerts and performances.

And today, a public memorial – for someone who had played no part in public life. What was the purpose of this ceremony? Abi felt like there was something important she was missing.

The crowds were thickening. There must be several thousand people here, all eager for a rare glimpse of the most powerful family in the land. Which was great from a not-getting-caught perspective, but problematic from a not-seeing-a-thing perspective. She wormed her way through to an elevated vantage point, on the steps of the building opposite.

When the motorcade arrived soon after, Abi was on tip-toes to see him. Jenner looked pale and handsome, dressed in a suit that must have cost more than most people earned in a year. His hair had been cut since she saw him last, trimmed very short at the sides. She imagined how it would prickle softly against her fingertips. His claret-red tie glinted gold – that would be a pattern of Parva-Jardine salaman-ders, breathing fire.

He stepped around the Bentley to open the door for Lady Thalia, whose eyes were covered by a tiny net veil. As Jenner put his hand on his mother's back to escort her inside, Abi saw another flash of gold – a signet ring. Only lords, ladies and heirs wore those.

Jenner was no longer the boy, overlooked even by his own family, who had worked late with her in the Estate Office. He'd moved on from giving rent breaks to struggling tenants. She remembered wistfully how they'd grinned as they'd diverted money from Gavar's credit line at the wine merchants, to improving the slave quarters on Kyneston properties.

He was a scion of the Founding Family. This was just what he'd always wanted.

Mother and son went into the chapel, followed by a stream of mourners. All were finely dressed, upright in their bearing and dignified in their grief. Abi recognized many from the Third Debate at Kyneston. Their joint appearance was causing a stir among the spectators, most of whom, Abi realized, would never have laid eyes on an Equal in the flesh before.

The size of the crowd itself was surprising. Euterpe Parva had lived unknown, and Abi had expected there would be few to praise her now she was gone. But Zelston's gory end had caught the public imagination, and now his would-be bride was dead of a broken heart. It was the stuff of stories.

As the service got underway it was relayed from the

chapel through loudspeakers outside. Several women in the crowd were weeping. Others waved red and white roses, some tossing the blooms towards the chapel doors.

Which was when Abi's brain finally connected it all.

Whittam Jardine's return to power had been abrupt: just barely legitimate, thanks to that parliamentary vote, and sealed in violence. He had then promptly suspended the parliamentary observers, the representatives of the commoners. His seizure of Great Britain had been opportunistic, unflinching and complete.

Now, having won the country, he intended to woo it.

'Fancy,' a voice rasped in her ear, 'seeing you here.'

Abi nearly had a heart attack. How had she not realized that a crowd would mean greater Security attention, not less?

But then she saw it wasn't Security.

It was worse.

'Like the – new look,' Dog growled, lifting a lock of Abi's newly short, dyed-dark hair.

His fingernails lightly scraped her neck. She remembered how they had dug into the skin of her ankle as he'd pleaded for help in the kennels. She saw his hands wrapping around the ends of the leash as he strode towards Hypatia Vernay in ruined Kyneston. The man reeked, as if he had been sleeping rough behind bins for days, although he looked clean enough.

She had a million and one questions – how had he got

here? Why was he here? – but there was only one thing she wanted. To get him as far from her as possible. She couldn't help but imagine their combined outlaw status sending alerts flashing on every Security system across the city.

'Go away,' she hissed, praying for those standing nearby to stop sending curious stares their way. 'Please.'

Dog huffed with laughter. 'Don't worry. Made my – own plans.'

He bumped something against her leg and Abi looked down. In his hand was a small sports holdall.

'See you around – Abigail.'

He bared his teeth and began to shoulder his way back through the crowd. Abi's legs went weak with relief, even as her brain started up worrying about that bag and what it contained. Once, she would have reported him immediately to Security. Whatever he intended here, what he'd done in the past was sufficiently heinous that he should be locked away. But it would be the height of madness for her to approach a Security officer herself now.

She fingered the phone in her pocket. Make an anonymous call to the emergency services, then chuck away this phone's card? Calls were recorded, though, weren't they, and maybe voice recognition software would identify her. Even if she ditched the phone, they'd know that she'd been here, in London.

But she had to raise the alert – Dog's presence boded nothing good.

'Excuse me,' she said, turning to the woman on her left, 'could I borrow your phone to make a quick call? It's quite important and my battery's died.'

The woman scowled, clearly unwilling – which was when the doors of the chapel opened and gave her an excuse as she lifted her phone and started filming.

'Sorry, love, using it right now.'

Jenner and Lady Thalia emerged from the chapel, flanked by a few more of the guests. Instead of walking back to the motorcade, the group formed a semicircle in the centre of the barricaded space before the crowd.

When Jenner stepped forward, Abi's stomach flip-flopped. He looked so perfect, and so very, very far away.

'My mother and I,' Jenner said, his voice picked up by a lapel mic and amplified, 'thank you from the bottom of our hearts for the kindness and respect you have shown our family by coming here today.'

Our family, thought Abi, turning the words over unhappily.

'Please know that recent events have been as challenging for us as they have been for you. Chancellor Zelston was a principled man who tried his best for our country. Ultimately, his best was not enough. But he never deserved the terrible fate that awaited him at the hands of a terrorist, a self-proclaimed supporter of commoners' rights.'

My brother, Abi thought, as Jenner's words tore her in two like a sheet of paper. He was talking about Luke.

'And now the tragic loss of my aunt, who lived only for her family and the man she loved. We are your Equals, and our hearts break as yours do.

'There are those who strive to stoke division between us. Who voice unhappiness at the current suspension of the Observers of Parliament. As someone who, by my aunt's sad passing, will now be entering parliament, I can tell you that your Equals already have your best interests at heart. And always have done. At Kyneston, I have personally overseen improvements to servant housing, and have forgiven debts to ease the lives of our tenants.'

Abi wished, then, that she had called Security – not for Dog, but simply because they might have broken up the crowd, aborted this speech. Because Abi wasn't sure she could listen to a minute more of it. Jenner hadn't written a word, she was certain. Perhaps his father had; perhaps even Bouda Matravers. It had her cruel inverted logic. Maybe his mother was using Skill even now to compel him to deliver it.

'He's kind of gorgeous,' Abi heard the woman next to her say to her friend. 'If only he wasn't the same age as my kid. Oh well, I suppose I could always *mother* him.' Her laugh was swollen with innuendo, and Abi hunched wretchedly into her scarf. Weren't they listening to what he was saying?

'You will be hearing more from my family, in the days to come, about how we intend to improve Britain for everyone. This country has lacked strong leadership for a long time. Now, in my father – in all of us – you have people who—'

Which was when something arced over the heads of the gathered spectators and landed, with remarkable accuracy, a few paces in front of Jenner. Abi's eye caught it as it descended. It was about the same size as a football, tatty and discoloured.

Someone at the front of the barrier screamed and there was a backward surge of people, opening a space around where the Equals stood.

It didn't look like a bomb – though Abi knew that these days, a bomb could look like anything: a parcel, a saucepan, or a child's school bag. It was round, and rocked to a still on the cobbles.

Jenner held out his hands, calmingly, just as he did with his horse. A few people were pushing their way backwards, trying to get away. Abi knew she should do the same, not least because Security might cordon off the area and question all those present. But just like everyone else, she wanted to know what was in the bag that Dog – because it had to have been Dog – had thrown.

Jenner crouched down. Those freckle-dusted features grimaced as he came close to the bag, as if it stank. That must have been the source of Dog's terrible smell, not the man himself.

With one hand, Jenner gripped the cloth; with the other,

311

he reached inside. Abi saw him recoil as his fingers found whatever was in there. What he pulled out was a horror.

A severed human head, the brown hair matted with blood. Where the eyes had been were jellied clots. The lips had been neatly sliced away, the head grinning at its own ghastly fate. Thanks to the lapel mic, everyone present heard Jenner's appalled whisper.

'Cousin Ragnarr.'

Security surged forward and swept Jenner, Lady Thalia and the rest of the Equals away to their cars, and Abi turned and pushed through the throng before a cordon went up. She walked as fast as she could while remaining inconspicuous, then jogged up a side street towards Piccadilly, where she lost herself in the crowds.

Abi was trembling, and made herself sit down on the steps of the Eros statue. All around, neon advertising hoardings flashed distractingly, and her thoughts were equally lurid and confused. What had just happened, there at the Queen's Chapel?

Dog had dispatched another Vernay. It was a personal vendetta. But what did it mean that he had launched his grisly trophy at Jenner and his mother? Was it no more than gloating provocation? Or was he now turning his murderous intent towards the Jardines?

And then there was Jenner's speech. That had disturbed her more than she cared to admit. It felt like a riddle she needed to solve, but the answer would be nothing good.

She bought coffee from one of the plaza's stalls, to try and sharpen her thoughts, then walked shakily to a bus stop.

As she turned the key of the Hackney house and pushed at the door, she heard voices. Abi froze halfway. It could be anyone. Had Security tracked her to this address?

But then a familiar voice said '. . . see who it is,' and Faiers' head appeared in the hallway. He beckoned Abi in.

'They've arrived,' he said. 'The first few from the Bore, friends and associates of the ones Bouda rounded up. Twelve prisoners were taken in all, and with what Bouda has planned, these guys are desperate to get their friends back – and cause a bit of trouble along the way. There's also one incredible surprise.'

'I hope it's a good one,' Abi muttered. 'Because you'll never guess what's been going on this morning.'

'The memorial,' Faiers said. 'You were there? Ragnarr Vernay's head? I was just sent a notification via Bouda's office.'

'Never mind the head,' said Abi, grimacing. 'You should have heard the speech.'

She followed Faiers into the sitting room, where half a dozen men sat talking. They were all ages – though really, their ages were unguessable, because what showed in their faces was the strain of harsh outdoor labour. All had rough, sun-darkened complexions, and their faces were deeply scored with lines.

Renie was cross-legged on the floor, leaning like a puppy

against the shin of a man on the sofa, a compactly built black guy whose face bore the pink shine of a burn. His hand rested lightly on her springy hair.

'Abi!' she called, waving with one hand, even as she wrapped the other around the man's calf. The kid looked like she hadn't slept in the days since Abi had seen her last. Her eyes had a raw, rubbed look about them.

'My uncle Wesley,' she explained. 'Ma's brother.'

So it really was good news. Except Abi then had to go and ruin it.

'And your brother Mickey – wasn't he in the Bore, too?'

As Renie turned her face into her uncle's knee, the reason for her swollen, pink eyes became all too apparent.

'Some bloke fell into a slurry tank last year,' said Wesley, petting Renie's hair. 'And Mickey got sent in after him. Neither of them made it out.

'It was devastating not being able to protect my own sister's kid. But now I've been sent another one. Nothing is going to happen to this precious girl. And I'm not gonna let the Equals destroy another family like they did mine – and yours, 'cause Renie's told me all about you, Abi Hadley. We're here to get our friends back. But not just for that. These folks' rule has gotta end.'

'So I guess it's time I told you what we're up against,' said Faiers, entering the room with a teapot. He set it down and folded his arms, like a doctor readying himself to break bad news.

'Heir Bouda and Chancellor Jardine are reviving an ancient tradition. The prisoners from the Bore will be executed at the first Blood Fair to stain this city in two centuries.'

Abi's gorge rose. Jardine was set on twisting the country into his own cruel image. Surely Britain wouldn't stand for it?

Then she remembered the crowd that morning. How people had jostled for a view of the Founding Family, and lapped up the awful speech Jenner had been made to deliver.

The most frightening thing wasn't that Jardine wanted a Blood Fair, she realized. It was that the people might want it, too.

20

Gavar

'Why choose between being either feared or loved?' Father said, turning his lion's smile around the table. 'The perfect authority is both.'

Gavar doubted Father would know what love was if it sent him a box of pink lingerie on Valentine's Day. In fact, he thought, looking round the intimate dining room in the Chancellor's suite at Westminster, they weren't a very lovable lot. Next to Father sat Gavar's ice queen wife, Bouda. Opposite Bouda was Silyen, who had turned up an hour earlier by helicopter, saying he'd just been visiting a friend. It was news to Gavar that Silyen had any friends. Mother had greeted Sil frostily. She was wounded that he had missed Aunty Terpy's memorial, especially given that he'd been with her at Orpen when she died.

Jenner was probably winning in the popularity stakes right now. Mother had spruced him up since his ennoblement, and the whole 'grieving nephew' routine had gone down well – particularly the horrible denouement with

Cousin Ragnarr's head. He sat opposite Gavar, pale and tense, holding himself upright as if practising for his new public role. What was going on in his head, Gavar wondered, thrust into a position beyond his wildest dreams? It was surprising, now that he thought about it, how little he understood either of his brothers.

'We are known as the Founding Family,' Father said. 'Because our ancestors Lycus, Cadmus, Aristide and the rest founded a new Britain. One ruled not by effete and Skilless monarchs, but by the Skilled and strong. However, I believe they made one regrettable error.'

Across the table, Silyen's eyebrows twitched.

'They instituted a parliament and a seven-year Chancellorship – understandably, to signal a break with the degenerate tradition of the kings. However, it denied the country the stability of enduring authority. An authority that it sorely needs in these troubled times, when our relationship with the other great powers of the world is in flux. I intend to change this.'

Father sat back in his chair, that penetrating gaze of his inspecting them one by one to see if his words had sunk in. Gavar knew what he thought he'd heard. He could almost see Father's fingers wrapped around the arms of the Chancellor's Chair, gripping tighter and tighter until they could never be prized off.

Opposite, Jenner looked startled, trying to make sense of it. Silyen was as inscrutable as ever, a smirk just visible behind his tangle of hair. Mother simply nodded; she had given up voicing opposition to Father on anything years ago.

No, the person most electrified by Father's pronouncement was the one person who Gavar thought might have heard it in advance: Bouda. She and Father were thick as thieves these days, cloistered for hours plotting new policy and legislation. At least that's what he presumed they were doing. Were it not for the fact that Bouda had a younger, handsomer version of Father at hand – to wit, Gavar himself – he might have suspected them of carrying on an affair. He wondered if he would care if they were.

Bouda was frowning. 'Are you proposing some kind of Chancellorship in perpetuity?'

'I prefer "of indeterminate term",' said Father. 'But yes. And around me, a First Family: all of you. When the people see us as mere politicians, they fail to respect us. Politicians are accountable, replaceable. They exist to serve the people. This was the error of Zelston's Chancellorship.

'We Equals are not politicians, beholden to the will and mandate of the masses. We are leaders and rulers. Our Skill sets us apart. It is time the commoners remember that – and that we remember it, too.'

Well. Gavar reached for his wine glass. Opposite, Silyen set up a slow handclap. All eyes turned to him.

'Bravo, Father,' Sil said. 'That last bit. I couldn't agree more, albeit we differ on the details.'

318

Gavar eyed his brother narrowly. Something about Silyen felt different tonight, though it was hard to say exactly what. You wouldn't think it possible for Sil to be any more arrogant than he already was, and yet he somehow radiated self-confidence.

Could it be his imminent elevation to the lordship of Far Carr? After which, Gavar realized with chagrin, Silyen would outrank him. His little brother's rise had been breathtakingly swift. And now even Mother and Jenner were getting in on the act, thanks to Aunt Euterpe's death.

Aunt Euterpe's *unexpected* death, when no one had been with her except Silyen.

People couldn't really die of a broken heart, could they?

Those old suspicions Gavar had harboured of Father and Silyen acting in cahoots came roaring back. Surely the pair of them hadn't planned all this? Rix's death in custody could have been Father's handiwork, delivering Far Carr to Silyen. While Aunty Terpy's death could have been Sil reciprocating in kind, clearing a path for the last two members of the 'First Family' to take a seat in the House of Light.

But Silyen had genuinely cared for their aunt – hadn't he?

Bouda interrupted his thoughts. She looked like a dinner guest gagging on an indigestible meal even as she strove to compliment the chef.

'It is an excellent plan. Our prestige has been dealt a

blow by Zelston's inadequacy. In this climate of unrest, it's essential that we reassert ourselves by every means at our disposal.

'And an "indeterminate term" is exactly right. We wouldn't wish to alarm the people – or, more pertinently, our Equals – with notions of a dictatorship, a Chancellor who will never be dislodged.'

Gavar snorted. Bouda was so painfully transparent. Why didn't she just say it? She didn't want Father hogging the Chancellor's Chair, because she had designs to sit on it herself one day.

Well, let the pair of them slug it out. Gavar's interest in the Chancellorship, never strong, was waning by the day. Even the attractions of London were dimming. All he wanted right now was to be back at Kyneston with his daughter.

Except Father had lost none of his proficiency at spoiling Gavar's life at every opportunity.

'I have had Aston House reopened,' he announced. 'It will become the official residence of the First Family. Your mother has been busy these past weeks ensuring that it will be ready for us to move into following tomorrow's ceremony. After the investiture of Thalia, Jenner and Silyen we will drive in convoy from the House of Light – accompanied by a Security escort, flags, that sort of flummery. We will then make a public appearance on the balcony. We must let the people see us.

'Furthermore, word has somehow leaked about Meilyr Tresco being stripped of his Skill. That such a thing is possible makes us look weak, never mind that it can be done by only one man, who is one of us. So by way of a corrective, your mother and I will provide a sufficiently showy demonstration of our ability.'

'Aston House?' Gavar asked. Surely that wasn't the one he thought it was? The vast, pompous building, all columns and windows, that stood at the end of the Mall. In Gavar's lifetime it had lain shuttered and sepulchral.

'You know, darling,' Mother chided him gently. 'The building the Last King gifted to one of his commoner favourites. After the Revolution his descendants remodelled it into that monstrosity, before realizing their mistake and handing it back to the nation to avoid being bankrupted by the running costs. Not a problem when staffed with slaves, of course, though I've had to recruit simply dozens of them.'

'The place has lain empty for decades,' Father said. 'It is the perfect symbol of commoner hubris, and the ideal beginning to our new regime.'

And that, it appeared, was that.

Which was how, a day later, Gavar came to be sitting beside Bouda, waving asininely as the motorcade turned into the Mall and crawled towards Aston House. The family was in four vehicles, three of them open convertibles: Mother and Father in front, followed by Gavar and Bouda, then Jenner and Silyen. The closed car at the back contained Libby, watched over by Daisy. All four vehicles writhed with coruscations of protective Skill, like the world's most expensive paint job.

Ahead rode cavalry in ceremonial uniform, preceded by a marching band, and the Mall was hung with national flags. Their red, white and blue was vivid against the bright sky. At the rate Father was going, the Jardine salamander would soon be worked into the design somewhere.

Gavar had almost hoped that Father's exhibitionism would fall flat, but it was as if half of London had turned out to see them. People stood a dozen deep behind temporary barricades. Security officers patrolled up and down, hands ready on the guns at their hips.

Some in the crowd waved flags, or held banners and signs. An excitable girl jumped up and down at the front of the barriers holding a gaily lettered placard. It read 'Future Mrs Silyen Jardine'. Gavar rolled his eyes. Good luck with that one. Another sign nearly made him choke – it was a photograph of himself and Bouda on their wedding day, cut into a heart shape and decorated all over with ribbons. Was it for real? He nudged Bouda, who looked as startled as he did before leaning across to direct a gracious wave at the person holding it, who emitted a joyful scream.

'Your father was right,' she murmured as she pulled back. 'They love us. How can they? Such sheep.'

But not all of them did. Here and there, towards the back

of the crowd, the occasional scuffle erupted. One man was yelling obscenities as he was dragged away. Gavar saw Kessler, his recruit from Millmoor Security, barking into his comm set as he identified potential troublemakers. The man was good. An utter brute, but good. He was Bouda's creature now. One less thing for Gavar to worry about.

The motorcade pulled up before the gate of the great house. It was a bog-standard wrought-iron affair, underwhelming after the pageantry Mother had woven into everything else.

Until the gate flared gold, fizzing and glittering. As Gavar watched, gilded vines and flowers unfurled, branched and blossomed. The entire structure glowed like liquid fire.

The crowd fell silent, watching the spectacle. The vines curved into two high arches. Across them both, snaking shoots met and twined in an intricate architrave. At its centre swelled a glowing orb, like some monstrous fruit. The orb burst in a spray of embers, revealing the familiar oval monogram of the entwined family initials, P and J. The onlookers ooohed and applauded. Even Gavar was impressed, despite himself. He hoped Libby had been able to see clearly from her car at the back, and hadn't been alarmed.

How would his daughter fit into this 'First Family' of Father's? Gavar suspected he'd have to pick his battles on that.

The glowing gates – perhaps their radiance would remain undimmed, a perpetual reminder of the power of those who lived behind them – swung open and the cars rolled forward. Security held the crowds at bay as the vehicles slowed to a halt before the house's pillared front entrance. Liveried slaves opened the Bentley's doors, and Gavar went immediately to collect his daughter.

'Was she okay with that?' he asked Daisy quietly, as he folded Libby's tiny hand in his and led her to the door. Mother's instructions had been for them to go straight inside and make their way to the balcony.

'She thought it was fireworks,' Daisy said, grinning. 'Your new place is rather grand, isn't it? Kyneston not posh enough for you any more?'

Gavar shot her a pained look. 'Just don't.'

The entrance hall was dominated by a diamond-shaped staircase. It bent outward to a mezzanine gallery, then back to a landing directly above, where tall French doors opened onto the balcony. Gavar scooped Libby into his arms and followed his family.

'Our new house,' he told his daughter, nuzzling her cheek and making her giggle. 'Draughty old dump.' The sea-green dress he had picked out for her was adorable, and he'd had Daisy coax her curls into an approximation of neatness with a matching ribbon. Gavar Jardine: infant stylist. He snorted. Maybe he should develop a second career. It looked as though Father's plans meant he wouldn't be required for the Chancellorship for several more decades. What was he supposed to do with himself his whole life long?

Bouda was waiting for him by the French doors, arms folded.

'You're not bringing her out,' she said in a low voice, as Gavar boosted Libby up against his shoulder.

'Just stop me.'

'Think about it,' Bouda persisted. 'This is about us versus them – showing them that their Equals are their betters. What sort of message will this send?'

'Libby isn't a message, Bouda. She's my daughter. And besides, I thought this was about making them love us. Who doesn't love a little child – except a frigid bitch with a shard of ice where her heart should be?'

He didn't stay to hear her retort. Gavar pushed the doors so hard the glass rattled, and strode onto the balcony. Mother and Father were already there, and Gavar went to his place beside them. Silyen was leaning on the balustrade, chin in his hands, studying the crowds below. Jenner was getting into the whole waving thing.

Libby swiftly got into the waving thing, too. As Gavar kissed her cheek, he felt Bouda step into position on his daughter's other side. A manicured hand wrapped lightly round Libby's back, and Bouda turned her perfect face and perfect smile towards their audience. Whatever she was feeling inside – if she felt anything at all – Bouda always knew what face to present in public. The control of the woman was terrifying.

The cordon had been lifted and, with Security supervision, the people of London were pressing closely around Aston House. As he looked at the sea of faces, Gavar was unpleasantly reminded of the last time he'd stood on a balcony before a massed crowd. It had been in Millmoor late last year, during the riot. A riot fomented, as they'd eventually discovered, by Meilyr Tresco.

Meilyr was part of the problem that Father was trying to solve.

Father was part of the problem that Meilyr had been trying to solve.

Were those really the only two choices?

He remembered the screaming fat woman, and her friend who'd launched the makeshift spear up at the Overseer. He remembered the hardboiled Security guy ordering open fire. The sight of people falling beneath the bullets, and the sickening realization that they still weren't going to stop advancing. He remembered his own voice calling 'No' and his Skill rolling out across the Millmoor square.

He'd done the right thing – everyone had said so. He'd not merely prevented bloodshed, he'd also given the commoners a lesson in knowing their place. That was what the slavetown's Overseer had said. Father, too. Gavar remembered saying something similar to Leah, during their frequent, final arguments – that she should know her place.

He looked at the daughter Leah had left him. Where was Libby's place? Up here among the Equals, or down there with the commoners? In this world of only two choices, his little darling belonged nowhere. He stroked her soft, flushed cheek.

Then thrust her, suddenly, into Bouda's startled arms as something arced towards them. Gavar lifted his hands and his Skill leapt out of him, just as it had in Millmoor. It caught the object on its upward trajectory, lifted it higher, enveloped it and *squeezed*.

The bomb – for that was what it was, Gavar's brain had finally registered – detonated inside a crackling sphere of his Skill. The sound was muffled but still shocking, and a wave of pressure reverberated through the air. Black smoke churned and billowed, held fast within the confines of his power.

Screaming started up in the crowd below, but all Gavar could hear was the shrill, terrified wail of his daughter in Bouda's arms. The bomb had been intended for all of them. It would have caught them unawares, just like the ballroom explosion at Kyneston but far more deadly, their Skillful reflex unable to save them.

Who had done this? His anger swelled and seemed to detonate just as the bomb had, engulfing him in a red-hot ball of rage. Skill burned in his veins and he screwed up his eyes against the pain of it.

When he opened them again, everything was different.

Slower. Magnified. The sounds that reached his ears were distorted. The only vibrant point in this stretched-out world was Gavar himself.

His heart was beating frenziedly. Staring down at the crowd, the sensory overload stabbed his skull. He could see lines at the corners of the eyes of a woman stood hundreds of metres away, powdered make-up clogging the creases. Could see that the hairs in the beard of the man who stood next to her were dark at the root, but orange-tipped.

He hadn't seen the direction the bomb came from. How far could a man throw? He identified the potential origin radius. Let his awareness expand out from it, like a bomb itself.

There.

The man was running now, but there was nothing suspicious about that. Everywhere people were running, and yelling, and calling, the sounds reverberating hollowly in Gavar's new hearing.

This man was different. Gavar saw the sweat on his forehead. Watched as a single bead welled up from a single pore and broke, slicking down his temple. He wore light cotton gloves. On one of them were snagged a few green microfibre strands. The green rucksack they were from had been discarded under a tree a few hundred metres away.

Gavar vaulted the balustrade and dropped from the balcony – an easy fall for an Equal. As his feet hit the ground, Gavar took off after his quarry. The chaos of the crowd

328

didn't touch him. It was as easy as dodging through a gallery of statues.

In the centre of Green Park, in no time at all, Gavar caught up.

He rugby-tackled his target – those years on the Oxford second team hadn't gone to waste – and felt the man's legs break as Gavar's shoulder crunched into him at astonishing speed. The bones shattered in four – six – nine places as he wrapped his arms around both knees. Once the man was down, Gavar punched him once, as gently as he could, because a man with his skull staved in would tell no tales. He heard the brain strike the inside of the man's skull, then ricochet – the coup and countercoup – and twist in its casing.

Then Gavar passed out.

He woke into a drab world. He wondered if he had torn something in his optic nerve, or somehow developed cataracts while he slept. The voices that swirled around him, on the contrary, were too fast, too high and twittering.

He wiped both hands down his face and groaned. He was in a bed, propped up on a stack of pillows.

'Libby,' he said, remembering the blast. The shimmering shell of his Skill containing the explosion before it could hurt his child – and everyone else.

'Absolutely fine and waiting for her daddy to wake up from his nap,' said a firm, small voice. 'She couldn't believe Daddy ran so fast, so of course he had to have a lie-down.'

Gavar focused. Daisy. The commoner kid was standing in the corner of the room. She gave him a massive smile, as if someone had handed her the best present ever.

That would be himself, in one piece, Gavar realized with astonishment.

'Darling,' his mother said, from right next to him. 'You were so brave. The television won't stop replaying it. You're London's hero.'

'And your Skill,' said another voice. 'I never knew you could do that.'

Gavar blinked with surprise. Bouda. The ice queen sat there beside his bed, pale and perfect, and Gavar saw something in her eyes he'd never seen there before – admiration.

'Neither did I,' he told his wife. 'I guess I'd never needed to, before.'

Already it was fading, his memory of that too-vivid world in which he had seen every vein on every leaf and heard the wind ruffling the down of ducklings on the lake. Had he really sensed those things? It must have been adrenaline.

But it wasn't, of course. It was Skill. Somehow he had surged far beyond the limits of what his body could ordinarily achieve. It had been spontaneous, involuntary.

Could he do it again? Deliberately?

Bouda was talking. He strained to pay attention.

'The man you captured. I had him taken to Westminster straight away for Astrid Halfdan to question. She didn't need long. He was paid by someone acting on behalf of the

Twelve Bore – that's what they're calling them, the twelve men I arrested in Lincolnshire a few days ago.

'I think it must have been them behind your Cousin Ragnarr, too. The timing makes sense: Ragnarr as a kind of curtain-raiser, then this. A literal decapitation, followed by a symbolic one. You did very well to catch him, Gavar.'

And astonishingly, Bouda leaned over and kissed him on the cheek. Not only that, she whispered in his ear.

'Your Skill. Something happened to me, too. In the Bore.'

She pulled back, squeezing his wrist in a way that was not exactly affectionate, but constituted more voluntary physical contact than she had shown at any point since their wedding.

'Get some sleep,' Mother murmured, petting his hand. 'My brave boy.'

Gavar's eyes were closing already.

When he woke for a second time, the light was almost gone. He shook his head to clear it – he felt back to normal again – and only then noticed that there was another visitor at his bedside.

Silyen was folded up in the armchair, hugging his knees to his chest and watching his brother over the top of them. The pose made him seem even younger than his eighteen years. It was hard to believe that only that morning Gavar had sat in the House of Light watching as Sil was installed as lord of Far Carr.

His little brother was as dishevelled as usual. There were even twigs in his hair, as if he had reached Aston House not by motorcade, but by crawling through a hedge.

Gavar peered closer. No, it wasn't simply a messy tangle, was it? The twigs had been woven together into a circlet. It almost, Gavar thought, resembled a crown.

He felt a sudden urge to slap some sense into his little brother, because this was lunacy. Crowns were forbidden, obscurely shameful icons. Emblematic of a time when commoners, not Equals, had ruled. During Aristide Jardine's Harrowing of the Princes, the blood-drunk people of London had rampaged through their city smashing the heads off statues of bygone monarchs. Royal portraits had been slashed, and even the signs of pubs unlucky enough to be named The Crown, The King's Head or The Queen's Arms had been pulled down and burned in the street.

But as he leaned forward to snatch the idiotic twig-crown, Sil's eyes flicked up to stare right into his, and it was all Gavar could do not to cry out.

In Silyen's dark, dark eyes, so like Mother's, the pupils burned like a hot drop of gold.

Then he blinked, and the gold dimmed to black.

'You were incredible earlier,' Sil said. 'I was so proud of you. How did it feel? Amazing – am I right?'

Gavar stared at him. There was no denying it.

'You're right.'

'I knew it. It's how we are, how we truly are. This is only the beginning. You'll see.'

Silyen smiled up into Gavar's face. His expression was radiant.

Despite the blankets that still covered him, Gavar's skin prickled cold at the sight.

21

Luke

'Luke?'

That was his name, wasn't it? Or it had been. He wasn't sure. He swayed unsteadily and gripped the edge of the door for support. The sun fell on his face but the breeze was cool.

'Luke!'

A hand seized his and tried to tug him away from the open doorway. He took a reluctant, stumbling step back.

'Let go of me.'

He shook himself free from her grasp. Her. The name swam up in his memory. Coira. The girl from the kitchen.

'What are you doing? This is the third night I've found you down here with the Last Door open.'

Her hands came up to his face and turned it from side to side, like he was a dropped pot being checked over for damage. Then she snapped her fingers right by his ear and Luke startled. It sounded like a gun going off.

A gun. He remembered Jackson here, in this place. And

Angel, too. And Abi. The girls had been outside, though. But Jackson had been in here. Then the gun had gone off, and Luke and Coira had put him through the door.

This door. He turned back to it. But Coira grabbed his hand again and pulled him round to face her.

'What's out there that's so fascinating? It's just the loch, in the middle of the night. Hardly even any stars, it's so cloudy.'

What was she talking about? Couldn't she see what Luke saw? A golden world. Fields of rippling grass. A forest. Mountains.

And somewhere – he had been straining for a glimpse of them – an eagle. A stag. And a king.

Luke swayed on his feet. He looked back over his shoulder. The sun was just lifting above the tufted treetops. As a breeze stirred, the leaves flashed and glittered like a dragon's heap of gold.

'He's there,' Luke said. 'I know he is.'

'Who's where?' Coira said angrily. 'Luke, snap out of this. You've not been right since Silyen Jardine came. What did he and Crovan do to you? I heard you scream, just after I took the coffee pot away, and I went straight back, but Devin wouldn't let me in, even when I kicked him.'

A high-pitched shriek came from out over the woods. Luke saw a spinning ball of wings: two hawks fighting, their talons locked together. The sun was high and the golden light was mesmerizing. If he stepped just a little closer, it would warm him.

'Luke, for pity's sake.' Coira grabbed the back of his shirt and pulled him away. 'We can't do this every night. I'll get a letter to Silyen Jardine somehow. Hide it in the supply boat. Whatever he did to you, he can come back and undo it.'

'I said, leave me alone.' Luke shook her off again, more brusquely than before.

Coira glared at him. Why was she so angry about this?

'Fine. It's not like I can stake out the entrance hall every night waiting for you. This is the Last Door. You know what it does. I was the one who told you, the day you arrived. You've even seen it at work. It kills, Luke.'

Coira's angular, pale face was flushed. She grabbed the door and swung it wider in invitation.

'But be my guest. Go on.'

She had quite the temper. Luke found her fierceness captivating.

But not as captivating as what lay through the door. His gaze slid from her face to the landscape beyond, and she realized he was going to do it just a moment too late to stop him.

'No,' she gasped, reaching out even as he pushed past her over the threshold.

Everything went dark, and the fuzziness in Luke's brain lifted for what must be a final, fractional clarity before he died. What had he been thinking? He knew that the Last Door killed. He'd seen it happen. What did he imagine was through here? There was no golden landscape. No forest. No eagle or stag. Only chilling cold and utter darkness. Was he dead already, and this sensation of a body some last trick of departing consciousness?

He looked at Coira, standing in the doorway, distraught. He should be crumpled on the threshold by now, just as he'd seen happen to the woman who'd confessed to sabotage. They said that your life flashed before your eyes as you died. Abi had once told him that was all nonsense, from a scientific point of view, but here he was, still thinking. Not yet a lifeless huddle. Was this all taking place in one drawn-out millisecond?

'Luke?'

It was Coira speaking, wonderingly. And could people talk to you in your near death experience – or actual death experience, or whatever this was?

'Luke, say something. Are you okay?'

He stared at her as she scrubbed at her face with the back of her hand. Was she crying? She couldn't take her eyes off him. He didn't want to take his eyes off her, but he darted a look back over his shoulder.

And saw not the golden woodland he had seen when he stood inside the castle, but instead, Loch nan Deur at night. Beyond it, the heather heathland sloped up to the helicopter pad. The water glinted darkly. When he lifted his face he saw that the darkness he had mistaken for death wasn't dark at all. It was the night sky, full of cloud. A sliver of moon jutted over the battlements.

'I'm here. I mean, I'm outside the castle. And it's night-time.'

'And you're alive!'

She actually started to laugh, a disbelieving, giddy laugh. It was infectious. Luke laid a hand on the wall and sagged against it. He wasn't in that golden world. Neither was he dead. He was standing outside Eilean Dòchais and it was dark and cold because it was the middle of the night. And he had just walked through the Last Door, which supposedly killed people, and yet he was very much un-killed. Luke was bent over, laughing hysterically.

He laughed until it hurt, with sheer relief.

He flopped to the ground, and although the cold of the rock seeped through his trousers, it was blissful to be out in the fresh air. He hadn't gone beyond the castle walls since he'd arrived, over a month ago. The others had been cooped up much longer – years, some of them.

Coira had been in there for all that she could remember of her life.

'Aren't you going to come out?' he asked her.

'Can I? Should I?'

'I just did.'

'But maybe there's something special about you.'

He grinned. 'I really don't think so.'

'Well, Crovan and Silyen Jardine might beg to differ.'

'So is it a lie, that this door kills?'

But he knew it couldn't be that. He had seen the woman step through it and drop dead right on the threshold. Jules had told him that others of the Condemned had done the same – and Coira must have seen them, too. On the day he arrived, even Crovan had confirmed it. *It takes your life, as all things that kill do*, he had told Luke.

So what had happened here tonight?

He calmed, and looked up at Coira, and saw the same question in her eyes. Was this to do with the door, or with him?

'You should go to the boat dock,' she said. 'Tomorrow's a delivery day. You can wait. Hide. From what you've told me of your Millmoor adventures, you'll have no problem concealing yourself on board.'

'I thought you said someone already tried that, and the boat stopped moving – couldn't make it to the shore?'

'That's true. But no one's ever walked through the Last Door and lived before. So there's something different about you, or about your collar. It must be worth a try.'

'It is.' Luke hesitated. 'But what about you?'

They looked at each other. Him outside in darkness; her inside, dimly lit by the light from the entryway's wall sconces.

'I'm not leaving you behind,' he said with finality. 'That's not what we did in the Club. It's not what I do.'

Should he urge her to walk through the Last Door and join him? Could they take that risk? What if she was right, and this really was due to something special about him.

He thought back to his time in the golden land, his meeting with the king. Those two churning, fiery lights. His thoughts had been too confused, the whole time he'd been in the castle, to fully remember or analyze what he'd seen. But out here his mind was as clear as the night sky. Memories joined up like stars mapped into constellations, and told a story.

Those fiery forms had been the two Equals. The one lashing savagely against the high wall: that had been Crovan, trying to break down the Silence laid on Luke. The other, the bright one: that must have been Silyen. Connected to him by a fine, golden thread.

What did it mean? Luke felt around his midriff, as if he'd find the end of the thread still anchored there, to tug on. There was nothing, of course. But as his hands touched the spot, he remembered.

Silyen at the gate, when Luke had first arrived at Kyneston in the van from Millmoor. That sensation of being disassembled, like one of Dad's engines. The feeling he'd had of a part being removed – or added.

Silyen at the gate a second time, when Luke became Crovan's property. The boy's glowing eyes as he broke Luke's binding to Kyneston. His whispered question: *You feel it?* The skin-crawling sensation that the broken estate bond was nothing compared to the bond that still connected him to the Young Master.

Was that it? Was Silyen protecting him – even watching over him, somehow? Yet Silyen had sat there as Crovan tore into Luke's brain. He had let him be Condemned, when he claimed to know who had used him to kill Zelston. That was hardly the behaviour of a protector.

'I think it's to do with Silyen,' he said eventually. 'But I've no idea what, or why. Don't come through. I don't want you to risk it.'

'You need to get away,' said Coira. 'The boat dock is easy to find – it's on the other side of the island. The boat is kept on the far shore of the loch; when they sail over, they unlock the outer door and unload. We're not allowed to open the inner door and take everything in until the boat has gone again. They take the castle waste, everything we can't burn, which is how we smuggled Rhys out last year.

'Like I told you, the boat stopped before it got all the way over. After they circled the loch endlessly trying to reach the shore, Rhys gave himself up. They brought him back and Crovan punished him, but he's still in one piece. For you, I think it's a risk worth taking. Maybe whatever Silyen did to you that means you can walk out of the Last Door also means the boat won't be held back.'

'But I'd be leaving you.' Luke hovered on the threshold. His fingers went to the collar at his throat, so tight and smooth it was almost like his own flesh. What he wouldn't give to be free of it. 'And the others. Some of them desperately need to get away as well: Rhys, Julian, the woman that brute goes after. Even Lavinia. What she did was criminal, but she doesn't deserve to be left here, terrorized by Blake.'

Which was when Luke saw Crovan stride up behind Coira and grab her hair.

'What is this?' the lord of Eilean Dòchais barked. He looked out of the door and saw Luke. 'Hadley. How?'

'Luke,' Coira called. 'Go! Get away!'

But where could he go? How could he get away? The boat was still on the other side of the loch, and he had no way of getting to it across the waters of Loch nan Deur.

'What have you done?' Crovan demanded, and when Coira didn't reply he backhanded her, and she reeled with the force of his blow.

Instinct took over, and Luke rushed to her – only to slam against an open doorway that was somehow as closed to him as if the door was shut. He could see them, he could hear them, he simply couldn't cross over to them.

Crovan spared him a glance.

'Fool. It only goes one way.'

Only goes one way. Crovan had told him that when he first arrived here. Both doors did. You went in the Door of Hours, and out of the Last Door. What else? What else had Crovan said? Something important.

Coira stood there, panting, glaring at their master. Her pale grey eyes flashed contempt. Crovan stared owlishly back, his eyes naked without his glasses. He had obviously risen from his bed to come and confront them, because he wore a belted dressing gown thrown over his trousers. His immaculate hair stuck up in places.

Luke was just about to hurry back through the Door of Hours to put himself between them, because the expression on Crovan's face boded nothing good, when he saw it.

He thought at first that he was mistaken. Or imagining it. But looking at the pair of them facing each other, he wondered only that he'd never seen it before.

It was the eyes, he realized. He had never seen Crovan's eyes unshielded by his creepy glasses.

They were the same cool grey as Coira's.

You wouldn't make the connection without a prior clue. Their hair colour was different; her face more angular. But with the knowledge he now had, Luke could see resemblances between Coira and this man – who must surely be her father.

Luke almost blurted out his discovery, to throw it in Crovan's face, this secret the man had concealed so that not even his own child knew it. But then his thoughts were racing ahead. Out here, in the crisp air, his brain felt preternaturally acute.

He remembered Jackson standing in this entryway, saying how the Crovans had been hostage-keepers, how someone who entered *could only leave with the say-so of the lord or heir.*

Coira's angry words to him, just minutes ago: *Be my guest. Go on.*

She was a Crovan. And she had given him permission to leave.

Who had Coira's mother been? Some commoner slave? One of the Condemned? Luke couldn't imagine any good scenario. Perhaps rape had been part of it. Perhaps murder.

But one thing was clear – if Crovan knew that he knew, Luke would never be let near the door again. He'd be locked up, and perhaps Coira would be, too. Whereas if he could just keep this knowledge from Crovan, they'd be able to try again another night, together. As a child of the castle, Coira must be able to leave by the same door she allowed others to pass through. Perhaps the boat might respond to her, too.

They wouldn't have time to co-ordinate it for tomorrow. But in a week, they could be on the boat, across the loch – and, just maybe, away to freedom. Coira could give them all permission to leave, all the Condemned. As the supply boat approached the castle, they could make a break through the door and be waiting for it, ready to overpower the crew and turn the vessel straight back round again.

'Hadley,' Crovan said, narrowing his eyes at Luke. 'Astonishingly, activity seems to be occurring in that brain of yours.'

'I've worked it out,' Luke announced. 'I've worked out how it happened, because I'm not supposed to be able to get out of this door, am I? I should be a very dead doornail right now. Well, you didn't think that someone would help me do it, did you?'

'And who would that be?'

'Silyen Jardine, of course. He's interested in what happens to me, I can tell. I had this sense, when he was here, that he wanted to help me. And I was right. He does. She tried to stop me, but I knew it would be fine. And it was.'

'Is this correct?'

Crovan turned to Coira, who scowled up at him.

'Of course I tried to stop him. It kills people; I know that, he knows that. But he wouldn't listen.'

'So you told him to go ahead and do it anyway?'

Luke had to prevent his fist clenching in triumph. Crovan was working through the same scenario. His theory had to be correct.

Coira nodded, sullenly.

'Such a good friend you are,' Crovan sneered. 'Well, yes, it seems that Silyen's meddling may have produced a surprise for all of us. But it won't be anything I can't take care of. Now come back inside, Hadley. There's nothing for you out there beyond a nice breath of fresh air – presuming that Bodina Matravers hasn't come back for you in my boat. But I didn't get the impression she'll be doing that, did you? No one will be coming for you, Luke.'

Crovan curled his fingers almost disdainfully, and Luke felt a warmth in the collar around his neck. He'd been foolish to celebrate prematurely, he realized. The man could still do anything he wanted to him. And while he had misdirected Crovan for now, he still had no reliable way off this island.

Luke's heart raced as he realized the Equal might take any memory of this night from him before he'd even had a chance to tell Coira. And there was no use shouting it out to her here and now – Crovan would simply take the knowledge from her, too.

'You don't need to make me,' he said. 'I'm coming.'

He moved towards the Door of Hours. As soon as he was out of their sight line he crouched and hunted around on the ground. It took a moment to find a shard sharp enough for his purposes. He dug it into the flesh of his palm and bit his tongue as he carved as deep as he could bear. There was no time for more than the two cuts, and he winced as he dragged the sharp stone tip through his skin.

'Hadley?'

Crovan's voice was imperious.

'The door handle,' Luke shot back, quickly licking his palm clean of blood. 'Can't see . . . ah, I remember, there isn't one.'

He pushed on the Door of Hours and it swung inward. Crovan stood there, smiling beneath his thin moustache.

'Welcome back,' he said.

Luke stepped inside and a sensation like drunkenness

came over him, clouding his brain. The castle's insidious influence.

Not entirely, though. He felt slow. Groggy. But the contours of what he'd learned were still there. Crovan. Coira. He looked between the two of them, trying to fix it in his mind. He flexed his left hand, and the pain in his palm reassured him that he had marked himself with the truth.

'Well, I'd better take care of what Silyen did to let you out of the door,' Crovan said, advancing. 'I can't have you slipping out again.'

Which didn't make sense. Silyen had done nothing about the door. Crovan knew that.

But he thought that was what Luke believed.

Then the first strike hit him and Luke's body became a lightning rod for pain. He howled as it sent him to the ground.

It was fake, he realized. Not the pain, but its purpose. Crovan would make him suffer, so Luke would believe he was burning away some gift from Silyen Jardine that had helped him open the door. But it was all a sham.

Luke was chilled by his own insight. He was thinking like them now. Would it help? Dare he dream that he could outsmart them? He'd have to hope so, because he couldn't out-anything-else them, that was for sure.

The second jolt of pain was so excruciating his brain nearly shorted. He jackknifed involuntarily onto his side, then rolled to lie face down so he felt less vulnerable.

Luke rested his forehead against the flagstones of the entryway, trying to control his breathing and his runaway heart. He let his eyes drift out of focus as he took in the meandering fissures of the slate. Jackson had lain more or less here, his skull blown away, his blood and brains leaking out.

There aren't any winners in our game, he remembered the Doc saying, a lifetime ago, as they'd talked in the Millmoor back office. *Not till it all ends.*

Please let it end soon. Please.

Tears ran down Luke's face: for Jackson and for Angel. For Coira, whose father was a man who had held her captive her entire life, but who didn't know it yet. For his sisters and parents, wherever they were (and please let that be somewhere safe).

For himself.

The third strike made him scream, and a shameful hot wetness bloomed beneath him. Not even Kessler and his tasers had managed that.

'That should do it,' said Crovan gloatingly, coming to stand over him.

The tassel of Crovan's dressing gown cord brushed against Luke's face, and to his sensitized nerves, it burned. Luke wished he'd kept the sharp stone so he could have jammed it into the man's ankle, maybe found a juicy vein that would drain him out like a pulled bath plug, faster than his Equal body could repair itself.

'Whatever Silyen did to you, it won't work again. So stay away from that door, Hadley. Death is a high price to pay for a breath of fresh air.'

The Equal crouched down and grabbed Luke's collar, hauling his head up. His other hand he splayed barely an inch from Luke's face, those fingers poised to plunge into eye sockets or pinch shut mouth and nostrils. He turned his head this way and that, assessing, like a hawk inspecting some furry scrap between its claws.

'I'll leave you with the memory of this evening so you can learn your lesson. As your canine friend used to complain: I let you keep the bad ones.'

Crovan pulled back, letting Luke drop to the floor.

'Get him cleaned up,' the Equal told Coira, as he stepped disdainfully over Luke's slumped form. 'Then get to bed. I'll have no more of these night-time disturbances. The next time he tries to leave, he dies – and I know you wouldn't want that. Caring for someone doesn't mean you can save them, girl. It just means it hurts more when they don't save themselves.'

With a billow of his dressing gown, the lord of Eilean Dòchais was gone.

Luke lay there, boneless and spent. He didn't protest as Coira rolled him over gently and helped him sit up, even though it revealed his soaked trousers. He hung his head, mortified at the reek of urine.

But also exultant. He had deceived Crovan, and he still

had the terrible knowledge safe in his head. It was knowledge that they could do something with, together, though he wasn't sure what.

Coira had turned his hand over and was inspecting his palm.

'Your nails must have done this,' she said wonderingly, her fingertips lightly tracing the bloody crescents there. 'You clenched your fists so hard you cut yourself.'

Luke looked down at what he had gouged: C C

Coira Crovan.

He closed his palm around her fingers, held them there a moment. He could feel her pulse beat softly against his wounds.

'No,' he said. 'There's something I need to tell you.'

22

Abi

'Jardine's good,' said Jon Faiers, looking around the room of the Dalston safe house where they were all gathered. 'The Aston House bomb that's been pinned on Twelve Bore sympathizers – that is, us. It was his idea.'

'Why would you put your family at risk like that?' asked Renie's uncle Wesley.

'There never was any risk,' Abi said, immediately grasping what Jon was saying. 'He knew it was coming and would have destroyed it. It's just that Gavar reacted first, right?'

'But why make yourself look unpopular?' Renie piped up, from where she was curled on the arm of the sofa at her uncle's side.

'They made themselves look strong,' Abi said, unwillingly awestruck by Jardine's cunning. 'Seriously. Gavar caught a bomb mid-air, blew it up harmlessly, then jumped off a balcony and sprinted superhumanly fast into a crowd of thousands and took down the person who did it. Even I was impressed, and I know he's actually an alcoholic, misogynistic jerk. How on earth did you find that out, Jon?'

Faiers grimaced.

'Heir Bouda's interrogation team is headed by a terrifying woman named Astrid Halfdan. Seems that the first person they picked up – the one Gavar caught – told her he'd been paid to do it by a man who identified himself as a Twelve Bore sympathizer. Which seems an unnecessary detail to mention. They pulled that man in, too, at which point Jardine turns up in the office and shuts down the inquiry by revealing it was all his handiwork. No one was ever meant to catch the first guy and investigate.

'Heir Bouda wasn't pleased. They had a row about it, in fact. Seems he'd told the family in advance that there would be a "demonstration of Skill", but she and Gavar had presumed that meant the stunt with the gate.'

Wes puffed his cheeks and exhaled – an expression of disbelief that Abi had learned to recognize over the past two days. She had come to like this guy and his comrades. Tough, matter-of-fact men who had seen one too many unnecessary accidents and avoidable fatalities. Men who had learned the hard way how little care the Equals had for their slaves.

The stories they'd shared with Abi had appalled her. It was strange, now she thought about it, how reticent those who had completed their slavedays were to speak of the experience.

Was that because those years were too depressing, or even too traumatic, to recall? Was it out of a desire to shield those who had yet to do their days from the knowledge of how bad it was? Or simply because that decade of your life was inevitable, and so not worth complaining about? 'Mustn't grumble,' Nan would say, whenever something rubbish happened, like a week of rain on her one annual holiday. Had she thought the same about her slavedays?

Was that what kept everyone quiet?

Or was it fear?

Fear of the Equals and their mysterious Skill. Fear of their enforcers, Security. In the everyday world, Security were just regular police, keeping the peace. But in the worktowns, she'd heard from Renie and others, they acted as though they were the lords and masters. And perhaps fear of them persisted long after your days were done, meaning no one dared complain too loudly.

Abi remembered the Millmoor brute who had come to take Luke away: his bull neck and bristling hair. In the worktown he had beaten Luke so hard his ribs broke, Renie had told her. Jon said he worked for Bouda Matravers now. Abi hadn't forgotten either his face or his name. It had been written on a strip across his chest: Kessler.

Was that what happened when the powerless were given power?

But no. Kessler aside, she wasn't going to start blaming commoners who turned on their own kind. It was the

Equals that were responsible. In the twenty-first century, they perpetuated a system created centuries earlier – when a man might think a decade's service to his lord a fair exchange for food and a roof over his head. The slavedays should have been swept away long ago.

So how to make people understand that it didn't have to be this way? How to show them that it was possible to stand up to the Equals? Millmoor's uprising had been a start. So had the burning of the Bore. Dina's planned shutdown of Riverhead was taking shape. The North was aflame with anger.

But London was different. The scruffiness of East London notwithstanding, this city was rich. Money the Equal families made from their factories in the slavetowns poured into this place. Tourists from around the world came to gawp at London's history and culture, and buy its slave-made luxury goods. Abi had seen them in their thousands on the day she'd gone to the Queen's Chapel.

This city maintained the facade that Britain was a civilized modern nation, when really it was barely one step up from feudalism.

'We need to talk about what else we're doing,' she said. 'Yes, we have to rescue those who were captured. That's what you're all here for. But the Bore burned in the first place as a protest. A message to our masters that conditions are atrocious and unjust.

'We have to keep sending that message. My brother was

Condemned. Meilyr Tresco was punished in the worst way imaginable. Dina Matravers and the Club members took a terrible risk to get out of Millmoor. And for what? Millmoor is practically back to business as usual; the Bore soon will be too. Whatever fire you started in the fields up there, we've got to keep it burning.'

They had all been talking among themselves before she spoke up, but the room fell gradually quiet.

'Go on,' Wes prompted. 'I don't think there's anyone here who disagrees with you.'

He looked around the room at his fellow fugitives from the Bore. They all shook their heads.

Abi drew a breath. There was no going back now. Would they understand where she wanted to lead them?

'There's no free internet and social media in this country. So there's no easy way to reach lots of people – except through something so big it can't be dismissed or ignored. And you *can't* ignore what happens in London. The bomb and the business with Heir Ragnarr's head proved that.'

'Makes me think of what you said earlier.' Renie looked up from where she perched on the sofa arm next to her uncle. Her jaw was remorselessly working some gum. 'About keeping the fires burning.'

Abi should have known she'd get it straight away. Renie Delaney had a talent for trouble.

'What're you saying, child?' Wesley elbowed his niece as

she squirmed away. 'You gittin' ideas from those old nursery rhymes?'

And he began to sing softly, *'London's burning, London's burning. Fetch the engine, fetch the engine. Fire, fire! Fire, fire!'*

Renie's wriggling ceased. She was transfixed by her uncle's voice.

'Used to sing you that when you was little,' he told her. 'My baby sister's baby girl. You were cute as a button in your frilly pink cot. Your da would lullaby you, too, with soppy old Irish ballads. But he didn't have no beautiful voice like mine.' He threw his head back and laughed.

Watching Renie's pinched face soften, Abi felt a surge of outrage. This hardbitten kid had been sent to somewhere far worse than an orphanage, after her whole family was rounded up when she was only eight years old. She had brothers, parents and a family that loved her, but they'd been split up. The same slavedays system had stolen away Abi's own siblings, and packed off her mum and dad to Millmoor.

No. It was time to stop talking about the 'slavedays system' as if it were an abstract thing. Time to stop thinking of it as some historical hangover – a bad idea dreamed up centuries ago, that Britain was regrettably still stuck with.

It was a group of people, right now, making a choice every single day, to let all this continue.

The Equals had done this. As directly as if Bouda Matravers had pushed Renie's brother into the slurry tank, or Thalia Jardine had personally chauffeured Luke up to Crovan's castle.

'They couldn't ignore London burning,' Abi said.

She felt her words electrify the room. These men had burned the fields they were enslaved in. Would they dare to burn the capital city?

Because she would, Abi realized.

When they'd gathered shell-shocked and despairing at Highwithel, in the aftermath of Meilyr's death, Abi hadn't been ready to join Dina Matravers' political crusade.

But she'd changed. Ragnarr's head and Whittam Jardine's bomb, Faiers and Midsummer, Wesley and the Bore had all seen to that.

'No, they couldn't ignore London burning,' agreed Wesley.

'They *won't* ignore it,' said Renie, as she flashed Abi a grin. 'When we do it.'

'Is this the point I should excuse myself?' said Jon Faiers. 'Only I do now work with Heir Bouda.'

He always called her that, Abi noticed, with annoyance. Deferential habits died hard. There was a practical reason, too, she supposed. It wouldn't do for him to omit the honorific when at Westminster, in the corridors of the House of Light.

'You think she suspects anything?' Wes asked urgently.

'I think I'd have a hot date with Astrid Halfdan in her

soundproof basement room if she did,' replied Jon. 'But still, I wonder if it's worth the risk – to all of you, I mean.'

'They can't find things out that easily, surely,' Abi said. 'It's not like watching a movie of everything that's ever happened to you, is it? I mean, look at when they were examining my brother, trying to discover what had happened at the Debate Ball. Obviously he'd been Silenced, but they didn't see further back – they never saw Bodina's involvement in Millmoor, did they? Even now, no one knows about Dina, apart from Crovan. And he has his own reasons for not telling.'

'I wonder how much longer it will stay like that,' said a new voice from the doorway. A new voice, but a familiar one.

The woman liked these kind of entrances, Abi decided, smiling despite herself as Midsummer Zelston came into the room. Renie launched herself at the Equal, and as they hugged Midsummer waved over the girl's head to Wesley and the other men of the Bore.

'Dina's plans are coming together,' the Equal announced. 'Any day now Riverhead's going to grind to a halt. The whole place.'

'All of it?'

Jon sounded impressed. Abi was, too.

Riverhead was the most northerly English slavetown and it specialized in shipbuilding. Vessels were welded together in the shipyards of Riverhead then floated down the Tyne.

These ranged from workaday ferries, to the gleaming cruise ships in which Confederate Americans visited their country's territories in the Caribbean (which the Union States forbade their own citizens from visiting). The idea that it might simply stop was almost unthinkable.

'From what I overheard back there just now,' Midsummer said, jerking her head to indicate the hallway, 'it sounded like you have some plans of your own. Incendiary plans. So what's the idea? Because we know Jardine's got this Blood Fair lined up for the first of May, just over a week's time. So we've got until then to rescue our lads in custody. And I reckon a shutdown in Riverhead, trouble here in London, and a breakout of prisoners will set off unrest in the Bore all over again. It could be just what we need to tip things over.'

'All this "Blood Fair" business,' one of the men said, speaking up. 'What is it exactly? I mean, the name ain't exactly promising, but what do they do? It's execution, right? Jardine's bringing back the death penalty. Like hanging?'

'There's not much blood at a hanging,' said Jon Faiers grimly.

'It's state-sponsored torture in the name of public entertainment, is what it is,' said Midsummer, a ferocious, disgusted look on her face. 'The sort of thing that's been outlawed by international statute across half the globe.'

359

'Yeah, yeah,' the man said. 'But what do they actually *do*?'

Faiers heaved a sigh, as if reluctant to talk about it. Abi soon realized why.

'There's a painting by Hogarth,' he said. 'It's been in the parliamentary vaults for decades, but at Jardine's suggestion Heir Bouda has put it up on the wall of what she's now calling the Office of Public Safety. It depicts the Southwark Blood Fair of 1732. Midsummer, maybe your phone can show us?'

The Equal pulled out her device – a Union American smartphone. All the Equals used them, but no one else in Britain was permitted them, even though the handsets were made here. Midsummer found an image via the unrestricted internet that only Equals could access, and passed her phone around. The looks of horror and revulsion on the faces of the men as they glanced at it set Abi's gut churning with apprehension. How bad could it be? She'd wanted to be a doctor; she wasn't squeamish about injury. And yet a doctor's first vow was to do no harm, and the thought of deliberate infliction of harm always sickened her.

When she saw the phone, she realized it was even worse than she'd imagined.

At first glance, the painting was merely a riot of innocent-seeming detail. A woman, whose yellow dress had the sort of neckline Gavar Jardine would appreciate, beat an enormous drum. A beggar's cat walked upright, a hat on its head. Flags and tavern signs flapped and swung, while an acrobat gyrated on a rope. Drunks quarrelled in the street, swords drawn.

It was so giddily distracting that it took Abi a moment to work out what was happening on an elevated platform in the centre of the canvas. And then she wondered how she could possibly have missed it.

One naked unfortunate was being swung over the edge by his ankles. The crowd below, holding aloft knives, were sawing at whatever bit of him they could reach. Another stripped figure, trussed to one of the balcony struts, was punctured by all manner of homely implements. These varied from a fish hook, to a toasting fork, to what appeared to be a cook's ladle jammed straight into one oozing eye socket. A child not much bigger than Libby Jardine was determinedly driving a large splinter of wood into the victim's shin.

Abi felt her gorge rise, and looked away. She hastily handed the phone back to Midsummer.

'Is he mad? That's not a show of strength – it's inhuman. It'll turn everyone against them.'

'You might be surprised,' Faiers said. 'Don't romanticize the common people, Abigail. There was no state executioner at the Blood Fairs. The prisoners were simply tied up and the public given free licence. Chancellor Jardine describes the Blood Fairs as celebrations of "people's justice".'

'British people would never do that,' said Wesley, one hand now protectively on Renie's shoulder.

'People anywhere will do it, given enough reason,' said Faiers.

'Hardly enough reason with these lads,' one of the Bore escapees protested. 'Burning fields and blowing up machinery sheds.'

'They'll be given a reason,' Abi said. 'Your friends will become enemies of the state – a threat to everyone.'

'I'm sure the mood will be helped along, too,' said Midsummer. 'I've seen at uni how drink and drugs can make normal people act like animals. I know girls who've had horrendous things done to them at parties. All you need is one messed-up person to start it off, then that gives everyone else permission. People forget themselves.'

The room fell quiet. It was such a bleak vision. Did everyone have a monster inside them, just waiting to be unleashed? Look at Dog, and the horror he'd become.

No, Abi wouldn't believe it.

Which was when she realized that the Blood Fairs weren't about converting everyone into bloodthirsty killers. Only a few would join in – the ones who, as Midsummer had said, were screwed up already. Its power over the rest would be as a threat. A grisly fate that awaited those who stepped out of line.

How to defeat that?

'Whatever they can do, we can do, too,' Abi said. 'If the

Equals think they can make everyone afraid, using the spectacle of the Blood Fair – well, we can make everyone brave using the spectacle of defiance.

'Let's fight their history with our history. When the kings fell, statues were smashed, portraits destroyed, royal buildings defaced and burned. Symbolic targets. We should do the same. No casualties; maximum visibility.

'Jardine's taken over Aston House because he thinks it represents commoner failure that only Equals can fix. Let's tell our side of the story. Let's go for the Queen's Chapel, where they staged the Blood Fair show trials. The Mayfair stores where they flog things made in slavetowns to the world's rich tourists. Those mansions along Aston Garden, where all the countries too ashamed to have an open diplomatic relationship with us cozy up discretely to their Equal neighbours. We can set this city on fire, and I don't just mean with matches.'

They were all staring at her: Renie and her uncle, Midsummer and Jon, the men of the Bore. Abi saw determination in their eyes.

'Don't know about you all,' Renie said, with an emphatic snap of her gum. 'But I reckon matches are a great place to start.'

And it turned out Renie was good with them. And with bricks. And with finding her way into and out of buildings, dodging CCTV, and hearing Security coming a full ten seconds before they turned the corner.

'Just as well I got *some* talents,' the kid said, as the two of them headed up Mountford Street. You could almost forget it was four in the morning, the light from the gilded, crystal-paned storefronts was so bright. 'Jackson tried to get me to write a banner once, but even he couldn't read it, and him being a doctor, that's saying something.'

She lapsed into silence. They were both thinking the same thing, Abi knew. Jackson hadn't been a real doctor at all.

'Yer brother dangled me off a roof one time, on just a bit of rope.'

'You know, that's really not much better as a conversation starter.'

Renie snorted. Both their voices were muffled by cotton scarves that covered most of their faces. 'I remember Jess sayin', when we was in Scotland, that you're more like Luke than you know. I don't think you believed it then. Do you see it now? You've changed, Abi.'

'It all changed when I ran from that car driving us to Millmoor,' Abi said. 'It's taken me till now to realize. I thought I'd be able to prove Luke's innocence, so they'd understand why I ran and everything would be all right. I was so naive. All I did was put myself in a place from which there's no going back.'

'Gives you a kind of freedom, though, don't it? When you've nothing to lose.'

It did. Abi felt for the spray can in her pocket. Tonight would be another line crossed. No, not just crossed. She was taking a run-up and would do a flying leap over it.

A leap into the unknown. Her heart was pumping.

'There are the others,' said Renie, nodding to where two more dark-clad figures, their faces similarly covered, appeared at the far end of the street. The girl looked at her watch, a plasticky BB thing from Millmoor. She might have just been checking when her bus was due, Abi thought. Her cool was astounding.

'Three – two – one – and, party time.'

Renie took off at a sprint. Speed would be of the essence here. These high-end stores would all have alarm systems linked directly to private security firms. They'd allowed themselves ninety seconds.

Abi ran for her target, one of the street's few modern stores. This was a boutique of couture supposedly designed by the wife of one of Lord Jardine's chums, where dresses sold for more than the average annual salary. That was pathetic enough, but the garments were hand-stitched in Exton, the Devon slavetown that was a favourite for the sorts of luxury brands showcased on this street.

The proprietress of this particular label believed the small hands and sharp eyes of Exton's children were best for the fine detailing prized by her international clients.

The expanse of window displaying her wares was perfect for their message. Abi tried to ignore the sounds of smashing glass and the smell of kerosene from all around her, as the other three did their work with bricks and petrol bombs. Her hand moved swiftly.

CHILD SLAVERY = SO LAST SEASON

As the hiss of spray paint died, Abi became aware that there was no more tinkling glass or thudding brick, only the crackle and roar of flame. She turned, but Renie was already at her shoulder.

'Pretty handwriting,' she said approvingly. 'The Doc woulda picked you every week. Let's go.'

They fled down the street, shopfront goods now luridly illuminated by awnings of flame.

The streets of Mayfair were a warren, but Renie's larcenous talents included an enviable sense of direction, and all Abi had to do was sprint in her wake. The two men from the Bore had split off southeast, towards the Queen's Chapel. Even though she'd suggested it as a target, Abi couldn't bring herself to be part of its destruction. It was a magnificent building that had survived centuries, but now its final moments were at hand. They would be the perfect distraction for the second task she had assigned herself and Renie.

Here was Hyde Park Corner. Only at this hour of night was it clear of the traffic that clogged it constantly. Then down along the edge of St James's Park towards Aston House. Where the former carriage lane met the great circular driveway of the First Family's new residence, an imposing statue loomed in the darkness. It was entirely unlit, though its position made it prominent in the daylight.

The statue was of King James I, father of the Last King. He had gifted the original Aston House to one of his numerous favourites. If you didn't already know his identity, though, you'd have a hard time guessing, because the statue's face had long ago been chiselled off.

'He was that ugly, eh?' Renie asked, hands on her narrow hips.

'He was no looker,' Abi agreed. 'But that's not why they gave him a facelift. Most of the royal statues were destroyed, but this one was left up as a reminder of the degeneracy of the monarchs. James actually wrote a book saying kings ruled by divine right – authorized by God. You can imagine what the Equals thought of that. But we'd better be quick.'

Abi shrugged off the backpack she carried and pulled out its contents, one wrapped around the other. The lighter one she passed to Renie, who had already vaulted onto the plinth and was preparing to shimmy up the king's stockinged legs.

Abi unfolded the sheet. Okay, so the slogan was in Latin, but everyone knew its meaning. *Sic semper tyrannis – Thus always to tyrants*. She fastened it securely to the railings. Above her, Renie was tying a knot tight around the curls of the king's stone wig.

The rumble and crunch of an explosion made them both look up. Less than half a mile away, the Queen's Chapel had just been reduced to rubble. A plume of powdery grey smoke rose into the air, its visibility reminding Abi that dawn was fast approaching. As they watched, the column of cloud was replaced by a gout of flame – the chapel's annihilation would soon be complete.

'Hurry,' said Abi. 'There'll be Security all over the place.'

'There you go.' Renie straightened the mask. Over the ruined visage of King James I now lay a ruddy-cheeked plaster-of-Paris mask of Chancellor Whittam Jardine. It was disturbingly lifelike, crafted by one of the men from the Bore who'd once had a talent for art.

'Much more handsome. How about a kiss from a filthy mongrel brat, eh?' Renie planted a smacker on the mask's cheek and cackled scornfully. Then from her vantage point, the kid twisted to look over her shoulder.

Right at Aston House.

She peered down at Abi.

'All this is just practice for the main event, right? Them.'

Abi gazed at the blank facade of Aston House – this building that Jardine had reclaimed solely as a rebuke to the common folk. The windows at the north end shone with reflected flame from the burning ruins of the chapel. Behind one of them, perhaps, Daisy was sleeping.

Jenner, too.

'Yeah,' she said, not meeting Renie's eye. 'Them.'

23

Bouda

'The resemblance is uncanny,' said Faiers, setting a spread of photographs and a takeaway coffee on Heir Bouda's desk.

Bouda sifted through the pictures. Onto the faceless statue had been tied a wretchedly convincing mask of Whittam. The characteristics were exaggerated – his skin wasn't that pink, nor his hair so orange; his eyes not quite so piggy – but it was instantly recognizable.

The image had gone round the world by the time Security had discovered the statue. The first person to see it had been an American jogger, pounding the parks in the early hours. He'd posted it to social media, where it had been spotted by an enterprising freelance photographer – another meddling foreign national – who had gone and shot proper images. Of the banner, for example.

Sic semper tyrannis.

The protesters had also made a mess of Mountford Street, and levelled the Queen's Chapel. Graffiti sprayed onto the wall opposite the ruined building read: *UN-FREE*

= *UN-FAIR*. A protest against the upcoming Blood Fair, then – which linked it to the disturbances in the Bore. Quite a web to disentangle.

'Two things,' she told Faiers, who had woken her with a call at 5 a.m. to break the news. 'How do we control this narrative, and how do we find out who's responsible? Your mother keeps asking for access to the Twelve Bore prisoners. Is she part of this?'

'The first point,' the commoner said, producing the two newspapers he held tucked under his arm, 'is already under control. I took the liberty of offering exclusives to two sympathetic editors – pictures and quotes in return for the right sort of headlines.'

He flattened the papers across the desk. A red-topped tabloid bore a photograph of the blaze on Mountford Street with the headline 'Flaming morons'. 'Yobs torch luxury street', read the subhead, and the article decried the impact on London's tourist industry. 'Vandals' was the header of the second paper, in which a picture of the Queen's Chapel looking elegant by candlelight was juxtaposed with the heap of smoking rubble it now was. A strapline along the bottom – accompanied by an inset of Thalia and Jenner looking weepily dignified at Euterpe's memorial – demanded 'Have they no respect?'

Of the masked statue, thankfully, there was no sign.

'We can't steer the international media, of course,' Faiers continued. 'Our best tactic there is simply to downplay it.

A period of uncertainty, the sort of minor unrest that occurs anywhere after a transition of power. We can turn that around to talk about Chancellor Jardine's vision of strong leadership, rejecting Zelston's technocratic approach, et cetera.'

Bouda stared at Faiers with surprise. He seemed almost too good to be true, this new adviser of hers.

Was he too good to be true?

'What?' he said, with a note of alarm. 'Did I say something wrong?'

'You understand how this works,' she said. 'So few do. But why are you here in my office, Jon Faiers? I asked about your mother just now. She's the Speaker of the Commons. *Was* the Speaker. And your father – as we know from that sensational little scene in my office – was an Equal who abandoned you both. Shouldn't you be out there participating in these sorts of protests, rather than in here helping me deal with them? Can I trust you?'

Anger flashed in those eyes that were the blue of cloudless skies over Grendelsham. How clear they were, and how unlike Gavar's bleary, bloodshot gaze.

'My mother is a hypocrite,' Faiers said. 'She prates about commoner rights, yet raised her child in a slavetown to avoid inconveniencing the Equal man she was infatuated with. My father, too. He imagined that doling out money to human rights organizations and fomenting

371

unrest among the common folk would atone for what he did.'

'So your motives are personal?'

'You know what my motives are. I told you on the clifftop at Grendelsham, before the Second Debate.'

A slight smile touched his lips, and the events of that night came back to Bouda vividly. Whittam's vulgar grop-ing; Faiers intervening and escorting her outside. The way the cigarette smoke had plumed from his mouth as he spoke, telling her that he'd noticed her out on the cliffs before every Second Debate.

'I believe there is a natural order,' Faiers continued. 'And that the common people not only cannot fight against it – they should not. But I also believe this country can be better governed. The slavedays do not make the best use of people's abilities. And weak Chancellors have apologized abroad for the way we conduct ourselves, while failing to make any changes at home. Our international prestige wanes. Your Skill is disregarded, by you and by us. Most ordinary people have no idea of what you are capable. And you are capable of so much.'

Bouda saw Gavar leap from the balcony and run super-humanly fast after a man whose actions no normal person could ever have discerned. She thought of Silyen Jardine at the heart of a vortex of glass, as shattered Kyneston reformed around him. She remembered what she had felt in the

Bore – the dizzying moment her Skill had passed into the water, and she knew it was at her command.

Faiers was right. If her own experience was anything to go by, few Equals used – or were even aware of – all that their Skill could do. But why did he care?

'What do you want, Jon Faiers?'

He rested both hands on the desk and bent down till his face was level with hers. And she could almost taste his words as he spoke them, just as she had breathed in his cigarette smoke on the clifftop that night.

'The same as you, Heir Bouda: to be greater than we are.'

'We?'

'Britain. Me. You. You want to be the first female Chancellor. Your ambition shines from you. There can't be one of your Equals that does not know it. Yet you trot at Jardine's side like a show pony, in the hope that one day he will take off the reins and let you run. He never will. You must know what he thinks of women. You are a diligent ally, an attractive vote-winner – a brood mare for his son. At least, I presume, for his son.'

Bouda leapt up, humiliated and incensed. How much had those pretty-boy eyes seen? She'd had the right word for Faiers the very first time they'd spoken: insolent. Criminally so.

Her Skill prickled in her fingertips. He wanted to know what Skill could do? Well, Bouda would gladly show him.

'Chancellor Jardine is doing exactly what you say is

required,' she told him, her chin high. 'Reasserting Equal rule and strengthening the nation.'

'Jardine will break Britain, and you know it.'

Her hand came up to slap him, but Faiers caught her wrist and held it. And damn him, she was stronger than any commoner man if she wished. She had only to let her power flow.

'Treason,' she hissed.

She glanced around the room, checking for any hitherto unseen witnesses hidden in corners, but of course there were none. Her eyes returned to Faiers, and didn't look away until he released her.

'So you want me to stop him?' she said, as his hand fell away. His fingers had left red marks on her wrist.

'On the contrary. Let him do it. And then when this country is broken, you put it back together again, claim the Chancellorship, and remake things as they ought to be.'

That was all Bouda had ever wanted.

Which was the only possible explanation for what she did next – which was to reach for Faiers and kiss him.

He pressed her back against the desk, his mouth hungry, his hands possessive. The intensity of him stole her breath. She had submitted to the pawings of Lord Jardine, and the overtures of her man-child husband. And yet here was a commoner – worse, a baseborn – who not only dared to lay a hand on her, but who was waking sensations she had never known. She scratched her nails into the short hair at the back of his neck and heard him groan.

He pulled back and tipped up her chin. 'Rule sternly, but gloriously,' he said, and leaned in for another kiss. 'Make Britain a country to be admired and feared around the world. And let me be at your side, your trusted adviser for the people. I believe in you, Bouda.'

This was madness. Madness itself. And yet she found she couldn't – didn't want to – stop, and stretched up to recapture his mouth.

It was only when she heard the outer door to her suite of offices open that she pushed him away. He cast his eyes to the floor as he straightened his clothes and wiped his mouth.

'Back to your desk,' he whispered. So she went, picking up the now-cold coffee and pressing the plastic lid to her lips.

'Bouda?'

Astrid Halfdan. Trid knocked and opened the door without waiting to be called in – testament to the years of friendship they'd enjoyed at university. But those days were gone. What had happened to her friend's little sister three years ago, Bouda thought, had changed Astrid almost as much as it had Athalie herself. Now, understandably, there appeared to be no bounds to the woman's deep hatred for commoners. The Blood Fair was supposed to be a spectacle of public violence, but if the people of London were slow to get started, Astrid would happily show them how it was done.

'I see you've heard,' said Astrid, nodding at the news-papers on the desk.

'Heard and acted,' said Bouda. 'Mr Faiers was quick to respond. Thank you, Faiers, you may leave us.'

She half longed for a burning glance as he went, but Faiers was no fool. He closed the door with a deferential 'Heir Bouda', and she was glad of it.

'Can I help you with anything, Trid?' she asked. 'It's just that it's going to be a busy day . . .'

She indicated the papers and photographs, but what she really needed was time and space to process what had just happened with Faiers. It was absurd, unseemly, to sully oneself with the touch of a baseborn – her own godfather's bastard child. And it was the last thing she needed with everything else going on.

And yet his dream was also hers. And he believed in her. Darling Daddy had never really understood her ambition, while DiDi simply wasn't interested in politics. Bouda's parliamentary groupies admired her mostly for her looks, she knew. And everything Faiers had said about Whittam? If she was honest with herself, it was all true.

'Sorry,' she told Astrid, rubbing her face. 'Hardly any sleep and a lot to wake up to.'

Astrid's dark eyes – her mother came from a Japanese

noble family, and had met Trid's father when he'd studied in Kyoto – passed no judgement.

'I thought you'd want to hear this as soon as possible. I was with Suspect Nine last night, and something interesting came out: Midsummer Zelston.'

'Midsummer? How do you mean?'

'I mean, she's in the thick of it with the Twelve Bore. Up to her neck. Practically co-ordinating them.'

Another traitor.

Bouda sat back, disgusted. First, Meilyr Tresco. Then the revelation that her own godfather, Rix, had been a commoner sympathizer – and Speaker Dawson's lover (and *don't* think about Faiers). Now this. Midsummer Zelston involved with the Twelve Bore.

She should have seen it a mile off, were it not still astonishing to her that an Equal could betray their own kind in this way. Midsummer was dating a commoner woman. Maybe that was it. People did strange things when their heads were turned. (And *definitely* don't think about Faiers.)

Was Midsummer still at Lindum, or here in London? Was she perhaps involved with those responsible for last night's stunts? If they had an Equal abettor or protector, it would explain their daring.

'We need to track her down,' Bouda said. 'Let's do it the soft way first, and find out who last saw her. I'll also have the data guys try and get a fix on her phone.'

And with that, Bouda's day began in earnest. Astrid

disappeared down to her silent basement, while one of the Overseer's minions took Bouda through to their small broadcast studio. Today, she had to get through the interviews Faiers had scheduled with foreign media. The Chinese one went smoothly – Bouda spoke the language fluently, having joined Daddy on many business trips from childhood. But her Japanese was rusty and she spent a fretful fifteen minutes trying to remember the specific verb forms used only by the Skilled.

When she stepped out of the studio, it was to find her office even more frenzied than usual. The Overseer pounced.

'Heir Bouda,' she said. 'We have a developing situation.'

The tech team was erecting a giant screen in front of the Hogarth painting. Nearby, a huge monitor displayed a map not of London, or even the Bore, as Bouda might have expected. Instead, Riverhead slavetown and the city of Newcastle were on display.

Whittam was standing in front of it, frowning. To one side waited Kessler and Faiers.

'Riverhead? Take us through it,' Bouda barked.

'At 6.15 a.m.,' the Overseer droned in her monotonous voice, 'a call was placed by a manager at the parts supply warehouse. Shifts there start at six, in advance of the yard-day beginning at seven. But no one had turned up. A check found that the buses that would have transported the workers hadn't left the depot. In fact, the whole vehicle depot is deserted.'

Bouda nodded. The dry docks were spread along the banks of the Tyne, so workers were bussed out to them from the slavetown hub. The transport depot would be an obvious strategic target. Shut it down, and you'd cause a lot of disruption with only a little effort. So this didn't have to be a large-scale protest.

But the rest of the Overseer's narrative put paid to that hope. Over the next two hours, no one in Riverhead had turned up. To anything. Not to the slavetown's own infrastructure services: sanitation, waste and maintenance. Nor to the shops or the canteens.

Riverhead served a huge area: Newcastle, Sunderland and North Tyneside. More than a hundred thousand people did their days there at any one time. There was no way the slavetown's Security could force that many people out of their beds and dorms, and onto buses to go to work.

This would have to be dealt with by penalties, then.

After conferring briefly with Whittam, she got her tecchies to patch her through to Riverhead's Overseer. While they tested the link, Bouda pondered unhappily that it should be Riverhead, of all places, that was causing such trouble.

Her mother, Angelica, had been the only daughter of an eccentric Tyneside lord. As young girls, Bouda and DiDi had loved shopping in Newcastle, hats pulled down over their distinctive white-blonde hair so they could roam anonymously. Their maternal grandfather, Lord Bligh, possessed a sprawling coastal estate north of the city, and had a weakness for building lighthouses.

Bouda rarely saw him now, though Dina still visited him regularly. Everything had changed after their mother died, killed in an act of sabotage when visiting the Portisbury BB plant with Daddy. Bouda had been thirteen. Bodina only eleven.

That had been the moment Bouda had realized that she and her kind weren't universally loved, as she had imagined up till then. No, they were feared and – by some – even hated. That day's awful insight had never left her.

Riverhead would need stern handling.

The slavetown's Overseer came fuzzily into view on the video link. He was a thin, anxious-looking man, but as the picture sharpened she saw that his eyes were flinty. The reassurances he offered that the ringleaders would be found were convincing too. He was taking tough measures, he promised.

A shame it was too late for that.

'For each missed shift, another year on their days,' she said. 'Do you understand? The usual penalty is a month. But for this flagrant mass disobedience, we must acknowledge that the stakes are higher – and so must they.'

'I will communicate it immediately,' the man said, his thin lips pursed. 'But it won't go down well. May I ask if there will be backup? Security detachments?'

'That's not out of the question. But if we need to intervene, it will mean authority has broken down in Riverhead.
Your authority. Do you understand me?'

If the man called in the guards, his career would be over.
That threat was usually enough to make the timid ones get
their act together. The incompetent ones, of course, would
have more to worry about than losing their job.

The line fizzed and sputtered as the man was speaking.
Bouda looked around in exasperation for the tech guy.
Could no one here do their job properly?

Then a voice crackled through the room. Amazingly, it
came from every speaker in the office.

'I'm the one you're looking for.'

Bouda stiffened in her seat. It was a woman's voice. Soft
and low. Almost, somehow, familiar. The Geordie accent
was like those she remembered from her childhood. Like
those of the slaves on her grandfather's estate. Almost, a
tiny bit, like her mother's, though that had been more
refined.

This must be the woman her people had hunted for all
this time. The one who ran the Riverhead railroad.

The bitch.

'Who are you?' Bouda asked.

There was no image to accompany the voice. All she
could see onscreen was the Riverhead Overseer, plainly
hearing the same as Bouda.

'Who am I?' The voice paused. 'You can call me the Angel of the North.'

Someone screamed as every monitor in the office cracked in an instant with the Skillful lash of Bouda's fury. She was unrepentant. If she had no Skill, she would have grabbed each screen and smashed it on the floor. How dare this bitch? How dare she?

The Angel of the North, the giant winged sculpture that watched over Riverhead, had been commissioned by heart-broken Daddy and Grandpa. Named for Bouda's murdered mother, sweet Angelica Bligh.

Bouda would have this commoner woman's head in a bag, just as her kind had done to Ragnarr Vernay.

'Meet me tonight,' the voice continued. 'Ten o'clock, in the middle of the Tyne Bridge. Just you and me. Leave your people on the Newcastle side, and I'll leave mine in Riverhead. No guns. No Security. No surveillance. You have Skill, so you've nothing to fear. Let's see if we can end this. Not just Riverhead. All of it.'

More crackling, and the line went dead.

On the video link, Bouda and the Riverhead Overseer stared at each other.

'Tell no one of this,' she snapped. 'Continue as discussed with the protocol. We'll review your progress later.'

Then she cut the link. Exhaled. Ran a hand along her ponytail to calm herself.

'We take her out,' said Whittam. 'Snipers. Easily done.'

At his side, Kessler nodded.

They talked casually of killing, these men. But could you really build a better Britain on the bodies of the dead? Was this what Faiers meant, when he said that Whittam would break Britain?

And what of Faiers' notion that she should let him?

Well, one kiss didn't make her beholden to Faiers any more than marriage made her bend the knee to Gavar Jardine. No one made Bouda's decisions for her.

'No,' she said. 'This woman has a whole slavetown behind her. As much as I could rip her apart with my bare hands for the way she's insulted my mother, killing her there and then would be mistaken. First, her little uprising needs to fail. Then her own people will turn her in.'

She looked at Whittam, to see how he'd respond to being overruled, but he merely grunted. Faiers nodded.

Bouda turned on her heel and issued instructions for helicopters to be made ready for the flight north.

It had been years since she'd last seen the Tyne Bridge at night. She'd forgotten how high it stood above the river. How much you could see of the surrounding city and slave-town.

Behind her, Newcastle glowed bright and many-coloured. Its party scene was in full swing. Carefree young people, their slavedays still years away, walked along the towpath far below, laughing, talking, and swigging from bottles. On the opposite riverbank, the slavetown burned a febrile sodium-yellow. Its low-rise apartment blocks stood in ranks against the curve of the hill.

On top of the hill: the silhouette of the Angel of the North.

The river flowed beneath, black and wide, rippling with light. And above was the high, criss-crossed iron parabola of the bridge's span. It was one of the few truly impressive structures in Britain built by slaves, not Skill. Bouda was certain the woman she was here to meet had chosen this spot on purpose.

She checked her watch. Five minutes to go. She nodded at her people – Faiers, the Overseer and Kessler all stood behind her. She had nothing to fear. Any move against her would be answered by annihilation of the slavetown rebels. She didn't think they'd be foolish enough to take that risk.

As she walked towards the centre of the bridge, she saw a figure detach itself from the far side and do the same. Female, tall and slim, wearing a black hat to render her silhouette anonymous.

The lights on the bridge had been doused, but Equal eyes were sharp. When Bouda saw who it was coming towards her, she stopped in her tracks, horror struck.

Her sister.

How had they taken Bodina? Was she some kind of hostage? Why had she not simply broken free with her Skill?

Perhaps – Bouda shuddered at the thought – they had somehow brainwashed her into supporting their cause. Taken advantage of her vulnerability since Meilyr's death, and sent her to intercede for them.

Bouda didn't think it was possible to hate the rebel leader, this "Angel", more than she already did. A Blood Fair would be no more than the woman deserved.

She sped up. She wanted to hurry to her sister, take her in her arms and tell her that it didn't matter why she was here, nobody would be cross with her. Bouda blamed herself. She'd known her sister would be hurting after Meilyr's death. She should have watched out for her, made more time for her. But there had been one thing after another to manage: the wedding, the slavetown purge, the Twelve Bore, and now Riverhead.

She would never again let it all come before family and her darling sister.

They were nearly level. Dina had stopped. Bouda halted too, about five metres away.

'What are you doing here, DiDi?' she asked. 'Did they make you? How did you get mixed up in this?'

'We've tried so many times to tell you,' Dina said, 'but no one's been listening. Not when Meilyr spoke out – and paid for it with his Skill. Not at your wedding, when I said in front of everyone that it didn't have to be this way. That it could be done with love and not with cruelty.'

Bouda trembled.

'What do you mean?' she said. 'These people are defying us, undermining us. Destabilizing the whole country.'

'Oh, Bouda. They simply want justice.'

'Justice? They're terrorists. Who filled your head with this rubbish? The Riverhead woman – this Angel of the North?'

'Do you really not understand?'

There was something like pity in her sister's face, and Bouda realized she did understand. She simply didn't want to believe it.

When Bodina spoke next, her voice was strangely altered. It had a strong Geordie accent. Like the slaves of their childhood. Like their mother.

'*I'm* the Angel of the North.'

Bouda stared at her. The words were meaningless.

'You can change things,' Dina said urgently. 'You're more important to Jardine than you know. His majority relies on your supporters' backing. You are the pretty face of his regime's ugliness. If you go back to him and say "enough", he will have to listen.'

'Stop it, darling,' Bouda said.

She longed to reach out to her sister, to fold her in her arms and rock her like she did when they were children and DiDi suffered nightmares. Like she had after their mother's funeral, when Bodina cried herself to sleep every night for months. Nothing would calm her except Bouda climbing into bed alongside her and holding her little sister until she quieted.

'It's not too late. No one knows you're mixed up in this. Come back with me now. I can say you were a hostage. You call yourself their leader, but without you this protest will fail, so there'll be no need for reprisals. No one will be hurt, no one need die.'

'Listen to yourself,' Dina said, the shine of tears in her eyes but her voice unwavering. 'People are hurt every day. People die every single day, thanks to what our regime does. Well, not in my name. Not any longer. When news of what's happening here goes out across the world, it won't be the voice of the Angel of the North they hear. It'll be me, Dina Matravers, Equal, sister-in-law of the First Family. I love you so much, Bouda, but I can't be quiet any more.'

When Bodina dropped to the ground, it took a second for the sound of the bullet that killed her to reach Bouda's ears.

It rang out with a crack like that of a heart breaking.

24

Abi

There had been silence when the news about Dina reached them at midnight. Then tears and shouting. Now, in the mid-afternoon, there was silence again. Renie was asleep on the sofa, and Abi laid a blanket over her. The kid had cried herself to exhaustion. Abi remembered how she'd been in the helicopter as they'd flown back from Eilean Dòchais after Meilyr's death: silent and stoical. Holding it all together. Just like Bodina herself, who had piloted the helicopter that flew the three of them out of there.

Renie had channelled that loss into a sense of purpose with the Bore, and the joy of discovering her uncle Wes. But now the tide had turned yet again, and deferred grief had come rushing back with a force as irresistible as the sea. Meilyr, Dina, and her brother Mickey. Her losses had finally crashed over Renie.

Abi was squashed at the end of the sofa, one hand absently stroking the girl's back, the other curled around a mug of tea. She was very still.

Her mind, though, was racing.

The television rolling news channel was playing. Abi had muted it, but the running captions told the story.

'HOSTAGE TRAGEDY' was one that flashed up again and again.

According to the looping news, a cell of known political terrorists had attempted a takeover of Riverhead slavetown. They had used a troubled Equal girl, Bodina Matravers, as a hostage. She was known to be emotionally vulnerable following her fiancé's suicide. He had been involved in commoner unrest, in Millmoor last year – and had been censured by parliament.

The possibility was left open that Bodina might have been with them willingly – due to her impaired judgement, of course. This segment was illustrated by all those paparazzi photographs that Abi had once flicked through: Dina holding a tiny dog up to the camera; Dina with a cocktail in hand, laughing. In each shot she looked extremely thin and even younger than her age. If you'd never met her, it was easy to imagine the sort of girl this was: fragile, sweet and gullible. Easily led.

Abi's heart ached. Yes, she and Bodina had had their differences. She would never forget the terror of the girl's Skill shoving her to the edge of Highwithel's law ledge. But Dina had been brilliant and brave. She had played her role of fun-loving party girl too well, and now that was how the world would remember her. What an insult. Abi closed her eyes against the stream of inane news images and pictured Bodina as she had been at Highwithel, standing on the jetty with Meilyr, Skill-light in hand.

Now both of them were gone.

The rolling bulletin continued its analysis. Dina had been targeted by the terrorists because her sister, Heir Bouda Matravers-Jardine, headed the Office of Public Safety. The Riverhead rebel leader, a woman calling herself the Angel of the North, had contacted the office. She'd challenged the Equal to meet her on the Tyne Bridge. Heir Bouda, unintimidated, had gone north immediately. The archive footage showed Bouda at the recent investiture, dignified in her heir's mantle, as beautiful as her sister but in every other respect her opposite.

Naturally, Security had provided an escort, including snipers. And it was one of those men who – not realizing the identity of the woman who had come forward from the rebel-held slavetown – had fired. He'd been alarmed by an apparent altercation between the two and had intended a disabling injury, rather than a kill. But it was pitch dark – an expert weighed in here on how night vision was notoriously challenging – and the bridge's girders obstructed sight lines.

Bodina Matravers had died instantly.

Security detachments had immediately been ordered across the bridge. Helicopters lifted up and over the city, their powerful spotlights lancing down. Armoured jeeps rolled in. For the umpteenth time Abi watched the images play out.

Those who stood at the end of the bridge were picked up first. Behind them, Riverhead's great gates had slammed shut. Unlike isolated slavetowns such as Millmoor, there was no exclusion zone around Riverhead. Only a high concrete wall with heavy-duty barriers inset at intervals.

Barriers that were never built to withstand explosives. Controlled detonations destroyed a few, the bars crumpling and concertinaing, and ground Security rushed in with choppers spotlighting their path. The way the pictures had been edited, including helmet-cam footage, made it look exciting – even immersive. It reminded Abi of a couple of Luke's console games of which Mum had particularly disapproved.

Maulers – the lowly slave units – distinguished themselves, one commentator said. Abi knew why that had been mentioned: this was 'good' slaves against 'bad'. Everything about this story was designed to put the viewer firmly on one side – and it wasn't the side of the protesters. 'INSURGENCY QUELLED', the scrolling caption flashed over scenes of arrest. Men and women were herded at gunpoint into the streets, hands above their heads in a seeming admission of guilt.

Then the caption cycled through to the last one, and Abi upped the volume slightly for what came next. She'd already heard it countless times, but she needed to hear it again. Needed to keep stoking her anger, so it burned hotter than her despair or her fear. Under her palm she felt Renie shift in her sleep, like a rabbit in its burrow when a fox walks past.

Whittam Jardine's face filled the screen. He was delivering his statement from the riverside terrace at Westminster. The House of Light glowed behind him.

'We condemn, in the strongest possible terms, the senseless actions of the past twenty-four hours. The welfare of every soul in Riverhead has been jeopardized by the behaviour of a small and vicious group of troublemakers. They are now in our custody and will receive the full weight of the law. I pledge to the people of Britain, here and now, that I will not permit the peace of our nation to be disturbed. The right of every man and woman to work out their days without intimidation or alarm will be protected.

'Finally, I would like to pay tribute to my colleague and daughter-in-law, Heir Bouda, on the appalling loss of her beautiful sister. Bodina Matravers was a complicated young woman, but much loved by those who knew her, and my family feels her absence deeply. Those to blame for her death will be brought to justice.'

'CHANCELLOR VOWS PEACE AND PROTECTION' cycled the caption.

Nauseated, Abi stabbed the remote and switched the television off.

Whittam could play the media like Silyen could play the violin – with a mastery that was itself a kind of Skill.

Riverhead had failed and fallen. Abi had dared imagine that the Equals' version of history could be fought with the truth, but how could you do that when they were making it up as they went along, and shouting it over and over and over through the media? They had everything at their disposal: power, money, connections. They hardly even needed Skill.

The speed and scale of the action against Riverhead exceeded anything they had anticipated. Dina had believed that her involvement would buy negotiating time, and that if Riverhead held out for one day, it could hold out for two, and then three, until the country had seen that it could be done. That Equals could be defied.

The lesson taught by Riverhead had turned out to be very different.

And there was something else Abi didn't want to think about. She had believed, ever since those early discussions in Highwithel, that any uprising for the people had to come from the people. It had felt wrong that commoners should need Equals – Meilyr, Dina, and Midsummer – to be their champions.

Except now two of those champions were gone, and Abi saw clearly how hard it would be without them. How difficult to rescue the Twelve Bore, and the new prisoners from Riverhead.

Let alone win freedom for the country.

Who should she turn to, now? Should she go join the men from the Bore, over in Dalston? That was where

Wesley had gone, though he'd refused to leave Renie's side until the girl had finally fallen asleep. Midsummer would surely be there, too.

Should she call Jon Faiers? He would be busy in Bouda's office, and given the circumstances, any contact might place him at terrible risk. If his sympathies were discovered at this stage, it would be disastrous for him.

Or should she call someone else?

Abi hadn't contacted Jenner since coming to London. She'd not wanted to put him in an impossible position with his family, or with Dina. Abi hadn't forgotten Dina's attempt at Highwithel to get Jenner to submit to the Quiet about what he had seen and heard. And then there was the fact that he was now an heir and would one day be a lord.

Her head and her heart warred constantly about Jenner, and it was easiest when she tried to push thoughts of him away altogether. But who else did she have to turn to? And who else knew her like he did? Not Wesley, or Faiers, or Midsummer, that was certain.

Easing herself from the sofa so as not to disturb Renie, she padded upstairs to the little back office for her phone. She was on her hands and knees groping under the camp bed when the front door was kicked in.

The downstairs hallway opened directly into the living room-cum-office where Renie was. Abi heard the girl shriek as several men, judging by the sound of their boots, burst into the house.

As Abi's fingers closed around her phone she heard a barked instruction from below: 'Check upstairs.'

'There ain't nobody here,' Renie yelled. 'Just me. Three of yer for a kid? You're so brave.'

Then a yelp, as one of them struck her.

It went against her every instinct not to rush to Renie's aid, but Abi didn't wait. She'd be no use to Renie arrested alongside her. She heaved up the sash window and climbed through, teetering on the sill outside to yank it back down so her exit wasn't instantly obvious.

If she jumped down, she'd be in the back garden with no way out, so she tested the strength of the guttering and swung herself up. The window was a dormer, its jut of tiles lying below the main roof ridge. Abi straddled it, hoping she was concealed from the sight of anyone in the road out front. She inhaled deeply to try and calm her breathing. What was going on inside the house? If they hurt Renie, Abi would never forgive herself.

Security must have had some lead to this place. Did they also know about the men of the Twelve Bore in Dalston? She couldn't be sure, but it plainly wouldn't be wise to go there straight away. Her options were dwindling fast.

Abi stifled a gasp as the sash rattled up beneath her. She couldn't see the speaker, but he must have thrust his head out because his words floated up clearly.

'Nah, upstairs is clear. Someone's been living here, there's a camp bed. But only one. Maybe the kid. If not, then whoever it is, they're not here right now. Let's leave someone out front to watch for them.'

The window frame rasped partway down, and the man was gone.

Abi waited a few moments, then rolled as carefully as she could onto her front and wriggled up to the ridge line. Who had Renie, and where were they taking her? The street lighting was in front of the house, while the gardens behind were in darkness, so she shouldn't be seen.

She recognized him immediately, the sodium lighting fuzzing off his shorn scalp. Luke's nemesis: Kessler. In front of him, two black-clad men were marching Renie between them. They were so big and she so little that her feet barely touched the ground as they dragged her down the pathway.

Waiting in the street were three vehicles: an anonymous black sedan, a van that could only be a prisoner transport vehicle, and behind it, a standard Security squad car. The two men shoved Renie against the van, then wrenched her arms back to handcuff them and roughly patted her down.

As they dragged open the side of the van to shove her in, Abi glimpsed movement and heard a distressed bellow that could only have been Wesley. The van slammed shut.

So they'd already been to Dalston, and rounded everyone up. Did they have Midsummer? Abi didn't see how Security could arrest an Equal, so she must not have been there when Kessler and his team arrived. She would surely have stopped them otherwise.

Kessler bent to speak to the patrol car's driver, and an officer climbed out of the back to take up position along the street. From there, he could watch the house. He had a gun, Abi noticed. A proper one, not a stun gun. Kessler and his crew were trading up.

Then the vehicles were gone and Abi was left alone, pressed against the roof. She gave it five minutes to make sure the watchman would stay where he was, before she slid down the tiles and back through the window. She grabbed the coat containing the last of the money she'd taken from Kyneston, and her phone charger. Who knew how long she might need to run for, or who was left to help.

Then it was out of the window again, and a short drop into the garden. She went over the fence into the neighbouring garden, down the side alley between that house and the next, and took off at a rapid walk south to Victoria Park. There'd be few people there to overhear her.

She sat down on a tree stump in a wooded area by the children's playground and pulled out her phone. There were only four numbers stored in it, and they belonged to the only four people who could help: Faiers, Midsummer, Jenner and Armeria Tresco. Which should she call?

She drew a deep breath before hitting the keypad. And the minute the phone connected and she heard that reassuring voice, Abi felt calmer. She could do this. Not everything was lost.

They arranged to meet that evening, four hours from

now, on the other side of the city. Abi decided to walk, crossing over onto the Thames' south bank. In Rotherhithe she dumped her coat in a charity bin and bought a new one off a market stall. Down a side street she found a small hairdresser's shop with no customers and a TV tuned to the sports channel. If the owner didn't keep up with the news, they'd hopefully miss it if Abi became a 'person of interest' and her photo was shared by the media.

After considering a super-short cut, Abi decided it would be better to have something to hide behind, so forked out for extensions. She grimaced in the mirror at the effect: on the run, with porn-star hair. But at least she looked different. This was about staying free.

The proprietor turfed her out and shut up for the night, and Abi couldn't put off her meeting any longer. Nor did she want to. Hopefully for a few hours she would have respite from the nightmare of the past night and day – and at the end of it, a plan for what to do next.

Westminster Bridge would have been the most direct route, but because it led to parliament, she skirted it, continuing to Lambeth. Even at a distance, she could see the House of Light illuminating the night sky with its flickering radiance.

London's burning, she thought. Burning with the Skill of the Equals. Could it ever be put out?

Crossing at Lambeth Bridge, she followed Horseferry Road. And then she was at the back wall of Aston House.

It seemed the height of folly, but when they'd spoken earlier, Jenner had argued that his family's new residence would be the safest place in all London. 'There are seven hundred and seventy-five rooms,' he told her. 'We're only using about thirty. You could probably move in and live here for years with no one noticing. It gets you off the streets, and in here there's no Security and no surveillance. Besides, Father and Bouda are at Westminster. Most likely, Mother and I will be the only ones home – and your sister and Libby, of course. I might be able to bring Daisy to you when Libby's sleeping.'

She felt a painful ache at the thought of Daisy. Abi would give anything just to see her little sister and hug her tight. She followed the wall, hat on and head down. As the hour began to strike in Aston's clock tower, she reached the doorway Jenner had mentioned. From the street, it looked long disused. But Abi had barely given the softest of knocks before it opened, and there he was. Pale face, warm freckles, and that wide, anxious smile.

'Come in quickly,' he said. 'No one saw you?'

Abi shook her head and squeezed through. Inside was a tangle of overgrown shrubs and grasses, newly hacked back to make a path. Once she was in, he refastened the door quickly with a padlock and drew an iron bar across.

'This was always a commoner residence,' he explained, seeing her surprise. 'So there's no residual Skillful protection. Mother has layered some family wards onto the central part of the house, the bit we're using, but Silyen's not been around much so no one's done the boundaries. Mother just got a chap to put new locks on anything that looked like a door or gate. I swear no one else knows this door is even here.' He slipped the key into his pocket. 'Now let me look at you. Oh, Abi.'

He reached for her and pulled her hard against him. As she let herself relax into his arms, Abi wished she had allowed herself to do this earlier. To come to him like this, despite the turmoil they had both endured in the weeks since they were last together at Highwithel.

'I saw you, you know,' she said, resting her chin on his chest and looking up at him. 'At the Queen's Chapel. The head. That awful speech – did your father make you say all that?'

Jenner looked mortified. Abi laughed, and stretched up to kiss him.

'Sorry,' she said. 'I shouldn't have mentioned it.'

'Where have you been for the past month?' he asked. 'What's been going on? I thought you'd given up on me.'

'I thought you'd want me to.' Abi paused. 'You're an heir, now. How does it feel?'

She reached for his right hand, and inspected the signet ring on the little finger. It bore the Parva emblem: the sala-mander.

'*I burn not shine,*' she murmured, remembering her con-versation about the family motto with Silyen Jardine in

Kyneston's library. 'I think that fits you rather well, don't you?'

'What's that supposed to mean?' He sounded annoyed and Abi could have kicked herself. She had meant only that unlike entitled Gavar, and eccentric Silyen, Jenner was steady, not showy. But he might have taken it as a reference to his lack of Skill. How much harder it must be for him, no longer in obscurity at Kyneston, but thrust among the most powerful Equals of the land. She'd imagined his new eminence would make things easier for him, but it struck her now that it might merely have made it worse.

She'd be no good at putting that into words, of course. So she squeezed his hand and kissed his cheek contritely.

He led her through a thicket of rhododendrons towards the rear of Aston House, and even though she was familiar with Kyneston, it was an imposing sight. Everyone knew the grand frontage that dominated the Mall, but you never saw the back. The front facade was just one side of a vast quadrangle. She truly could lose herself in here, Abi thought – and the idea was so very tempting.

'This way,' Jenner said, leading her by the hand. They went through an archway in the rear wing and emerged in an inner courtyard. It was square and massive; two tiers of windows, of which only a few were lit, lined every side of the quadrangle. On the outer frontage, not visible from here, was the balcony from which Gavar Jardine had leapt.

And beyond that sat the defaced royal statue to which she and Renie had given Whittam Jardine's face.

Abi's skin prickled. Here she was, in the Jardine home itself. Whittam slept here. Gavar too – and presumably Bouda, now that they were married.

As if sensing her unease, Jenner squeezed her fingers. 'Nearly there.'

He put an arm round her as two servants crossed the quad, bearing trays with empty dishes, their silver covers rolling gently. The servants never once turned their heads. Perhaps they were house-slaves brought up from Kyneston. You learned to ignore a lot there.

Then they were inside a warmly lit, richly carpeted corridor, with elaborately carved wooden doors leading off the length of it. Abi felt more exposed in here than outside. What if they were to meet Thalia Jardine? The Equal would be sure to recognize her.

So she was grateful when Jenner turned into a quieter corridor and paused outside a door.

'We'll sort it all out,' he said.

He opened the door and motioned Abi inside, stepping in behind her.

As her eyes adjusted to the dim lighting, Abi saw that there was already someone there, sitting in an armchair.

Lord Whittam Jardine.

Horrified, she turned to try and bundle Jenner back out. Perhaps Whittam wouldn't recognize her. Perhaps he'd think she was just another commoner trollop dragged in for a night of fun by one of his sons.

But Jenner was stood in front of the door, turning a key in the lock. He looked up when she thumped his shoulder, panicked and afraid, and caught her wrists in one hand. With the other, he reached out and stroked her cheek.

'You'll be with your brother,' he said gently. 'That's what you want, isn't it? Just as I am now finally equal with mine.'

Then he turned her around to face his father.

'No!' Abi said, struggling. 'No, Jenner.' But he held her tight.

Whittam prowled over. Abi had never been close to him before, and she recoiled. Power and cruelty rolled off him in waves. He grabbed her face between his thick fingers, and they gripped Abi's cheekbones like a vice. She felt suddenly, terrifyingly fragile. One squeeze of that hand and she would break irreparably.

'She's young,' Whittam said sceptically.

'Nineteen,' Jenner supplied. 'Nearly twenty. But her brother was only seventeen when he killed Zelston.'

'True.' Whittam released Abi, but continued to pad around her. 'They were obviously part of the same network. Corrupted together. After her brother's Condemnation, she fled from Kyneston, knowing that she would surely be discovered next. She made her way up to Riverhead to plan the next move in their campaign of unrest and intimidation.'

'What?' Abi wasn't sure what she was hearing. 'Jenner, you know where I was. You were there with us.'

'Yes, you went first to Highwithel, to Meilyr,' Jenner said, gripping her arm a little more tightly behind her back. There was a robotic quality to his voice, as if reciting something he had learned by rote. 'Meilyr, who openly confessed to stirring commoner revolt. You and he decided that you should go to Riverhead, to try and succeed where your brother had failed in Millmoor. Poor, besotted Dina Matravers, who could never deny Meilyr anything, agreed to help. You decided that when you shut down the slavetown, she would lure her sister up.'

'Jenner, no.' Abi tried to shake herself free. 'What are you saying? You know none of that's true.'

She cried out as Whittam Jardine backhanded her across the face.

'Stupid girl,' he said. 'Truth isn't what happened, it's what people will believe happened. I managed to get rid of that deluded little bitch, Bodina, without arousing her sister's suspicions. But recasting her as a tragic bit-part player leaves me with no leading lady in this drama.

'There are women among those we detained, of course. But the best tales are those that require the least embellishment. So it was perfect when my middle son, newly awoken to his responsibilities as a parliamentarian and heir, came to me after your phone call. He said he'd found me a new

Angel of the North. Yes, I think you'll fill the role admirably – just in time for the finale.'

It was a nightmare that had rushed over her so fast Abi could barely comprehend it. She twisted around to look at Jenner. Tried to lift her hands to him, but he still held them as tight as the cuffs had gripped Renie.

'Is he making you say this? Jenner, please, this isn't you.'

'I'm an heir now, Abi. For the first time I know how much my family really values me. And Father says that with Crovan able to strip Skill, it'll only be a matter of time before he can restore it, too. I did tell you all, at Highwithel, that there wasn't anything I wouldn't do for that.'

'I loved you.' It was both truth and accusation.

'And I cared for you too,' Jenner said, a soft, sad smile on that lovely mouth. 'But I think I can do better than a commoner girl, don't you? Besides, you'll be Condemned alongside your brother. You'll be together. So it's what you wanted, too, in a way.'

'Condemned?' Lord Jardine barked with laughter, and Abi trembled to hear it. 'You know how this story ends, Jenner. With Friday's Blood Fair. Enough of this maudlin nonsense.'

Terrified, Abi jerked her head to see if Jenner would protest, but Lord Jardine was already between them. He pressed those thick fingers to her forehead and Abi went down into a darkness that held no mercy.

25

Luke

'Yet another helicopter. How tiresome,' said Jules, with a sarcastic drawl. 'I blame you, Luke. We had a nice, quiet life before you turned up.'

Luke rolled his eyes at his friend, but his heart was racing. The first chopper that came had brought Meilyr, Dina and Abi. The second, Silyen Jardine. Who would this be?

He fidgeted in his armchair, unable to continue reading the book in his hand – a mouldering account of the castle and the Crovan family. He'd trawled every shelf in the library for anything that might tell him more about what had happened that night at the Last Door. He was confident in his deduction about Coira's identity. But given that his life – and hers – would depend on them both being able to walk safely out of the door again, he needed to discover all that he could. Something that he couldn't put his finger on was nagging at him.

'It's a woman,' Jules announced. 'Alone.'

Just as they had previously, the guests stampeded onto the landing and staircase to watch for the new arrival. Left in peace, Luke forced his eyes over the relevant paragraphs one more time. What was he not understanding?

One bloody year eight centuries ago, when Scotland's *mormaer* earls vied for power, a king-presumptive and his son were murdered beneath their own roof by a treacherous guest. So the *mormaer* Crovan set about ensuring that no one would do the same to him.

The Door of Hours and the Last Door were crafted. Only the castle's lord or its heir could grant guests safe passage back to the world outside. Far from making the Crovans pariahs, this made it a mark of good faith to visit the castle, and many negotiations between rival parties were held there. That was what Jackson had been relying on, Luke thought sadly, as he closed the book. If only Crovan had been as honourable as his medieval ancestors.

He tucked the volume down the side of the chair, and went to join the others watching for the new arrival. But he'd already missed her, because as he reached the door Jules barged back in past him. His friend went straight through to the adjoining billiard room, where a bottle stood chilling in an ice bucket ready for champagne o'clock. Julian's throat worked as he drank deeply, then he slammed the bottle down, belched, and wiped his mouth.

'Jules?'

'The bitch.'

'What?'

'Who is she?' someone else asked. The rest of the guests had followed Julian back in from the landing, all as curious as Luke at his violent response.

'She's the reason I'm here,' Jules snarled, drawing another glug. 'She's my girlfriend's older sister, Heir Astrid Halfdan.'

Bottle in hand, he stormed out of the room.

Well.

Luke wanted to hurry after him, to offer encouraging words. Jules had always been insistent that he was only here because Athalie's family disapproved of her seeing a commoner, and that they had fabricated charges against him. Perhaps they'd had a change of heart. Or perhaps someone had proved his innocence and Astrid was here to notify Crovan. Maybe Athalie was getting married, and Jules was no longer considered a threat to their family's well-being, so he could be released.

But in his heart, Luke knew it would be none of these. And that it would be nothing good.

Would the Jardines have done something similar to Abi, if her relationship with Jenner had continued? He wouldn't put it past them. Jenner would have fought for her, though. Luke worried often about his big sister's safety, and where she was now, but in Dina and Jenner, she surely had powerful protectors.

Daisy was under Gavar Jardine's wing – he hoped. Luke

sometimes forgot that it was Gavar who had sprung him out of Millmoor, at Daisy's request. It sat oddly with his recollections of the boorish, swaggering heir – other than the moment Luke had paused from his woodcutting to watch the three of them out walking, Gavar holding Libby, and Daisy chattering animatedly at their side.

Libby's mother had tried to flee through Kyneston's gate with her child, but the baby had been unable to open it. And Jenner, too, had needed Silyen to open the gate the night Luke had been dumped outside the estate wall.

Both had Jardine blood in their veins, yet were incapable of opening the gate.

What was he not understanding?

His brain was so clouded. He remembered the clarity he'd experienced outside the castle, yet it was impossible to think clearly in here. Luke retrieved the history book and went to shower and dress for dinner. One more read through wouldn't hurt.

He knocked on Julian's door before going down. Jules opened it, wild-eyed and reeking of booze. Plainly the champagne wasn't the only alcohol he'd got his hands on. He wasn't in black tie.

'I'm not going,' said Julian. 'She lies. It'll all be lies. They hate me, and that one's the worst of all.'

'She might not even be at dinner.'

'Of course she will be, Hadley,' said a voice behind Luke, and he spun, horrified, to see Crovan standing there.

'She's here for you, Julian. You'll be accompanying Astrid to London tomorrow. So scrub up.'

Maybe his wild imaginings were correct, Luke thought, astonished. Maybe Athalie had been pining for his friend so badly that the family had relented.

'Interesting news for you, too, Hadley,' Crovan said, before stalking off.

'I have no idea,' Luke said to Jules's questioning look. 'None at all. Go get ready.'

Astrid Halfdan was dwarfed by Crovan as the two Equals entered the dining room where the rest of them waited. Her dark hair had a glossy, bird's-wing sheen. Her lipstick was a classy coral. And something about her was absolutely terrifying.

'Julian,' she said, breaking off her conversation with Crovan. 'Such a pleasure to see you here. Arailt assures me you've been a model prisoner, responding just as we'd hoped.'

Luke's stomach flopped. He knew what that meant – how Crovan tormented his guests with their own crimes. He'd never forget the horrifying demonstration in which Devin was slashed and stabbed by nothing but Skill. Not knowing Julian's supposed crime, Luke couldn't guess what Crovan did to him.

The lord of Eilean Dòchais pulled out a chair for Astrid, and she sat. She had been placed directly opposite Julian, who blanched.

'Athalie has been making progress, too,' she continued. 'My sister never recovered use of her hands, despite the efforts of some of the most Skilled. There were several unsuccessful rounds of neurosurgery, too. Eventually, amputation was recommended, to at least enable her to regain a semblance of function with prosthetics. She's got the prettiest little robot fingers you could hope to see. They can manipulate almost anything – as you'll find out.'

'Julian,' Crovan said, pausing for the servant to set a plate of pheasant terrine in front of him before leaning across the table. 'You've been chosen for a singular honour. Lord Jardine has revived the venerable tradition of the Blood Fair, to deliver justice to enemies of the state. But you know, people sometimes find it hard to get outraged about political crimes. So he's asked me to provide a few warm-up acts. The kind of thing that makes people's blood boil. And Athalie put in a special request for you.'

Crovan leaned back in his seat. Both he and his guest watched Julian.

Everyone watched Julian.

Luke felt sick. He didn't know what a Blood Fair was, but with a name like that it was a sure bet it didn't involve carousels and candyfloss. And while he still wasn't sure what Julian was accused of, Luke didn't need more details on anything that required amputating a girl's hands.

'I didn't do a thing to Athalie,' Julian said, his face gone very pale. 'Except love her.'

411

'So you've always claimed,' Astrid Halfdan replied. 'You loved her so much that you drugged her with veterinary-grade anaesthesia to inhibit her Skill's protective reflex – a dosage you administered every four hours during the nineteen days you held her captive. You chained her so tightly, in that basement, that the nerve damage to her wrists was irreparable, even by us.

'You loved my little sister so much that during those nineteen days you violated her repeatedly, in every way imaginable, and recorded yourself doing so. The videos show that every time you judged her insufficiently appreciative, you blocked off her airways until she passed out, then carried right on.

'Thanks to our Skill, Athalie's body has recovered from the less grievous injuries you inflicted: the twelve broken bones, the spinal fracture where you stamped on her, and the internal lacerations. But not her dear little hands. And maybe never, despite her amazing strength and spirit, her mind. If there's one night a week she sleeps through, we count ourselves lucky.'

Luke pushed his chair backwards and scrambled to his feet, anything to get away from this person he'd called his friend.

And weirdly, it was to him that Julian turned his resentful gaze.

'You suddenly believe them too, do you? I told you how

things were with me and Athalie. Punting. Parties. It was beautiful – and they ruined everything.'

'Your friend is a fantasist,' Crovan said. 'An obsessive, psychopathic fantasist. I did try to tell you when you first arrived, Hadley: this is human nature. Your precious moral superiority is pure delusion.'

Luke cringed against the wall.

'Just in case an abductor-rapist isn't enough to get the good people of London worked up to a murderous frenzy, I thought a child molester would do nicely, too. Blake, you'll also be accompanying us.' Crovan picked up his knife and fork. 'Do try the mustard, Astrid. I have it pre-pared at one of my family's properties in Dijon.'

For a few moments, the only sound in the room was the clink of Arailt Crovan and Astrid Halfdan's silver cutlery against the china plates as they ate.

'What is this?' Blake said icily, from where he sat on Julian's other side.

'The Blood Fair?' Crovan wiped his moustache with a spotless napkin. 'A primitive but wholly entertaining spec-tacle of retributive justice. The people get to vent their disgust at criminal behaviour in what you could call a hands-on fashion.'

'Not just hands,' Astrid added. 'Anything goes, really, as long as it's not fatal. Obviously cumulatively, it'll be fatal, but the idea is for it to take a while.'

Luke looked at Blake and Julian, and saw his own empty seat beside them. Three of them, all in a row.

Crovan had promised 'interesting news' for him, too. He leaned against the wall, his legs gone boneless with fear.

'Me too?' he forced out through a throat that had closed to try and keep the words in.

'You?' Crovan looked up, candlelight glittering in the lenses of his glasses. Luke was glad of the creepy reflection – glad he didn't have to see Coira's eyes looking out at him from the face of this maniac. 'You stay right here. Silyen and I aren't done with you yet. No, it's your sister Abigail who gets top billing at the Blood Fair.'

'No!' The word exploded out of Luke. Horror. Astonishment. Denial. It was all of these and more.

'It seems you set quite the revolutionary example. She stirred up trouble in Riverhead and got Dina Matravers killed. Calls herself the Angel of the North – a poetic touch. Once the mob's through with Julian and Blake, I'm sure they'll be ready for Jardine's *pièce de resistance* of a fallen angel.'

It took a moment to sort that out. Dina, dead. Abi supposedly stirring up Riverhead and calling herself the Angel of the North. And Jardine going to punish her for it?

'You know that's just not true.' Luke was shouting now. 'Dina is the Angel, not my sister. You must have seen that in my memories.'

He never received a reply, because Julian seized the

414

moment to lunge across the table at Crovan with a steak knife. It was madness with a second Equal in the room. It was madness anyway, because of the collars. Which was when Luke wondered if Julian didn't want – or didn't expect – to kill Crovan. He wanted Crovan to kill him, to spare him what was coming next.

Jules would be disappointed. He barely made it halfway across the table before Crovan's Skill, or the collar's restraining power, flipped him onto his back and slammed him against the mahogany. Astrid leaned forward with her own knife and stabbed it hard through Julian's palm, transfixing him.

She surveyed the effect, before taking the knife from the diner to her left and slamming that through the other hand. Julian howled.

'Get used to it,' Astrid said, before resuming her seat.

Dinner passed in a haze. Luke didn't dare try and meet Coira's gaze as she directed the servants in with the next courses. Julian wept and writhed, a grotesque centrepiece. Blake cut his food into minuscule pieces and ate them, one by one, like a condemned man eking out his last meal. Which was exactly what he was.

Dinner concluded, Crovan summoned Blake to his side, and the pair of them left with Astrid. The others filed out in silence, unable to look at Julian, who was plainly fastened to the table by more than just two lengths of sharpened silver.

Luke lingered a moment. The easy thing would be simply to walk out like all the rest. But Julian had been a friend to him in here; Luke had chosen not to see the darkness inside his heart.

'I'm sorry,' he said. 'What you did to that girl sounds horrific, but . . .'

He couldn't finish the sentence. Was he going to say that he didn't think Julian deserved what lay in store for him? Because he wasn't sure that was true.

He shook his head. Maybe Julian did deserve such a fate, but no society could do it and still call itself civilized. And Luke refused to subscribe to Crovan's nihilistic view of humanity. Julian's evil wasn't a judgement on the entire commoner class, and answering atrocity with atrocity could never be justified.

Julian's throat was working, as if he was trying not to cry. Then Luke began to panic that maybe he was choking.

Then he wondered if the kindest thing was to let him – until Julian released a gob of spit straight into his face. Luke recoiled, wiping his eyes, as Julian began to thrash his head and shout and swear.

It was all too much. Julian. Abi. Surely his sister couldn't be destined for the same fate? Luke shook his head, feeling desperate.

'Easy, easy.' A hand was on his shoulder and Coira was there, turning him to her and folding her arms around him. 'It's not all lost. Not yet. You heard – Crovan won't be here tomorrow. He's going with her.' She looked over at Julian. 'We can't talk here.'

Luke lifted his face from her shoulder and followed her gaze. Julian had fallen silent again, his head thudding back onto the table.

'Perhaps I could – a pillow or . . .'

Coira shook Luke gently by the shoulders, then not so gently took his face between her hands and made him look at her.

'You've got to pick your battles, Luke. He's not your battle. If Crovan and Heir Astrid find him dead in the morning, they might decide to take someone else – like the Angel of the North's brother. You can't risk it. Sleep. Tomorrow the castle is ours.'

Coira leaned in as if she might kiss him, but she simply pressed their foreheads together before spinning away into the kitchen. Luke didn't know if he was disappointed or relieved. He couldn't cope with anything more tonight. His legs barely worked to trudge up the stairs to his room, where he fell face down onto the bed.

In the middle of the night Luke came to, gasping. Dark images churned through his mind, all of them of his sister.

Abi, suffering.

He saw Astrid Halfdan pin her to a table with knives through her hands. He saw Julian, leering, as he stamped down hard on her midriff. He saw a collar flare golden at her throat and the lord of Eilean Dòchais bend to clip a leash to it and tug her onto all fours. His sister was whimpering as she crawled on bleeding hands. She had Dog's broken-backed gait because Julian had shattered her spine. Crovan paraded her through the streets of London and the people jeered and applauded.

Luke ran to the sink and was violently sick. It was all he could manage not to punch the enamel, furious and powerless. He glanced at the clock on the wall. Three in the morning. It was Thursday now. The Blood Fair would take place on Friday – called as a public holiday. Unless he could stop it, Abi's fate would be everything his nightmares had shown him, and worse.

Had she no defenders down there in London? Did Daisy know about any of this? Luke desperately hoped his little sis was blissfully ignorant. And yet, might Daisy be able to beg Gavar to rescue Abi, as she had persuaded him to rescue Luke? It didn't seem likely that the heir would thwart his father's plans so publicly. There was Jenner Jardine, but he was Skilless and unable even to open his own estate gate. How could he snatch a girl from the middle of a public killing ground?

Skilless, and unable to open the Kyneston gate.

Like Gavar's baseborn daughter, Libby: also unable to open the Kyneston gate, and also Skilless.

And yet the Last Door had obeyed Coira.

Did that – could that – mean what he thought?

Luke was no expert in Equal genealogy, but he was

418

pretty sure baseborn children weren't considered Equals. That was what the long-running drama of Libby Jardine was all about: Gavar wanting his daughter recognized, and his parents refusing.

Yet blood alone wasn't enough for a Skillful boundary to obey you – as shown by Jenner Jardine. You needed Skill as well.

Luke reached for the book he'd been reading earlier. Yes. There it was, set out plainly. Only the lord *or heir* could grant safe passage through the door. For the door to obey her, Coira had to be the castle's heir – and to be heir, she had to be Equal-born.

And if she was Equal-born, she would have Skill.

It hardly seemed possible.

If she had Skill, she could summon the boat. They could sail over the loch, make their way to the town that supplied the castle. Find the nearest railway station. Get to London. Coira's Skill might even help rescue Abi.

The despair he'd felt, as he'd fallen on his bed the previous night, was replaced by a sudden, surging hope.

He lay down, unable to go back to sleep, drifting fitfully in and out of consciousness until dawn knocked at his window. He dressed mechanically, every minute or so reminding himself of his deduction, as if to embed it too deep for forgetting. He found a pencil and scribbled it down, too, in the history book, because who knew what might happen between now and the time Crovan left.

As he came down for breakfast, a ghastly sight awaited. Julian and Blake were standing in the hallway unmoving; their eyes were open but seemingly unseeing, plainly bound by Skill.

The breakfast table was deathly silent, except for Crovan and Astrid Halfdan's inconsequential talk. The guests all listened, wretchedly, as he urged her to try the salmon, caught in a stream on the Crovan estate and smoked to a recipe unchanged since the days of the *mormaer*. She told him about the preparations for the fair and the great platform being erected in Gorregan Square. It would be sited right at the heart of things, at the axis of Aston House and the Mall, and the House of Light and Whitehall.

After breakfast, the whole household gathered in the hallway to watch the two Equals and their prisoners depart. Luke kept his head down, saying nothing, trying not to draw attention to himself.

Except his silence itself drew attention.

'You've been quiet, Hadley,' Crovan said, and Luke's veins iced up.

'I was trying to work out how to hide in your suitcase so I can go and rescue my sister,' he said, as insolently as he could.

Crovan barked with amusement. 'No suitcase needed. I keep a townhouse in Belgravia. No, the best thing you can do for your sister, Hadley, is wish her a quick death. Maybe a heart attack as the first blade goes in. Devin, I'll be back

in two days. Astrid my dear, after you. Julian, Blake, follow
us.'

He held the Last Door open for Astrid Halfdan, all cour-
tesy. Blake and Julian stepped robotically after her, their
movements no longer theirs to command. Then the lord of
Eilean Dòchais was gone. As one, the guests swarmed up
to the library and watched out of the window as the boat
sailed into view, crossed the loch, and the helicopter lifted
off.

There wasn't a minute to waste. Luke hurtled down the
stairs and pelted towards the kitchen – only to run into
Coira coming out.

'Steady,' she said, holding him at arm's length.
'Everything becomes that bit more difficult if you've got a
broken leg.'

'Please,' he said, leading her into one of the small side
rooms and closing the door. 'You have to listen. I can't
quite believe it, but it has to be true.'

He unfolded his deduction. And to his astonishment,
her first question wasn't about her Skill.

'So where's my mother?' she said sceptically. 'If she was
an Equal, she wouldn't be someone Crovan could just
dispose of. And then why have I led a life like this, collared
like a servant?'

Luke's brain raced for an explanation.

'Perhaps he was cruel to her and she left him, but had to
leave you behind. Or she was unfaithful, or he thought she

was, and they separated and Crovan took it out on you? Who knows. We'll find out, I promise. But first, please, I have to get out of here. My sister dies tomorrow if I don't. You have to call the boat over so we can get away. I know you can do it.'

'If I have Skill, then why have I never felt it? You'd think I'd know.'

This knocked the breath from Luke like a punch. Maybe Coira was like Jenner after all. Maybe she had no Skill, and *that* was why Crovan had separated from her mother, and why Coira lived collared with the servants. Maybe she'd lived upstairs until her father had finally given up hope that her Skill would appear. Then, disgusted, he had sent her below.

But there was still the fact of the door.

'I don't know,' he said desperately. 'I've no idea. But I know that what happened at the door before was real. And Crovan knew it too, I could tell. Please.'

'We have to try,' she agreed. '"I've gathered some things for you, money from Devin's cash box and some normal clothes. Get changed, then we can go.'

She led him to the pantry, where he found his old trousers laid out alongside a shirt and a chunky, high-necked jumper that would conceal his collar. A fisherman's satchel contained a roll of bank notes, food and water. Then they crept through the deserted entrance hall.

Luke and Coira stood in front of the Last Door side by side. He reached for her hand and squeezed it.

'I should probably say something,' she said. 'He did, just now, when showing Heir Astrid out – "after you", he said. That's permission to leave.'

She pulled open the door, and Luke saw two things: one was the rain-washed morning of Loch nan Deur, clouds dulling the glinting water.

But laid over it, Luke saw a different, twilit land, where a breeze ruffled copper grass. As Luke looked up, the silhouette of a great owl passed across the silver disk of the moon. And by its pale light, he saw something he'd not noticed before – on a mountainside, the gleam of a golden tower.

Luke's heart felt like it might burst. In that tower was the king. He knew it.

'Go on,' Coira urged him.

Luke shook his head to clear it. His sister needed him. He couldn't afford to step through that door to anywhere but the shore of Crovan's island.

He blinked furiously, as if that shining land was a mote he could dislodge from his eye. When he focused again, all he could see was the the rocky shore of Eilean Dòchais, beneath a light Highland drizzle that dimpled the loch.

Coira would think he was hesitating because he was afraid.

He stepped through and felt the rain soft against his cheek.

He turned to Coira, behind him, to check.

'You're still here,' she said, with one of her rare smiles.

'Yes.'

She meant that he was still alive. But Luke tried to hide the strange disappointment he felt at being here, and not *there*, in the king's twilit realm.

No. He was where he needed to be. Where Abi needed him to be.

'Your turn – if you're sure you want to do this.'

He watched her pale, determined face, and realized the depth of her courage. He knew they were right, that she was this castle's heir and that the door was hers to bind or loose.

But if they were wrong. If they were wrong . . .

Coira stepped through and he seized her and swung her around joyfully.

'You did it! Oh, you did it.'

And with an extravagant flourish he went down on one knee and kissed her hand, and didn't even care that he went bright red as he did so.

'Heir Coira.'

'We're not there yet,' she said, pulling her fingers gently from his grasp. She was frowning. 'This is where my Skill wakes up and summons the boat, right? Because I'm still waiting for that to happen.'

Luke stood up immediately. He had assumed . . .

He had assumed . . .

'You're not feeling anything?'

'No. And I haven't for my whole life. Why would that change now?' Her hands went to the band at her throat. 'Maybe it's this? He controls people with these collars, so perhaps mine controls Skill too? Or maybe I just don't have any.'

She held out her hands, as if willing them to flare with power, like something from a movie. But they remained empty. Just her own chapped-raw palms and slender fingers, red-knuckled from all the scrubbing in the kitchens.

Luke's throat constricted, as if the collar there was tightening. What was the problem?

'I'm sorry, Luke.' Coira looked up, and for the first time on that strong, sensible face he saw something like hopelessness. 'There's just nothing there. I'm so sorry.'

Her eyes shone, and as he watched, a single tear welled up and spilled over, running shining down her cheek. She reached up to wipe it away.

And as she did, the fire came back into her eyes. She took his hand, and pulled.

'We forgot,' she said. 'There's another way.'

26

Luke

She did it like she did everything: boldly. As she went down the steps to the glittering dark water, it was Luke's turn to panic. Her reasoning was that the loch, like the door, would respond to her simply as a Crovan, rather than needing any Skillful command. But he knew the agonizing price she'd pay if it didn't.

So when the water parted beneath her foot, as she left the final step above the water margin, he sagged with relief.

'Wait, I need to stay close.'

He kept one hand on her back as they entered the water and crossed the loch. The chasm of water was chilling, the trickling walls on either side blocking the sunlight. But Luke's hand was warm where it rested on Coira's shoulder and his heart sang with expectation.

'I hope nothing stops us reaching the shore,' Coira said as the loch bed began to slope upwards again. 'The boat wouldn't land with Rhys still on board, remember.'

But plainly the Crovan land and the Crovan loch would

not deny their heir, because first Coira and Luke's heads emerged above the waterline, then their shoulders, until finally it was at their ankles and they stepped free of the dark water onto the gleaming gravel.

'Phew.' Coira pushed back her hair. 'I'm glad that's over. Though I've got the walk back to look forward to.'

'What? Why would you ever go back? We're free now. You never have to see this place again.'

'It's not that simple, Luke.'

The look in her grey eyes didn't bode well.

'Think about it. I've never left this castle. It's my whole world. I've never seen a train, or a . . . shop. Never even been in a village, much less a city, much less London. And I don't have any Skill to help you save your sister. I'm not the person you need with you for this. I'd get run over or something before we even reached Edinburgh.

'And there are the others. There are people here who need to escape. I have to get them out. And there's my . . . father, and my mother. I need answers, Luke. Who am I? I need to know.'

Luke couldn't believe it. 'If he's kept your parentage hidden for seventeen years, why do you think he'd tell you now? And he'll punish you for helping me and the others to escape. He'll make you forget that you ever knew a thing about yourself. You'll be back to being a Condemned servant girl, when really you're this castle's heir.'

'Well, it's good that you'll be out and free with that

knowledge in your head then, isn't it? You'll be okay, Luke. You have more allies than you know. I've seen how Silyen Jardine looks at you. You're important to him, though I've no idea why.

'You are going to rescue your sister, and you are not going to forget about me. And when things are calmer, if I still haven't found you, then you must come back for me. But I can't go with you now.'

Unexpectedly, quickly – too quickly for Luke to follow – she broke away and darted back into the loch and he'd lost her. He called her name, yelled it with everything in his lungs, but he could see the turbulence in the water as she went deeper, walking away from him.

He couldn't believe it. Had he done something wrong? Said something wrong?

But no, there was no time for that. He had to reach London – and Abi. The supply boat crossed from the opposite side of the loch, and it was serviced by a delivery truck that came down a track to the shore. At the other end of that track would be a shop, a village, and a bigger road.

The wheel-rutted-track was where he started. His shoulders were hunched with every step he took, as if anticipating – what? A yelled alert to his escape? A bullet from Devin's rifle? The village proved even worse. Luke held his breath as he passed through. Paranoid, he imagined every house here having a sheet pinned up with photos of all the

Condemned, in case any of them escaped. But of course, none ever did.

The track away from the village soon became a tarmac road – practically a highway in this part of Scotland. At a T-junction, a sign pointed in one direction to the Isle of Skye bridge, so he turned the other way and stuck his thumb out. He struck lucky when two blokes on their way to a stag weekend in Inverness gave him a ride. They'd already opened the beer so the conversation required from him was minimal, which avoided any super-awkward 'What are you doing up here?' questions.

A couple of hours later they dropped him at the railway station, pressed a can of beer on him 'for the journey', then pulled away tooting their horn. Luke bolted into the departure hall. Coira had given him enough money for the ticket, but the timetable had no good news. Inverness was the other end of the country to London and it would take nearly nine hours to get there, with a change at Edinburgh. The next train left just before 1 p.m.

They were the longest nine hours of Luke's life – worse even than the day he'd spent shut in Kyneston's cellars after his trial. He'd used the time at Inverness station to buy a baseball cap to hide under, and a visitor guidebook to London. He'd only been in the city twice, once on a school trip and once as a family treat when Mum received a promotion. His memories were of the tourist spots, individual places with no idea how they connected.

He remembered Astrid mentioning the Blood Fair's location – in Gorregan Square, where the roads from Aston House and the House of Light met. He traced the map with his fingers, trying to commit the streets to memory. But beyond mastering some basic orientation, Luke had so little information that formulating a plan was beyond him. He'd received the impression that the prisoners were held at the parliamentary complex at Westminster. Breaking them out of there would be a non-starter.

Gorregan Square was the best bet. If the Blood Fair relied on ordinary people being frenzied enough to murder defenceless prisoners, the mood would be close to anarchy. Who knew at what moment it might all spin out of control and give Luke an opening. That thought wasn't much, but it was something.

Once they were past Durham, he pulled the cap down and hunched in his seat. He'd lost sleep due to the nightmares about Abi, and knew he'd likely be awake much of the night. The train conductor nudged him once, to check his ticket again. Then when he next woke, it was dark and he was in London.

Security stood on the other side of the ticket barriers, rifles tucked into their elbows. Were they waiting for him? But no, he saw them stopping people as they left the platform. It looked like a spot check of some kind.

'Curfew for all under-eighteens,' he heard one say.

'Twenty-four hours, until six o'clock tomorrow night. Please get your children indoors directly.'

Luke hoped his stubble was bristling, and thanked his time in the Machine Park for a chest that was broader than most boys' his age, as he squared back his shoulders and walked confidently past. A band was playing in the plaza outside the station, and punters were crowding around a temporary bar lit up with neon. Women in short dresses walked around handing out drinks from trays. On the stage behind the band, a digital clock counted down from its current position of just over thirteen hours.

It was the number of hours until the executions began, Luke realized. The number of hours his sister had left to live.

Choked, he pushed past a girl who held out a drink to him, not stopping to apologize when he knocked it flying. He needed to get to Gorregan Square right now.

Traffic was flowing as normal, but signs warned of closures from midnight. Many streets were already dark and deserted, but here and there – in Russell Square and Covent Garden – were more bands, more bars. In the darkness, on park benches, squatting on the steps of churches and among the shadows of Covent Garden's grand arcade, he saw people passing around bottles, cigarettes, joints, and more.

'You want something?' a shaven-headed guy said, shaking

a little ziplock bag full of what Luke was very sure weren't headache pills. 'Special rates tonight.'

Luke shook his head and picked up his pace.

You could hear Gorregan half a mile away. His progress slowed as the streets became busier; he wasn't the only one heading to the square. It sounded like the biggest party London had ever seen was underway. Soon, the air itself was reverberating to the thud of bass from massive speakers.

As he approached the National Gallery, he could hardly believe what he was seeing. It looked as though the whole population of London was there, crammed into the square and spilling down the radiating roads.

Immense statues stood at three of the square's four corners. At the fourth was an empty plinth, intended to hold the statue of a king, but abandoned and symbolically left empty after the Equal Revolution. It afforded Luke an excellent vantage point over the seething mass below.

Unignorable, in the centre of the square, was the scaffold. It encircled the base of Nelson's Column, built on the backs of the four monumental bronze lions that guarded the admiral's monument. Another low platform surrounded it. That would be so the crowd could reach the victims, Luke realized with a shudder.

On the scaffolding, set at intervals and close to its edge, were thick metal posts. As Luke pushed closer, he saw that long chains hung down from each post: two from the top, ending in small cuffs, and one from the centre, terminating in a secondary loop of metal. Again, the chains were long enough that the person attached to them could be reached easily.

Crash barriers edged the platform. People were already camped down there, Luke saw with disgust. Who were they? Who could be so sick in the head that they'd want to be first in line to inflict pain on someone they'd never met, whose crime hadn't affected them in the slightest?

The numbers were against Abi and the rest. London had a population of more than six million. It stood to reason that among so many, there would be a few – and it would only need to be a few – twisted enough to grab this opportunity.

How could he stop this? Join the fray around Abi, with bolt cutters to sever her chains? But he wouldn't know which post would be hers. And Security would just haul her off again – and probably pull him up there, too, for good measure.

Some sort of diversion, then. Maybe he could steal some tear gas canisters from Security, let them off just as the first victims – that would be Blake and Jules – were being led out. Or maybe a bomb alert, to evacuate the area before the spectacle even started? It was such a long shot, but he had to try something. No one had searched his bag as he came into the square. Anyone here could be carrying anything.

He did a lap of the square, checking for opportunities. As he walked, he turned over idea after idea, but came up with nothing better. On his third circuit, he saw a Security officer enjoying his beat near one of the pop-up bars. A flirtatious bar girl was plying the man with drinks. The situation had potential, and Luke settled in to watch.

He waited as the officer became progressively more intoxicated, then he allowed the crowd to jostle him in close. Grateful for all he'd learned from Renie during the Club's 'games', Luke managed to snag one of the tear gas cylinders from the man's utility belt. He made a note to try for his stun gun later, if the guy was out completely cold, but when he circled around again, the officer was gone.

He'd need a phone to make a bomb-threat call. That bit was simple. The square was full of people either drunk or high or both. His momentary qualm about lifting a woman's handbag was quickly squashed. Anyone whose idea of fun included drunk-dancing the night before people were publicly tortured to death deserved the inconvenience of losing their bag. The woman's phone was a standard touch-key model, so unlike the smartphones used by the Equals, there'd be no worry about unlocking it. He dialled a number at random to check, and heard the dial tone. No problems there.

Then it was time to hunker down and wait.

27

Luke

As dawn rose, Gorregan's bronze lions and marble statues gazed imperturbably across a party that was showing no signs of stopping. A reek of sweat and vomit hung over the imposing square. Given the state of most people here, half of them would happily stab a penknife in a prisoner's leg if their mates told them it'd be a laugh.

But no. Luke wouldn't believe that. Not until the evidence of his own eyes convinced him. That was Crovan's view of human nature. Never Luke's.

With the fair scheduled to begin at ten that morning, he resolved to make the call at half eight – enough time for an evacuation, but not long enough for them to discover that there was no bomb and restart the whole thing. Worming his way through the thick of the crowd, he skulked round the back of St Martin in the Fields. He rehearsed his words, then, with sweaty fingers, dialled the emergency services.

'Okay, thank you for your call,' said the male voice at the

other end when he'd delivered his piece. It sounded almost bored.

'You don't understand. I said, I have a bomb, and I will detonate it if the Blood Fair goes ahead.'

'Yes, you and the hundreds of other people who've called this morning saying the same thing. Student, are you, sonny? One of these "social justice warriors"? Do us a favour and stop wasting our time.'

'No, wait, I'm none of that. This isn't a threat – it's real. I'll do it. I'm . . . family.'

'Ah.' The voice paused a moment. 'Well, I'm sorry to hear that, son. But you've got to understand, what these people did was against the law, and that needs to be punished. I can see from the location of your phone that you're near Gorregan. Here's my advice. Go home. Whatever you do, don't stay there and watch it, kid.'

The line went dead.

Luke let out a stream of curse words that would have given Mum a heart attack if she'd heard them. What options were left? Almost none. He fingered the tear gas cylinder. He'd intended to throw it into the crowd, to create chaos just as they led Abi out. In the confusion, he would grab her and perhaps they could make an escape – although how, and where to, was the point at which that particular plan started to fall apart.

But another idea occurred. Maybe a way to bring the show to a halt before it even began. An elevated viewing box had been constructed, from which the Equals would watch everything. A gas canister tossed in there might abort the whole event. He needed to get back fast, before the square became so densely packed he'd have no chance of finding a spot.

It was well past nine by the time he'd wriggled his way into the press of people around the platform. At one point, he thought he'd have to drop to his hands and knees and crawl through the thicket of legs. He lost count of the number of times he was elbowed in the eye, trodden on, or shoved so hard it winded him.

But eventually he reached the front. Just a few people stood between him and the scaffold, while behind him – erected over a statue of some women standing on a wave, so it would be solid and immovable – was the Equals' elaborately decorated viewing box. At the right moment, he could toss the canister either onto the platform, or up into the box. He reached for his satchel, to check it was still safely there.

And discovered to his horror that the satchel was gone. The strap must have ripped in the press of bodies. Or maybe someone had done to him what he had done to the dancing woman whose bag he'd nicked. A knife brought to stab a victim of the Blood Fair could just as easily slice through a bag strap.

He let out a howl of despair. All his ideas, come to nothing.

'What's up?' said the person next to him. 'Lost something?'

He turned, wound tight enough to punch the speaker, some bloke in a hoodie, when in the shadow of the hood he glimpsed a flicker of gold. The guy blinked, and it was gone.

'I should have known you wouldn't miss it, Luke,' said Silyen Jardine. 'Though I'm intrigued as to how you escaped from an inescapable, blood-bound castle. You'll have to tell me over a coffee sometime. My treat.'

'Don't say another word to me,' Luke said, 'unless it's to explain that you're here to rescue my sister.'

'Me? I'm here to let the Dog off the leash for a bit. You know what he's like about rapists, and he has such fond memories of Julian and Blake.'

Luke followed Silyen's gaze, and there was Dog at the very front, pressed up against the crash barriers.

'What's wrong with you? People are going to die here, and you've brought him along to help?'

'You're surprised, after I let an innocent boy be Condemned for a crime he didn't commit? After I encouraged Zelston to make a Proposal that could only ruin him? When I was the only one there when my aunt died? Either you're less intelligent than I thought, or you have a touchingly high opinion of me, despite all the evidence to the contrary.'

Half concealed by the hoodie, Silyen's mouth curved up

into a smile. Luke's fingers itched to smack it. But right now, the Equal was the only hope he had of rescuing his sister – because he could, Luke was certain. With the merest lift of his fingers, Silyen Jardine could save Abi's life.

'How did you even know I'd be here?'

'I had no idea you were coming. You *are* supposed to be a prisoner in Scotland. But I felt you right away once I got here, thanks to our … *special* connection.' Silyen stepped closer, so that his hood framed both their faces. He grabbed the front of Luke's sweater and twisted, pulling their bodies together. 'When something's stuck to a spider's web, she can feel it wriggling, no matter where she is.'

Luke wasn't even going to think about what that might mean. Only that it was somehow, possibly, useful. *You're important to Silyen Jardine*, Coira had said. Well, if he was, he could do something with that.

'It's a shame our little bond will be broken,' he said, keeping his voice level, 'when I die up on that scaffold alongside my sister, when my rescue goes horribly wrong. Unless you do something.'

Silyen let go and Luke stumbled back.

'Ahh,' the Equal said, his smile even wider, if that was possible. 'I knew you'd be perfect, Luke. From the minute we met, I knew. But I doubt I'll need to do a thing. Look, here comes my family.'

A peal of trumpets sounded. The crowd pressed and swayed as Security opened a path for the Jardines: Lord

Whittam and Lady Thalia, Gavar and Bouda, then Jenner. They took their seats; the sixth chair was empty.

'Ooops,' Luke heard Silyen mutter. 'Forgot to put that in my diary. And I'd keep your head down, Luke.'

Luke needed no telling, because he'd just glimpsed those arriving to occupy the next two rows of seats. He could barely see the petite forms of Astrid Halfdan and the girl alongside her. But he saw Astrid's companion lift a hand to push back her long hair, and her slender arm ended in a gleaming robotic claw. After her huffed a humongous man that Luke recognized as Lord Matravers, Dina's father. He was too out of breath to speak, but was listening intently to Crovan.

'Yes, we should do something about that.' Silyen reached out to Luke's throat and teased down the neck of the jumper. His fingertips brushed across skin and collar. 'It's a shame, because it's a good look on you. But we don't want any unnecessary fuss.'

As easily as if it had been a ribbon tied around Luke's neck, Silyen slipped a finger beneath the golden band. Luke watched him draw it off and almost cried with relief.

Silyen held it up to inspect for a moment, then tipped his hand and let it fall to the ground. The band evanesced in a shimmer before it hit.

Luke remembered when the Equal had plucked the padlock from Dog's cage. He dispensed freedom so casually, did Silyen Jardine. As if it was nothing at all.

'Pay attention,' Silyen mouthed, pointing towards the platform.

The horror was already beginning.

Julian, clad in only a pair of white shorts, had been frog-marched onto the platform. Gone was the Skill-induced blankness of yesterday morning. He was fully alert – and plainly terrified. He was begging and whimpering as Security moved around him, fixing the chains: two at his wrists, a third looped around his waist. On the far side of the platform, Luke could see Blake receiving the same treatment, unresisting and contemptuous.

'People of Britain!' Lord Jardine's voice carried across the square. 'The ties that bind us are greater than the forces that seek to tear us apart. You serve us, and we protect you. This is how it has always been.

'And more than merely protecting you, we want you to flourish. We live to keep our country strong, and to improve life for each one of you. As a token of that pledge, today we deliver for your judgement those who have grievously wronged you, and our country.'

London was lapping it up. Those gathered in the square were baying and applauding. Luke couldn't believe it. They were cheering a man who was telling them that their place was to serve. They must be intoxicated beyond reason.

Jardine continued. 'This pair are convicted of the rape of children and the mutilation of a young woman. After them will come more. Seditionists who burned the crops that make your children's bread. Wreckers who terrorized the quiet and honest labour of the worktowns. We give them to you.

'Act without fear of retribution. Against these creatures, here and now, no crime can be committed. Today we entrust our justice to your hands.'

The trumpets blasted. Security dragged back the crash barriers. Then, with a roar, those at the front of the crowd surged forward. Luke swayed on his feet, partly from the motion, partly because he was dizzy with horror and amazement.

He felt Silyen's hand at his elbow, holding him steady.

'Watch,' the boy murmured. 'Watch and understand.'

'What am I supposed to understand?'

'That you don't get to save everybody.'

Luke shook him off.

Julian's wailing was inhuman, a piglike squealing. Blood fountained up. Something followed it, tossed high above the crowd. A finger. Then another.

'For Miss Athalie!' someone cried, as an apple corer stabbed down roughly where Julian's eyes might be. Jules's scream was as jagged as broken glass. Luke turned away, and glimpsed, in the box behind, the gleam of two robot hands applauding.

It went on and on. Torn scraps of bloodstained white cloth were trampled, unregarded. Luke saw what looked like a fan of steel, and could have sworn he heard Dog's demented laughter. Then came a piercing, ululating shriek from Julian that Luke didn't think he'd ever forget, as something resembling offal was flung into the air and there was a lavatorial stink.

Luke doubled over and vomited. A soul-deep nausea wrung out his stomach. Julian's screaming ceased, and Luke heaved one last time.

He saw a glint on the ground. Someone had dropped a knife. He curled his fingers around it. As he straightened up, the mess that had been Julian was being dragged to the rear of the platform.

A column of prisoners was marched up the steps to take his place: half a dozen men, then at the back of the group, Abi.

No, not quite the back. After her came Renie.

In a moment, Luke's knife was at Silyen Jardine's throat.

'If you've a plan for rescuing my sister, now would be a really good time.'

Silyen *tsk*ed, making no move to push the blade away.

'Only dull people have plans, Luke. "Go here. Do this. Hope other people do that." It never works. No, clever people embrace possibilities. Seize opportunities. For example, there are several intriguing possibilities for what will happen here next. And in only one of those does your sister die.'

'That's one too many.'

Then a powerful voice roared out, 'Get that child off there!'

'Oooh,' Silyen murmured quietly at his side. 'Not the one I was expecting.'

Luke had heard that voice before, in another crowded square where hell was breaking loose. He turned to look. Gavar Jardine was on his feet, standing at the front of the box, gesturing furiously.

'We believe she's sixteen, Heir Gavar,' a voice replied from the stage. And Luke recognized that one, too, though he glanced over his shoulder to check. Yep. Kessler, his Millmoor nemesis.

'She looks more like twelve, but I don't give a damn either way. I'm not going to watch a child be ripped to pieces. Nor a young woman, either.'

'Sit down, Gavar,' said Bouda Matravers icily. 'This is the justice they deserve.'

'It's nothing of the sort,' Gavar snarled.

Which was when the sculptured marble wave the Equals' box rested on somehow, impossibly, lifted higher, and the air quivered with a roar that could only have originated deep in the throats of the square's monumental bronze lions. The stone wave curled and crashed in a jaw-dropping display of Skill, smashing the box to the ground. Equals tumbled and fell, the people nearby yelling and pushing to get out of the way.

Luke looked at Silyen in astonishment. The Equal boy shrugged, in an unmistakable 'not me'.

Then a light came into his eyes and he pointed. Away across the square, standing tall on Gorregan Square's empty fourth plinth, was a young woman Luke didn't recognize, her head half shaved and hands uplifted.

'Good old Midsummer,' Silyen whispered, grinning.

Behind them, the lions roared again.

Then with a scorching uprush of air, the platform surrounding the scaffold burst into flames.

28

Abi

The stage beneath her feet heaved as if the earth itself had shrugged. Abi staggered, grabbing the metal post for support. The Security man who'd been holding her cuffs, ready to fasten them, was thrown violently sideways.

'Renie!', she yelled – but the scaffolding between them tore in two, Renie's section jutting up even as Abi's tilted downwards. The kid scrabbled to hold on to the edge of it with her fingertips, while Abi's knees buckled and she fell.

The ground shook with a monstrous rumbling, as if a Tube train was somehow tunnelling up to the surface. And as Abi watched, Renie's portion of the scaffold was lifted high on the back of a monstrous bronze lion that tossed its head and roared.

Was she going mad? Had they put a chain around her neck and tightened it – and, starved of oxygen, was she hallucinating this?

The platform surrounding them burst into flames, as did

the shattered viewing box. Everywhere people were running and screaming.

Abi tensed for the Security man to grab her. If he fastened the chains, either the people of London would swarm over her with steel in their hands and murder in their eyes, or the fire would burn her up. She'd fight him with her last strength.

But no-one touched her.

Behind her, Abi heard the guard's groans. Perhaps he'd been injured. But there was no time to look. The flames were hot on her face and the scaffold would catch fire next. She had to jump – but it would be blind, a leap through flame and smoke. She rocked back on her heel for propulsion, then launched herself forward.

Hot, black air seared her throat as the exertion forced her to drag in a breath. But she made it through the flames – only for her feet to catch the top of the crash barrier. Abi fell in a tangle of clattering metal, sharp pain shooting through her elbow and ankle.

Something roared and a giant bronze paw smashed down beside her.

'Abi!'

She looked up. Renie was perched on the back of the gargantuan metal lion. She sat astride its shoulders, her fingers dug deep into its rippling mane.

'Come on,' the kid shouted, reaching down. But Renie was too small and the lion too large. And Abi's arm hurt too much to lift it, and her ankle too much to stand. So though Renie's fingers strained to reach her, they never had a hope of pulling her up.

The lion roared again and sprang away. Renie twisted on its back, still hopelessly reaching out. Abi shook her head, willing the kid to turn round and hang on.

The bronze beast cleared the flaming wreckage of the Equals' box in a single bound. The noise in the square was deafening, now, as people fled. Another throaty rumble came from somewhere nearby, and the crowd heaved and turned again to get away from the path of a second lion, then a third and fourth. Mounted on one, Abi thought she saw Renie's uncle Wes. Pulled up behind him were several men of the Bore.

The four lions stalked across Gorregan Square, and Abi saw where they were headed. On the empty fourth plinth in front of the National Gallery stood Midsummer Zelston, arms stretched wide. She looked like a bronze statue herself, monumental and magnificent.

Two of the great lions reached her side and stayed there, tails lashing angrily. From the other two, the riders dismounted and the creatures readied themselves to spring back down the steps to retrieve the remaining Bore workers – and Abi, she devoutly hoped. She dragged herself to her feet, wincing.

'No,' said Bouda Matravers, in a voice loud enough to be heard half a mile away in the House of Light.

The blonde woman was immaculate as ever, despite having been thrown from the box like all the others. She stretched out one hand across the square, and Abi wondered if she was somehow going to pluck Midsummer from where she stood, or throttle her with nothing but the power of Skill.

Instead, the fountains blew.

At the heart of Gorregan Square was a massive ornamental pool of water. At each of its four corners, fountains in the shape of Nelson's ships poured ceaseless streams from their bowsprits. In the centre, a giant bowl spumed water high into the air. As Bouda's hands pinched and twisted in the air, the bowl flew off, the ships cracked open, and the ornamental cascades turned into geysers.

The water poured up in a torrent, then flowed outward like a high curtain, forming a glassy, rippling wall that divided the square in two. Walled off, the lions prowled and snarled.

At the near side of the pool, water spiralled upwards in a twisting, turning column – then lashed down with a terrible power towards the burning scaffold.

The force of it was incredible. It doused the flames in a deafening sizzle, sending up a wave of acrid smoke. The debris – Abi included – was blasted away in a foaming flotsam of wood, ash, metal poles and chains, and wrecked crash barriers. Other people caught in the torrent slammed into her – were they spectators? Security? Something torn and bloody washed over her, perhaps from the man they'd ripped apart first.

As she was swept away Abi thought she heard a voice shout her name, but she must have been mistaken because it sounded like Luke.

Then something struck her head and her ears rang, her vision swam, and she felt herself sink.

It could have been immediately, or it could have been minutes later that a hand roughly pulled back her hair. Another slapped her face. She couldn't move, Abi realized. Something heavy pinned her down.

'Abigail.'

This stern voice definitely wasn't Luke. She tried to look, but could barely open her eyes. The person gave a growl of annoyance and pressed two fingers against one puffy eyelid despite her yelps. There was a violent tingling, and when she blinked, she found that she could see.

The sight was a surprise.

'The kid got away okay?' her rescuer asked. 'I thought I saw her on one of those bloody lions.'

'She did,' Abi rasped, her throat hoarse from the smoke.

'And what about you?' said Gavar Jardine. 'You're all bashed up, but that's better than what they had planned for you. Come on, I'm getting you out of here, and away from this shitshow my family laid on.'

Gavar. What did this mean? Abi had never liked the

boorish heir: he was too fond of the bottle and treated women despicably.

And yet he'd fetched Luke out of Millmoor, hadn't he? At Daisy's request. Was that what this was?

'Did Daisy ask you to rescue me?' Abi croaked, as the heir of Kyneston pulled the wreckage of the scaffolding off her as easily as a kid picking clothes off his bedroom floor.

'Daisy? No, she doesn't know a thing about all this. I had no idea you were the star of the show either, until I saw you up there just now. The fire was me. Sorry about that. It happens when I'm angry.'

'And this made you angry? Wasn't it all your family's idea? Your father. Your wife. Your *brother.*'

She remembered what Jenner had done, the depth of his betrayal, and just for a moment wanted to close her eyes and tell Gavar Jardine to leave her, because nothing was fixable after this.

'I'm *not,*' Gavar said through gritted teeth, as he lifted a final piece of twisted metal and tossed it aside, 'my *family.*'

Then he bent down and scooped her up carefully.

'Wait,' Abi said, urgently. 'My brother. I thought I heard his voice.'

'Your brother is at that madman's castle. I'm sorry, Abigail, but we need to go while everyone's still watching the circus that's happening back there.'

'Yes,' she said, coughing, the last of her strength leaching from her. 'Of course he's not here. I'm being ridiculous.'

451

'I'll take you to your sister, if she'll do?'

Daisy would certainly do. Abi's heart sang at the thought of seeing her little sis again.

Gavar's grip around her tightened as he strode through the wreckage of Gorregan like it was nothing at all.

Abi studied him. The past two months had been incomprehensible: from the moment Highwithel had suddenly reared out of the sea, to Jenner's betrayal – still too raw even to consider. Being rescued by Gavar Jardine was merely one more thing that defied explanation.

'Your family won't be happy with what you did,' she said.

'My family has lost its senses,' Gavar said. 'As has everyone else, apparently. I've never seen anything more disgusting in my entire life. I'm not saying Meilyr and Dina were right. But I'm not being a part of whatever my father and Bouda think they're doing.'

An ally, Abi thought. That was what Gavar Jardine was – or could be.

'As Father keeps pointing out,' the heir continued, digging a key from his pocket as he lowered Abi onto the saddle of a motorbike. 'I have no idea how to run a country. But I'm pretty sure it's not like this.'

'Well,' Abi croaked, 'I have a few ideas.'

And Gavar Jardine snorted as he swung his leg over the bike behind her and kicked it into gear.

Abi felt the engine's vibrations thrum through her. Then

and so many more. Your support and enthusiasm means the world to me. So do you.

To Mike, Fiona, Jacques and Jay, for not letting me quit my 'other dream job'. Paddy, Jeremy and Mark for patience and unfailing good humour on location and in the edit. (Greg, if you could write half of my next book that would be marvellous.)

To the readers who loved *Gilded Cage*, and the bloggers who use their time to give books exposure: you warm my heart. You are so appreciated.

And not least to my family: Mum, Jonathan and Dad. Sis-in-law Justine. Isabella and Rufus, at last you know what your auntie does! I'm so proud of you both.

Acknowledgements

To my agents, Robert Kirby, Ginger Clark and Jane Willis: treasured dream makers.

To my editors, Bella Pagan and Tricia Narwani: beloved book alchemists.

To the incredible inner circle at Pan Mac and Del Rey: Alice, Abbie, Phoebe, Jo, Kate, Lorraine, Emily, Julie, Keith, Ryan, Dave. The gloss of 'sine qua non' in the dictionary is a list of all your names.

To all those at Pan Macmillan and Random House who champion books to librarians, booksellers and readers of all kinds. This year I've learned how very much you do, and I am so grateful.

To my international editors and translators, for taking this series round the world with such style and enthusiasm, and sending me awesome translation questions.

To friends old and new: Hilary, Giles, Tanya, Taran, Rachel, Mark, Tim, Debbie, John, Mira, Nick, Kristina

her hair was in her eyes and she couldn't see, as Gavar turned the motorbike into the thick of the crowd and roared away through the filthy streets of London.